nothing to lose

christina jones

nothing to lose

HarperCollins*Publishers*

HarperCollins*Publishers*
77–85 Fulham Palace Road,
Hammersmith, London W6 8JB

www.**fire**and**water**.com

A Paperback Original
Published by HarperCollins*Publishers* 2001

3 5 7 9 8 6 4

This novel is entirely a work of fiction. The names,
characters and incidents portrayed in it are the work
of the author's imagination. Any resemblance to actual
persons, living or dead, events or localities
is entirely coincidental

A catalogue record for this book
is available from the British Library

ISBN 0 00 651363 8

Set in Perpetua by
Rowland Phototypesetting Ltd,
Bury St Edmunds, Suffolk

Printed and bound in Great Britain by
Clays Ltd, St Ives plc

for Paul Lovelock:

biker, musician and my lifelong friend. A kind,
gentle, funny, happy man who should have lived for ever.
I will always miss you. I will always remember.
You were simply the best.

also for Nenagh Johnson,

the most beautiful greyhound in the world.
May she continue to enjoy a long and happy
retirement filled with luxury and love.

A man travels the world in search of
what he needs and returns home to find it.

George Moore

chapter one

The chorus of 'Zip a Dee-Doo-Dah' roared along the aisle, poured through the nave, then soared sacrilegiously up into the sixteenth-century rafters of St Edith's. The organist, more used to wheezing out 'The Old Rugged Cross', gamely tried to keep pace with the toe-tapping mourners. Even the vicar, his elbows resting on the pulpit's worn carve-work, was clapping his hands to the back beat.

Sandwiched between her fiancé, Andrew, and her parents in the front pew, Jasmine Clegg sang '. . . my oh my, what a wonderful day . . .' as the tears coursed down her cheeks. Her grandfather, currently reposing in his silk-lined, oak-veneered coffin at the top of the chancel steps, would have loved every minute of it.

It was, Jasmine thought sadly, exactly what he'd wanted – exactly what he'd detailed more than three years earlier while he and Jasmine had been sheltering from a coastal gale, sharing cheese and onion baps and a tomato Cup a Soup.

'When my time comes,' Benny Clegg had waved his crusts under her nose, 'don't you dare let your father go for anything mournful like "The Lord is my Shepherd" or "Abide With Me" or – God forbid! – "The Day Thou Gavest".'

1

Jasmine had swallowed her mouthful of soup quickly, raising her voice above the crashing of the sea. 'What? Oh, Grandpa – I don't want to even think about it!'

'Well I do. When I go, I want a damn good shindig. I want all my friends tapping their feet and smiling. No – listen, love. I want my coffin to go into St Edith's to "Entry of the Gladiators", come out to "In The Mood" . . .' Benny had gurgled happily here. 'Me and your gran had some right old times to Glenn Miller . . . and I want everyone to have a rip-snorting singsong in the middle. That Zippy tune would be about right . . .'

He'd started to whistle it cheerfully between his teeth. Bits of bap had sprayed onto the wet shingle, and a seagull had swooped down and scooped them up with a shriek of triumph. Jasmine had looked at Benny in horror. He meant it! He was planning to die! He couldn't! Her grandfather was the only person in the world whom she truly loved. He couldn't die and leave her.

'Grandpa! Stop it, please!' She'd shaken the raindrops from her hair, and shouted against the salt-tanged screech of the wind. 'I don't want to hear this! I won't listen. Anyway, you'd never get away with even a partial-humanist funeral in Ampney Crucis. Not with that new vicar.'

Benny had swigged at the soup and emerged with a vibrant orange moustache. 'No? You don't reckon he'd stand for it? Maybe not – he seemed a bit of a miserable sod at Harvest Festival, now I come to think about it. He never saw the funny side of the marrows and –' he'd suddenly regarded Jasmine fiercely – 'don't you try to change tack, young lady. This is very important to me.'

'And you're the most important thing in the world to me and I don't want you to die!'

'Lord love you, I'm not planning on going yet awhile. I just want to get this clear. When I'm dead it'll be too

2

late, and if I leave the arrangements to your father he'll go for dirges and things. You know he will, don't you?'

Jasmine had nodded. The Clegg sense of fun seemed to have bypassed Benny's only child with a vengeance. Her father was the least humorous person she had ever known.

The raindrops were drumming steadily on the corrugated-iron roof, which slapped and flapped above their heads. She'd sighed.

'If you're being serious, you'll have to have some hymns and prayers, especially if you want the service to be at St Edith's.'

'OK then, I'll have a couple of rousing hymns and some nice cheery prayers as a sop to you and the Good Lord, then you lay me to rest on the leeward side of that oak tree with your gran, so that I get the sound of the sea, the smell of the rain, and the warmth of the evening sun. You'll see to it. Jasmine, love, won't you?'

And Jasmine, the last remnant of cheese and onion bap stuck miserably in her throat, had nodded.

'Good girl.' Benny had hugged her. 'That's settled, then. And the rain's easing, so how about cheering ourselves up with a pint or three in the Crumpled Horn?'

Now they were in the Crumpled Horn again – without Benny, of course, but all his wishes had been carried out to the letter, and the post-funeral party was in full swing. Jasmine, still numbed with grief, clutched half a pint of Old Ampney ale, and hunched in a window seat. The afternoon sky was pale and luminescent, more like January than early May, sweeping down to the sea. The earlier rain had left everything looking shiny and cold, like stainless steel. It was bleak and cheerless, as only an English seaside village can be on a damp spring day, and the crowded pub was empty without Benny's throaty laughter.

His closest friends, Allan, Peg and Roger, were huddled in the inglenook, their faces woebegone, their elderly hands still clutching handkerchiefs. They'd wept copiously at the graveside, hugging Jasmine, sharing the devastation of her loss. Roger had said that she'd done a wonderful job for Benny. Allan, nodding, had added that if he had to choose a way to die then Benny's had been just perfect: falling asleep in his favourite armchair, as he had, with a glass of beer in one hand and a plate of egg and chips just finished in front of him, and greyhound racing on the telly.

They looked at her now and smiled sadly. Jasmine smiled back, without using her lips, just stretching her face slightly. She'd probably never smile properly again.

Across the crowded bar she could see her mother, looking even more pointed than usual, dressed in stark black, pecking at a sandwich, mentally working out the calorie content. She looked, Jasmine thought, like a hard-eyed, glossy crow raking at a piece of carrion. Her father, dark lounge suit. black tie and too many whiskies, was back-slapping with his council cronies. Andrew, her fiancé, was, as always, networking. Jasmine wondered how many cars he'd managed to sell to the funeral director. Andrew never missed an opportunity to do business.

Neither her mother nor Andrew would miss Benny at all, and her father would soon recover. They'd found Benny an embarrassment to their social standing, and had avoided even mentioning him if at all possible. To them he'd been an eccentric, scruffy old man with little money. There had been times, Jasmine knew, when her parents had denied that Benny was even part of their family. He'd known it too, and been bitterly hurt by the denial. And now it was far too late for anyone to make amends. She wiped away a solitary tear. She'd never felt more lonely.

'Jasmine – may I join you?'

4

She shrugged. 'Yes, of course. But I'm not good company.'

John Bestley, Ampney Crucis's sole solicitor, nodded as he sat down. 'No, I understand, my dear. A very sad day. Especially for you.'

Jasmine sniffed back further tears. They hurt her throat. She always cried more when people were kind.

John Bestley played with the stem of his sherry glass. 'You are aware that Benny left his will with me? And that he'd asked for the contents to be divulged here after the funeral?'

'Yes.' She bit her lower lip and exhaled. 'He also told me that you'd said that public will reading was practically a dead art. That it rarely happens these days — except in films.'

'Very true. But your grandfather always had a sense of the dramatic.' John Bestley's eyes crinkled. 'He fancied that this would be a rather theatrical finale to the day.'

Jasmine chased a beer mat round the table. 'He didn't have anything much to leave though, did he? He didn't even own his house. He was always broke. And Dad's his only son, so there doesn't seem to be a lot of point.' She picked up the beer mat and tapped its edge fiercely against her glass. 'I mean, John, that if people are going to *laugh* —'

'No one will make a fool of your grandfather, my dear. Certainly not me.'

'OK. Sorry. I just didn't want it to be embarrassing for him. Mum was always so condescending to him about it, you know . . . The little bits and pieces he had were priceless to him, but probably . . . probably . . . just, well, tat to other people . . . Oh, I'm sorry . . .'

John Bestley hurriedly handed her a very stiffly starched handkerchief from his breast pocket. 'There, there, my dear . . . It'll be fine. Trust me. Shall we get it over with, then?'

Jasmine wiped her eyes, blew her nose, and nodded.

John stood up, clapping his hands. 'Ladies and gentlemen! If I could just command a few minutes of your time!'

The hubbub died slowly. Heads turned. Jasmine's parents move closer together, as if to shield each other from the coming humiliation.

Andrew slid into the seat that John had just vacated and squeezed Jasmine's shoulder. 'Cheer up. This won't take long, will it? After all, Benny had nothing to leave.'

Jasmine narrowed her eyes. Through the blur of her tears, Andrew's regular features and neatly cropped fair hair all shifted sideways a fraction. 'He had *everything* to leave! Everything!'

'Yes, well,' Andrew fumbled his words, 'of course he did. I just meant that in terms of material possessions, and, well, hard cash, it's hardly going to amount to the legacy of a lifetime, is it?'

Benny had never liked Andrew; couldn't see why Jasmine had agreed to marry him. She was beginning to think the same – but she was far too emotional to face any further life-changes· at the moment. She needed all the constants she could get.

John, having covered the preliminaries, had started on the bequests in solicitous tones.

'*To my son, Philip Clegg –*'

Several of her father's councillor chums immediately looked slightly askance and Jasmine bit back a smile. Nice one, Grandpa! Her father, believing that Clegg was a dead giveaway of his humble origins, had changed his and her mother's surname to Clayton several years earlier. Jasmine, who had always been proud to be a Clegg, had torn up her deed poll forms.

'Excuse me,' John peered over his half-moon glasses, 'could we have silence, please? Thank you. *To my son, Philip Clegg, I leave my good wishes for his future, my sorrow that he had no interest in the family business, and my binoculars to enable him to see what is happening under his nose.*'

The Crumpled Horn erupted in hoots of laughter. Jasmine, watching her father's face pucker in non-comprehension, sighed. Benny's jokes had always been wasted on Philip.

'The old sod,' Andrew hissed. 'There was no need for that!'

John tapped on the table. 'Please! Let's get on! *To my daughter-in-law, Yvonne Clegg, I leave my chip pan in the hope that she will use it daily and put some flesh on that scrawny frame. While this may broaden her hips, unfortunately I am not in a position to leave her anything which might broaden her mind.*'

Yvonne clutched at her husband with a shriek. Philip patted her hand. Jasmine wished that she could rush across and comfort her parents. She wished that she wanted to. Sadly, she reckoned, considering the way they'd treated her grandfather, Benny had let them off very lightly indeed.

'That's totally uncalled for!' Andrew hissed. 'Your mother has got a wonderful figure. All the blokes at the dealership think she's top totty.'

'What?' Jasmine wrinkled her nose. 'My mother? That's disgusting . . .'

'Of course it isn't. Any woman with an ounce of self-respect would take care of herself, just as Yvonne has done. I bet she's still a size ten, and with that fabulous hair . . .' He trailed off.

'Yes?' Jasmine's voice was dangerously calm. 'Go on.'

'Well, nothing, of course, I mean . . .'

7

John Bestley was still speaking. Jasmine stared at the handkerchief, damp and twisted in her hands. She didn't need Andrew to draw the comparison between her petite, blonde, designer-dressed mother and her dark, plump, untidy self. Yvonne had always seemed rather shocked that her only daughter had the brown eyes, the clumsiness, and the overwhelming desire to please of a capering Labrador puppy. And Jasmine herself knew that she was as far removed from being anyone's top totty as it was possible to get. But the thought of Andrew's smarmy car salesmen friends leering over Yvonne was still stomach-churningly appalling.

John cleared his throat. '*To my three dear friends, Allan Lovelock, Roger Foster and Peg Dunstable, I leave the sum of twenty thousand pounds each.*'

Andrew let out a low whistle.

'Bloody hell!' Yvonne stopped clutching her husband and, rocking on her stilettos, clutched at the bar instead. 'This is ridiculous! That money should go to Philip! The will's invalid!'

'On the contrary,' John said smoothly, beaming at Peg, Roger and Allan, who looked about as poleaxed as Yvonne, 'the will is perfectly legal. Now, please, no more interruptions. The last legacies are fairly brief.'

Jasmine was silent. Sixty thousand pounds! Where the hell had Benny got that sort of money? He'd always lived so frugally, he must have been squirrelling it away for ever. Still, no one deserved it more than Allan, Peg and Roger – they'd been true friends for many, many years.

'*To my granddaughter, Jasmine Clegg,*' John Bestley's voice softened as he motioned his head towards her, '*I leave all my love. She has been the best pal a man could have, and it has been both a privilege and a pleasure to share her life for twenty-eight years . . .*'

This time Jasmine couldn't stop the tears. They fell soundlessly, the sobs rocking her body. Andrew patted her clumsily.

'*To her I wish health, good fortune and, above all, lifelong happiness. I would hope that she will always have the strength to follow her own path in life without hindrance from others. She will understand. I also leave her the residue of my estate —*'

'Christ,' Andrew sighed. 'A council house full of second-hand furniture.'

John Bestley adjusted his glasses and looked directly at Jasmine. 'Would you like to see me privately at the office to go through the specifics, my dear?'

Jasmine sniffed into the hankie and shook her head. It didn't matter. She'd find a home for Benny's bits and pieces somewhere. It was time she looked for a place to rent, anyway. She couldn't go on living with her parents for ever. It was some scant comfort that her grandfather's possessions could one day furnish her own little flat.

'Very well,' John cleared his throat. '*I also leave Jasmine Clegg the residue of my estate in its entirety: my furniture and all my personal possessions for her to do with as she pleases. I also leave her my beach hut —*'

Jasmine caught her breath. The beach hut! She'd almost forgotten that Benny and her grandmother had actually owned the sea-front chalet where she'd spent most of her childhood summer days. It had been her bolt hole all her life. Oh, that was wonderful . . .

'Council's intending to bulldoze them, so I've been told,' Andrew said, looking disappointed. 'You won't get much for it.'

John coughed. '*Also to my granddaughter, Jasmine Clegg, I bequeath fifty thousand pounds.*'

'Fifty grand!' Andrew had perked up. He kissed her

cheek. 'Wow, Jas! That's amazing! You could invest it in the dealership — become a partner.'

Jasmine's mouth dropped open. She wasn't listening to Andrew. She didn't dare to look at her parents. She worked some saliva into her mouth. She couldn't take this in. There had to be some mistake. 'Er — John . . . maybe I should come and see you. I mean . . .'

'Whatever you think best, my dear.' John's voice was avuncular. 'We'll make an appointment later. And there's just one more thing.' He looked down at the papers in front of him. '*To Jasmine Clegg I leave my business. I know she loves it as much as I do. I have had the licence transferred to her name to come into effect six weeks after my death.*'

'Business? What business?' Andrew looked quizzical, then his eyes widened in horror. 'Jesus Christ! He doesn't mean . . . ?'

Jasmine started to laugh. Her parents were gaping at her across the bar. Roger, Allan and Peg were all beaming.

John Bestley gathered the pages of the will together tidily. 'Congratulations, my dear. You are now the proud proprietor of Benny Clegg — the Punters' Friend.'

Jasmine, not knowing whether to laugh or cry now, was slightly disturbed to find she was doing both.

Benny had left her his bookmaker's pitch at Ampney Crucis Greyhound Stadium.

chapter two

'And just what do you intend to do with this?'

Jasmine sat down heavily, puffing from her exertions, and surveyed both her best friend, Clara, and the Victorian chiffonier, with grave doubt. 'Goodness knows. I thought it'd sort of slot in.'

'It'd sort of slot in,' Clara said, 'to the mansion it was designed for. It was a tight squeeze in Benny's front room. It is never – never, ever – going to fit into a beach hut.'

It was a month after the funeral. June had come to Dorset, bringing with it fine weather and the first rush of holidaymakers. The beach hut, one in a row of two dozen perfect 1920s specimens, had a wooden slatted veranda, two main rooms, a minuscule bathroom, a kitchenette comprising two sockets and a gas ring, net curtains, and a line for hanging up wet bathing costumes; and, like its neighbours, was painted in sugared-almond colours. The huts stood in proud defiance along the Ampney Crucis sea front; with the skewwhiff wooden steps down to the sands in front of them, and the undulating gradient of the cliffs behind.

Jasmine had already transferred most of Benny's furniture into the beach hut. The chiffonier was the last to go. Clara, in one of her rare moments either not at work or in the gym, had been co-opted in as heaver-and-shover-in-chief. The chiffonier's move had taken far longer than Jasmine had anticipated, and they now had an interested audience of small children in shorts.

Scrambling to her feet, Jasmine once again grabbed a corner of the chiffonier. For a few minutes they seemed to be making some headway, then Clara dropped her end of the enormous cabinet with a groan.

'There! That's it! I've broken a fingernail! Andrew should be helping you with this. I can't believe he's let you do the house clearance on your own.'

'I wasn't on my own,' Jasmine panted, tugging futilely at the immovable object. 'Roger and Allan and Peg helped.'

'Get real! They're all eighty at least!'

'No they're not. And anyway, they helped me with respect and sympathy, and didn't mind me crying all the time. Andrew would have mocked.'

'Yeah, he probably would, the bastard. But still, Allan and Roger must be pensionable by now, and Peg Dunstable is away with the fairies.'

'She is not!' Jasmine giggled. 'Just because she thinks she's Doris Day doesn't mean that she hasn't got all her marbles. She's a very astute businesswoman, she's just got a bit of a fixation –'

Clara picked at the flaking nail. 'You are so naïve, Jas, do you know that? Peg Dunstable is totally barking. God – you'll make a right team.'

'Yes, we probably will. Now forget your manicure and my sanity and lift your end.'

They lifted and pushed, but the chiffonier was still wedged at an angle across the veranda. Clara, again examining the damaged fingernail, leaned against the cabinet with a sigh. 'What we need is a strategy – and the help of a couple of rugby teams. Why couldn't you have got yourself engaged to a man with biceps, instead of . . . ?'

'Go on, you can say it. You've said it often enough. A smarmy showroom-bound wimp like Andrew.'

Clara disliked Andrew even more than Benny had, if that were possible. Jasmine, who had known Andrew ever since schooldays, and who had had no previous serious boyfriend, had been engaged to him for the last three years. They'd sort of drifted into it, sort of stuck together, and certainly Jasmine had never considered ending it. So what if it wasn't a Grand Passion? Neither of them had expected that, had they? It was safe, it was familiar, and both sets of parents approved.

She grimaced. Her parents would never, ever approve of anything she did again . . .

Philip and Yvonne had been incandescent since the day of the funeral. The rows in their five-bedroomed mock Tudor detached had raged for weeks. They had culminated in Jasmine, for the first time in her life, leaving home. Silently, she'd packed her suitcase and decamped to the beach hut. Andrew had joined in on the parental front at this point, and told her that there was no way she could live, like some down-and-out, in a dilapidated chalet that was due for demolition.

Fired by a fierce determination that she hadn't even known she possessed, Jasmine had told him to mind his own business, and had also evaded both her father's and Andrew's insistence that she must invest her nest egg wisely – either in Andrew's car dealership or Philip's portfolio – and had deposited her inheritance in her building society account.

She had a feeling she hadn't heard the last of the matter.

'Tell you what.' Jasmine fanned herself with the flapping hem of her T-shirt. 'Shall we abandon this for a bit and go to the Crumpled Horn?'

13

Clara shook her head. 'We will not. We'll finish the job first.'

'God, you're so bloody focused.'

Clara looked smug. 'Which is why I'm Sales Director of Makings Paper, while you're – well, God knows what you are.'

'I'm a bookie.' Jasmine grinned at her. 'Or at least I will be as soon as I've had a few lessons.'

Clara gave her a withering look, and once again applied her shoulder to the cluster of carved beechnuts dangling from the chiffonier's corner. 'And have you told your parents and the squirmy Andrew that you've jacked your job in yet?'

'Hell, no. They're still getting over Grandpa's legacies and the fact that I've left home. Telling them that I'm no longer inputting boring figures on to boring computers in the boring accounts department at Watertite Windows would possibly be a scrap of information too far at the moment. Hey – I think we've done it! It moved!'

With a lot of scraping and cursing and a shriek from Clara as another fingernail splintered, the chiffonier was finally heaved into place. Sweaty, grimy, and triumphant, Jasmine surveyed it with pleasure.

'Doesn't it look lovely? Oh, thanks, Clara – you're a real pal.'

'I'm mad and so are you. Look, Jasmine, you do know you don't have to live here, don't you? My flat is huge, and it'd be really fun to share and –'

'And I'd drive you crazy by filling it with clutter and making a mess and knocking things over.' Jasmine said, thinking of Clara's pristine minimalism with a shudder. 'No, thanks so much, it's really kind of you – but I don't think even our rock-solid friendship would survive being together twenty-four hours a day. Anyway, I love this hut.'

Clara grinned. 'Rather you than me then – but the offer stands should things get desperate. Right, so now you can stay here and play house while I go and get a takeout from the pub. Any preference in crisp flavour?'

'Not cheese and onion. They make me cry.'

Clara gave her a swift hug. 'Poor thing. Is it still awful?'

'Yup. It's getting a bit better, though. I usually only cry at night now.'

'I should have been here for the funeral.'

'You couldn't help being in Guatemala.'

'Guadeloupe. And it was naff timing for a holiday. I can't bear to think of you having to cope with it all on your own.'

'Well, I did, so maybe it was a good thing that you weren't here. Mum and Dad and Andrew were useless, so I had to just get on with it. Anyway, could we not talk about it any more, please?'

'Yeah, sure. Sorry. So, it's a pint of Old Ampney and a packet of smoky bacon?'

'Make it half a pint. I want to keep a clear head. I'm going to meet Peg at the greyhound stadium later for my initiation.'

'Bloody hell!' Clara forced her way through the inquisitive audience of children who were now three-deep on the veranda. 'She'll have you doing sugar-sweet smiles and singing "The Deadwood Stage" complete with whip noises and thigh slapping. I know – I've seen her do it in Sainsbury's. I'd better make it a treble whisky at least.'

Laughing, Jasmine watched Clara disappear towards the prom road and the Crumpled Horn, and then looked proudly at the chiffonier now firmly wedged at the back of the hut. The place was possibly a mite overcrowded, but at least she now had everything she needed to call it home. It'd be fine for the summer months. The winter, with the notorious Dorset gales swooshing in from the English Channel, coupled with plunging temperatures, could be another matter altogether, but she'd deal with that when it arose. Right now, she thought, as she delved into one of the dozens of cardboard boxes she'd brought from her grandfather's house, she was relishing her new-found independence.

'Bugger off!' Clara, balancing a tray of beer and crisps, climbed back on to the veranda and glared at the children. 'The show's over. Go and watch Punch and Judy. Although, on second thoughts, this is probably funnier.'

'There!' Jasmine stood back to admire her handiwork. The chiffonier was now adorned with various pieces of her inheritance – two Staffordshire highwayman figurines, a walnut carriage clock which had stopped five years before, and a pair of slightly verdigrised brass candlesticks. She'd also added her grandparents' wedding photograph in a silver frame. 'How does that look?'

'Like it belongs in a mausoleum.' Clara shook her head. 'You can't be serious about this, Jas, can you?'

'Deadly serious. Never more serious about anything in my life. Now, where's the beer?'

Ampney Crucis Greyhound Stadium was possibly a bit of an overstatement. An oval sand track surrounded by dirty and disintegrating white railings, enclosed by three tiers of rickety stands, with a snack bar at one end and a Portaloo at the other, it probably wasn't anyone's idea of a good night out at the dogs. However, Jasmine, who had grown up there, standing on a box beside Benny as he set prices, took bets, and hopefully didn't pay out too much too often, absolutely adored it.

She lingered for a moment in the evening shadows, looking at the deserted track, biting back the tears. It was the first time she'd been here since her grandfather's death, and she could see him everywhere, hear his voice barking the odds, feel the comforting touch of his worn tweed jacket as she'd snuggled against him on cold nights when the wind came straight off the sea.

The bookmakers' pitches, three of them, were permanently sited at the foot of the stands. Greyhound racing at Ampney Crucis was very far removed from the bright lights and glamour of the big stadiums. The site had been in the Dunstable family for generations, and Peg was fiercely proud that it was one of the few surviving independent tracks in the country.

God knew, Jasmine thought, trailing her fingers along the wobbling rails, how it had survived at all. With meetings three times a week, all year round – solely for the Dorset locals in winter and with the addition of the bemused Ampney Crucis holidaymakers in the high season – they somehow seemed to manage to scrape a living. Quite a good living really, she supposed, if Benny's legacies were anything to go by.

Completely alone in the stadium, Jasmine wandered towards the bookmakers' pitches, shivering slightly as she plunged from the warm evening sun into the towering shadows of the stands. 'Benny Clegg – The Punters' Friend' stood in the middle of the three, 'Roger Foster – Bookmaker to Royalty' was to the left, and 'Allan Lovelock – Honesty is my Middle Name' to the right. Roger and Allan, both of her grandfather's generation, like Peg, had been permanent fixtures at the Ampney Crucis track all her life. This was the only place – apart, of course, from the beach hut now – where she really felt at home.

She sat forlornly on one of the three orange boxes which made up the rest of her inheritance, and wondered briefly if she could really make a go of it. Could she, in all honesty, become a successful bookmaker? Oh, sure, she'd written up the books for Benny ever since she'd been able to add up: standing beside him at the meetings, writing down the bets in the ledger as the punters put them on, able to work out winnings quicker than any calculator. But being in charge? Setting prices? Calling the odds? Actually running the business? Would she ever be any good at that? Her grandfather had entrusted everything to her – she prayed that she wouldn't let him down.

'Sorry to have kept you waiting, darling.'

Peg Dunstable swept down the stand steps, her flicked-up hair swinging jauntily, kept in place by a broad Alice band. With her swirling skirt cinched in by a black patent belt, the collar of her poplin blouse standing up, a two-ply cardigan slung round her shoulders, and wearing ankle socks and flatties, from a distance she looked the spitting image of her heroine. It was only close to that anyone could see the wrinkles on the papery skin beneath the panstick, the mesh round the base of the blonde wig, or spot that the inky curly lashes weren't securely attached at the corners. No one in Ampney Crucis would ever have been brave enough to point this out.

'No problem.' Jasmine stood up and brushed the dust from the seat of her jeans. 'I needed a little bit of time alone – to – um – get used to Grandpa not being here.'

Peg hugged her. 'I know, pet. I know. I miss him so much too.'

It was an awkward hug, Jasmine felt, as Peg only reached her shoulder. She could see all the intricate knotted roots of the Doris Day wig.

They stood in silence for a moment, remembering Benny. Then, because she was going to cry, Jasmine shrugged herself free. 'So, where do we stand? The licence is mine in two weeks' time – I know that. And I know

18

Roger and Allan have been very kind and said they'll help me to get started – which is nice of them as we're supposed to be rivals for the same business – and that the meetings are every Tuesday, Friday and Saturday. I don't know exactly what I'm supposed to do.'

'Make money,' Peg grinned. 'And lots of it. That's what Benny did. The money he left was the bit that the tax man didn't get wind of. Oh, I know they say you'll never meet a poor bookie, but at a small venue like this one – and with virtually the same punters backing virtually the same dogs every session – it's a miracle that he managed to stash away anything at all.'

Jasmine sighed. 'I know. I was amazed that he had so much.'

'Any ideas what you're going to do with yours?'

'Keep it in the building society just in case I go belly up as the Punters' Friend. No, really. I've walked out of the only job I've ever had. I'm not qualified to do anything else, and if I make a mess of this –.'

'You won't,' Peg said stoutly. 'Once you get the licence through we'll all help you out. I thought you might be thinking of using Benny's cash for the deposit on a house.'

'No, there's no need. I've got the beach hut for the time being, and Andrew and I are getting married next year and –'.

'Pah!' Peg clicked her fingers dismissively. A false nail fell off. 'Andrew Pease is a waste of space! He's a free-loader, Jasmine, a smarmy, nasty piece of work, just like your dad.'

'Don't spare my feelings,' Jasmine smiled. 'Say what you really think.'

'Oh, darling! I'm so sorry! Me and my mouth! It just all comes out.'

'I'm glad it does.' Jasmine moved her hand to touch

19

Peg, then withdrew it in case she dislodged the hairpiece or something awful. 'It's about time people were honest with me. I've always just bumbled along, living at home, having Andrew, doing a job I loathed – because Grandpa was there to make everything all right. Now I've got to stand on my own two feet.'

Peg looked up at her and winked. 'That's the spirit. You're not Benny Clegg's granddaughter for nothing, you know. Now, I didn't really ask you to come along here this evening just to bad-mouth your family – fun though it is – I wanted to ask for your thoughts on something I've been pondering for ages. Shall we go up to the office?'

Peg's office, at the top of the rickety stands, was a sort of Portakabin on stilts. The bits of it that weren't buried under the racing papers and greyhound form books, were covered with photographs of Doris Day and Rock Hudson. There had been an awful patch, Jasmine remembered, at the time when Rock had been outed. Peg had worn deep mourning and closed the stadium for a fortnight. However, if the pictures were anything to go by, his sexual *faux pas* had now been forgiven.

From the window Jasmine could see the sea; the evening tide was going out in little sunburst ripples, leaving the sands flat and clean and pale. The roofs of the beach huts, looking like a child's pastel necklace, were just visible, as was the Crumpled Horn and the narrow streets climbing away from the front towards the church and the housing estates. Bathed gently in the sun's last rays, the village looked peaceful and time-warped. Jasmine allowed the familiar scene to soak into her like a balm and prayed that it would never change.

Pouring two pints of Old Ampney ale from a selection of bottles in the fridge, and switching on the stereo system to allow 'Secret Love' to billow round the plasterboard walls. Peg indicated that Jasmine should sit down.

'I've discussed this with Allan and Roger, pet, and they're all in favour. Now, as you're part of the syndicate, we'll need your agreement before we go ahead.'

Jasmine was intrigued. 'It all sounds very hush-hush. You're not planning to nick the Greyhound Derby from Wimbledon, are you?'

'Oh!' Peg looked affronted. 'Who told you?'

'What! You're kidding!'

'Yes, actually, I am.' Peg put her head on one side in a coquettish manner. 'But you're not too far off the mark, to be honest. Now – just take a look at these . . .'

Peg pushed a pile of glossy, laminated brochures through the heaps of newsprint on her desk. Jasmine flipped through them. Romford, Crayford, Wimbledon, Hackney, Walthamstow . . . all the huge and famous greyhound stadiums were represented.

'Very impressive, but I don't see . . .'

Peg fished another highly coloured brochure from her desk drawer. 'It's time we were competitive. Oh, I know we can't compete with these big boys as such, but we can certainly do more than we've been doing. I've heard on the grapevine that the Greyhound Racing Association are having a big push this year to update and improve the industry's image; bring dog racing into the twenty-first century – you know, fun for all the family . . .'

Jasmine nodded. The change within the sport had been going on for some time. There were all sorts of family packages on offer, and corporate hospitality, and things like that – every single one of them way out of Ampney Crucis's league.

'And that Sky telly are going to be moving away from the established BAGS tracks and covering the smaller meetings. But this,' Peg continued, brandishing the remaining

21

brochure under Jasmine's nose, 'is what really sparked it off, pet. That new stadium at Bixford. Look at it – it looks like an art deco mutation of the damn Millennium Dome! And they're raking it in! And they've just pitched for the Platinum Trophy for next February . . .'

Jasmine leafed through the brochure. Bixford was in Essex, in the heart of dog-racing territory, and the Gillespie Stadium had been making the headlines for several months. The new Platinum Trophy race, sponsored by Frobisher's Brewery, would definitely be the jewel in their cloth cap.

She sighed. 'Yes, well, good luck to them, but –'

The telephone on Peg's desk shrilled. Peg hurled papers aside in a frantic attempt to locate it. Holding up her hand to Jasmine, she snatched at the receiver. The conversation was brief, cooed, and punctuated by besotted smiles.

'Ewan,' Peg said softly, replacing the receiver. 'He's done something silly and left Katrina again. He's coming to stay for a while to let the dust settle. Won't that be a hoot?'

Jasmine nodded because it would be. She and Ewan had grown up together. Dark, dangerous, delicious Ewan Dunstable, Peg's beloved nephew, was every woman's wildest fantasy. He was a serial cheater – but lovely with it. The last time he'd left his wife and holed up with Peg, he and Clara had had an affair that left Ampney Crucis reeling. Andrew absolutely loathed him.

'Now, back to business.' Peg patted the golden hair. 'Where were we before that naughty boy interrupted? Oh, yes. Bixford and the Platinum Trophy . . . Now what we'd thought – me and Roger and Allan – was that, if you're agreeable, we'd pool Benny's legacy money together, give this place a bit of a spruce up, and rename it the Benny Clegg Stadium.'

'Oh!' Jasmine fumbled in the sleeve of her T-shirt for

a tissue. 'Oh, Peg! That would be absolutely brilliant.'

Peg leaned across the desk and jabbed at the Bixford brochure. 'And, once we've done that, we thought we'd really put the old place on the map, and give these Essex geezers a run for their money, by applying to stage the Frobisher Platinum Trophy!'

chapter three

Eighty miles away from Ampney Crucis, on that same
June evening, April Padgett was having one of the
worst nights of her life – and that was saying something. In her twenty-three years she'd managed to have
some humdingers.

The Gillespie Greyhound Stadium's Copacabana Cocktail
Bar was packed with its usual designer-dressed Bixford
clientele; the air conditioning had packed up; the ice-maker
had jammed and immediately defrosted; and someone had
been sick behind the token plastic palm tree.

However, far worse than any of these was the sight of
Martina Gillespie, April's boss, behind the bar, with the till
wide open, clawing her magenta talons through the takings.

'You've been giving them buggers freebies again!' Her
squawk quite drowned out the soothing tones of Barry
Manilow inside the bar, and the orgasmic shouts of the
track commentator outside it. 'Don't deny it! I've been
watching you most of the evening. I know what drinks
you've served and I know what the float was, and I know
this till is short! How did you manage it, eh? My back was
only turned for five minutes while I went to check on that
fracas in the lavs.'

April groaned. Martina Gillespie had eyes like a hawk,
a voice like a strangled donkey, and a face like a ferret. A

crew-cut in Tequila Sunrise orange, more make-up than Danny La Rue, and copious amounts of post-menopausal body-piercing, completed the picture.

Oh God! Why hadn't she put the money in straight away? Why had Jix appeared in the Copacabana while Martina was sorting out the loo punch-up? Why did she always feel so sorry for him? Why had she given him that damn drink?

April tried smiling. 'Well, no, it's not short really. . . '

'Yes, it is not really!' Martina shrieked, somewhat ungrammatically. 'Do you want this bar job, my lady, or don't you?'

Bloody, bloody stupid question, April thought, still managing to look confused and innocent at the same time. 'Of course I do, but –'

'But nothing!'

A large part of the designer brigade had turned from gawping at the on-track excitement through the huge plate-glass windows, and were listening with interest. As they were all sweating profusely because of the lack of air conditioning and ice, it seemed that a good row might just take their minds off their discomfort.

April shifted her balance on her borrowed Manolo Blahniks, and winced as the circulation started pumping into her toes. 'I was going to put the money in myself later. I just got busy. Anyway, it was only a Fuzzy Navel – without the ice, of course, because of the machine.'

'Only a Fuzzy Navel!' Martina howled, clutching her Versace-clad bosom. 'Only a Fuzzy Navel! Dear God! Have you any idea how much a Fuzzy Navel costs?'

'Of course I have. I've been working in this bar for long enough to know the price of the damn drinks!'

'And don't you come the old acid with me, my girl! I don't want none of your smart backchat, OK?'

God, April thought wearily, Martina was dog-rough under the posh frock. Her vowels, which before the invective had started might have had their origins somewhere around Knightsbridge, were rapidly floating down the Estuary.

'Look, Martina, it was one drink. Just one drink. And like I said, I was going to put the money in.'

'Don't you Martina me, young lady!' The pointed chin had performed some sort of upward manoeuvre and was nearly touching the beaky nose. The selection of diamond ear-studs all winked under the deep-set ceiling spotlights. 'I'm Mrs Gillespie to you – understand? And whose bloody freebie was it tonight? Another one of your freeloading pals with a sob story about having lost everything on the last race and –'

'Yeah,' April said, sliding back along the bar, easing her feet. There was no way on earth that she'd tell Martina the drink had been for Jix. It would have meant instant dismissal for both of them. 'That's right.'

Martina gave a triumphant snort. 'I knew it. Well, it'll come out of your wages, O K? Double.'

Bitch, bitch, bitch, April thought, giving a subservient nod. God, the woman must be wired up to the bloody electronic workings of the till to know exactly how much there was supposed to be at any one time.

'Martina – er – Mrs Gillespie – I wasn't trying to steal from you. I fully intended to make the till up at the end of the shift. Oh – and look – I think the ice machine's working again! Everyone will want drinks.'

They both stared at the contraption in some consternation, mainly because neither of them understood it. However, where it had been dribbling lukewarm water only minutes earlier, it was now crackling and frosty. That was a start.

'O K.' Martina, immediately sensing a Gillespie-moneymaking opportunity slipping away, shoved her cropped head towards April. She looked like an aggressive Swan Vestas. 'But I'm watching you, my girl. Now, get serving – that's what you're paid for!'

'Cow!' April muttered under her breath, as Martina teetered out of Copacabana to spread a little happiness elsewhere. 'Hateful, spiteful, mean-minded cow!'

'Two Alabama Slammers and a Freddy Fuddpucker.' A fairly well-known footballer from the lower echelons, with a simpering brunette on each arm, thrust his way to the front of the perspiring queue. 'And whatever you'll let me give you, darling . . .'

April mixed the drinks, smiling her professional bimbette smile. Any minute now he was going to mention Long Slow Comfortable Screws, or Screaming Orgasms, or Slippery Knobs – or any of the hundred and one risqué names that cocktails had these days. And she would laugh, and look coy, and he'd think he was the funniest man since Chaplin with the most original lines since Mark Twain. And then she'd take his money and he'd give her a knowing look and swagger away, and the whole thing would start all over again.

The footballer had one of those little wispy beardy things that David Beckham had made so popular ages before. He stroked it in what he obviously considered a seductive manner, leaning forward across the bar. 'I bet you're just dying for a Hard Dick.'

April upped the smile, closed her ears, and mixed the drinks.

Oh, how she hated this job! How she hated the stupid frilly French maid costume – God only knew where Martina thought Copacabana was! – which showed her knickers when she bent over, and the stupid lacy nippie cap which meant that however tightly she screwed up her curly fair hair, tendrils of it always escaped. And how she hated the loud, rude people she had to serve, and the even louder and ruder people she had to work for.

One day, she thought, viciously shaking a Kaytusha Rocket for a girl with pink hair and crossed eyes, she'd be out of here. But not yet, of course. Not until she'd saved enough money to achieve her goals.

One day, she thought, as she poured the concoction into a glass and added two umbrellas, a sparkler, and a selection of impaled fruit and the cross-eyed girl didn't say thank you, she'd get as far away from Bixford as possible.

One day, when her debts were paid and her savings account was full, she'd move to the country and have a house of her own, with a garden, and a dog, and a proper family . . . It was the dream that kept her going: the dream that made working at three jobs a day, nearly every day of the week, even remotely bearable.

The course commentator was announcing the last race of the evening, and the cocktail crowd all swarmed towards the doors, either to savour the atmosphere from the glass and chrome terraces, or to place their bets with the Tote behind the restaurants. None of the designer crowd who frequented the Copacabana, April was sure, ever went trackside to part with their money; they probably didn't even know that there were ranks of bookies on the rails. Greyhound racing at Bixford, for the cocktail brigade, was purely incidental.

She listened to the fruity amplified words, extolling the qualities of each of the dogs, with a thump of pleasure. Another half-hour at most, and then all she had to do was clear up, cash up, and go home.

An hour later, with a black shrug over the top of the frilly maid outfit, the till dutifully balanced, and everything in

28

the Copacabana neat and tidy, April stumbled down the series of spiral chrome staircases. The borrowed Manolo Blahniks were crippling her, but at least she'd managed to wrench off the stupid cap and shake her hair free. The crowds hadn't quite dispersed, and there were still raucous shouts echoing from the shadows as she slipped out of the main doors and into brilliant splashes of floodlighting.

The stadium was lovely like this, she thought, picking her way through an ankle-deep pile of discarded betting slips and fast-food containers: like a huge palatial ocean-going liner, towering into the hot night sky, with lights gleaming from a thousand windows. Oliver Gillespie had certainly hit on a winner, siting the stadium as he had between Romford and the M25, and its art deco design meant it was visible for miles. Oliver, she'd decided when he and Martina had interviewed her for the Copacabana, was OK. A bit bluff and brusque, but straight enough – for a self-made spiv, that was.

Oliver Gillespie had made his fortune during the Thatcher years of enterprise for all, by installing snack-food vending machines in an epidemic rash across the country's motorway service areas. There probably wasn't a pre-packed pasty not disgorged by a Gillespie Guzzler anywhere in the country. But for all that, and his other more sinister sidelines, Oliver had proved to be a fair employer. However, Martina the shrew was a completely different matter.

April had sensed that Martina, in a desperate attempt to shake off her Canvey Island roots, was always going to lord it over her employee. And she'd been right. Martina had made her life hell. If it hadn't been for the dream, April would have chucked it all in ages ago.

April paused in the darkness, and lit a cigarette. It was her one luxury. Ten cigarettes lasted her for nearly four days if she rationed them to one in the morning with her

29

first cup of coffee, one last thing at night with a glass of plonk before she went to bed, and this one – the best one of all – immediately she had finished her five hours in the Copacabana. She loved the almost-silence after the frenzy, the smell of the dogs, and the lazy, soporific chat from the bookies as they packed up their carpet bags.

If ever a girl deserved a shot of nicotine, she thought, dragging the smoke into her lungs with relish, she did. Especially tonight. She smiled good-nights at a posse of security guards as they passed, their backs to her, poking underneath the stands for inebriated punters or bombs or both. She listened to the excited yelps from the kennels as the last greyhounds were reunited with their owners and swished off in luxury in the back of four-wheel drives. She watched the litter-pickers start their rounds, and the groundsmen with their motorised rakes chug round the track. All the after-the-show people were springing into action, which meant that Jix should have finished his shift soon too. Not much longer to wait.

April had been doing this for two years, ever since Oliver Gillespie had piled his Guzzler fortune into the born-again glamour world of greyhound racing, and opened the Bixford stadium. It was close to her flat, the hours suited her and slotted in nicely with her other two part-time jobs, and she usually got some tips, which she secreted away in a Roses chocolate tin under her bed. She loved the greyhounds too. The racing side of Bixford wasn't of much interest, mainly because she'd never had enough spare cash to gamble with, but the dogs themselves were gorgeous.

She was captivated by their lean muscled beauty, their good humour, the way they always laughed at their handlers, their enthusiasm, and their huge, beautiful eyes. She'd decided early on that when the cottage in the country with

30

the roses and the family became a reality, the dog frolicking on the manicured lawn would definitely be a greyhound.

She was just grinding out her cigarette stub with a toe of one of the Manolo Blahniks, when Jix, dressed as always in purple velvet flares, a soft black leather jacket and more bangles than Accessorize, arrived to escort her home.

'You shouldn't be smoking.' He flicked his hair from his eyes and looked accusing. 'You said you'd stop on New Year's Eve.'

'I said a lot of things on New Year's Eve, most of them inebriated rubbish. Anyway, it's my only vice – unlike some . . .'

Jix laughed. '*Touché*. Do I gather that Martina sussed out the Fluffy Navel?'

'You do. She did.' April fell into step beside him. 'And she was not best pleased.'

'You didn't tell her it was for me?'

'Course not. Do you think I'm mad? Look, she thinks I'm the dregs of the Gillespie setup – but you . . .' She grinned at him. 'You're definitely the underclass's underbelly.'

'Cheers. And you should have let me pay.'

'It was my treat. You deserve it. It was just a shame Martina had to be playing I-spy.'

Because they had flats in the same house, Jix always walked home with April. He said it wasn't safe for her to be wandering around Bixford's back streets so late at night. She secretly thought that, should push come to shove, she would probably be the one to protect Jix. Tall, slender to the point of skinny, with long silky hair and the pale, beautiful, androgynous face of a Jonathan Rhys Meyers clone, Jix looked far too delicate and otherworldly ever to inflict any physical damage on anyone.

When she'd first moved into the flat below his, Jix had

31

been like a walking directory. Not only had he pointed out the places to go, and those it was best to avoid, but he'd also – when it became essential to her survival – helped her find all three of her part-time jobs. Jix, it turned out, knew everyone and everything in Bixford. He'd apparently started working for Oliver ten years previously – at the tender age of fifteen – and had been involved not only in the Guzzlers, but several other less edifying Gillespie enterprises throughout Essex. Jix was now on the Gillespie Stadium books as a financial assistant. Jix, April had decided long ago, was the least likely-looking debt-collector that she had ever seen.

They left the stadium, and turned into a narrow street of dark-windowed, three-storey houses, boarded-up shops that had once sold meat and veg and knitting patterns to the older generation and were now the graffiti-ists' dream, and Antonio's Pasta Place, which was still open. The scents of garlic and red wine floated out into the heavy darkness, the candles guttered on the tables, and several Bixford winners were doing justice to ravioli and chips.

April waved at Antonio and his wife, Sofia, through the open door.

'Don't be late in the morning!' Antonio called in a broad Southend accent.

'As if!' April called back.

The exchange was the same every night. To April it was as routine as brushing her teeth. Comforting, really. By midday she'd be dressed in a short black skirt and neat white blouse and be serving pasta to Antonio's business lunchers. Bixford was rapidly becoming very fashionable, like Stepney and Walthamstow, and the streets were buzzing with bright young city traders, or twentysomethings all excited at making Internet millions. Soon, she supposed, the boarded-up shops would become cybercafés and multimedia takeaways and estate agents. It was another really good reason for leaving Bixford as soon as possible.

'You got your key?' Jix asked as they stopped outside number 51. 'I don't want to wake the boys upstairs by ringing the bell.'

April fumbled in her pocket and, finding the key, let them into the hall. Number 51 was divided into three flats: hers on the ground, Jix's above, and the top one shared by Joel and Rusty, a mixed race gay couple who worked from home in aromatherapy and ethnic cooking respectively. The hall always smelled as though someone were taking a bath in a curry house.

She opened her front door and Jix followed her in. The lamps were alight and April sighed a small sigh of pleasure. It was her home and she loved it. The country cottage and the family and the dog would be heaps better, of course, but until they came along, this would do nicely.

Three rooms – four if you counted the bathroom, which April didn't because it was about the size of a coffin – all furnished with second-hand junk painted bright colours, the chairs and sofa covered with throws, the dirty carpet hidden under vibrant rugs, and a selection of primary-coloured abstract paintings on the walls. The paintings would have to go, April knew that, but she was hanging on to them for old times' sake; or at least until she'd achieved her dream.

'All OK, sweets?' Daphne, Jix's mum, looked up from the sofa in front of the television. She'd obviously been enjoying the twin delights of a word-search puzzle book and Granada Men and Motors. 'No problems?'

'None.' April smiled blissfully as she eased off the Manolo Blahniks. The run-in with Martina didn't count. That was par for the course. 'What about you?'

Daphne shook her head, gathering her books and pens and magazines together. 'Not a peep from the little love. Sleeping like an angel.' She stood up stiffly and smiled adoringly at Jix. 'Time to take your old mum home, then. Thank the Lord it's only up half a dozen stairs. I'm fair whacked tonight.'

'Me too,' April yawned. 'Thanks a lot, Daff. See you tomorrow. Sleep tight. 'Night, Jix.'

The door closed behind them, and April slid on the chain and clicked the two locks into place. Daphne was like a storybook mother, April always thought: round and soft and comfortable. Jix was so lucky. Her own parents had separated years before, instantly divorced, and immediately remarried. April had never felt truly wanted by either of their new partners. She'd left home at eighteen, and now they only exchanged cards at Christmas and the occasional telephone call. She'd love to have a mother who was there, like Daff, all the time, to talk to, laugh with, share shopping trips — that sort of thing.

Not that Jix could share shopping trips with Daff, of course. Daphne hadn't left number 51 for over ten years because of her agoraphobia. It suited her admirably, she said, giving her tons of time for following all the soaps; and, of course, from April's point of view, the combination of her affliction and close proximity made her an absolutely perfect baby-sitter.

'It's an ill wind, sweet . . .' Daff always said.

April tiptoed into the dimly lit bedroom and peeped at the tiny truckle bed alongside hers. Her daughter, Beatrice-Eugenie, two and a half years old, the most gorgeous child in the universe, and the reason behind the roses-round-the-door dream, slept peacefully. Tired as she was, April allowed herself a few moments of sheer indulgence, just staring with total love, then dropped a kiss on the smooth

34

forehead, pulled the discarded duvet over the tiny shoulders, and crept back out of the room.

Sliding out of the appalling French maid's costume, too tired to put it on a hanger and knowing that if she didn't she'd be too tired to iron it tomorrow, she went for the half-measure and folded it over the arm of the chair. Then pouring the dregs from the one remaining bottle of wine in the fridge, she slumped onto the sofa. It was a hot and sultry night. Gone midnight. Beatrice-Eugenie would be awake by six. And April had all three of her part-time jobs to do tomorrow. She lit her last cigarette of the day, and squinted through the smoke at the gallery of paintings around the wall.

Sometimes she really hated Noah for leaving her with all this. Sometimes. Most of the time she still loved him more than life. She wondered if she would ever see him again.

Because of her unhappy home situation, Noah had been the answer to all her prayers. At thirty he'd been the only grown-up boyfriend she'd ever had. He was tall, with a rugby player's physique – even down to the broken nose – and she hadn't believed him when he'd said he was an artist. Artists, she'd imagined, were – well – like Jix. All sort of ethereal. Noah was anything but. His paintings were screaming blocks of colour which she didn't understand, but which apparently were exactly what the loft-livers were looking for. When he asked her to move in with him, in his flat in up-and-coming Bixford, she hadn't thought twice.

So number 51 had become her home, and Jix and Daff, and Joel and Rusty had become her neighbours, and life had been wonderful. She and Noah had lived on love and commissions for two years. Then, without warning, he'd decamped with one of the warehouse-living, share-dealing women for whom he'd been doing two paintings.

April blew a plume of smoke into the living room. It hovered in a blue stream on the still night air. The memory still hurt. Finding the note, finding Noah's side of the wardrobe empty, finding his brushes and canvases gone from the kitchen cupboard . . .

She stubbed out the cigarette and hauled herself to her feet. Five hours' sleep if she was lucky. Her eyes were already gritty at the thought as she switched off the lamps and the television and drifted into the bedroom. Beatrice-Eugenie stirred in her sleep, her straight hair fanned out in a halo on the pillow. Bending down to kiss her, April wondered how long it would take to give her child a proper life. A year? Two? Could she cope with another two years of non-stop work and scrimping and scraping?

With luck, though, she thought, sliding into bed, it would be sooner rather than later. All she had to do was to find Noah and tell him that he had a daughter. She pushed her head into the pillow, listening to the Bixford night-noises outside. With Jix's help and contacts she'd already searched for Noah for over two years without success, but she was sure she'd find him one day.

April closed her eyes and felt sleep rush in. Noah hadn't even known she was pregnant when he left. But when she found him, when he saw Beatrice-Eugenie, he'd come back, she knew he would.

chapter four

'Make that three tricolore salads, then and one green. Two lasagnes, a spag bol and a seafood risotto. Garlic bread all round, fizzy water – oh, and a carafe of Frascati. OK, darling? Got all that?'

April nodded, smiling her bimbette waitress smile, the one that came slightly lower down the scale than her bimbette cocktail-bar one, and flicked closed her little spiral-bound notebook. Easing herself between the Pasta Place's crowded tables, she padded towards the kitchen's swing doors. It was almost two o'clock, and the hordes of lunchtime grazers were showing no intention of returning to their offices. Not that she blamed them: the temperature was in the mid-nineties.

In the kitchen Sofia was leaning out of the trattoria's window, sucking in the foetid air from Bixford High Street, while Antonio, listening to the greyhound results on a 1960s transistor radio, flipped pasta with confident dexterity.

April wiped the perspiration from beneath her eyes and above her upper lip, and started to fan her face with the notebook. 'Oh, sorry – yeah, table twelve's finally made a decision.' She ripped out the top page and handed it to Sofia. 'They should be the last, and I put the closed sign up ten minutes ago. God, it's so hot! Maybe we'll get a storm to break it up.'

'Maybe.' Sofia hauled herself in from the window, studied the order, nudged her husband aside and began frying onions and garlic on autopilot. 'But, of course, coming from Umbria. I'm used to this weather.'

'Get away!' April grinned. 'You're from Dagenham!'

'But my genes are from Umbria,' Sofia said, snatching at a handful of fresh basil. 'It makes all the difference.'

April untied her white apron, and flexed her toes inside her sandals. Well, Daff's sandals really. She seemed destined to spend her life in other people's shoes. The previous night's Manolo Blahniks were Sofia's pride and joy. One day, when she'd found Noah and reunited her family, and got the cottage-in-the-country dream sorted out, she'd really have to buy a pair of shoes of her very own.

'Will it be OK if I leave you to wait on table twelve? Only I'm due to meet Jix at the stadium in half an hour and I'd like to see Bee first.'

'Of course,' Sofia nodded. 'You must spend some time with the little 'un. You work too hard, *cara*.'

'Have to. Can't pay the rent otherwise – and I certainly don't want my landlord hammering on my door. do I?'

She and Sofia pulled mocking faces at one another. The thought was too awful to contemplate. Number 51 and the Pasta Place, and in fact a good-sized chunk of Bixford High Street, belonged to the Gillespies. Oliver and Martina had bestowed the leases of the properties to their only son on his twenty-first birthday eight years previously, when the Gillespie Greyhound Stadium was in its embryonic design stages and Oliver was still passing backhanders to the planners. As landlords went, Rachman was sweet and peachy in comparison to Sebastian Gillespie.

'Sod it!' Antonio dropped the pasta on to the counter with a sticky slap and snapped off the radio. 'Beijing Bob has just won the two o'clock at Crayford!'

April and Sofia regarded him without sympathy. Living in Bixford, they both knew that gambling was a mug's game, and that heaping any sort of fortune on to the nose of a greyhound was asking for trouble.

'How much?' Sofia raised her voice above the sizzling pan. 'Not the bloody business tax money again?'

Antonio shook his head. 'It's not the money, Sofia, as I keep telling you. It's the form what damages the odds. Beijing Bob is due to run here at Gillespie's next Saturday, and I'd hoped to do him ante-post. Now he'll be odds on. No one will give me a decent price.'

April winked at Antonio, shrugged at Sofia, and headed for number 51.

Beatrice-Eugenie, wearing just pants and a floppy sun hat, was splashing happily in and out of a washing-up bowl in the back yard. April paused in the kitchen doorway, watching her with love, and thinking that even if the country cottage and the lawn were not a million miles away, those refinements would currently be wasted on her daughter. At this moment, screaming with laughter, and having a water battle with Jix's mum. Beatrice-Eugenie was obviously in heaven.

Daff was crouched on an upturned bucket, to the left of the doorstep in the high-walled yard. April knew it was just far enough outside not to bring on one of Daff's panic attacks, but still close enough for her to rescue Beatrice-Eugenie in case of an emergency.

'You finished? God, is that the time already?' Daff squinted up at her, temporarily abandoning squirting plumes of water from a washing-up liquid bottle much to Beatrice-Eugenie's chagrin. 'We've been having a smashing time, sweet – and I've put loads of sun block on her so's she won't get burned.'

'Thanks.' April squatted beside the bowl and splashed water over her daughter's smooth golden shoulders. 'You be a good girl for Daff, Bee. Mummy won't be long . . . and when I come back we'll go to the park.'

Beatrice-Eugenie wrinkled her small nose, tilted back the sun hat with the nonchalant air of a junior Frank Sinatra, and gave her mother a gappy smile. 'Ducks?'

'Ducks,' April confirmed, kissing the top of the sun hat. It had come from the charity shop next door to the Pasta Place, and despite frequent washings still smelled mouldy. 'And we'll go on the swing too. And then we'll have tea in the garden . . .'

Some garden, April thought, kissing her damp daughter again and standing up: a six-foot-square piece of concrete, walled on all sides, with only the persistent weeds adding any greenery. Still, one day, when she was a proper mother, it would all be different. Right now, she had to shimmy out of the waitress uniform, scramble into something suitable for the afternoon, and be at the stadium before Jix left. Then tonight, in the frilly French maid outfit in the Copacabana, she'd start the treadmill all over again.

'You had something to eat?' Daff resumed the water-squirting. 'I could get you a quick sandwich if you like. Me and Bee had Marmite.'

'No, I'm fine. Sofia and Tonio fed me, thanks. And I've got to dash.'

With a last check to make sure that Daff and Beatrice-Eugenie were fully equipped with Nivea, lemon barley water and Pringles, April trudged indoors.

'I thought you weren't coming.' Jix unpeeled himself from the deserted stands and stood up. 'I thought you'd skived off to do a spot of sunbathing in the park.'

'I wish.' April pushed the stray strands of hair back into

her scrunchie. 'It's so hot! I really wanted to stay with your mum and Bee and the washing-up bowl.'

Jix laughed. 'Sounds tempting . . . So – what do you want to do today? Stick together and take pot luck, or split and offer specials?'

'You stick to offering the specials. I prefer keeping my clothes on, thank you. And anyway, it depends who we've got this afternoon. You know I'm no good with the sad ones. I can't bear it when they cry.'

'Me neither.' Jix flipped through his clipboard. 'And I always believe them when they say they can't afford to pay – and I've been doing this for years. Sometimes I wonder why Oliver keeps me on.'

'Because you know far too much about him for him to let you go. And anyway, as debt-collectors go, you're ace. You never get heavy, and your softly-softly approach seems to work brilliantly. Even if it does take a bit longer to rake in all the money.' She smiled at him. 'And you don't look scary, which has to be a bonus. I mean, if you turned up on my doorstep looking like that, I'd definitely give you my last quid.'

Wearing the velvet flares, with a trailing multicoloured scarf round his waist, a tie-dye vest, a wondrous New Age array of beads and bangles, and with his long hair freshly washed and silky, Jix looked like an early Mick Jagger. Only, of course, April decided, far better-looking. Prettier. Nothing at all like the rest of Oliver Gillespie's henchmen, who were all scowling and pit-bullish.

'Stop it – you'll make me blush. Not. And you look pretty cool yourself.'

Cool, April thought, was absolutely the last thing she felt. The skimpy denim dress – like Bee's hat, from the charity shop – was already sticking to her, and her bare feet were slippery inside Daff's sandals. Still, the dress and

41

shoes would do for tramping the back streets of Bixford, trying to persuade people even more broke than she was to repay Oliver Gillespie's interest-loaded loans.

She'd been sharing Jix's debt-collecting round for nearly two years. Unofficially, of course. Oliver would have had a fit if he knew that she knew his secrets. And Martina would squawk so loudly that they'd have no trouble hearing her on the Isle of Dogs, and without doubt April would lose her job at the Copacabana, which would completely defeat the object.

At first April had been reluctant to become involved in this truly dingy side of the Gillespie enterprise, but without support from Noah, and with an abhorrence of turning to the State for aid, she needed all the money she could lay her hands on for Beatrice-Eugenie. Jix said it saved him time, and was scrupulously fair about splitting his percentage with her, and to be honest, she thought wryly, they made a good team.

Jix wooed the women with his beauty and quiet charm, while April flirted with men who would otherwise have slammed the door in her face, and persuaded them to part at least with something. That was why she always wore low-cut, short, tightly fitting clothes for the debt-collecting. That was why she flirted and teased and vamped until the men paid up. Despite frequent propositions, and one or two pretty scary moments, she'd so far managed to keep her dealings above board. She knew that Jix went to bed with most of the ladies who owed Oliver cash. They said they'd happily pay him for sex, and if he decided to use the money to pay off their Gillespie debt then that was his choice.

If it was extortion, or prostitution, or a bit of both. April simply couldn't afford to care. She and Bee had to survive, the dream had to be saved for, so it simply had

42

to be done. If she lay awake at night wondering with hot shame whether the means she was employing could ever justify the end, by the close of each afternoon when she added another wodge of notes to the under-the-bed chocolate tin, her moral scruples were mollified.

'I'll do from Anthony Eden Close to Nye Bevan Walk.' Jix was studying the clipboard. 'Which'll leave you Hugh Gaitskell House. OK?'

April groaned. 'God – not Mr Reynolds again! His terms were a fiver a kiss last week.'

Jix grinned. 'You wouldn't have to give me a fiver. I'd kiss you for nothing.'

'No. he meant *I* had to kiss him and *he'd* pay a – Oh!' She thumped him none too lightly on the arm. 'Sod off, Jix! Come on, then – let's make a move before I'm spotted here and given the third degree. I'm sure security must have clocked me a million times – and even if they are one burger short of a McDonald's – they're bound to put two and two together before long.'

April and Jix started to skirt the track's perimeter. The stadium, even in its shimmering early afternoon silence, was still awe-inspiring. The sandy track was silver smooth, the thousand windows reflected the sun in white-hot prisms, and the paintwork gleamed. The unseen army, employed to keep the stadium looking as luxurious as any palace, certainly knew their onions. Tonight, when the moths bumbled against the floodlights, and the dogs' excited yelping split the air, and the shouts of the punters hovered in a roar above Essex, it would all spring once more into glorious tacky life, but now it stood again like a cruise liner in dock, just waiting.

A large dark red car purred up to the imposing wrought-iron gates with the greyhounds rampant, slowed, and let down electric windows, allowing expensive air conditioning and Mahler to pour into the stifling afternoon. April and Jix stopped walking and squinted, then Jix motioned his head towards the visitor. 'I'll go and see what they want. You'd better keep out of sight just in case Oliver and Martina are around. Don't want too many questions, do we?'

April immediately ducked behind a chromium-plated pillar. The plum-coloured Daimler with the personalised number plate wasn't a car she recognised: definitely not belonging to one of the Gillespies' usual celeb cronies – sports stars, entertainers, politicians; she'd seen most of them hobnobbing with Oliver and Martina in the Copacabana. Jix, who was also in charge of car-parking for the chosen few, always gave her the lowdown on their bank-breaking vehicles on their nightly walks home. The Daimler was a stranger.

She watched Jix lope long-leggedly towards the gates, looking for all the world like a time-warped escapee from Woodstock. She watched him duck his head inside the car's open window, then point towards the offices at the far end of the stadium. He was smiling. The visitor was probably a woman. No, April corrected herself with a grin, it was *definitely* a woman.

Within five minutes he was back, the Daimler purring its silent way round the outside of the track in the direction of Oliver's suite of offices.

'Female?' April hazarded, sliding from behind the pillar. 'Middle-aged? HRT'd? Well-upholstered? Stinking rich? Invited you to visit her hotel room this evening?'

Jix gave her a withering stare as they headed towards the High Street. 'No, not at all. Female, yes. About twenty-one, I'd say. Posh Spice-thin. Definitely loaded. And we're probably going to meet up in the Copacabana tonight – if she's finished her meeting with the Gillespie tribe. Any other little details you'd like thrown in? Frock by Issy Miyake? Hair by Nicky? Scent by Calvin Klein?'

'Christ,' April sighed as the splendour of the stadium turned into the grey, scorching dross of Bixford. 'For a hippie, you're so bloody materialistic.'

'Realistic,' Jix said happily. 'Where there's brass there's usually more brass. And anyway, I knew her.'

'Get off! You don't know anyone with a Daimler – at least, not legally.'

'I mean I know who she is. So do you. She's everywhere – on chat shows, in the glossies, all over the broadsheets. She's Brittany Frobisher.'

April was stunned into momentary silence. Brittany Frobisher, brewery heiress, was currently the media's favourite It Girl. Brittany Frobisher, however, unlike most others of her ilk, actually seemed to work for her millions. Regularly photographed at film premieres and at hot clubs and parties, usually in the company of similarly loaded children of the famous-for-being-famous, Brittany Frobisher was also seriously beautiful.

'Why is Brittany Frobisher meeting Oliver and Martina, then? Is she one of Sebastian's girlies? Are they announcing their engagement?'

'Seb and Brittany? God, no! Actually, she's here strictly on business. We – as in we the Gillespie Stadium – are tendering for the Frobisher Platinum Trophy. It's going to be the biggest dog race ever next year. Biggest prize money, massive telly coverage, huge advertising sponsorship all putting greyhound racing firmly on the must-do map for the entire family – and Oliver wants it more than he wants another million quid.'

'Told you, did he? In one of your chummy little chats?'

Jix shook his head. 'I read it off his confidential e-mails. And the beautiful Brittany just confirmed it.' He paused, managing to look slightly ashamed. 'I – um – sort of hinted that as Oliver's ace PA, I had his ear. She says she'll be delighted to tell me more tonight over a drink . . .'

'She'll chew you up and spit out the pieces.'

'In my dreams.' Jix sighed blissfully.

April wrinkled her nose. 'Your mum'll go mad. You hip-grinding with the Tara Palmer-Tomkinson of the yeast and hops dynasty. It's not what she voted New Labour for.'

'Democracy and the devolution of the class system have always been my mum's strongest suits, actually. She voted for Tony Blair on those issues alone.' Jix came to a halt outside a block of high-rise cement flats. 'So I'll merely be living out her expectations. Now, are you ready for Mr Reynolds?'

'Nope.' April looked at the tower block and shuddered. 'And that was John Major.'

'John Major owes Oliver money?'

'No, dope – John Major was always banging on about the classless society.'

'Was he?' Jix flicked through his clipboard. 'Don't remember that far back. And don't change the subject. There are seven customers in the flats. Six should be easy-peasy. The seventh is Mr Reynolds. Now, Mr Reynolds still owes thirteen hundred. He's three payments behind. We need at least fifty. So, by my reckoning, that's ten kisses . . .'

April punched him again. 'Pack it in. I won't stoop to your level. Anyway, why are Frobishers here now if this prestigious race isn't until next year? I think you've got it wrong. I reckon she's one of Sebastian's women ready to bang in a paternity suit.'

'Don't you know nothing?' Jix poked out his tongue. 'These things take for ever to organise, like the Olympics or Glastonbury. Every dog track in the country's going to be tendering for the Platinum Trophy – and it's in February, only eight months away. Brittany's probably going to have to visit each stadium before Frobishers make their choice.'

'Nobody will outbid Oliver though, surely? Not even Wimbledon or Walthamstow? We all know what Oliver's like when he sets his greedy little heart on something.' April tipped her head back and gazed up at the thirty-two floors of Hugh Gaitskell House. 'And do I really have to do this one?'

'Yeah.' Jix blew her a kiss. 'Unless you'd rather do Freda Cope? She only owes twenty-five quid – but collecting it would involve putting on a bri-nylon wig and miming to *Cliff Richard's Greatest Hits* – not to mention the baby oil and strawberry yoghurt . . .'

'Mr Reynolds, here I come,' April scowled, easing her feet inside Daff's sandals. 'And as the lift is always vandalised, I'll meet you back here in about an hour, then?'

'Make it an hour and half,' Jix grinned. 'Freda's got a pretty horny daughter . . .'

Jix had been right, April thought as she thundered on Mr Reynolds' peeling and graffiti'd door. The first half-dozen of this afternoon's customers had grumbled about the heat, grumbled about having to cough up, grumbled about life in Hugh Gaitskell house, and eventually parted with their money. She'd written the receipts, stuffed the cash into the triple-lock satchel, and thanked them with a grateful smile.

The heat was all-enveloping, rising from the stairwell in clouds of ammonia and decay. April, trying to breathe through her mouth, wriggled inside the denim dress and knocked again.

'Yeah?' Mr Reynolds, wearing a dirty vest, dirtier trousers, and the sort of bad perm that Kevin Keegan had made his own in the seventies, peered through a crack in the door. 'Oh, it's you. I ain't got no money.'

'Please, Mr Reynolds.' April smiled, which proved difficult when she'd stopped breathing. 'Just something. Anything. Just enough to stop Mr Gillespie losing his temper . . .'

''E can lose 'is bleeding temper all 'e bleeding likes,' Mr Reynolds affirmed vigorously. 'I ain't got no money.'

In danger of passing out, April sucked in some air. The waft of stale cigarette smoke and unwashed body emanating from Mr Reynolds made her gag. 'Oh God – look – you owe so much. I can't go away empty-handed again – and no, don't even think about it. You're not coming any damn closer . . .'

Mr Reynolds gave a hideous wink. 'Pity. Nice little bit of skirt, you are. Dirty job for a pretty little thing like you . . . Tell you what – what if I gives you something you can sell? What about if I gives you something that's worth even more than I owes old Olly? What do you say?'

April shook her head. She knew that Jix sometimes took electrical goods in lieu and sold them in the market to raise Oliver's cash. She shrugged. 'Well, maybe . . . but it's got to be worth it. Not just some old tat.'

'This ain't no tat.' Mr Reynolds gave a stumpy-toothed grin. 'This'll make old Olly's eyes light up and no mistake.'

He closed the door. April, envisaging having to stagger down thirty-two floors carrying an armful of porn, somehow doubted that Oliver Gillespie would be exactly thrilled to ribbons with her business acumen.

''Ere.' Mr Reynolds yanked the door open again. 'Worth a fortune. That's me sorted, then. Full and final. What do you think?'

What April thought was obviously irrelevant as Mr Reynolds had slammed the door again and started shooting bolts into place. April stared at the piece of dirty string in her hands, then at the animal attached to the other end.

'Jesus.'

The greyhound blinked soft brown eyes at her and wagged a spindly brindled tail.

'Mr Reynolds!' April thundered on the door. 'Mr Reynolds! I can't take him!'

'You've taken 'im!' The voice echoed from the far side of the graffiti. ''E's all yours! 'Is name's Care Paravel. The castle thing. Out of that kids' story. The lion in the wardrobe one.'

Cair Paravel, April thought wildly. Brilliant. One of her childhood favourite bedtime stories. She pulled herself up quickly. 'I don't care what his name is – I can't take him! Mr Gillespie won't want him and –'

'You take him home then. 'E'll make a nice pet.'

'I can't take him home! I'm not allowed animals in my flat.'

'Tough tit, love. You could train 'im on and win a fortune. Now bugger off – I'm busy!'

April looked down at the greyhound, who was happily licking between her toes. God Almighty. Jix would go mad. Not to mention Sebastian Gillespie, the killer landlord. Not only was there a no-pets clause in her tenancy agreement, there was also a no-children one. She'd managed to keep Beatrice-Eugenie a secret from the Gillespies for two and half years, but she'd never manage to keep a greyhound hidden in number 51 as well – would she?

chapter five

J asmine stared at the trickle of people sifting through
the rusty turnstiles, and felt a prickle of apprehension
shifting along her spine. Would she ever, ever, be able
to live up to her grandfather's reputation?

'Benny Clegg – The Punters' Friend': the signs still
stood proudly beside her pile of upturned pallets and above
her ancient blackboard. Having told Peg that she had no
intention of changing the pitch's name, Jasmine had thought
that simply having the sign there would give her the courage
she needed for her first official appearance as a bookie.
Now she realised that even six pints of Old Ampney probably wouldn't provide enough Dutch pluck to get her
through this ordeal.

With less than an hour to go until the start of the
meeting, the greyhounds, along with the Ampney Crucis
holidaymaking punters, were already arriving expectantly
in the stadium. Roger and Allan, their joints set up on
either side of her, had drifted away to chew the form fat
with owners and trainers, and others in the know. Jasmine,
who was suddenly convinced that she now knew absolutely
nothing, stayed resolutely glued to her post.

It was the last Saturday of June, the evening sun was
low and still warm over the sea, and the bookmaker's
licence in her name had arrived from the Levy Board on

Wednesday morning. Well, it had arrived at the beach hut on Wednesday. It had been delivered to her parents' address some days before, if the postmark was anything to go by. As Jasmine's relationship with Philip and Yvonne was still frosty verging on cryogenic, Andrew had brought the fat envelope with him on one of his infrequent visits.

Jasmine sighed and sat down on the edge of a pallet, remembering. She'd ripped open the envelope, her eyes filling with tears and making the words on the official-looking forms all blurry. It was Benny's legacy, and she'd wished so much that she hadn't got it; she just wanted him to be alive more than anything in the world.

Andrew had been exasperated by the tears, and had clattered around the overcrowded beach hut, muttering that she should be over it by now, and that she should be pulling herself together, and eventually that she was making a laughing stock of her parents and him. Especially him. Then she'd cried some more, and Andrew had flounced out and she hadn't seen him since.

She'd probably never see him again. Watching the holi-daymakers in their shorts and T-shirts, and the Ampney Crucis residents in their dog-going best, all wandering amongst the dilapidated stands, Jasmine wondered if she cared. She'd lost Benny, and she'd alienated her parents – why not break off her engagement to Andrew and make it a disastrous personal hat trick? She'd miss him, of course. She'd got into the habit of loving him. She probably loved him in the sort of way that you loved a favourite, comfort-able sweater. Not that Andrew was always comfortable: more often than not he was definitely overwashed and scratchy. But he'd always been there. And she didn't hold out much hope of a replacement.

Andrew's tirade, she knew, had been caused only by the apparent ignominy of the bookie-and-beach-hut part of

51

her life. He was blissfully unaware that Benny's money was going to be pumped back into glamorising the stadium, or that she and Peg were going to tender for the Frobisher Platinum Trophy, or even that Ewan Dunstable was due back on the scene. Andrew, like her parents, simply couldn't believe that she'd chucked up the security of Watertite Windows, and the comfy family nest on the Chewton Estate, to become a bookmaker.

A bookmaker – like Benny . . . Jasmine took a deep breath. Benny had left her the pitch because he *knew* she could do it, so why on earth was she dithering around like a neurotic gnat? She'd been helping Benny for as long as she could remember; he'd always said all it took to be a successful bookie was tickets and chalk and a bit of nous. She'd listened to him chatting with Roger and Allan in the Crumpled Horn for most of her life; it was simply a matter, he'd claimed, of changing the prices, taking the mugs' money – and winning. Simple as that. A child could do it.

Jasmine stood up, brushing down her jeans. She *could* do it. No, more than that – she *would* do it, and make a success of it. It would be easier, of course, if she had someone writing up the bets for her, the way she had for Benny, but the crowd wasn't large, so she presumed she'd manage somehow. If only Andrew was more supportive, he might have come along tonight to help her. She giggled, imagining him in his chinos and immaculate shirts, frantic-ally scribbling on the foolscap sheet at the back of the joint as she doled out tickets and yelled, 'Eleven pounds to five, twenty three!'

'Jasmine! Darling!' Peg Dunstable suddenly powered her way out of the stands. 'How are you feeling?'

'Nervous,' Jasmine admitted, 'but more confident than I was half an hour ago. I was just thinking I could do with someone to do the writing up. I'm scared I'll make a mess of it.'

'We'll try and find someone,' Peg nodded, her race-night Doris Day wig – one with impossibly bubbly layers and a fringe – dancing in time. 'Of course Ewan will be able to help you out when he arrives. It'll do him good to have a little job. Keep him out of mischief.'

Jasmine squeaked and puffed out her cheeks in a gesture of disbelief. Andrew would definitely break off the engagement – if she hadn't already done it first, of course – if he thought she and Ewan were snuggled up together under Benny's banner. Not that Ewan would be interested in her *that* way, she reminded herself quickly. Even if they hadn't known each other so long that they were like brother and sister, Ewan had always been attracted to such beautiful women – oh, and, of course, he was still married to Katrina – even if he seemed to forget the fact on a regular basis.

'I thought he'd have arrived by now.'

'So did I.' Peg flicked at the Peter Pan collar of her white shirt. It sat neatly over the lapels of a tightly fitting fifties-style black suit. It was definitely a steal from *Move Over Darling*. 'I telephoned Katrina to see if they'd had a reconciliation and gathered from the invective that they hadn't. As far as she knew he was in London – and she was more than happy for him to stay there from what I gathered.' She sighed. 'You know, I do think he's got himself mixed up in something iffy this time.'

'Of course he hasn't,' Jasmine grinned. 'It'll just be another married woman or something like that. He'll be hiding from an irate husband.'

'I don't think so, pet, not this time. He told me he was in trouble, some undercover work or something, and Katrina said that he'd got involved with freedom fighters.'

'Freedom fighters? Ewan?' Jasmine rocked with laughter.

'Idealistic he may be, but he's also bone idle. I'm sure natural sloth and procrastination are not top of a mercenary's must-have list. Katrina was probably just shit-stirring. And he was far more likely to have said underwear than undercover. Don't worry, Peg. Ewan will turn up here before long.'

'I sincerely hope so. I do like to be able to keep an eye on him.' Peg patted Jasmine's arm, pausing to peer into the distance as a volley of high-pitched yapping splintered the Tannoy's version of 'By the Light of the Silvery Moon'. 'Damn! It sounds like one of the tourists has interfered with a dog! I'll have to go and raise Cain. Now, you try your best tonight for Benny's sake – and to cock a snook at your boring family – and I'll pop along as often as I can. OK?'

Jasmine nodded as Peg marched away to bring order to the chaos which looked like erupting at the kennel end of the stadium. *For Benny's sake* . . . She straightened her shoulders and picked up the chalk. As neither Roger nor Allan had put up their opening prices, she knew she'd just have to wing it. She'd always taken it so much for granted – the names of the dogs for each race just miraculously appeared, the prices beside each runner doing the same. For all her involvement, it had never occurred to her to ask her grandfather how these things actually materialised.

Of course, she knew that at the larger stadiums the bookmakers all had pre-printed disposable sheets to pin up prior to each race, and wrote the odds against them with fat marker pens. Such innovations had not yet reached Ampney Crucis.

Oh well, the names at least were easy. They were listed on the race card. Jasmine chalked up each of the six dogs for the first race in their trap order, her capital letters sloping downwards more each time until it would be beneficial to be standing on a slope in order to read them. She stared at them critically. They'd have to do – she'd try harder for the next race.

Now for the prices . . . She frowned. That shouldn't be too difficult, surely? Ampney Crucis attracted the same trainers and owners, and the same greyhounds and their offspring year after year. She knew them all. The stadium didn't attract big owners or trainers from far afield, and the only time a stranger infiltrated their ranks it was to try out a novice greyhound far away from the touts' prying eyes.

She knew well enough that anything trained by Bess Higgins might be expected to win, and anything trained by Able Nelson wouldn't. Then there were the regular names who occasionally chucked up winners, but more often than not fielded the also-rans. Having sorted out the pros and cons in her mind, Jasmine beamed and hummed along with *Doris Day's Greatest Hits*, chalking up the relevant starting prices. Bess's had the shortest odds and Able's the longest; the others sort of fudged somewhere in between. Piece of cake really, she thought, finally making Mariner Queen twenty to one and blowing the chalk dust from her fingers.

The public address system suddenly ceased its nasal interpretation of 'Love Me or Leave Me', and Gilbert, who doubled up as the snack bar's hot-dog seller in between races, coughed chestily into the microphone.

'Ladies and gentlemen, welcome to Ampney Crucis Greyhound Stadium. The first race will begin in fifteen minutes' time, which should, by my reckoning – he paused here for a chuckle at his own wit – 'give you just quarter of an hour to place your wagers. May I wish you, on behalf of the management, an enjoyable and prosperous evening.' The microphone clicked off, then immediately screeched on again. Gilbert was still wheezy. 'Oh, and there will be hot and cold drinks and a selection of refreshments, all at very reasonable prices, available from the kiosk between races. Thank you.'

Confident that she was now ready for anything, Jasmine opened her foolscap double-entry ledger, made sure the money satchel was out of reach of sticky fingers, and felt a punch of excitement land just beneath her ribs. The greyhounds were coming out for the parade!

The handlers, in their buff-coloured coats, led the six dogs along the sandy track in front of the stands. The dogs' jackets, red, blue, white, black, orange, and black and white stripes – always in that order from one to six – blurred as Jasmine sniffed back tears. Benny always loved this bit: the first sight of the dogs as they pranced away from the visitors' kennels, sniffing the air and each other, clashing leather muzzles, wagging whippy tails.

The holidaymaking crowds were getting excited now, pushing towards the rails, calling to each other. Jasmine, with her float of £500 beginning to appear merely small change, swallowed nervously. Casting surreptitious glances across at Allan and Roger's boards, she could see that her odds on Mariner Queen, the five dog, were far too generous.

Just as she reached for her cloth to amend the mistake, a weasely-looking man in vest and braces thrust himself forward.

'I'll take the twenties on Mariner Queen, my duck.'

She groaned. Sod it! Too late. She glanced down at the fifty-pound note clutched in the scrawny, freckled hand. Christ! If the five dog won she'd be paying out twice her float – and then some! She handed over the ticket. 'Er – one thousand to fifty – seventy-six.'

She hastily rubbed out the twenty to one and replaced it with twos.

Allan shook his head across the knot of punters. 'You'll regret that one, Jasmine. Better lay some off.'

What? Oh yeah – dead easy. With whom exactly? It was OK for Roger and Allan, they packed up their joints occasionally and decamped to race courses across the south of England, taking in horses as well as dogs. They had contingency plans. Laying off unwelcome high bets on a potential winner was easy when the ranks of bookmakers stretched into infinity. There was no mug bookie here who would happily take her money on the favourite, simply to watch his own profits slump. Allan and Roger had probably had their own little wagers during the week, cancelling out any would-be losses with bookies at Brighton and Plumpton.

Praying that Mariner Queen would catch a cold on the first bend, Jasmine shoved the foolscap ledger under her chin and doled out a rush of nice and simple pound bets to a clutch of women in white cardigans and cross-over sandals. Only another thousand of those and she'd be able to pay out the weasely man should the worst happen.

As the minutes ticked away, and the odds fluctuated with each bet, Jasmine chalked and rubbed, took cash and handed out slips, and made sure that each transaction was marked in the ledger. God! Much more of this and she was going to meet herself coming back!

'Very impressive,' Clara, wearing pale linen trousers and a handkerchief top, grinned. 'If I didn't know you better, Jas, I'd say you looked pretty organised.'

'I am organised,' Jasmine hissed, taking a last-minute ten-pound bet on the favourite. 'I'm amazingly organised, thank you. A little frazzled because I haven't got three pairs of hands, but coping admirably.'

'Give us that book thing, then.' Clara held out an elegant hand. 'And tell me what I have to do.'

Jasmine passed her the ledger, and wiped the blackboard. 'Nothing at all until the next race. All bets are finished on this one. The dogs are going behind.'

'Behind? Behind what?'

'The traps. Haven't you learned anything in your years in Ampney Crucis?'

Clara shook her head. 'I've tried really hard not to make the greyhound stadium one of my priority places to enjoy a glass of Chardonnay.'

'Just as well then, because Gilbert's never got beyond tea or coffee – and you don't know what you're missing. Still, there's no time to educate you now. The first race is about to start. I'll give you a crash course in bookmaking during the lull between races.'

'How many are there?'

'Thirteen tonight.'

'Thirteen?' Clara's eyebrows rocketed into her hair. 'Thirteen? Wake me up when it's all over!'

Jasmine poked out her tongue. 'Watch and learn. You'll soon be hooked, believe me.'

Unclipping the leashes, the dog-handlers were already manoeuvring their quivering charges into their respective traps. The crowd was hushed as Gilbert chestily built the tension for the off. Jasmine, uttering a quick prayer that Mariner Queen wouldn't win, watched as Bunny, the hare boy, took up his position behind the start. She smiled to herself. That was something else they'd have to sort out before the Frobisher's Brewery high-ups descended on them to check out the track's suitability. All the massive stadiums had automated hares: huge remote-controlled beasts in fluorescent colours which zinged aggressively round the track like enraged feather dusters. Ampney Crucis still retained the antiquated equivalent of Peter Rabbit.

Bunny, who had refused to change jobs even when his

care worker had found him a nice little trolley-pushing number at Tesco, now held the hare in place, kept his eye on the starter, and, at the signal, pushed the button. The moth-eaten fur ball hurtled away on its rail, rattling teasingly past the traps, then the six gates shot open, and six canine streaks hit the track.

The roar from the stands instantly drowned Gilbert's screeching commentary, and Jasmine, on tiptoe, watched as the greyhounds tore past. A blur of brindle and black and white. A gash of coloured jackets. A flurry of kicked-up sand. They were round the first bend in a nanosecond.

'Who's winning?' Clara clutched Jasmine's arm, all feigned disinterest forgotten. 'Is it the orange one?'

As the orange one was Mariner Queen, Jasmine pulled an agonised face. 'God, I hope not! No – it's the six dog in the stripes.' That was OK. One of Able Nelson's less favoured runners. 'With the two dog catching fast.' Not so good. Bess Higgins's second favourite.

The volley of cheering from the punters seemed to act as a spur, and in a super-canine effort to catch the hare, the greyhounds accelerated into the home straight. Twenty-four elegantly muscled legs pumping like pistons, six sets of powerful shoulders bumping and barging, they belted after their quarry.

'It's the orange one!' Clara screamed triumphantly. 'He's out in front! He's going to win!'

'He's a she, and no, she isn't. Battling Bertie's going to take it!'

Battling Bertie, coal black, and wearing the red jacket, literally threw himself across the finish line. The three judges, all Ampney Crucis worthies, gave a unanimous thumbs-up and Jasmine punched the air in triumph. Battling Bertie was one of Able Nelson's least-fancied dogs. Hallelujah!

'Bless them,' Clara said. 'How sweet! Look – they're all still running after the rabbit!'

'Hare – and of course they are. They don't know they're racing – and don't look at me like that. No one's ever bothered to explain it to them. They just think they're having a good time. Now, make yourself useful – grab this.' Jasmine thrust the bulging satchel into Clara's hands. 'When a winning punter gives me their ticket, I'll check it off in the ledger and tell you how much to pay out. OK? Clara – OK?'

'Jesus, Jas!' Clara's eyes were huge as she peered into the money bag. 'Do you know how much cash you've got in here? Hundreds and hundreds of pounds – maybe thousands! And that's just on one race! And there's another twelve to go! My God! You'll be a millionaire by the end of the week!'

'I wish. At least half of this will have to go to the punters who backed Battling Bertie – and God knows what will happen in the next few races.' Jasmine braced herself as the successful punters all converged from the stands, waving their tickets. 'Ready for the onslaught?'

For a frantic five minutes, she took winning tickets, checked them with the ledger entries, and instructed Clara how much money to pay out on each one. Roger and Allan, engaged in the same occupation, gave her conspiratorial grins across the holidaymaking heads. Jasmine felt a surge of blissful happiness. She'd done it! Her first race! She was a bookie – a real bookie – just like Benny had intended.

'All going OK, pet?' Peg powered her way through the crowds. 'No probs?'

'None. Clara's been a star – and Mariner Queen didn't win.' Jasmine was still suffused in the afterglow of triumph. 'And I'm going to do this for the rest of my life! I'll be like Grandpa, still taking bets when I'm -' She stopped and looked at Peg's face. 'What's up? It's not Ewan, is it?'

Clara, counting out fivers like she'd been born to it, paused momentarily at the mention of the name.

'Much closer to home.' Peg shrugged her padded shoulders. 'Your bloody father.'

'Dad? He's *here*?'

'No, unfortunately. If he'd been here I'd have cheerfully removed his head from his bloody smarmy shoulders!'

Jasmine blinked. 'What's he done this time?'

'According to the latest kennel gossip, he,' the Doris Day wig wobbled angrily, 'and his bloody planning committee sodding cronies, have apparently filed a motion for the north-east corner of Ampney Crucis to be redeveloped into the Merry Orchard Shopping Plaza.'

'Oh, wow! Really?' Clara was practically jigging up and down 'With designer outlets and stuff like that?'

'Precisely stuff like that.' Peg's glare was withering. 'You stupid child.'

Jasmine frowned. 'Hey, come on, Peg. There's no need to be snotty to Clara. Ampney Crucis could do with a bit of a spruce up and –'

'And we're on the north-east corner!' Peg roared. 'This stadium is slap-bang in the middle of it! And your beach hut's on the periphery, pet, so I wouldn't look too damned smug!'

Jasmine felt the euphoria drain away from her like the air from a punctured balloon: slowly, and with a plaintive hiss. Her father couldn't do it! Could he? Her head reeled. Of course he could. And probably would – especially with her mother's strident voice nagging him. How better to get their revenge on Benny's humiliating words in the Crumpled Horn on the day of the funeral? How better to make sure their only daughter toed the party line and returned to the family home, the dutiful fiancé, and the

61

proper job? How better to wipe away the last ignominious traces of Philip and Yvonne Clayton, pillars of Ampney Crucis society, having once been related to Benny Clegg – the Punters' Friend?

'Bastard!'

'Couldn't have phrased it better myself.' Peg gave a grim smile. 'We'll have to put our heads together on this one. I'll speak to Roger and Allan and –'

'Ladies and gentlemen!' Gilbert rasped rudely into the conversation. 'The runners for the second race are just starting their parade. This race, a 480 metre sprint, is sponsored by Eddie Deebley's Fish Bar, with a trophy for the winning owner and trainer – and a piece of cod and six penn'orth for the losers!' Gilbert's voice disappeared into paroxysms of laughter.

'Silly sod!' Peg glared at the speaker trumpeting above their heads. 'Thinks he's bloody Tommy Cooper!' She patted Jasmine's arm. 'I'll leave it with you, pet. You best have a word with your damned father as soon as possible.'

chapter six

'So that makes two thousand, three hundred, and forty-two pounds!' Clara, her voice rising an entire octave in amazement, called towards the open door. Sitting on the edge of Jasmine's bed, balancing a beaker of Old Ampney shandy on her knees, and with the night's takings arranged in heaps across the duvet, she gave a further whoop of delight. 'Good God, Jas – two and a half grand in one night – three nights a week – that'll mean your annual salary is – bloody hell!'

Jasmine, perched on the top step of the beach hut's veranda in the darkness, was only half listening. It should have been wonderful, her first night. She'd made a profit and she'd done Benny proud. But even without being there, her parents and Andrew – she lumped Andrew in with them purely out of pique – had completely ruined it.

Taking another mouthful of celebratory beer, she pushed her fringe away from her eyes and sighed heavily. She was pretty sure that her father's council planning committee had no intention at all of demolishing the stadium – after all, it had been tried before and come to nothing – but just the mention of it was enough to stir the local anti-greyhound contingent into protests and boycotts and similar aggravation. Whether it was genuine or not, it had taken the shine off the night somehow; sown seeds of doubt over her bookmaking future. Probably just as they'd planned it would.

'Jasmine! Are you listening to me? I said –'

Jasmine bit her lip. 'Sorry. I know . . . yes, it's great. But don't forget, the good nights at the track are usually only in the summer months. Grandpa always had to balance out his holidaymaking profits against weeks and weeks in the winter when you were hard-pressed to get more than twenty people into a meeting, and every night meant a loss.'

'I'm sure we can come up with some business plan to tide you over the closed season.' Clara, ever the businesswoman, staggered through the assault course of cramped furniture and nudged in beside Jasmine on the step. 'And Benny must have pulled off some major coups if his legacies were anything to go by.'

Jasmine heaved a sigh. She supposed he must. She just wished he'd let her in on one or two of his secrets. Nights like this one definitely weren't going to be the norm.

Clara's eyes were gleaming. 'You know, much as I hate to say it, it's been bloody impressive. I thought you'd make a right hash of it –'

'Like I have everything else? Give me time.'

'Dope!' Clara hugged her. 'You're only just starting, Jas. You're just a late beginner in the finding-your-feet stakes – and this is something you can make a success of all on your own.'

'Maybe . . .' Jasmine listened to the invisible sea tugging at the shoreline shingle as the tide receded. 'As long as Mum and Dad don't foul it up for me first.'

Clara drained her half-pint glass. 'God! You don't really believe what Peg said, do you? This place thrives on gossip and speculation. Not that a shopping mall wouldn't be much appreciated – but not, of course, at the expense of the stadium.'

Despite her gloom, Jasmine laughed. Clara's addiction to retail therapy was legendary. It had passed into local folklore ever since they were at school – she and Clara and Andrew and Ewan, together since Ampney Crucis Junior Mixed. They'd taken their pocket money into Bournemouth on Saturday mornings, and while Clara had always bought high-fashion girlie things like pretty tiny tinselled purses or patterned tights or palettes of eye make-up, Jasmine had spent hers on sweets and comics. Clara had always seemed grown-up, somehow. Jasmine felt that even now, by comparison, she was still at the twenty something equivalent of gobstobbers and *Bunty*.

She drained her glass and closed her eyes in the soft darkness. All those years ago . . . when Clara had wanted to be the next Margaret Thatcher, and Andrew had wanted to be rich, and Ewan, because he and Andrew were rivals even then and had wanted to go one better, had wanted to be rich and famous, and she – she grinned, remembering. She'd wanted to be like Benny . . .

Clara balanced her beaker on the sandy step and stood up. 'I ought to be going. I've got a breakfast meeting tomorrow, despite it being Sunday, with some saddies who are here for a golf-and-business weekend. But thanks for tonight. It was good fun. I've spent my life avoiding the stadium like the plague. I always thought getting mixed up in greyhound racing was a bit sleazy, but it was a real blast.'

'Does that mean you'll be writing up for me again?'

'Maybe . . .' Clara twirled her car keys. 'Especially if Ewan is back on the scene.'

Jasmine sat for a little longer in the darkness after the red taillights of Clara's hatchback had disappeared along the cliff road. If only Ewan hadn't married Katrina, he and Clara would have been perfect for one another, she was sure. They'd enjoyed teenage flirtations – and, of course, had had the celebrated affair a couple of years back – and it was because of Ewan, Jasmine knew, that Clara never stayed long in any of her relationships.

She sighed, leaning back against the open door. They'd both made a mess of the lurve thing, really, hadn't they? She because she'd got Andrew, and Clara because she hadn't got Ewan. Maybe they should both have moved away from Ampney Crucis years ago – but Clara was busy climbing the Makings Paper corporate ladder, while Jasmine had been blissfully happy simply to be here with Benny.

Feeling the tears once again rising unbidden behind her eyes, Jasmine swallowed quickly. It must be the Old Ampney ale that was causing all this depressive introspection. What she needed, she decided, trying to work out where the darkness of the sky and the blackness of the sea actually met, was a rollicking, heady, just-for-fun affair. Oh well, after she'd broken off her engagement, of course. A girl had to retain some standards.

There were still a few night sounds: the rushing of the surf, the distant voices of home-going Ampney-Crucians, the shrill giggling of teenagers somewhere up by the beer garden of the Crumpled Horn. Had she ever giggled shrilly as a teenager? She feared she probably hadn't. Andrew had never been given to sudden lunges of passion in shadowy places. It was one of the many things she'd missed out on. Maybe she should start catching up? It would be a bit complicated, of course, having her first grown-up taste of self-employment *and* rejuvenating herself into an adolescent at the same time, but she was sure, if she put her mind to it, she'd manage it somehow.

Still, she thought, grabbing hold of the handrail and

pulling herself to her feet, first things first. Before she started to enjoy herself at any level, she'd really have to speak to her father about whether the Merry Orchard Shopping Plaza was simply a nasty rumour intended solely to put a dampener on her new career, or a glass-and-chromium reality.

Tugging closed the beach hut's warped wooden doors, she paused. Had she heard something? Someone? Holding her breath, she listened again. Yes – there were definitely footsteps plodding slowly down the cliff steps. One set? Two? It was difficult to tell. Her palms were suddenly sticky, and for the first time since she'd left home, she questioned the wisdom of living in the hut with doors which only held together with a sort of hook-and-eye contraption and one rusty bolt.

While Ampney Crucis was way down the list of Dorset's crime hot spots, nevertheless, there were enough people who knew that she lived here alone, who knew she'd taken over Benny's pitch, and who would therefore be aware that she'd pocketed substantial winnings that evening.

Damn! Sod! Damn! She fumbled with the fastener. Why hadn't she taken Clara up on her offer of driving into Bournemouth and depositing the takings in the night safe? She held the doors together, her hands shaking. The bolt wouldn't shoot home. She rattled at it again, her anxiety making her even more clumsy than usual.

'Jasmine! It's me!'

She jumped at the voice echoing from the other side of the scarlet panels, then felt a surge of relief, immediately followed by a wave of anger. Andrew? What the hell did he want at gone midnight?

Wriggling the bolt free and pushing the door open again, she peered out into the sultry darkness. 'God – you scared me. I was just going to bed.'

Andrew, outlined against the black sky, looked slightly encouraged by the statement. 'I saw your lights on down here. I thought I ought to check on you.'

'Why?' She pulled the door open wide enough for him to step inside the beach hut. With both of them in there it was very crowded. She was pressed up against the chiffonier. 'I don't need looking after.'

Andrew, who was in danger of being garrotted by the washing line, ducked under it. 'Don't you? I beg to differ.'

Jasmine wrinkled her nose. Why did Andrew always have to sound so pompous? Why hadn't she noticed it before? Maybe she had; maybe she'd simply chosen to ignore it as part of the comfort thing.

'Jasmine?' He'd manage to extricate himself from the towels draped on the line and was looking round at the clutter with some exasperation. 'Are you listening to me?'

'Not really. It's late and I'm tired and I don't think there's anything to say. Not tonight, anyway.' She pressed even closer to the chiffonier. 'Did my parents send you?'

'What?'

Jasmine narrowed her eyes. Andrew looked – what? Shifty? Worried? Whatever it was, it passed immediately and he'd regained his equilibrium within a split second.

'Your parents? No, of course not. I've been in the Crumpled Horn with the blokes from the dealership. Quiz night. We beat the Old Speckled Hen.'

'To a pulp? How cruel.'

Andrew, who obviously didn't see the funny side, frowned. 'There were crowds of holidaymakers coming in right on last orders. They'd been to the stadium. I remembered it was your first night as a . . .' He looked embarrassed and trailed off.

'Go on. You can say it. It won't contaminate you. A bookie. Try it. B-o-o-k-i-e.'

'You've changed, Jasmine, do you know that? There's an air of flippancy about you. Something of the dark side.'

'God – now you sound like Ann Widdecombe – or Pink Floyd. Or maybe even –'

'My point proved, I think.' Andrew looked smug. 'Anyway, as I was saying, I remembered that you would be working as a – er – as well, your grandfather's replacement – and I thought I'd see how it went.'

'What the hell for?' Jasmine felt truculent. She was tired and longed for a shower and to crawl into the downy feather bed which had served her grandparents well for the entirety of their married life. 'As I recall, the last time the subject was raised, you chucked the Levy Board licence at me, told me to stop snivelling, and stormed off out of here before I got tear stains all over your Fred Perry.'

'Yes, well, maybe I was a little hasty. I should have been more sympathetic, I realise that with hindsight.' Andrew shrugged. 'And despite our previous disagreements on the subject, I do care about what happens to you. If you're determined to see this thing through, then I suppose I should be supportive. We're engaged, for heaven's sake.'

'Are we?' Jasmine stared at her grandparents' wedding photo on top of the chiffonier. Would she and Andrew ever stand, dusted with rose petals, beneath the lich-gate of St Edith's, looking that besotted? Somehow she doubted it.

'Of course we are.' Andrew looked a little affronted. 'You're still wearing the ring.'

Jasmine stared at the diamond chip on her wedding finger. 'Only because I've eaten too many doughnuts recently and can't get it off.'

Andrew sort of smiled. It tweaked at the corners of his mouth but got no further. Jasmine really didn't care whether he thought she was joking or not. She was sure

69

he'd only sneaked up on her hoping to find her sobbing into her Horlicks after making a complete dog's breakfast of her first night. Or maybe her parents had suggested that he should visit her and find out if she'd already capitulated beneath the threat of the Merry Orchard Shopping Plaza. Whatever the reason for his visit, she just wanted to cut it short.

Andrew obviously wasn't taking the hint. The smile moved up a fraction to somewhere just short of jaunty. 'So, you're not going to offer me a drink or anything?'

She shook her head. 'No. Sorry. Clara and I finished up the Old Ampney about an hour ago. So, if you don't mind –'

'Jesus Christ!' His eyes were suddenly riveted on the folding door separating the two rooms.

'What? What's the matter?' Jasmine levered herself off the chiffonier and sucked in her breath to negotiate Benny's fireside chair.

Andrew remained rooted to the spot, slack-jawed, gazing into the bedroom. Clara had left the lamp on. The night's takings were still tumbled across the poppy and daisy duvet.

Jasmine bit back a grin of triumph. 'Oh, goodness! I'd forgotten to put away my small change. Is that what shocked you? The sight of so much money.' She pushed past him and, pulling open the drawer of the bedside cabinet, scooped the notes and coins inside and slammed it shut. 'Don't worry, Andrew. I promise not to spend it all at once.'

'Jasmine . . .' His voice was almost awe-struck. 'Please, please stop talking like Clara. Please start being yourself again. And please tell me you're not intending to keep all that cash in here.'

'Of course I am. I'll bank it on Monday.'

'You're going to keep it in here? For two days? There must be –'

70

'Two thousand three hundred and forty-two pounds exactly.' Jasmine sighed. 'And yes, it's my takings from tonight. Less my float. Not a bad profit. Now, would you mind very much just clearing off? I really want to go to bed.'

'We could go together.'

Jasmine whimpered. Please, no. She flapped her hands. 'Not a good idea. You can't ignore me for weeks then come breezing back in here expecting to snatch up your conjugals at the drop of a hat.'

'Jas . . . Darling . . .' He moved towards her, his progress only slightly impeded by the bulk of the furniture. 'I've missed you so much. I hated falling out. And you really need someone here to keep an eye on all that cash.'

Casting a frantic look around her, knowing there was nowhere to go, Jasmine toyed with the idea of leaping across the bed like a demented trampoline artist and triple somersaulting out of the window. It would never work. She'd never get her eleven and a half stones off the ground.

If she couldn't do athletic stunt woman, she was pretty sure she could pull off simpering and girlie. 'Well – er – actually, I've got a terrible headache . . .'

'Poor baby . . .' Andrew reached out and practically tugged her across the top of the Lloyd Loom ottoman. 'Let me kiss it better.'

Jasmine, muttering a strangled oath into the recesses of his polo shirt, tried to push him away. Andrew, damn him, was clinging to her like a limpet on superglue. After a few seconds of futile and embarrassing struggling, she gave up the fight.

'There,' Andrew said in what he patently thought was a sexy whisper. 'Isn't it lovely to be back together again?'

Jasmine clenched her teeth and groaned, 'Yeah. Lovely . . .'

*

In the pink and pearly light of an Ampney Crucis morning, Andrew really didn't look his best. With his mouth wide open and his hair lank, and most of the poppy and daisy duvet clutched to his groin, he really was an unprepossessing sight.

Jasmine, furious with herself for being such a pushover, edged away from him and slid her feet to the floorboards. They were warm beneath her skin, and the mingled scents of desiccated seaweed and salt and hot sand rose through the cracks to greet her. As quietly as possible, she pulled on her discarded T-shirt to cover her nakedness, and tiptoed out of the bedroom.

'Bugger!'

The ottoman, as always, caught her unawares. Pulling an agonised face she glimpsed back into the bedroom. Apart from a little burst of staccato snorting and a twitch of the poppies and daisies, Andrew continued to sleep soundly.

Deciding it was far kinder to allow him a prolonged Sunday morning lie-in, Jasmine quietly rinsed out one mug and filled it with a tea bag, a dollop of milk and two sugars. Then, setting the kettle to boil on the gas ring, she unbolted the double doors and hooked them back against the flaking wooden walls. The longer Andrew slept, the better. She really didn't want a rerun of the previous night's one-sided display of unbridled passion. Money, she'd decided, must be one heck of an aphrodisiac. Andrew had almost indulged in foreplay.

The veranda was already warm from the morning sun, which scattered sequins across the sea, and slightly gritty beneath her bare feet. Settling down in one of the canvas chairs to wait while the kettle boiled, Jasmine watched as Ampney Crucis slowly unfurled.

Other beach-hut residents, those who simply used their chalets for daytime use, were arriving with portable barbecues and cool bags and bathing costumes and the Sunday papers. Jasmine waved along the row as they opened their doors and switched on their radios. Everyone waved back, shouting greetings about it being another scorcher, and this being the life. Jasmine nodded and returned the greetings, albeit sotto voce so as not to disturb Andrew.

Shifting her gaze to the cliff path, she watched lazily as the holidaymakers, fortified by a full English inclusive of fried slice, began to emerge from the road behind the Crumpled Horn, strolling from their B&Bs, carrying enough paraphernalia to see Ranulph Fiennes through at least two more expeditions. The village still attracted families not brave enough or rich enough to attempt flights to Orlando or Majorca. The women, all of a type, had white cardigans, and tight holiday perms, and sunburned foreheads, while their menfolk sported replica football shirts in stiff nylon, and uniform baggy shorts. Jasmine smiled as small children in neon bright beachwear scampered down the wobbling wooden steps to the beach, just as their parents and grandparents had before them. Just as she had throughout her childhood.

These annual visitors were more than happy with Eddie Deebley's Fish Bar and the Crow's Nest Caff and the ice-cream kiosk, all of which were waking and stretching and putting out their canopies and tables and chairs. The Crow's Nest also did a fine line in buckets and spades, Lilos and risqué postcards. It suited the unsophisticated Ampney Crucis holidaymakers – and Jasmine – down to the ground.

Hearing the kettle rattling its lid with impatient hisses, Jasmine hauled herself to her feet, and made tea as silently as possible. Andrew, thankfully, was still sleeping, undisturbed by the early morning noises, and she shuffled back to the veranda with her mug. The sun caught on the facets of her engagement ring, shooting tiny iridescent stars across her finger. She twisted it, thinking how pretty it looked. Was this going to be enough? Walking in Benny's shoes, married to Andrew, living in Ampney Crucis until it was her turn to be interred in St Edith's churchyard?

She sipped her tea, watching a sand castle take shape at the bottom of the steps, knowing that it would be crumbled within the hour by the gentle swell of the incoming tide. Yes, she knew, was definitely the answer to the first and third questions. And the second? She sighed. Possibly. Probably. After all, what other choice did she have?

chapter seven

'Ready?' April screwed up her eyes against the fierce glare of the afternoon sun, and peered into the grey misty distance of Bixford's municipal park. 'Shall I let him go?'

Jix, who was perched on a second-hand mountain bike purloined from Joel and Rusty upstairs at number 51, was merely a blurred outline against the lavatera bushes, owing to the heat haze and low-hanging industrial smog. However, as far as April could see, he was nodding.

'Was that a yes?'

She clutched more tightly at Cair Paravel's collar. The greyhound was already squirming himself into a frenzy of excitement.

'Yes!' Jix's shout echoed above the screams of the roller-bladers and the Can-Can tinkle of the ice-cream van as it Formula One'd round the park's perimeter. 'Yes! Let him go! Three-two-one! Now!'

Giving Cair Paravel's blue brindled head an encouraging pat and uttering a prayer to the god of greyhound racing, April let go of the collar. In a whirl of long legs and rotor-blade tail, Cair Paravel shot across the scorched grass like an Exocet missile. Jix, pedalling like fury, and with one of Beatrice-Eugenie's teddy bears trailing from the bicycle's rear spokes, disappeared round a bend in the shrubbery. Within seconds, Cair Paravel had also vanished from view, leaving only puffs of dust and debris in his wake. April, beaming with maternal pride, clapped her hands and ran to catch up with them.

Summer in the city, she reckoned, was definitely nothing to sing about. The air was clogged and festering, and despite her charity shop cut-off denims and a skimpy T-shirt, the sweat was trickling uncomfortably between her breasts. She'd long ago discarded Daff's sandals, and her bare feet were slippery and dirty from the grass.

Turning the shrubbery corner, forcing her way between a drooping flowering currant and a scrubby lilac, April ground to a halt. 'Oh, sod it!'

Jix, the bike discarded at the edge of a bed of wilting Busy Lizzies and cigarette ends, looked at her and shrugged. 'Maybe we haven't explained it to him properly?'

'We can't make it any clearer, surely?' April gave a piercing whistle. 'Cairey! Stop! Now!'

Cair Paravel, having completely ignored Jix and the training bike, was belting away towards the kiddies' play area. With its unpleasant concrete blocks and water-pipe tunnels, April always thought it looked a bit like a land-reclamation site. However, Beatrice-Eugenie, unused to other more elegant child-friendly playgrounds, loved it. The council had tried to prevent infant fatalities by laying thick layers of bark chippings beneath the more obvious hazards. Cair Paravel was now yomping his way through this with relish.

April whistled again. The greyhound changed gear, slowed, and looked over his shoulder. Then executing a perfect circle, he lolloped happily back towards them, tongue lolling, eyes smiling. When he reached them, he stood on his hind legs and gave both April and Jix slobbery kisses before dropping to all fours and turning his attention to the teddy bear.

76

Exasperated, April looked down at Cair Paravel, who fleetingly returned her gaze with an apologetic one of his own, and thumped his tail. Sprawled on the grass, with the captured teddy bear beneath his tapering front paws, he was washing it delicately.

April sighed. 'He still thinks it's a puppy. He runs like the wind, he's a natural star, yet he's got no killer instinct whatsoever. He won't chase the hare.'

'P'raps it's because it doesn't look like a hare.'

'Don't make excuses for him.' April dropped to her knees beside the dog and kissed the top of his head. 'He doesn't chase anything. He didn't chase you or the bike, did he? He just ran because he likes running, but not in the right direction. And even when he does come in contact with the teddy –'

'He mothers it.' Jix fondled Cair Paravel's silky ears. 'It could explain why Mr Reynolds was so keen to get rid of him. What use is a greyhound that won't chase?'

None at all, April thought. But she'd never say so. Not in Cair Paravel's hearing at least. 'He'll just have to stay a pet, then, won't he? He's good at that. I just thought if I could race him, he may be able to add a bit to the chocolate tin under the bed.'

Jix, looking beautifully summer-hippie, April felt, in patchwork flared jeans and a tie-dye vest, stretched out on the grass with languid elegance. 'Of course, if my mum could get over her agoraphobia, it would definitely be the answer.'

In the five scorching weeks since Cair Paravel had left Hugh Gaitskell House and taken up illegal residence in number 51, he and April had fallen deeply in love. He also adored Beatrice-Eugenie and Jix, and had been known to scrabble up the three flights of stairs to be pampered by Joel and Rusty. Sadly, he absolutely detested Daff.

April giggled, picturing Daff, her skirt tucked up into her knickers, sprinting across the grimy wasteland with Cair Paravel in hot pursuit. 'I think her psychotherapist might have something to say about that. Anyway, she's very hurt that her affection is unreciprocated.'

Poor Daff. Bursting with love for everyone, delighted to have another unlawful occupant at number 51 to entertain her in her incarceration, she'd been heartbroken when, on introduction, the greyhound had sniffed her, whimpered, and backed away growling.

'Maybe she reminds him of something nasty in his past.' Jix was staring at the sky. 'Maybe Mr Reynolds was into cross-dressing.'

'Possibly. Very probably, in fact. In which case I don't blame Cairey.' April wrinkled her nose at the memory of the dirty vest and the bad perm. Given a pinny and a headscarf, Mr Reynolds could have walked straight out of *The League of Gentlemen*. Reaching out a lazy hand, she fondled Cair Paravel's velvet muzzle. The discarded teddy bear, now washed to within an inch of its life, was drying stiffly in the sun. 'So, are we going to give up on trying to train him, or what?'

'Or what.' Jix rolled over onto his stomach, his hair falling across his face. 'We'll just need to find him a proper circuit. Perhaps that's all he needs – a track, and other dogs. At least then he'd have to run in the right direction.'

'Would he? I wouldn't bank on it. Anyway, I was never intending to enter him for the Derby or anything. I just thought that he might be OK in some of the smaller races at tracks outside London. Reckoned I might make some money from him, you know. At least enough to earn his keep.'

They surveyed Cair Paravel with grave disappointment. April was pretty sure that Jix was right. If only they could try him out at the Gillespie Stadium, introduce him to a real track, he might improve. Might actually realise what he was supposed to do. If he could race alongside other dogs, he may just grasp that there was a purpose to running like the wind on the trail of his quarry. But the Gillespie Stadium, handy though it was, was a definite no-go area. Even if they sneaked in at midnight and bribed the security patrol, there was still the awful risk that Sebastian, Oliver, or – worst of all – Martina would get wind of their sessions.

Then there'd be a dawn raid on number 51 and they'd discover not only Cair Paravel but Bee as well, and April could see herself turfed out onto the streets with her waifs and strays in tow. No, she shook her head, if Cair Paravel was going to earn his keep it would have to be somewhere miles away from Bixford.

Still, even that would probably bring all sorts of complications. To be able to race legally, even at an anonymous small stadium out in the sticks, Cair Paravel would have to be registered – and if Mr Reynolds had come by him duplicitously, then he probably already was. Which would mean the Greyhound Racing Association asking all sorts of probing questions about his ownership.

'Come on.' April glanced at her watch and scrambled to her feet. 'It's nearly five o'clock! I'm going to be late and so are you. Martina will have us on toast.'

Clipping the lead to Cair Paravel's collar, and stuffing the saliva-rigid teddy bear into her handbag, she waited while Jix picked up the bike, then, skirting the dust-encrusted lavatera, they hightailed it towards the constant swoosh of traffic on Bixford High Street.

'Sit!' April commanded as they reached the pelican crossing. Cair Paravel sat. Jix looked like he wanted to. April grinned. 'Late night?'

'Early morning, actually.'

'Not the stunning Brittany Frobisher?'

'Nah. As you well know.'

April smirked as the little green man appeared and the signal beeped listlessly. Jix had failed miserably with the delectable Brittany. Despite her alleged promises to meet him in the Copacabana on the day she'd arrived to discuss the Platinum Trophy with the Gillespie clan, she'd stood him up. Since then, she and Seb Gillespie had been publicly inseparable. It had taken Jix weeks to recover from the humiliation.

Darting across the road, dragging Cair Paravel behind her and hoping that Jix and the mountain bike made it in one piece, April calculated that she'd just have her hour with Bee before she had to don the French maid's outfit and sweat it out in the cocktail bar. They'd agreed not to take Bee on any of Cair Paravel's abortive training sessions in case she said something to someone. Her conversation was just reaching the charmingly indiscreet stage.

The tailback of halted traffic snaked along the High Street, engulfing the Pasta Place and the boarded-up shops in a wreath of carbon monoxide. The restaurant's doors were shuttered and the blinds drawn as they passed. April knew that Sofia and Tonio would be upstairs in the flat, grabbing the last moments of their siesta, sprawled, exhausted by the heat and the lunch-time rush, on their vast canopied bed, building their strength for the next onslaught.

By taking off-cuts of chicken and steak instead of her waitressing tips, April had so far managed to feed Cair Paravel without verging further on bankruptcy. Antonio had offered to give her the meat for free but she'd declined, because it simply wasn't in the game plan. She would never accept handouts of any sort. Everything that funded the roses-round-the-door dream had to be earned by honest toil. Well, almost honest. April could never quite square the debt-collecting with gainful employment.

However, the lack of Pasta Place tips in the chocolate tin now meant that Cair Paravel would soon have to start earning his keep in one way or another. If becoming a champion racer was going to be out of the question, April decided she might have to try and get him a paper round.

They'd just reached number 51, and Jix was reaching for his keys, when the traffic rumble was splintered by a piercing blast of car horn. Cair Paravel leaped into the air and on landing, immediately wound himself wimpishly round April's legs. Glaring into the string of vehicles for the offender, April groaned.

Everything had ground to a halt again by the pelican crossing. Lounging behind the wheel of his navy-blue Mercedes sports car, smiling quizzically, and with Brittany Frobisher beside him, was Sebastian Gillespie.

To be honest, April thought, rapidly trying to thrust the still-quivering Cair Paravel out of sight behind the mountain bike and failing, if Sebastian hadn't been the spawn of Oliver and Martina, and hadn't been her killer landlord, she would have allowed herself to find him very attractive. Tall, blue-eyed, with brown hair the colour of a peat stream, and a lopsided smile, he was certainly a high-scorer on the lustometer. However, as Daff was so fond of saying, handsome is as handsome does, and if he found out that she was breaking her tenancy rules, Sebastian could – and definitely would – see her homeless and jobless.

Still trying to disguise Cair Paravel as a bicycle spoke, April raised her hand in acknowledgement, forcing what she hoped was a cheerful employee smile. Jix, she noticed from the corner of her eye, was jabbing the key into the lock and not even trying.

'Nice-looking dog!' Sebastian called. 'Not yours, I hope?'

'What?' April glanced down at Cair Paravel in theatrical amazement as if he'd just metamorphosed on the end of the lead. 'God, no! Just – er – exercising him for a friend!'

'Right . . .' Sebastian nodded. 'One of our owners?'

April shook her head, tugging the reluctant greyhound away from galloping through the now-open door of number 51. 'Um – no – well, not exactly. He's – er – not a racer . . . more a family pet . . . That is, of course, his owner's family pet. Not mine – ha-ha!'

Brittany, who was wearing sunglasses and very little else, lifted them, glanced at April, and looked bored. The little green man had stopped flashing. The traffic was starting to move. Sebastian nodded again in a sort of detached way and released the handbrake. April allowed herself to exhale.

'Mummeee!!! Caireee!!!'

Bee, wearing only knickers and the battered sunhat, dashed through the open door, darted through Jix's legs and hurled herself at April. Cair Paravel did a neat circular turn, and with his ears at full prick, leaped on Beatrice-Eugenie and licked her exultantly.

Ignoring both dog and daughter, April fixed a rictus smile in Sebastian's direction and was wildly disturbed to notice that he was still watching the scenario in his rear-view mirror as the Mercedes purred away.

'Do you think he twigged?' Jix lugged the bike into the hall as April disentangled Bee and the greyhound on the dusty pavement.

'Twigged? Full branch, trunk, and bloody rooted!' April snorted. 'Gorgeous and spoiled rotten he maybe, but sadly Sebby is nobody's himbo. Oh, bugger . . .'

*

By ten o'clock, the Copacabana was in the middle of its nightly heave. April, shaking and pouring Purple Rains, Pink Squirrels and Yellow Fevers until she was almost colour blind, had earlier rehearsed and re-rehearsed her explanations, should she require them, with Jix and Daff. Cair Paravel would belong, as she'd said, to a friend. Bee, they'd decided, would be Jix's progeny, visiting her paternal grandmother for the afternoon. Should Sebastian by any chance have heard the giveaway M word, they'd decided – may God forgive them – to credit Bee with a pronounced speech impediment.

The tenth race of the evening had just taken place in the glitter-ball stadium; drinkers who had picked the winner were surging away from the bar towards the Tote, while those who hadn't were making inebriated selections for race eleven.

Martina, in a white lacy sprayed-on frock and with diamanté dust in her crew cut, spiked her way on vertiginous stilettos behind the bar. 'April! I'll take over here for a sec. Table forty-seven wants another bottle of shampoo.'

'OK.' April gave Martina a wild-eyed stare. 'Don't you want to serve them?'

Table forty-seven were celebrating a wedding anniversary. Loudly. They'd already had half a dozen bottles of the Stadium's overpriced Moët. None of them seemed to have the slightest interest in greyhound racing. Most of them were singing football anthems.

Clattering the champagne from the fridge, swooshing the bucket under the ice-maker, then ramming the bottle into the blue-white crackles, April was sure Martina must have an ulterior motive. On the rare occasions that she worked in the Copacabana, she always preferred to serve the high spenders herself. High spenders were frequently high tippers, and many a twenty-pound note had found its way into Martina's crepey cleavage. Was this just a ploy to get April to drop her guard? Was she to serve champagne to the partygoers and then collect her cards on the way out for keeping a dog and child in a Gillespie flat?

Swamped with guilt and fear, April ventured the question again.

Martina's heavily creased turquoise eyelids flickered rapidly. 'No, I don't want to bloody serve them. They're mouthy scum. Anyway, that's what I pay you for. And while you're doing it, I'll check the till – so there better not have been any freebies tonight, or else.'

'There haven't been.' April almost kissed the scrawny pancaked cheek in delight. It was merely her light fingers that were causing the Gillespies concern – not the existence of her family. 'I've learned my lesson . . .'

She winced. Maybe that was a Uriah Heep too far. Martina obviously didn't think so. The oil-slick lips oozed into a death's-head smile.

'Good. That's what I like to hear. Now, get that poo out to the punters. Cheap trouncers they may be, but they're pouring money into our pockets. Go on! Shift!'

Ramming the cap on to her curls, making sure that her knickers weren't showing, April wrapped the ice bucket in a cloth, placed it on a tray, and shimmied her way out into the throng.

'Ouch!'

Two bottom pinches before she'd even reached the plastic palm tree. This was certainly no job for Shere Hite.

Table forty-seven snatched at the champagne in delight, not even breaking off in the chorus of 'Football's Coming Home'. The cork exploded into the multitude of twinkling ceiling lights and several people cheered. Down below them, in a blaze of floodlit glory, the blue-jacketed greyhound had just sped to victory in the eleventh race of the

evening. No one on table forty-seven took the slightest
notice. The wedding anniversary couple, April noticed,
both had black eyes.

'Here you are, darling.' A fat man in bri-nylon waved
a flabby hand towards her. 'Come and get your tip!'

April smiled her sweetest fuck-off smile and shook her
head. 'We're not allowed to accept tips, I'm afraid. All
gratuities have to be placed in the communal jar on the
bar and – Oh!'

The fat man, shaking his head and laughing gummily,
had grabbed hold of the frilly skirt and tugged her towards
him. Dropping the tray with a clatter, April found herself
anchored firmly on to his lap.

'Couldn't put that in a jar, eh, darling?'

Struggling to escape, April almost gagged with disgust.
The fat man clung on, digging podgy fingers through the
crisscross gaps in her fishnet tights.

'I like a babe with a bit of spirit.'

'If it's spirit you want,' April muttered, 'try this.' And
balling her fist, she punched him neatly on the nose.

'Bugger me!'

The fat hands stopped gripping her thighs and rushed to
his face. The football anthems faltered to a halt. The wedding anniversary wife clapped rather half-heartedly. April
stood up, straightened her cap, and staggered shakily away
from the table – straight into the T-shirted chest of Sebastian Gillespie.

'You just punched a customer!'

Oh God. 'Yes, I know. He mauled me.'

'He's supposed to maul you. That's why you're dressed
like a tart.'

'He's not and I'm not!'

Sebastian's eyes narrowed to slits. 'Get back to the bar.
I'll deal with this. We'll talk later.'

'But he —'

'April — leave it!'

Remembering that Sebastian almost definitely knew about Beatrice-Eugenie and Cair Paravel, April left it. Slinking back towards the bar, burning with outraged indignation, she wondered where she'd get another job. God, no tips from the Pasta Place and no wage from here — she'd be fighting Cair Paravel for a share in his paper-round.

Martina, just closing the till, cocked her shorn sparkly head towards the window seats. 'Bit of a disturbance, was there?'

'Something like that,' April muttered, still squirming inside from the intimacy with the fat mauler. 'Sebby's sorting it.'

'Sebastian to you,' Martina corrected with a disapproving sniff. 'Sebby is what he's called at home — oh, and by his girlfriend, of course . . .' She waggled bony claws along the bar.

April whimpered. Brittany Frobisher, in tiny crushed-velvet shorts and a beaded bikini top, was perched on a stool at the counter, stirring something opaque with a twizzle stick and looking pretty cheesed off.

Martina edged her way out from behind the bar. 'Sebastian said it looked as though they were getting a bit rowdy. Not our usual class of punter at all, but you can't turn 'em away on the grounds of being common, that's what I say. Did they give you a tip?'

April shook her head. Should she tell Martina she'd punched a customer or leave that little gem of information for Seb? 'Nothing, I'm afraid. Oh, it looks as though Sebby — um — Sebastian has got it all organised.'

Martina frowned as Sebastian, gripping the fat man by his bri-nylon neck, parted the Copacabana faithful like a floppy-haired Moses. She blinked blue Eylure lashes as her son and fifteen stones of perspiring flab disappeared through the gold-plated doors.

'Gets it from his gramp,' she said admiringly. 'He could still chuck out an entire pub on the Old Kent Road when he was well into his eighties.'

Sebastian returned within minutes, running his fingers through his hair. The layers immediately fell into place, April noticed, indicating that the cut had probably cost more than she earned in a month.

'Barred for life,' he informed his mother. 'None of his party seemed at all sorry to see him go.' He raised his eyebrows towards April. 'You're not hurt?'

'No. Furious and insulted, that's all. Thanks.'

'No problem.' Sebastian smiled along the bar at Brittany. 'Pour us a couple of Godfathers then, and we'll say no more about it.'

April's hands shook as she heaped ice into two squat crystal-cut glasses. Martina, having had a quick whispered conversation in Brittany's perfect peachy ear, had tottered off to spread more sunshine and happiness throughout her empire. Pouring two measures of bourbon and one of amaretto over the heaps of ice, April wondered what Sebastian was going to say no more about: her thumping the fat man – or the flouting of the tenancy agreement? She had a pretty awful feeling it wasn't going to be the latter.

'Thank you.' Brittany accepted her glass with a smile – a genuine smile that made her, April realised with irritation, even more beautiful. 'Seb told me about the trouble with that customer. How awful for you.'

'It wasn't pleasant,' April admitted, warming towards Brittany for this show of female solidarity, and pushing the second Godfather across the bar to Sebastian. 'But as your boyfriend so kindly pointed out, dressed like this, it's all I can expect.'

87

Brittany frowned at Sebastian. 'I hope you didn't say that at all. That's like saying every woman who wears a short skirt is asking to be assaulted. If I thought –'

'Hey!' Sebastian held up his hands in supplication. 'Back off, both of you. All I meant was that to certain lowlifes, a pretty girl in a fantasy costume is fair game. It's not April's fault – it's my mother's for making her wear that bloody outfit in the first place.'

April, torn away to serve Dirty Harrys to a selection of the QPR reserve team, wanted to punch the air in triumph. Oh, please God, she thought, gleefully crushing ice, let Sebastian be the one to tell Martina that for her next stint behind the Copacabana's filigreed bar, April would be dressed as a librarian.

'Anyway,' Sebastian leaned across the bar towards her, studying the contents of his glass, 'your clothing wasn't really what I wanted to discuss with you. I'm far more interested in talking about your secret life . . .'

chapter eight

Strange really, Sebastian thought, as he stared from his sitting-room window, how defensive April had become. Almost as though she'd had something to hide. The poor kid had looked scared to death when he'd started talking to her. Did she really consider him to be that much of an ogre?

He had no idea why the abortive conversation with April should have suddenly come into his mind on this overcast Sunday morning, ten days after that embarrassing night in the Copacabana. Probably, he thought, leaning his hands flat on the sill and gazing down from the third floor of Marliver House – which he privately called Tacky Towers – on to acres of turf regimentally striped like the Wembley pitch, it was because of Jix.

Jix, dressed like a rainbow wraith and looking as always like a refugee from Glastonbury, was currently strolling about the Gillespie garden – which was overloaded with neon roses, and dotted with gazebos and decking and water features – with Oliver. Jix and April were somehow inextricably linked in Sebastian's mind. They were always together. Were they an item? He employed both of them and owned their homes, and yet he knew nothing much about either of them.

The night that he'd ejected the objectionable drunk,

April had parried his questions about the greyhound, and the – what he'd considered at the time – friendly chat regarding the toddler, who had surprisingly turned out to be Jix's child. Her answers had been firm and monosyllabic, not encouraging any further probing. Almost as though she had anticipated his questions. He'd tried, for the first time in his life, to unbend with someone who relied on him for their living, and had got very short shrift.

He knew April had been outraged by that greasy sod touching her, and who could blame her? Sebastian had been furiously angry that his mother had insisted that the all-female bar staff wore those French maids' outfits, and very ashamed that he, as a Gillespie, had condoned it. Had he taken that anger out on April? Transferred his guilt? He shouldn't have let it happen, should he? Chucking the groper out after the event wasn't really good enough. The situation should never have been allowed to arise.

And, as far as he knew, April and the other girls were still wearing the costumes behind the bar because Martina had insisted on it. Would April be happier being allowed to wear jeans? Did she mind being dressed up as a male fantasy in an attempt to sell more cocktails to punters who chucked them down their necks like lemonade?

He shrugged. What did he really know about April? Stuff all. What the hell did he know about women like her? What the hell, to be honest, did he know about most things? How much had he learned in his thirty-three years about life outside the confines of the Gillespie empire?

Cushioned from ever really having to earn a living by the success of the Gillespie Guzzler vending machines, privately educated to a standard never once called upon in his capacity as Stadium Manager, gifted an entire street of properties on his coming-of-age, he'd never been brought into contact with the real world.

And much as he'd have liked to talk to April further about the greyhound and the child, it hadn't been his real reason for making conversation. One of the stadium's security guys had mentioned to him that April worked in the Italian restaurant, and helped Jix with Oliver's debt-collecting too. It had intrigued and bothered him. He'd really wanted to ask her how she managed to juggle three jobs, and if she needed a pay rise in the cocktail bar.

He knew he could easily have persuaded his mother to increase April's salary by a couple of pounds an hour, if it would mean she didn't have to get involved in the more murky areas of Oliver's empire. Maybe that was it: the debt-collecting. Maybe April hadn't wanted him to know that she was part in that. Not that he could blame her – he wasn't too keen on it himself.

The little girl had been pretty, though, and had sparked what – on that hot afternoon? A sort of jealousy that Jix, years younger than he was, and a hippie wide boy, should have already experienced the joy of fatherhood? Probably. He'd known Jix for ten years, ever since he'd first been employed by Oliver as a teenager, and never once had they discussed women or football or anything on a personal level. And somewhere in that time Jix had become a father – and none of the Gillespies had known.

Sebastian sighed again. He'd like to have a child. He'd give it a proper life – not a cushioned and cosseted and pigeonholed one, but a life with choices and freedom. Jix would, by his very nature, offer his daughter a life like that . . . And the greyhound had made them – April, Jix and the little girl – look like a real family.

Sebastian liked greyhounds; he loved all animals, but again he'd never been close to any. Animals had never been allowed at home, and the dogs at the Stadium were mere accessories. They were probably as important to him, as a businessman, as – oh, a good single malt was to the manufacturer of pure crystal glasses. A necessary accoutrement; nothing more.

So, really, he thought, that whole day had been the catalyst; seeing Jix and April together with the child and the dog, and then doing his Sir Galahad bit with the drunken slob in the evening. All the minor irritants and dissatisfactions had been brought to the surface by those two simple events. Everything that was wrong with his life had suddenly sort of concertinaed together.

'Sebby! You're not ready!'

He gritted his teeth and turned from the window as his mother barged into the room. She never knocked. The only way to keep her out of his flat was to lock the door and he always forgot. She insisted on treating him as if he were twelve.

'Yeah, I am. It's only lunch, Ma. It's not black tie.'

'It's lunch,' Martina said frostily, 'with Rod and Emily Frobisher. Not to mention Brittany. We want to make a good impression – and jeans and T-shirt are not acceptable.'

He grinned at her. 'It's either jeans or nothing. Take your pick.'

Martina, dressed in a stretchy outfit in sugar pink, with frills at neck and cuffs, and wearing more heavy gold jewellery than Big Ron Atkinson, obviously thought she looked the last word in chic. Knowing that Brittany's mother favoured the stark classic lines of Chanel, Sebastian wondered if he should say something. He decided against it. He was pretty sure that the Frobishers would find enough nouveau riche bad taste in the Gillespie mansion to keep them in after-supper small talk for years. Martina's dress sense probably wouldn't even get a look in.

'Dad's just sorting out the luncheon seating with Jix,' Martina continued, her sharp eyes darting around the room.

'The forecast says it'll be sunny later. We'll still eat in the garden.'

'And I need a tuxedo for that, do I?'

'No need to be sarky, Sebby. A nice pair of slacks and an open-necked shirt will be fitting.' Martina cast a glance into the bedroom. 'And you haven't even made your bed!'

'Ma, leave it out, I'm not a child . . .'

But he was, Sebastian thought sadly. He was Oliver and Martina's only child, and everything was still laid on for him as it had been all his life. His clothes were washed and ironed, his meals cooked, his life organised. He only had himself to blame if Martina spent every day snooping round his rooms – like she had when he was a teenager home for the holidays and she had a fear that he was into pornography or dope or both. It was his own fault for not moving out years ago.

It had been so easy, after university, moving back into Tacky Towers, and not having to do a thing. Oliver and Martina, generous to a fault, had given him six rooms converted into a self-contained flat. He had his own front door, a new car each year, holidays, everything else on tap, access to the indoor and outdoor swimming pools, the gym in the cellar, the solarium in the attic. How ungrateful was he then, to envy people like Jix and April, who lived alone and scrimped and saved and worked hard and budgeted for their lives?

How could he tell his parents, who thought that showering him with money and material possessions would make him happy, that he envied them the poverty of their beginnings, and almost lusted after the hardship of their past? Wouldn't it really have been more fun to have started with nothing, and to have slogged and sweated for the dream – or was that just a safe option now when viewed from his privileged position? Was it so wrong for him to be itching to leave the Gillespie Stadium, the property-owning, the security of his home, the claustrophobia of his family, and strike out on his own?

Martina had now opened his wardrobe and was rattling through the hangers, surveying his shirts with her head on one side like an inquisitive lurid-coloured bird. God, he thought, any minute now she'll be spitting on a hankie and wiping my face.

'Ma, I'm wearing jeans. Brittany will be wearing jeans. Probably Rod will be wearing jeans.'

'Christ! I hope not!' Martina squawked, pausing between a black polo shirt and a denim jacket. 'Your father is wearing his new Paul Smith.'

Sebastian shook his head. Oliver, portly and looking like an East End market trader, could kill Paul Smith's suave and sophisticated styling stone dead.

'And which particular two-birds-and-one-stone job is this lunch supposed to be?'

Martina arched etched orange eyebrows. 'Are you hinting at a hidden agenda, Seb? You know as well as I do that this is just us, as a family, meeting Brittany's parents.'

'Oh, yeah? Brittany and I have seen each other – what? Half a dozen times? And how come that you haven't needed to meet the parents of any of my former girlfriends?'

Martina refused to look fazed. 'OK, so it's imperative – absolutely imperative – that we get the Frobisher Platinum Trophy at Bixford. We're up against Walthamstow and Wimbledon and every other damn track in the country. But that's by the bye. Should it come up in conversation over lunch, however, it'd be very handy . . .'

Sebastian smiled ruefully. 'So you're expecting Brittany and me to plight our troth over the consommé, are you, thus making the Platinum Trophy a definite?'

'Nah.' Martina momentarily forgot her vowels. 'Not

that it wouldn't be a bit of a coup. And you're not thinking along those lines, I suppose?'

'Not at all. At least, not yet. Brittany is good fun and good company – and very beautiful, but –'

The bit after the but was left dangling. There was a crash from downstairs, followed by thundering footsteps, then Oliver exploded into the flat.

'Bastard caterers! They've sent salad cream!'

Sebastian bit back a grin, while Martina went into the sort of hand-wringing routine that normally accompanied national disasters of cataclysmic proportions. In any other house in the country, surely, the larder would offer up salad cream or mayonnaise or both? Were his parents the only people who relied totally on outside caterers for even the simplest lunch party?

'I'll go to the 8 'til Late and get some mayo, shall I?'

His parents looked at him as though he'd just suggested the ritual slaughter of all new-born infants.

'You?' Oliver puffed out his cheeks. 'What the hell do you want to go to the shop for? We have people to do that. I'll get Jix to do it as soon as he's done the table and stuff.'

'I'd quite like to go. Get a paper. You know . . .'

Martina looked shocked. 'Get a paper? From the 8 'til Late? We have all the newspapers delivered. They're in the conservatory.'

Sebastian knew. He also knew that the broadsheets would remain on pristine view while his parents devoured the *News of the World* and the *People* in private. Oh, God. He didn't want to be having this lunch with the Frobishers; he wanted to be like other men of his age and have a family and privacy. He wanted to wander down to the corner shop and buy a Sunday newspaper, and go to the pub and discuss football and cricket and cars and sex.

He gathered up his car keys from one of the mirror-varnished side tables. Even the furnishings in his flat had been organised and supplied, wall-to-wall, by outside designers. It was his own fault. As with everything else, he'd allowed it to happen simply because he didn't have the energy, interest, or inclination to do otherwise.

'I'll go and see if Jix needs a lift to the shop, then.' And before his parents could protest, he was leaping down the gold and marble spiral staircase, three steps at a time.

Outside, the air was sultry and warm and hung with perfume. The roses exuded heavy, heady scent, and the grass was damp and earthy. Jix was dragging wooden chairs round the oblong table, adjusting the umbrella, plumping the matching navy and white striped cushions.

'Do you need a hand?'

Jix stopped, pushed his hair away from his eyes, and blinked. 'Sorry?'

'I wondered if I could help.'

With a shake of the head, Jix pushed the last chair under the table. 'No, thanks. Your old man would have my guts if he thought I'd asked you.'

'But you didn't bloody ask me – I offered.' Sebastian frowned. 'Anyway, they need mayo. I'm going to get some.'

Jix shook his head again. 'I'll go. It's what I'm paid for. I'm a gofer. A fixit. Are you trying to do me out of a job?'

'Of course I'm not. I'm trying to be – well – friendly.'

Jix looked more frightened by this remark than anything. 'Why?'

'Fuck knows. How long have we known each other?'

'We don't know each other, Seb, that's the point. I work for you. For your family. I live in your house. It's been like that for ten years – why the hell have you suddenly decided that we need to be mates?'

'I haven't. Christ — I don't know . . .' Sebastian kicked at the perfect turf. 'Maybe I've seen the error of my ways.'

Jix took a deep breath. 'You haven't been brainwashed, have you? Got at? Not by Jehovah's Witnesses or someone? My mum had a bout of that. You know, with her agoraphobia she likes having people in. We couldn't move for tracts and prayer sheets for weeks. Only got shot of them by telling them she'd turned Satanist.'

Sebastian grinned in triumph. There! He now knew something about Jix that he hadn't before. Daphne had agoraphobia! They'd known there was something wrong with her, of course, but had always believed it to be arthritis.

'Do you find it funny or something?' Jix was looking po-faced. 'Agoraphobia? Only it's not amusing for my mum, I can assure you.'

Sebastian quickly sucked the grin into tight lips. 'God — no. It must be awful for her. For both of you. It's just that you've told me something personal . . . Something else. Until the other day, I didn't even know you were a father —'

'What?' Jix jerked his head up, his mane of hair swirling with an astonished life of its own. 'Who? Jesus! I never —'

'It's OK.' Sebastian gave what he hoped was a man-of-the-world smile. 'It can happen to any of us. She's a pretty little thing too. I suppose you have access rights? That must be tough — just seeing her occasionally . . . What's her name?'

Jix remained looking poleaxed. 'Who?'

'Your daughter. April told me all about her — Oh, shit. Maybe she shouldn't have . . .'

Jix suddenly seemed to need to rearrange the six place settings. 'She doesn't live with us. She doesn't even stay

overnight. We know about the tenancy rules and everything. Don't think –'

Bloody hell! Sebastian longed to sweep the crystal and
bone china to the ground and stamp on it. 'Jix, I'm only
making conversation. I'm not interrogating you –'

'Bee. She's called Bee. Short for Beatrice-Eugenie.'

Sebastian tried hard not to laugh. Well, hell, Sebastian
wasn't that great, was it? Especially not for someone who,
despite the ministrations of various elocution teachers, still
sounded as if he came from Stepney. 'Oh, right. Are you
a royalist, then?'

'Nah, not really – um – but Bee's mum thinks – that
is, thought – that Sarah Ferguson got a raw deal. Er – that
is, she reckoned that she was a bit of a star to dig herself
out of the mess she was in. She – um – thought that
Beatrice-Eugenie was like a fitting tribute . . .'

Sebastian grinned again. O K , maybe it wasn't quite like
propping up the bar in the Goat and Turnip with a bottle
of Bud and discussing Chelsea's dismal away form and the
previous night's conquests, but it ran a pretty close second.

'And – er – are you still seeing each other?'

'What?' Jix gave a sigh of exasperation. 'Me and Bee?
Of course. And look, Seb, nice as it is to chat, your old
man's got me on a deadline here and if you need mayo as
well –'

'I'll get the bloody mayo. And I meant you and – um
– Bee's mother. Do you still see her?'

For some unfathomable reason, Jix seemed to find this
highly amusing. 'Oh, yeah – I see Bee's mother all the
time . . .'

'More wine, Emily?' Martina proffered the bottle across
the table. 'Or perhaps some fizzy water? That sushi was a
bit saline.'

Sebastian, his knees – still in jeans – resting comfortably against Brittany's bare ones, leaned back in his chair. Brittany, who was wearing a tiny cream slip dress, some slender gold chains and possibly nothing else, had cheered him up considerably. So far so good. Rod Frobisher had turned up in jeans and a CK T-shirt. Oliver had promptly gone to change. Emily, in white trousers and a severe navy overblouse, had sadly had no such sartorial influence on his mother. However, he had noticed that as the meal went on, Martina's accent was more and more aping Emily's clipped Home Counties tone.

'Ten to one they mention the Platinum Trophy before we get to pudding,' Brittany whispered. 'Either that, or how super the Seychelles are for honeymoons.'

'Make that evens.' Seb saluted her with his wine glass. 'On both counts.'

The conversation had been lunch-party polite so far; there had been four-way non-confrontational discussions on politics, the joys of having your children working for you in the family business, exotic holidays, the current tax system – and how to avoid it. Both sets had amusingly skirted round the main topic like mongrels eyeing the same bone.

Martina's weather forecast having been correct, the sun was now simmering in a cloudless sky, and the lawn was dazzling dizzily with its jade and emerald stripes. The umbrellas cast welcome shade over the table, and threw sharp black shadows onto the nearest water feature. Sebastian hated the Tacky Towers water features. They were irritating trickles and bubbles, tiny plumes of water being regurgitated endlessly over pebbles. They played havoc with his bladder, and made him long for wild, unfettered oceans, roaring and crashing on to deserted beaches.

'So –' Oliver pushed a piece of oil-drizzled lamb's

lettuce round his plate. 'Have you reached your decision on the Platinum Trophy yet?'

Seb and Brittany exchanged grins.

'Not yet, no.' Rod Frobisher concentrated hard on an olive that seemed determined to avoid his fork prongs. 'Anyway, that's Brittany's province. She'll collate all the reports from the tracks which have tendered, and will make the final decision.'

Oliver's attention shifted immediately. 'And have you visited all the interested stadiums yet, my love?'

Sebastian flinched a bit at his father's familiarity. Brittany was an ardent feminist.

She smiled sweetly. 'No, Oliver, love – I haven't. No one has yet been ruled out – or ruled in for that matter. I know what the television boys are looking for – and obviously I know what Frobishers need by way of publicity and promotion. There are some places I've visited that probably won't do on either count – but I still have several out-of-town stadiums to see throughout the summer. I'll have made my final decision by the end of the year.'

'But it'll stay in the London area?' Oliver's tone had an edge of urgency.

Martina gave a little scream. 'Lord love us! Of course it'll stay in the London area! All the big boys know about the city tracks. It's where the crowds come to – where the money is. It'd be madness to go outside – to somewhere where there's no transport, no facilities –'

'Oh, there has to be all that, of course.' Brittany stretched her bare legs under the table, so that they brushed silkily along Sebastian's. 'But if we're going to be linked with something so high-profile I think we'll need originality too. After all, the well-known stadiums may be a bit – jaded . . .'

'Jaded? Jaded?' Oliver rocked dangerously on his chair.

Then he stopped. 'Ah, right . . . yes, I can see where you're coming from, love. You mean, with Wimbledon and Walthamstow already having the big meetings, the punters might be looking for something a little newer? A bit different?'

Sebastian, his concentration shattered by the proximity and movement of Brittany's legs, held his breath. Brittany stopped her seductive sliding and leaned across the table towards his father.

'Exactly. Which is why I've planned to ask Sebastian if he'd accompany me when I visit the smaller tracks. Naturally, I will expect him to be impartial, but I do need his expertise.'

chapter nine

Eleven thirty. Only another half-hour to go, and he'd be there. Ampney Crucis. Home. By midnight. Like a returning Cinderella.

Ewan Dunstable turned up the CD player in his ancient Citroën, flooding the interior warmth with the hippie harmonies of the Moody Blues, and pressed the accelerator to the floor. The car rattled through the humid July night, catching freefall moths in the bouncing headlight beams. He was longing to be with Peg again; with her outspokenness and her honesty and her complete eccentricity. Peg had taken him on through his disruptive teenage years after his parents had emigrated to New Zealand and he'd elected to stay and finish his schooling. The plan then had been that he'd join them in Christchurch after A levels, or in vacations if he went on to university. He'd done neither. He'd fluffed his exams, stayed on with Peg, living in Ampney Crucis, and then he'd met Katrina.

He saw his parents once every couple of years; they had happy reunions and all parties seemed quite relieved when they were over. Peg, he knew, meant more to him now than his own mother. Of course he should have been in Ampney Crucis weeks ago as promised; he should at least have let Peg know that he'd be delayed; but things had got rather out of control.

His life, Ewan thought as he turned from the bypass on to the coast road, had a habit of getting out of control lately. Well, not just lately, if he were honest. Things had been haywire ever since he'd married Katrina. He hadn't made many mistakes in his life – being naturally lazy he'd just taken whatever came along and made the best of it – but marrying Katrina in that first hot flush of lust had been the biggest mistake ever. Not fair on either of them: not then – and definitely not now.

Whether Katrina knew or cared where he was at the moment was immaterial. They both knew that divorce was the only answer to their problems, but neither had so far had the inclination to make the first move. Living apart had been sufficient. Katrina had her career, earned her own money, had her own savings, and had more or less kept him throughout their marriage. Ewan shrugged ruefully. While Katrina may or may not miss him when they eventually split, she'd definitely be pleased to see the back of the financial burden.

The coastal roads were deserted. High-banked verges like waves breaking over an ocean gully surrounded the car on either side, their tops white-crested with shepherd's-purse foam. Ewan felt the tension draining away as the surroundings became more familiar. More dear. What a fool he'd been to leave.

All those years ago, when he'd joined Katrina in Cambridge, hopelessly infatuated, and sure that his idealism would lead him into charity work, or the social services, or maybe even local politics, he'd considered Ampney Crucis far too insignificant a place for his talents. He'd bragged to Clara and Andrew and Jasmine that they'd be stuck in the village rut for ever while he went out and set the world alight.

He grinned as he turned at the rickety Ampney Crucis

signpost; his crusades had led him into more trouble than he wanted to think about – and, each time, when everything got too much, the very place he headed for was the one he had been so eager to leave.

Slowing the Citroën to a respectable speed, he cruised through the sleeping village. Down the hill past St Edith's, where Benny was now buried. Ewan felt a pang of regret; Benny had been one of the constants throughout his young life in Ampney Crucis; everyone had loved him. He couldn't imagine how devastated Jasmine must have felt when he died. Must still feel. The love Benny and Jas had shared would live on for ever. The Moody Blues had reached a sad track, so Ewan switched off the CD player. He'd sent a card, of course, but not until afterwards – which had really been far too late. He hoped Jasmine would forgive him, but he'd been busy in Spain and postal communications had been at a minimum, and by the time Peg had eventually managed to get hold of him, even the funeral was over.

Towards the village now. The new estate – which was actually not new at all any more – was in darkness. Ewan thought of Jasmine again: was she still living at home here with Yvonne and Philip, or had she and Andrew married by now? He shook his head. Peg would have let him know, and he'd have been invited to that – surely? He felt a pang of guilt about letting his contact with Ampney Crucis slip in such a cavalier fashion. Peg, Jas, Clara – God, even Andrew – meant more to him than anyone else. They were his roots. He'd been far too hasty in ripping them up and thinking that Cambridge and Katrina and the educational élite were all he needed to flourish.

Still cruising, he now drove along the harbour road – past the old three-tier fishing huts, which had been bought up by property developers and optimistically rechristened

'Marina View' – where Clara had her minimalist loft conversion overlooking half a dozen lobster boats and the occasional pleasure cruiser offering trips around the bay.

Clara . . . Was it too late to make amends? Stupid of him really to have ignored what was under his nose, and left Ampney Crucis for Katrina's ice-cool intelligence. Then, of course, he'd fouled up big-time a couple of years ago when he'd sworn that he'd left Katrina for good – and Clara had believed him . . .

He drove on slowly, still savouring the familiarity. The Crumpled Horn, Eddie Deebley's Fish Bar, the Crow's Nest Caff . . . – everything was the same as it had been in his childhood, and probably as it would be in another fifty years. It was so good to be back.

Jesus! Pulling the car to a halt, Ewan slapped his hand on the steering wheel. Back where? Where the hell was he going? Peg's, obviously eventually – but not at this time of night. Once Peg had removed the Doris Day persona, had a cup of Bournvita and two Thin Arrowroots, and a blast of 'I'll See You in My Dreams', there was no waking her until *Today* filtered through the radio alarm. He groaned. He'd have to park on the cliff top and sleep in the car.

He shrugged and drove on again. It would mean waking cold and cramped and with a mouth like burned sandpaper, but what other choice was there? Anyway, he'd slept in far worse places recently, and survived, hadn't he? As usual, he'd planned to get to Ampney Crucis in daylight; as usual, his plans had gone slightly awry.

Of course, there was always Clara . . . He switched on the CD player again, the Moodies swamping the Citroën with mystic chords. No, not Clara. Not after the acrimonious break-up. He had bridges to build with Clara, and turning up in the middle of the night would definitely not be the best way to lay the foundations.

Would Jasmine still be awake? Probably, but he'd never liked her parents, and they'd always disapproved of him, so he couldn't see them welcoming him with open arms at any time, and definitely not at gone midnight. Who did that leave? Andrew? He shook his head. Definitely not.

Driving across the scrunchy shale and bouncing over tussocks of coarse grass, Ewan pulled the Citroën on to the cliff top and switched off the engine. The music was low now, and the sea and sky both black and welded together like melted tar. The only outside sound was the rush and pull of the tide on the shingle, and the occasional desultory slap of a wave splashing over the groynes.

Ewan pushed the headrest back and leaned into it, stretching out his legs. He was dog-tired, longed for sleep, but didn't want to close his eyes. When he closed his eyes the horrors rushed in from nowhere. He was hungry too. And thirsty. And most of all he needed a pee.

Sighing, he climbed from the car. There were no handily placed bushes, no privacy, and the public conveniences at the top of the cliff steps were always locked at sundown. He wandered to the edge of the gentle chalky fall. Several scrubby gorse bushes halfway down offered some minimal seclusion, but were at a precipitous angle . . . He grinned to himself: below him, their pointy roofs in zigzag relief against the darkness, stood his salvation. The beach huts.

Ewan started to scramble down the undulations, dislodging bits of stone and pebbles beneath his trainers. No one would know, would they? There was no one to see him. OK, it was hardly sanitary, but he really didn't have a choice. Hopefully it'd rain in the night, or there'd be a heavy sea fret, and tomorrow's beach-hut users would be none the wiser. He rattled down the last few feet, skidding over clumps of candytuft and crushing ferns, before landing in a slither behind the huts.

It was pitch-dark, silent, secluded. Everything he needed.

Oh, the relief!

'What the hell do you think you're doing?' An angry female voice and the blinding flash of a torch cut the relief pretty short. 'Jesus! That's disgusting!'

Mentally juggling with whether to stay and apologise, or run like hell, Ewan faltered for a minute. Christ! How embarrassing! And it was bound to be one of the Ampney Crucis blue-rinse brigade making sure her beach hut's net curtains were up to scratch, or something. That was exactly the sort of thing they did in the small hours here. Skulked. Unless, of course, the village had moved on a bit and was now into Neighbourhood Watch. Jesus! That really didn't bear thinking about – and hadn't one of the Rolling Stones once been arrested for urinating in public? What chance would he have?

The torch light wavered a bit. The footsteps came a fraction closer. 'Ewan?'

He screwed up his eyes, trying to see past the dazzle. Christ – not someone who knew him? Not one of Peg's cronies? They'd have a field day in the Crumpled Horn retelling this one

'Um . . . yes . . . Actually . . .' He blinked. 'Er – look, you seem to have the advantage. I can't see a bloody thing with that light on.'

'Ewan!' The voice sounded amazed and quite happy. The torch's beam dropped. 'It's me – Jasmine. You scared me to death.'

'Jas?' This was even more embarrassing. 'What on earth are you doing here? It's past midnight.'

107

'I live here, silly.' She'd moved closer still and was smiling at him. 'Didn't Peg tell you?'

Ewan shook his head wordlessly. He wasn't sure whether Jasmine could see the denial or not. It didn't matter. It was all so bizarre. Why the hell would Jasmine, whom he could now see was wearing some sort of nightshirt thing with kittens on it, be living on the seafront like a summer dropout?

She seemed to have regained her equilibrium far faster than he had. She still smiled expansively. 'God – I'm sorry if I frightened you – but really, why were you having a pee behind my beach hut?'

'*Your* beach hut? God Almighty, Jas – you don't mean that you and Andrew are shacked up in that chalet, do you? What happened? Did his dealership go belly up or something?'

'No, of course not.' Her laughter rolled up the cliff path. 'It's a long story – and where the hell have you been, anyway? Peg said you were arriving weeks ago.'

'Yeah,' Ewan nodded. 'I was supposed to be. And that's an even longer story . . .'

The walnut carriage clock on the chiffonier said a quarter to three. Mind you, Ewan reckoned it had said quarter to three two hours ago. He stretched comfortably in his armchair, and drained his fourth bottle of Old Ampney. 'Is that clock right? Or are we stuck in the Ampney Crucis time warp?'

'It's half-past two, almost. Do you want to go to bed?' Jasmine pushed her dark hair away from her eyes, then wrinkled her nose. 'Hey, pack it in! Don't use your seduction look on me. It's totally wasted. I simply meant, if you're tired I'll drag out the spare eiderdown for you.'

108

He grinned back at her, shaking his head. 'No, I'm fine as long as you are. We can both sleep in in the morning – and I wasn't being seductive. I've lost the art.'

'Bollocks,' Jasmine said cheerfully. 'You never found the art with me. I was always immune. Now, carry on with your story – you've heard all my news.'

He had. Looking round the crowded beach hut, which was now furnished exactly as he remembered Benny's house from his childhood, he thought Jasmine had worked miracles with her life. He couldn't wait to see her in action as Benny Clegg – the Punters' Friend – and as for having the guts to leave the security of the house on the Chewton Estate, and shacking up here in the hut – his admiration knew no bounds.

'I got a bit involved in a cause . . .'

Jasmine, tugging the kitten nightshirt firmly round her curves as she curled on the deeply cushioned sofa, stopped and leaned forward. 'Really? Crikey. Peg said you'd joined some mercenaries or something. Like guerrilla warfare or gun-running, but we thought she'd got it wrong. What was it then?'

'Greyhounds.'

'Uh? Greyhound-running? Doesn't sound like an under-cover operation to me. We do it all the time here – Tuesday, Friday and Saturday nights, every week of the year.'

'Jasmine! This is serious. I've become involved in a rescue operation.'

She beamed at him then, looking exactly as she had in Ampney Crucis Junior Mixed. 'That's sweet of you, but there's no need. The stadium is going to be OK. Didn't Peg tell you? We're – me and Peg and Allan and Roger – investing Grandpa's money into making it – oh, almost as good as Bixford!'

'Not the stadium, Jas. I'm rescuing greyhounds. Abandoned ones, ill-treated ones. Ones that have served their moneymaking purpose. You have no idea what happens to them when their racing life is over.'

'Of course I have!' Jasmine looked indignant. 'There are all sorts of organisations that make sure they have long and happy retirements. The Greyhound Industry and the Greyhound Trust both work like crazy to ensure that the dogs are well looked after. And round here all the owners just keep them as pets when they've finished running, and weep buckets when they die and —'

'Not everyone is like that, though.' Ewan gave an involuntary shudder. 'That's why I've been in Spain. So many greyhounds are sent out to the Continent to continue racing in appalling conditions and are treated unbelievably badly. God, Jas, you've no idea of some of the things I've seen . . . The Spanish boys have a great rescue mission going on. This particular group that I've joined is co-ordinated from there. We've been snatching dogs, getting them the right veterinary treatment, and finding them homes across Europe.'

'Really? Wow!' Jasmine untangled herself from the kitten nightshirt and stumbled across the obstacle course of furniture. Throwing her arms round his neck she kissed him. 'You're a star!'

Slightly winded by her exuberance, he pushed her to arm's length. 'Thanks, but Katrina didn't think so.'

'Why on earth not?' Jasmine sat down again. 'God, Ewan, I can't think of anything better to be doing with your life. I'd have thought she'd be so proud.'

'Not really. She thought it was stupid. She's not an animal lover.' And that, Ewan reckoned, was the biggest understatement so far. Katrina had been scathing in her contempt. Especially as the rescue operations *cost* money rather than made any.

110

'Sod her, then.' Jasmine carried on smiling. 'So, is it all over now? This particular crusade? Or are you still involved?'

'I'll always be involved. Once you've witnessed that sort of horror – and been able to do something about it – you can't give it up. I've left the European side of things now, but I'm going to be raising awareness over here, canvassing for people to take retired greyhounds as pets, that sort of thing.'

Jasmine nodded her approval. 'Count us in, then. I mean, there's no problems round here, but no doubt there are unscrupulous people hidden away all over the place.'

Ewan looked at her, plump and warm and kind. He couldn't tell her just how unscrupulous some of the people he'd dealt with, duped, and double-crossed were. And how they would happily break his legs if they ever caught up with him again. Greyhounds meant big money to so many unregistered and unlicensed people. Greyhounds weren't flesh and blood – just a means to a financial end.

'Oh, and one more thing – it's probably better not to mention any of this to Peg just yet. She's no mug, and she'll only panic if she thinks I've got embroiled in something nasty.'

'Whatever.' Jasmine yawned. 'Oh, I'm really sorry, but I'm going to have to go to bed. Do you want the eiderdown?'

Ewan grinned. 'Please. And a good-night kiss.'

'Think yourself lucky you've got the eiderdown.' Jasmine hauled herself to her feet and poked out her tongue. 'I don't do extras.'

Less than twelve hours later, after having been given the full Prodigal treatment by Peg, Ewan was sitting in her office high above the deserted greyhound track. The windows were open to the summer sounds of the beach, and an ozone-loaded breeze rattled round the edges of faded posters from long-demolished cinemas called the Roxy or the Gaumont. Roger and Allan, leather-faced, and with their braces rakishly on show over their open-necked shirts in deference to the heat wave, were each gummily munching their way through one of Gilbert's 'whoppa' hot dogs. Bunny, the hare boy, was adding ice, very slowly, to a jug of lemon barley, and Peg and Jasmine were totting up figures on the back of an old envelope. As board meetings went, it was very relaxed.

Peg stopped in her mathematical equations and adjusted her wig. It was a French pleat today, to go with a sheath dress and very unsuitable – Ewan considered – stiletto sandals. They didn't sit well with the corn plasters.

'Right, then. We're all agreed. Jasmine will go and approach her damned father about the proposals for the Merry Orchard Shopping Plaza. Yes, I know it was put forward at the last meeting, but Jasmine wasn't keen then, were you, pet?'

Jasmine shook her head.

'Right, but now she is.' Peg tapped along with the bass line of 'Whatever Will Be Will Be', her biro becoming quite agitated on the chorus. 'And, anyway, now we've got our figures together – and we know what alterations we want to make – I'm going to tell Frobishers that the new Benny Clegg Stadium is getting ready to stage the Platinum Trophy.'

Roger dislodged a piece of caramelised onion from between his false teeth. 'Won't that mean they'll have to come and inspect? What if we're not up to speed by then?'

'We'll just show them the plans, of course.' Peg frowned at this display of leaden-footedness. 'They're business people.

112

They'll understand. But according to the bumph, all tendering tracks have to be inspected by the end of August – so we'll have to get a shift on.'

'But what if bloody Philip – sorry, Jasmine – says the place is definitely going to be demolished?' Allan rolled his greasy paper napkin into a neat ball. 'What then?'

Peg anchored the French pleat more firmly into place. 'Good Lord! We won't say anything about it! Have you never heard of subterfuge? No, we'll welcome the Frobisher's contingent with open arms, lie through our teeth, and we'll tackle the planners this end. They'll have to carry me out of here in chains before they demolish one inch, believe me.'

Ewan smiled to himself. She meant it. He could see it happening. But really . . . he looked fondly at them all: Peg, Allan and Roger, all well past retirement; Jasmine, far too innocent for her own good; Gilbert, Ampney Crucis's one-man answer to McDonald's; and Bunny, the hare boy – what chance would they have against the might of the planning committee? What chance, in God's name, did they have of staging the biggest race in the greyhound calendar? Surely it would be kinder to disillusion them now, before it all went too far?

'And you, pet,' Peg zipped round and fixed Ewan with a beady stare, 'you'll have your part to play, of course.'

'Look, I hate to be a wet blanket, but – '

'Frigging 'ell!' Bunny, the hare boy, catapulted into the room at that point, tripping over his plimsoll laces and simultaneously losing his grip on the jug of lemon barley and his own centre of gravity. Ice cubes rained down on the board members like hailstones in a summer downpour.

Peg removed melting ice from her cleavage without a word. Jasmine had quietly stood up and was mopping down the distraught Bunny. Roger, Allan and Gilbert were resignedly dabbing at sticky pools on the top of the table with their hot-dog papers.

Ewan felt his grip on reality slipping slowly away. He was getting sucked deeper and deeper into Frank Capra country with every passing second. He sighed. 'OK. What have I got to do?'

Peg dropped the ice cubes into the wastepaper basket and gave him one of her killer smiles. 'Well, we're all going to use our strengths, of course, darling. So I thought you'd have guessed.'

Jasmine giggled. Ewan shook his head. What strengths did he have that would possibly be of any use here? Well, he supposed he could heft and heave with the best of them when it came to demolishing the old stadium and building the new. Or public relations work? That might be quite good fun. And he'd still have time to slope off and rescue greyhounds without anyone asking awkward questions. And, anyway, it would be a good thing to keep his head down in the wilds of Ampney Crucis for the time being. It would mean he could keep an eye on Peg, too – and of course, rekindle the flames with Clara. He could think of worse ways of spending a summer.

'OK, I'm up for it. Put me out of my misery. Tell me what I'm going to do.'

Peg burst into a little bit of 'Move Over Darling', then stopped and smiled flirtatiously. 'You, sweetheart, are going to seduce the pants off Brittany Frobisher.'

chapter ten

It was going to be easier said than done, Jasmine thought, as she clambered over the kitchen furniture and tried to peer into the mirror: getting her father to regale her with his plans for the greyhound stadium. She balanced on two chairs and took a closer look. God! She looked like a clown! Why was she so ham-fisted when it came to putting on make-up? Why hadn't she asked Clara to give her a hand? And why – she stopped, balancing precariously on the edge of the draining board on her way down – was she bothering anyway?

She was only going home to see her parents on an ordinary Tuesday afternoon, after all. Oh, and possibly Andrew. He'd threatened to abandon the dealership for a couple of hours to be there. It was her mother's afternoon off, and she knew that Philip always escaped the Tuesday committee meetings if possible. It seemed the perfect time to catch them unawares. But even so, why would any of them even notice that she was wearing make-up? They'd probably just open the door a fraction, recognise her, and slam it shut again with a cursory, 'Not today, thank you.'

She somehow felt that, despite Peg's enthusiasm in the boardroom the previous day, tackling her father about the council's plans for the Merry Orchard Shopping Plaza wasn't going to be a piece of cake. Like everything put off for too long, there came a time when it was simply far, far too late. She should have gone home weeks ago. And there was a greyhound meeting tonight as well. And Clara was helping her write up – and she hadn't yet got round to telling Clara that Ewan was back in town, or that his sole mission for Peg was to become the next notch on Brittany Frobisher's bedpost.

'Oi!' A small child in a sand-encrusted bathing costume stood on the veranda gazing in at her. 'You do ice creams?'

'What? No, sorry. Shit.' Jasmine jabbed the mascara brush in her eye and blinked damply at the child which had now turned fuzzy at the edges. 'Try the kiosk.'

'This is the kiosk. My mum said.'

'It's a beach hut.' Jasmine scrubbed at the affected eye with a tea towel. The black streaks spread down her cheek. 'Bugger. It's my home.'

'Stone me.' The child kicked dismissively at the veranda with the toe of its pink jelly shoe. 'Ain't you got no ice creams, then?'

'No. Nor hot dogs, nor chips, nor whelks nor – oh God!' Jasmine surveyed the result of her scrubbing in the mirror. She looked like Alice Cooper.

'Sod you, then.' The child turned on its heel and climbed carefully back down the steps. 'This ain't a proper holiday place, this ain't. They does ice creams in Benidorm.'

'Naff off back to Benidorm, then,' Jasmine muttered under her breath, trying to repair the mascara damage. 'And if this afternoon goes the way I think it will, I'll probably join you.'

The house on the Chewton Estate stood back from the road, a mirror image of the other ten houses in the crescent. Its allotted semi-circle of turf was protected by a low-slung link of white chains, a pampas grass stood dead centre, and a tub of geraniums was placed with geometric precision on either side of the front door. It had been the only house in which she had lived and yet, Jasmine thought, surveying it almost impartially now, it had never been home at all. Home had always been Benny's jumbled, comfortable, cornucopia of a council house, where the larder always offered up forbidden treats, and the rooms were stuffed full of child-proof glories in primary colours.

'Tasteless tat,' Yvonne had always said. 'Glittery, tacky, tawdry, outdated junk.'

Jasmine had loved it. And now she lived with it. And the beach hut had quickly become far more her home than this place had ever been.

There were no cars in the drive, but that didn't mean that her parents weren't at home. Jasmine reckoned that Philip and Yvonne must be the only people in the world who actually used their double garage for its intended purpose. The cars – purchased from Andrew's dealership, of course – were not only status symbols to her parents but also prized possessions. They were, as was everything in the house, to be admired and boasted about, but not enjoyed.

As she scrunched her way up the shingle drive, Jasmine was uncertain as to whether she should just walk in or ring the bell. How strange . . . She opted for skirting the side of the house, and tiptoeing in through the open kitchen door. There was no welcoming smell of familiarity; no cooking, no animals, not even bleach or disinfectant. It was like a show house: everything colour co-ordinated, neat, clean. Sterile. Nothing out of place. It didn't look as though people actually lived and ate and slept in this house. Well, really she supposed they didn't. Not any more. She'd been the only one who ate anything. Everything.

When she'd lived here, returning bored and frazzled

from the accounts department at Watertite Windows, Jasmine had had a secret carbohydrate stash behind the 98% Fat Free section in the top cupboard. As Yvonne spent all day spreading fear and loathing at one of her two posh frock shops – she resolutely refused to refer to them as boutiques – and Philip had always been out on council business, Jasmine had eaten gluttonously and alone. Her parents' meals arrived hygienically packed from the once-a-month supermarket shop, and if they couldn't be microwaved and contained more than ten calories then they simply weren't served up. Her father, she knew, made furtive evening sorties to the Crumpled Horn, and necked back massive portions of shepherd's pie with chips and baked beans.

Jasmine leaned from the kitchen window. The garden was empty too. The pool, Yvonne's pride and joy, sat in its turquoise rectangle beneath the sun's relentless glare, its surface unruffled, its surrounding honey-coloured flagstones bone dry. The garden furniture, ordered in from Scotts of Stow, still looked as untouched as the day it had been delivered. It was all soulless, anonymous, dead.

'Jasmine! Goodness! This is a surprise!' Yvonne was standing beneath the arch to the dining area, looking slightly startled. 'Why didn't you ring to say you were coming?'

Jasmine jumped guiltily. 'Hello, Mum . . .' As soon as the words were out, she was aware how ridiculous they sounded. 'I suppose I should have phoned you.'

Yvonne, wearing skimpy shorts and a brief sun-top, with her golden curls pinned neatly on top of her head, was barefooted. Jasmine presumed that was why she hadn't heard her come into the kitchen. The bone-thin body was an all-over even caramel colour, her make-up was salon-perfect, and her finger- and toenails glistened with some expensive opalescence. Jasmine, with her smudged mas-

118

cara, baggy denims and an extra large T-shirt, felt that her mother had done it on purpose.

'Well, we offered enough invitations.' Yvonne looked martyred. 'Andrew said that he'd told you that you were welcome to come home on more than one occasion. Even when you refused to return my calls.'

Jasmine shuffled her feet. 'Yeah, I know. After what happened, I just – well, I didn't want to. Sorry. And, anyway, there would have been conditions attached, wouldn't there?'

Yvonne shrugged. 'Maybe. Like giving up this ridiculous pretence of being a – a bookmaker.'

Her mother's lips, Jasmine noticed, made a fat pouting *moue* round the word. She wondered suddenly if Yvonne had had collagen treatment.

'There's no point in saying anything else, Mum. I love being a bookie. I'm getting quite good at it, actually.'

'Dear God in heaven! That's like saying you're making a success of being a prostitute!'

Jasmine heaved a huge sigh. Her immediate reaction was to turn tail and walk out – but then Peg and Roger and Allan would never forgive her if she left before she'd accomplished her task, would they? 'Don't be so insulting! Being a bookie was good enough for Grandpa. Anyway, you know it's what I've always wanted – to be like him.'

Yvonne swept an immaculately manicured hand across her brow in a theatrical gesture. 'And I've spent my entire married life trying to live it down! Being related, albeit only by my wedding vows, to Benny Clegg! Your father and I have struggled against the slur for years – and we'd both lived, prayed, for the day when he was no longer with us and we could hold our heads up in the golf club and –'

'Mum! How can you say that? I loved him!' Jasmine's

119

eyes filled with tears. She had to clench her teeth together to stop the tears from spilling down her cheeks. 'I miss him so much! He was the best, the kindest, most wonderful person in the world!'

Yvonne's tongue clicked against her teeth in irritation. 'To be honest, Jasmine, we've had this conversation a thousand times. I really don't want to hear it any more. So, if you haven't come here to offer the olive branch, and you're not intending to stop making a fool of yourself with those geriatric reprobates at the greyhound track, just why are you here?'

'I was asking myself the same question.' Jasmine was bitingly angry. 'But actually I've come to see Dad.'

'Your father's not here. He's playing golf at Poole and then going on for a back-slapping dinner. I've no idea when he'll be home. And sorry to be blunt, but I'm just going out – so if you're not coming home to stay, there's not much point in you hanging around, is there?'

None at all, Jasmine thought sadly. She'd have to ring the council offices and make an appointment to see Philip, just as if she was planning to add a porch or extend her conservatory or something. Yvonne was looking quite twitchy, and the house was beginning to stifle Jasmine.

She took a deep breath. 'Fine. I'll go, then. Can I use the loo first?'

'This is still your home. You don't have to ask.'

'Oh, I think I do.' Jasmine brushed past her mother, far too angry to look at her. If she saw the flint in Yvonne's eyes she'd only cry. 'Up or down?'

'Whichever . . .' Yvonne held herself away as Jasmine passed.

Jasmine chose up. The downstairs cloakroom, with its frills and flounces and the crinoline lady hiding the spare loo roll, had always depressed her. She belted through the familiar stripped pine and cream rooms, up the cream and pale pink staircase, and into the cream and eau-de-Nil bathroom. Everything was as it had always been. Like a pastel stage set.

It was only on her way downstairs again that she noticed the spare bedroom door was open. Of the five bedrooms, Yvonne and Philip had the master with the en-suite overlooking the crescent, Jasmine's had been at the back of the house, and two of the remaining rooms were turned into a study and a mini gym. The cream and ice-blue guest room, at the end of the landing, was usually stripped and clinical, waiting for visitors who rarely materialised. Today, though, there were clothes on the end of the bed and the curtains weren't quite properly pulled back.

Jasmine frowned. Had her parents got someone staying? A colleague or a distant relative? Funny, with all the time he seemed to spend here, that Andrew hadn't mentioned it. She trotted downstairs again, curious, but really not wanting the curiosity to show. She'd ask the identity of the mystery guest, though, she decided, just in case it was someone she knew. Someone who might be a friend or ally. Someone, like ancient Aunt Edna from Scotland, who could share memories of Benny.

'Mum? Who's sleeping –'

Yvonne's voice, obviously on the telephone, floated up the staircase. '. . . just leaving. Give it half an hour, eh? Just to be on the safe side. Yes, of course it'll be worth the wait . . . Isn't it always?'

Was that her father on the phone? Surely not? She'd never heard that coquettish tone in her mother's voice before. Intrigued now, Jasmine noisily thumped down the last few stairs but by the time she'd reached the kitchen, Yvonne was staring out at the swimming pool and the phone was back on the wall.

'I'll be going now, then.' It seemed a ludicrous parting shot. 'Who was on the phone?'

'No one.' Yvonne didn't turn round. 'Just the pool man.'

Jasmine blinked. The pool man, who was grubby, and reeked of chlorine, and had a perpetual cigarette dangling from the corner of his mouth, seemed an unlikely target for on-line seduction.

Yvonne's shoulders tensed. 'It doesn't need to be like this, Jasmine. You know it doesn't.'

'It does. I'm really happy in the beach hut – and at the stadium – and I should have moved out years ago. Anyway, if I stay away maybe one day things will be all right.'

'If you stopped sullying the family name, maybe they would.'

'Which family name would that be? Clayton? That's not my name. I'm a Clegg – and proud of it. No, really, Mum, I'm sorry, but I think it's for the best. Tell Dad I came round, won't you? I'll have to catch him some other time. Oh – and, by the way, who's sleeping in the spare room?'

Yvonne gave a sort of sniffy laugh. 'Goodness! You're a real little Miss Marple, aren't you? Your dad is, actually.'

Jasmine's mouth fell open. 'Dad? Why?'

Yvonne turned round then, her eyes wide, her lips down-turned. 'Because he snores, that's why. He flatly refuses to do anything about it. Won't see the doctor, won't take any of the remedies I've suggested – so it was the only way I could get a decent night's sleep.'

'But he's always snored.'

'Not like this, he hasn't. And it's getting worse. Like trying to sleep with a pneumatic drill. Betty at the salon has had a hell of a job debagging my eyes. She thinks I'm a star to have put up with it for so long. Now, sorry to shoo you out but – Oh, bloody hell!' Yvonne's head suddenly whizzed round like the child's in *The Exorcist*. 'That

122

sodding cat! It'll poo on the patio! Scram, you scraggy bugger! If I catch you I'll –'

Jasmine watched as Yvonne sprinted out of the kitchen door and away across the crew-cut lawn in pursuit of the tabby from two doors down. It was, she knew, no contest. The tabby picked its way daintily across the flagstones, strolled through the herbaceous border and disappeared through a convenient gap in the fence. Yvonne, her arms windmilling wildly, watched, scowling, as it squeezed its tabby plus fours through the larch-lap panels.

Seizing the moment, Jasmine picked up the phone and dialled 1471. She hadn't heard it ring, so maybe her mother had dialled out. No – she listened to the nasal voice – there had been a call ten minutes ago . . . Withheld number . . . She replaced the phone, pursing her lips, cogs whirring. The pool man would have no reason to withhold his number, would he? And Yvonne's voice had been purring and sensual. And her father was sleeping in the spare room . . .

As she watched her mother undulate back across the lawn towards the house, Jasmine's heart plummeted. It made sense . . . It all added up. Yvonne was having an affair.

'So that's twenty-five pounds, and your stake makes thirty.' Jasmine managed to smile at the youth proudly waving his winning ticket in front of her. Then she nudged Clara. 'Thirty quid! Number two-three-eight.'

'Uh? Oh, yeah. Right.' Clara dreamily doled out the allotted notes.

The favourite – one of Bess Higgins's graders – had just won the third race of the evening. Favourites had also won the first two. With ten races still to go and a queue of winning punters to pay out, Jasmine was well aware that if the trend continued it would result in a substantial loss. And Clara had been told about Ewan's return, but not about Brittany Frobisher, and was being about as much use as a tissue-paper umbrella, and all the time the only thing Jasmine could think about was her mother – and who? Not the pool man, that was for sure. Possibly one of her father's council chums, or a mutual mate from the golf club. Whoever it was, it was disgusting.

Paying out the winners with about a quarter of her brain, Jasmine mulled over the other possibilities. There didn't seem to be any. Philip may not be perfect – but neither was Yvonne – and anyway, it was always other people's parents who had affairs, whose grandparents died . . .

'Bit of a bugger, that one,' Clara was raking through the depleted contents of the leather satchel as the last winning ticket had been handed in. 'Let's hope the next one isn't a favourite. Is that why you're looking terminally pissed off?'

Jasmine nodded. She couldn't tell anyone about her suspicions regarding Yvonne. Especially not Clara. Clara would think it was hootingly funny. Clara's mother had had gentlemen callers for as long as Ampney Crucis could remember, and as a child Clara had had so many courtesy uncles that at Christmas their house had resembled Hamleys.

'Yeah, that and not being able to find out anything about the Merry Plaza Shopping Centre. Peg was not best pleased. She's itching to go ahead with the Frobishers.'

'So what's happening now? About this rebuild and the platinum thing?'

Jasmine scrubbed at the runners from the previous race with her duster, and laboriously chalked up the next six. She wished she knew. She wished she could think straight. The stadium was jammed noisily with holidaymakers, and

124

the greyhounds were filling the hot evening air with their yelps of excitement. With the Tannoy playing a selection from Doris's *Greatest Hits*, and the scent of frying onions wafting from Gilbert's snack stand, it was reminiscent of a fairground.

She reined in her thoughts. 'Oh, I reckon Peg'll go ahead anyway. That's what everyone else wants to do. They all think Dad's bluffing.'

'And you don't?'

'I haven't got a clue. Probably, knowing him. And Mum was pretty poisonous this afternoon so they're probably in it together.' She stopped. They actually probably weren't. Like they weren't sharing the same bed any more. She couldn't think about it. 'Have you seen Ewan yet?'

Clara shook her head. 'I thought he might be here.'

That would explain the skimpy white strappy dress, then, Jasmine thought. And the Jimmy Choos. Not to mention the knockout waft of something bank-breakingly pungent.

'He probably will be later. He was sorting out the electrics at Peg's – you know how dodgy she is about practical things. Apparently all the fuses keep blowing and Ewan doesn't want to be fried in his bed – Oh, come on! Don't go gooey-eyed on me. That was not a sexy remark. And anyway, you're supposed to hate him more than any man who ever lived.'

'I didn't actually say that.' Clara managed to look a bit embarrassed. 'Did I?'

'That and much, much more.' Jasmine took a rush of bets on the one dog, Fickle Finger, and marked it down to evens on the blackboard. 'Like having his extremities shrunk and wearing them as a trophy necklace, I seem to recall.'

Clara shrugged. 'Maybe. But that was then. I've grown

up a lot – and apart from that he's amazing in bed and my sex life has been so boring recently that I may just forgive him.'

'Christ. Whatever happened to feminine solidarity, the rules of which I believe we set down in the playground, regarding men who dump on you?'

'It all flies out the window when there's a drop-dead gorgeous man around, I'm afraid. As you'll discover.'

Despite her brain-churning, Jasmine giggled. Hardly. Andrew was still paying her infrequent visits at the beach hut, which meant those nights were filled with fumbling, rapid lovemaking and a lot of post-coital snoring – his, not hers. The engagement was still on, just. She somehow could never visualise the wedding, though. She'd wondered if it was some sort of premonition – like poor Princess Diana had had when she'd said so publicly that she could never see herself becoming Queen of England. Was that all there was going to be for her and Andrew? Rigid, uncomfortable encounters – with no tulle and confetti at the end of it?

The greyhounds were being led out for the next pre-race parade, leaving no more time for speculation. The holidaymakers had shoved their way to the front of the rickety stands to get a better look, and several last-minute punters were crowding round her and Roger and Allan, pushing fivers at them like there was no tomorrow.

'You're going to be buggered if Fickle Finger wins,' Clara said laconically. 'This could be your worst night ever.'

Jasmine knew. But so far it had been a wonderful summer. She'd had nights when she'd pocketed a small fortune, others when she'd only just broken even, but at least the weather had been fine, and the stadium had been full. There were going to be plenty of nights in the future when the rain would be dripping morosely from the corrugated iron roofing, and the wind would howl in from the sea, and she wouldn't take a single bet. She'd been around Benny long enough to know that it wasn't going to be roses all the way.

The handlers were easing the dogs into the traps, and Bunny, all aquiver with excitement, was poised with the hare. Then the whole shebang began again. The hare rattled away, the traps shot open, the dogs streaked sideways round the sandy track, and the Ampney Crucis air was filled with excited yells.

Fickle Finger won by a mile.

It was gone midnight before Jasmine and Clara and the sadly depleted leather satchel returned to the beach hut. The mood was not carefree. There was the infidelity problem to mull over, as well as the financial deficit. And Ewan hadn't shown up at the stadium, so Clara was sulking. Not even the pleasure of cod and chips from Eddie Deebley's Fish Bar, eaten from the paper along the cliff path walk, had managed to cheer them up.

They slouched down the cliff steps, Clara's Jimmy Choos making the descent far more precarious than usual. Jasmine, knowing every inch of the route, stared out into the fathomless darkness, wondering if she felt sorry for her father, and deciding she didn't.

Clara grabbed her arm, tumbling chips into the candytuft clumps. 'There's someone down there! Look, Jas, by your hut.'

There was. Jasmine, her eyes accustomed to the gloom, didn't even need the faint illumination scattered from the upper rooms of the Crumpled Horn to know it was Andrew. She'd recognise that stocky outline, that cropped head, anywhere.

'Sod it. Not tonight . . . I'm just not in the mood . . .'

Jasmine and Clara shuffled slowly along the path in front of the beach huts.

'Jas!' Andrew appeared from the shadows. 'Thank God! I've been waiting for ages. You'll never guess who else has shown up – Oh, hi, Clara.'

Clara sketched a smile. Then the smile radiated shooting stars into the darkness. Jasmine groaned. Ewan had just levered himself up from one of the canvas chairs on the veranda and was bearing down on Clara with all the amorous intent of Rhett Butler after a carpetbagging session.

chapter eleven

'Cairey! Heel! No – stop!' April hurled herself across the walled yard of number 51, sloshing through the weedy puddles in desperation. 'Caireee!!!'

The greyhound, having loped across the small expanse in three easy strides, had cornered Daff, and was now crouched, snarling, ready to go for the throat. Beatrice-Eugenie, in red Wellingtons and a second-hand plastic mac, gurgled delightedly at this impromptu entertainment. Daff, who had obviously only poked her head out of the back door to sniff at the rain, huddled against the dingy brickwork and sighed resignedly.

'Sorry.' April tugged Cair Paravel away from Jix's mum. 'I didn't know you were coming out.'

Daff gave a shrug. 'Wouldn't have bothered if I'd known he was going to be here. Only wanted a spot of fresh air – being cooped up inside when it's wet fair gets on my nerves. And I wasn't intending to venture any further afield than the doorstep, of course, even if he thought I was.'

'I'm so sorry. We've just come back from our run in the park, so he's still a bit frisky,' April said apologetically, feeling really awful that she'd spoiled Daff's tiny daily trip into freedom. 'And, of course, I have to smuggle him in through the back way in case anyone sees him. I had no idea you'd be taking a breather.'

Cair Paravel had now rolled on to his back in a puddle and was laughing up at Bee, who was sitting astride him, tickling his tummy. April shook her head. Not only was he never going to chase the hare or run in a straight line or any of the things he was supposed to do, he was obviously never going to get over his intense dislike of Daff. Not that he'd ever bitten her, of course. Things had never gone that far; Cair Paravel was simply too much of a pacifist. Still gentle to the point of soppiness with all other humans and animals, Cair Paravel seemed to be hellbent on making Daff's life a misery. To give her her due, Daff was still optimistically hoping for a reconciliation.

April and Jix had serious doubts about the way Cair Paravel had been treated by the less-than-fragrant Mr Reynolds in his previous ownership. Maybe there was some truth in the rumours circulating Bixford that Mr Reynolds was into a rather sad sort of middle-aged cross-dressing. These had confirmed their earlier suspicions – and would certainly explain Cair Paravel's distrust of all things polyester.

'Maybe,' Jix had frequently said, 'if we could get my mum to dress in cotton and silk, the problem would be solved.'

To be honest, April reckoned, as the rain dripped sadly from the bleak rooftops, getting Daff out of her man-made floral frocks and headscarves would be about as easy as convincing the sceptical British public that they were simply gagging for another Millennium Dome.

'I'll get him indoors and give him his dinner,' April said, manfully removing her daughter from the greyhound's inverted midriff. 'Then I'll bring Bee up to you for lunch before I dash off to Antonio's, if that's OK.'

'Finc, sweet.' Fortunately, Daff was never one to bear a grudge. 'We can play rainy-day games. Jix used to love them.'

Lucky Jix, lucky Bee, April thought as she shepherded her two damp and muddy charges inside the flat. Her own recollections of wet childhood days were far from happy.

She'd just managed to stuff the last of the Pasta Place's leftover meat into Cair Paravel, sponged the worst of the park's traces from Bee, and scrambled into her waitressing black skirt and white blouse, when the doorbell rang.

She looked warningly at dog and child. 'Not a peep while Mummy answers the door – OK?'

Beatrice-Eugenie nodded diligently. Cair Paravel didn't.

Since that awful day when Seb Gillespie had spotted them outside number 51, and then asked so many weird questions in the Copacabana – and apparently also given Jix the third degree – April had been paranoid about unexpected callers. Fortunately another of Cair Paravel's failings was his reluctance to bark at strangers, and while this may have made him pretty useless as a guard dog, it was certainly a blessing in disguise as far as April was concerned.

She slid back the bolts, unlatched the lock, and pulled the door open.

'You April Padgett?' An androgynous teenager, with bleached dreadlocks dripping from beneath a fleecy hood, flashed a wide toothpaste-ad smile at her. 'You got a greyhound?'

'Yes I am and no I haven't.'

The teenager scuffed its soaking trainers. 'You sure? Belonged to Nobby Reynolds? Blue dog? Cair Paravel?'

April whimpered. Sebby was obviously hiring teenage hit men. Again she shook her head.

The teenager pursed its lips. 'Nobby said you 'ad 'im. Debt settlement. You passed 'im on?'

'If I didn't have him, I couldn't pass him on, could I?'

April's teeth were chattering. 'Why do you want to know anyway? Who sent you?'

'My dad sent me.'

April blinked. Sebby was this child's father? Never in the world! Seb was far too young. 'Who's your dad?'

'Clive Outhwaite.'

Outhwaite . . . Outhwaite . . . The name seemed familiar. Was he another well-known Bixford knee-capper? Then the penny sort of clunked into place. April knew exactly where she'd heard the name before. Every night at the stadium, broadcast loudly across the Tannoy. She sucked in her breath. 'Clive Outhwaite? Not the greyhound owner from Bixford North?'

'Yeah!' The Outhwaite offspring looked delighted. 'Right, well, Nobby Reynolds – 'e's right weird by the way – 'e bought Cair Paravel cheap off my dad because 'e was crap. But 'e never took 'is papers, see. Registration, vaccinations, races run – all the guff. I went round to give them to old Nobby, and 'e says that the dog belongs to you now. See?'

April saw. She saw very clearly indeed. She just wished she knew what to do with the seeing. She decided to go for the easy route. Lying through the teeth. 'Um, well, yes – I did collect him from Nob – er – Mr Reynolds. But not for me. Oh, definitely not for me. But – er – look, to save you the bother of getting even wetter, why don't you give me the papers and stuff and I'll pass them on to Cair P – er – that is, to the greyhound's new owner?'

The smile dazzled even more brightly against the gloomy day as the teenager fished beneath the voluminous recesses of the fleece. 'Sounds good to me – and me dad'll be chuffed to be shot of the whole business, to tell the truth. Right 'ere we go . . .' Producing a bulky folder, the youth handed it over, then suddenly erupted in a burst of almost manic laughter. ''E's a crap dog, mind. That's why my dad stitched up old Nobby! 'E don't want to run after the bloody 'are!'

'Really? Blimey!' Feeling completely hysterical anyway, April joined in the laughter. 'Just as well I passed him on then, eh?'

'Just as bloody well,' the junior Outhwaite chuckled enormously. 'If you'd kept 'im and thought you were going to race 'im, you'd be in serious shit! See ya!'

Two hours later, after dishing up the last order of ravioli and chips to a traffic warden, April tucked her notebook into the waistband of her pinny, eased her feet inside her new waitressing shoes, and wearily made her way back to the Pasta Place's kitchen.

Tonio and Sofia were enjoying the garlic-scented fug, watching the raindrops trickle down the steamy windows. April poured herself a glass of milk from the fridge, then forked up the remainder of her salad which had been sitting on the table since her shift began.

'Bloody wet August,' Antonio sighed. 'Bloody hate it.'

Sofia looked askance. 'Brings the munchers in, though. They don't want to sit around outside in weather like this. Good for trade. Anyway, it'll clear up before Bank Holiday Monday – my corns are telling me so.' Her eyes trailed down to April's feet. 'Ooh, new shoes?'

'New to me.' April also looked down at the flat pink canvas crossovers. 'Charity shop – fifty pence. Brilliant for work.'

'Bit dowdy, though,' Sofia sniffed. 'Not flattering on the legs. You can't beat a nice pair of Manolos to add oomph to the legs.'

'Maybe not, but these are bloody marvellous on the feet. And they're mine all mine. Not yours, not Daff's . . .' April chewed on the last mouthful of her lunch. 'And I don't care what Martina says, I'll be wearing them in the Copacabana tonight too. They'll set the fishnets off a treat.'

Despite a mass protest from the cocktail-bar waitresses, Martina had totally refused to allow them to ditch the French maids' outfits. April secretly hoped that the addition of the pink mumsy sandals would go some way to ruining the overall effect of available sexuality.

Antonio, who had continued to gaze dismally at the sodden High Street, suddenly rapped on the window. 'Hey! Jix! You just finished work?'

April, desperate to impart the news about Cair Paravel, finished the glass of milk and headed back towards the restaurant. 'Tonio – ask him to pop in for a moment, will you, please? Can I give him a cappuccino?'

'Course, love. And a pastry.' Sofia had bustled towards the machine. 'Poor lad always looks half-starved.'

The traffic warden, obviously in no hurry to head back into the downpour, was still chasing ravioli around his plate. Several other tables were occupied by people delaying their return to the afternoon's work for as long as possible. The restaurant was as warm and steamy as a sauna. April placed the cappuccino and Danish on a corner table and pulled out a second chair as Jix dripped into the Pasta Place from his debt-collecting round.

'You look nice,' she grinned at him. 'Been somewhere special?'

'Leave it out . . .'

Jix shrugged off his long black P V C trench coat and unwound several chiffon scarves. On any other man, April thought, the outfit would be gay to the point of capriciousness; on Jix, however, the effect was astoundingly sexy. Freda Cope had obviously thought so.

April raised her eyebrows. 'You've still got strawberry yoghurt in your hair.'

'Christ!' Jix pulled several strands forward and surveyed them with horror. 'She's supposed to get it all out before I leave.'

'What exactly does she get you to do for your money – or rather, Oliver's money?'

Jix looked gloomy. 'Don't ask. To be honest I'm losing my taste for it – and it's ruined me for yoghurt. Is everything OK at home? Mum, Bee, Cairey?'

'Fine . . .' April watched as Jix tore into the Danish pastry with strong white teeth. Whatever contortions he performed for the sad Freda Cope, it certainly seemed to have given him an appetite. 'But I've got something to show you.'

She pulled the folder out from her bag and pushed it towards him across the table. While he demolished the coffee and pastry she filled him in on the finer details of the visit of the junior Outhwaite.

'Ace!' Jix said when she'd finished. 'All we have to do now is to change his ownership on the registration forms – not as our dog, though . . . maybe in Mum's name, or Bee's even, then we'll get him racing.'

'You haven't been listening. Clive Outhwaite's child says he's a duffer.'

Jix tapped the racing papers in front of him with a slender finger. 'Because they've only ever tried him out at Bixford. He's had seven starts and loused them all up. Not completed a race. So it could be the track he hates. We're going to take him somewhere completely different.'

April shook her head. She wanted a cigarette but knew she'd have to wait. 'Like where exactly?'

'No idea yet. But Sebby's got a list of all the stadiums that have tendered for the Frobisher Platinum in his office. Some of them are in places I didn't even know existed. I'll pinch a copy of them and we can get the map out and find somewhere really out of the way. I reckon if I get Cair Paravel's papers up to scratch when I finish this afternoon's collecting, we could have him in for a race somewhere on Bank Holiday Monday.'

April squeaked. 'That soon! And how are we both going to get time off? And then there's transport – neither of us has a car, and I somehow can't see us managing to smuggle a racing greyhound on to public transport and –'

Jix leaned across the table and placed his fingers on her lips. They smelled disturbingly of yoghurt. 'Shut up. Leave it with me. I'll sort something out and see you later. OK?'

'OK. Oh, and is it also OK if I don't do the collecting this afternoon? I'm really wiped out. And I've got to work tonight.'

'Course it is. You go and get you feet up for an hour – but please take those dreggy sandals off first. You look just like my mum!'

Giggling, April punched him. Happiness swept through her. She had an afternoon off – and even if she used part of it to catch up on her sleep, it would still mean being able to join in the rainy-day games with Daff and Bee. Cair Paravel ever running in a proper greyhound race was probably out of the question, of course, but it was nice to have a new dream. Life, she thought as she stood up and automatically gathered together Jix's mug and plate, was definitely on the up.

Daff's rainy-day games had been great fun. They'd involved a lot of kneeling on the window seat, each of them choosing a fat raindrop sliding down the outside of the pane, giving it a name, and then watching them race. It was like a sort of vertical Poohsticks, and had kept the three of them happily involved for hours.

136

Now back downstairs in her own flat, with Bee watching cartoons and Cair Paravel stretched out on the sofa, his long muscular legs overlapping the arms at both ends, April had managed not only to catch up her sleep, but also on having a bath and washing her hair. And there were still several hours to go before she signed in at the Copacabana. She sang as she ironed the pile of second-hand clothes, the feeling of elation still with her.

'April!' Jix's voice echoed from outside the door. 'Let me in, please.'

Still humming, April unbolted the door. Jix had shed the PVC trench coat and most of the scarves and seemed to have removed the yoghurt from his hair. He waved the folder under her nose.

'Bingo! Cair Paravel is now officially owned by Beatrice-Eugenie Padgett! Everything else passed muster with the GRA, and we're free to let him rip!'

'Great.' April smiled at his enthusiasm. And it did seem very apt that Bee should own the dog, as neither of them was supposed to exist. It made it all very Brigadoon. 'And where and when exactly is this amazing event going to take place?'

'Ampney Crucis.' Jix budged up next to Cair Paravel on the sofa and gazed at the television over Bee's head. 'Bank Holiday Monday. They have meetings three days a week, but are apparently putting on a special for the August Bank Ho – What are you looking at me like that for?'

'Amply Who?' April turned down the television cartoon's volume, and ignored Beatrice-Eugenie's grumbling. 'Where the hell is that?'

'Not sure.' Jix looked a bit abashed. 'I nicked the list off Seb's desk, like I said. Sebby and Brittany are supposed to be inspecting the place, but not on that day, so I guess they've tendered for the Platinum. Anyway, it's definitely the smallest and most obscure circuit on the list.'

April switched off the iron and reached for the dog-eared and out-of-date atlas of Britain which was stuffed into her bookshelves along with dozens of other bargain-basement buys. Opening it on the ironing board, she scanned down the list of As.

'A-m-p? Is that right? A-m-p-n-e-y? No . . . can't see it – Oh, yes I can! It's in Dorset! Miles away!' She flicked to the appropriate page. 'God, Jix, look! It's a pinprick! Why the hell would they want to tender for the Platinum? They haven't got an earthly . . .'

Jix had uncurled himself from Cair Paravel and was leaning over her shoulder. His hair was silky on her cheek and she brushed it away. He exhaled. 'Yeah, see what you mean. It does look pretty titchy – but that's all to the good, isn't it? No one will know us from Adam there. And look at the location. It's really near to Bournemouth – that means it's right on the coast. Just think of it: we can all go and have a day at the seaside!'

'Oh, wow! Yes!'

April closed her eyes. She'd known it was going to be a lovely day. Bee had never, ever seen the sea – and she hadn't had a day at the coast for years . . . She hardly dared think about it.

She opened her eyes to the reality. 'How on earth are we going to get there, though? We haven't got transport. And you can hardly borrow one of the Gillespie motors for this particular outing.'

'True – but we could hire a car . . .' Jix sat down again, squeezing underneath Cair Paravel's front legs. Bee, feeling left out, scrambled on to his lap. 'I've been asking around. For a couple of hundred quid, plus a deposit, we could have one for two days –'

'A couple of hundred!' April blinked. 'We can't afford that – can we? I mean, I know I can't – not unless I use the chocolate-tin money.'

'You're not touching that. That's spoken for. It's for the future. And I'm as skint as you are – but I've got an idea. Mind you, you're not going to like it much . . .'

'Oh, no! No way!' April held up her hands in horror. 'I am not performing special favours for Oliver's debtors! Not even for a hundred pounds a time. Not a bloody chance!'

'Hey,' Jix looked indignant, 'as if! No, it's nothing like that – although it is pretty personal.'

April stared at him. He'd turned his head and was gazing at the paintings on the wall.

She groaned. 'Sell another one of Noah's pictures, you mean? God – do I have to? I really wanted to hang on for them for Bee – and for when Noah comes back.'

'Yeah, I know. But when he comes back, he can paint you as many as you want, can't he? And this is for Bee too, isn't it? Seeing if Cair Paravel can make you some money?'

April grimaced. She knew she couldn't argue with the reasoning. It was just that the few of Noah's paintings that were left were her only link with her happy past. The only thing she had of his – apart from Beatrice-Eugenie, of course.

'And,' Jix tickled Bee, making her laugh, 'you know how much his paintings are going for now, don't you?'

'Roughly . . . I mean, I know what the others fetched. And the woman at the gallery said they were rocketing in price every day. Maybe it'd be best to cash in on them now – before he goes out of fashion, I mean.'

Jix stopped tickling Bee. 'Look, I don't want you to be forced into doing something that you really don't want to do. You know that. I could always sort of borrow the money from work.'

'Forget that!' April glared at him. 'You've never been dishonest. That's why you've survived with the Gillespies as long as you have. They may be bloody villains themselves, but they trust you implicitly. And Daff relies on every penny you earn. She'd die if you got the push. Don't you ever, ever suggest anything like that again, OK?'

'OK, Mum.' Jix winked at her.

'So, yes, I'll sell a painting. But only one – and it'll be the last time.' April sucked in her breath. 'And I'll want a really good price. I suppose it'll mean having to hike it up West.'

Jix grinned. 'It won't, actually. There's a new gallery opened up in Bixford South. One of my – um – contacts mentioned that he'd – er – sold a few paintings there. I thought, as you're not waitressing tomorrow, that we could take the picture along at lunch time.'

chapter twelve

It had stopped raining, but only just, and the pavements gleamed and steamed in the humidity. April, struggling from the bus with the painting wrapped in sheets of yesterday's *Guardian*, was already uncomfortably sticky. Jix took the parcel from her as she negotiated the hordes of students and tourists all trying to get on and off the bus at the same time. They'd left Bee with Daff, while Joel and Rusty had agreed to take Cair Paravel on his usual undercover pipe-opener in the park, getting quite excited about being seen with something as daringly butch as a greyhound.

Bixford South was far more arty than the other two parts of the borough: there was no industry here, no greyhound stadium, no back-to-back terraces or boarded-up shops. Bixford South had wide roads and leafy pavements, with tall elegant houses and green open spaces. Its residents all worked in publishing and the media, drank caffelàtte in mock-Manhattan coffee lounges, and had wisteria-walled gardens which featured in the Sunday supplements.

April took the painting from Jix again, cradling it against her to protect it from the rushing lunch-time crowds. They'd chosen the smallest one simply for ease of man-oeuvring, but even so it was heavy and bulky. 'How much further?'

'Just along here,' Jix said. 'Round the next bend. Are you sure you don't want me to take it?'

April shook her head. She had a knot of sadness in her stomach at the thought of parting with it. It had been one of her favourites: a mass of greens and blues and turquoises, representing, Noah had said, the ocean calming after a storm. She'd watched him paint it, laying the colours on top of one another, scraping them away in swirling curves just before each one dried, to give movement and depth. She hadn't understood it, certainly hadn't seen it through his eyes, but the finished picture reminded her of the blissful weeks they'd shared together as it grew.

The gallery was elegant, quiet and well lit, with lots of white walls and pale wooden floors. Each of the two windows displayed a single painting beneath spotlights: both were abstract, vivid jags of colour on black canvas. Inside, there was one rather ugly floral arrangement, all dried thistles and bits of curling twig, towering in a pale vase in a corner, Beethoven tinkled the *Moonlight Sonata* unobtrusively from hidden speakers, and a ceiling fan whirred continuously. April thought it gave the place the air of an upmarket funeral parlour.

A woman, presumably in charge, glided out from an antechamber as though on castors. 'May I help you?' The matching set of raised eyebrows and pursed lips immediately suggested that she couldn't possibly.

April, wearing the pink sandals and a denim dress, quailed in front of this vision in fawn suede and co-ordinated make-up, and shifted the parcel under her arm. 'Er – yes, I hope so.'

The woman, whose minimalist name badge strained at having to encompass the words Penelope Grieves-Harrison, surveyed Jix in his Glastonbury best and looked as though she would like to telephone the police. 'Are you browsing?'

Jix shook his head. Several necklaces jangled. 'No, we'd like you to look at this painting with a view to buying it.'

April winced slightly at Jix's no-nonsense approach to the matter in hand. She'd have skirted around it a bit, made nervous apologetic noises, and probably said sorry a lot.

Penelope Grieves-Harrison seemed a little taken aback too. The pale gold eyebrows took on a life of their own. April could see 'Stolen! Stolen!! Stolen!!!' flashing through the cool brain. The lips peeled apart.

'We don't buy paintings from casual vendors.'

April, deciding that Jix needed backup, worked some saliva into her dry mouth. 'It's a Noah Matlock.'

Penelope's sculpted lips drew back even further, now revealing a set of teeth that wouldn't have disgraced a racehorse. 'I don't think it is.'

Holding herself back from shrieking 'Of course it is, you daft bat – I should know – have a bloody look!', April tried a woman-to-woman smile. 'It was painted three years ago. During his return-to-nature elemental period.'

Penelope Grieves-Harrison gave a well-bred snort. 'Oh no, my dear. I think not. All the Matlocks of that particular period are on permanent exhibition at the Stroud Gallery.'

April counted to ten. 'I know. Three for earth, three for air, three for fire – and two for water. This is the third water one. *Oceanic Calming* . . .'

Jix seized the moment and, having wrested the parcel from April, laid it flat on the desk and began ripping off the layers of newsprint. Despite her cool indifference, Penelope, April noticed, moved a little closer. As the tumbling colours came into view she gave a small gasping intake of breath.

'There,' Jix said, when the whole thing was uncovered. 'See. It's genuine.'

Penelope was poring over it, peering at the chunks of paint, looking like a greedy child at a birthday party spotting the food for the first time. 'It's certainly a remarkable copy.'

'It's not a damn copy,' April said, exasperated. 'It's not a forgery. It's the real thing. Look at the signature – it's his trademark.'

Noah, being highly original April had thought at the time, always drew a tiny ark complete with Lowry-type stick animals beneath his name, in the left-hand corner of each of his paintings beside the completion date.

Penelope had fumbled in the desk drawer for an eyeglass and was scrutinising the signature, her fawn hair all-of-a-piece with the soft suede dress. April exchanged glances with Jix. It had never been like this when they'd sold the other paintings. Then, so soon after Noah's defection and sick with early pregnancy but not realising it, she had gone sadly with Jix to one of the big West End galleries, off-loaded the pictures and pocketed the cheque and no questions had been asked.

'I do have other proof, both of the painting's originality and my ownership.' April really hadn't wanted to do this. Jix had warned her against it. But push was coming to shove here and they needed the money. 'There's this . . .'

She took the letter from her handbag and passed it to Penelope Grieves-Harrison. April knew the contents off by heart. She watched as the tawny eyes scanned the pages, taking in the huge scrawled words, knowing exactly at which point the eyebrows would raise, at which part the tongue would dare to protrude between the gin-trap teeth.

Darling April, my love, my inspiration,

Without you these paintings would not exist. Without you I would be as sterile as other men, working in dark futility.

144

My elemental work is dedicated to you. Should I leave you – and I swear I never will – *Oceanic Calming* is your insurance that I will return. It was created out of the roaring, surging torrent of our love; it siren-calls our passion teasingly to all those lonely souls unlucky enough never to have known such emotion. It is yours. Always. When you part with it you will have parted with my heart.

Your devoted and adoring, Noah.

When April had first shown it to Jix, he'd shrieked with laughter. 'What a load of old cobblers! God Almighty, April – what the hell was he on? Who wrote this for him? No, don't tell me – my mum's got similar stuff upstairs. The love letters of Godfrey Winn! Jesus!'

Then he'd seen April's tears, and handed the letter back quickly and made her a cup of tea.

She'd told him this morning that she'd brought it with her, and proof of her identity – and his reaction had been predictable. 'For God's sake don't show it to anyone. They'll laugh in your face.'

But Penelope wasn't laughing.

'Very well.' She folded the pages and handed them back to April. 'I'll need to speak with my co-owners, of course – so if you could leave the painting with me for a day or so . . .'

'No way.' Jix pushed his hair from his face. It immediately tumbled back again. 'The painting and April stay together. We want an immediate decision.'

Penelope stared longingly at the two-foot-square daubs of colour. April held her breath. The tape had worked its way round and Beethoven was tinkling the *Moonlight Sonata* again.

Penelope opened the bidding. 'Two thousand pounds.'

'Four,' Jix said quickly.

'Two and a half.' Penelope hadn't even broken into a sweat.

'I'll take three.' April's lips had gummed themselves together. She prised them apart. She hoped Penelope wouldn't see the urgency in her eyes. 'Three thousand pounds. Now. In cash . . .'

Penelope winced. 'Cheque.'

'Sorry. Only cash.' April could already visualise the notes, crammed together, fresh and crisp, in the chocolate tin under the bed.

'Very well.' It was a rapid capitulation. 'You'll have to wait while I go to the bank. We don't hold cash reserves here. I'll call one of my assistants to wait with you until I return.'

The assistant, young and slender and a pale imitation of the splendid Penelope, must have been listening to every word, if the speed with which she appeared from the antechamber was anything to go by.

'Elise will take care of you in my absence.' Penelope was striding towards the door. 'I won't be long.'

Elise eyed them warily. April wanted to rush round the silent room punching the air. Three thousand pounds! Three thousand! And she still had at least ten more of Noah's pictures at home. Not, of course, that she'd get rid of them. This was the last time. But – oh, what an investment for Bee's future!

'You could have got a lot more,' Jix said. 'She settled for three so quickly that she'd probably have parted with double.'

'I know, but I'm useless at haggling, and a definite three thousands pounds right now is a damn sight better than six thousand maybe. We can hire a car, and pay for all sorts of things, and get Cairey racing and –'

Jix shook his head. 'The money is for you and Bee. Yes,

sure, we'll use some now. But the rest must be saved for when you and Noah get back together and move to the roses-round-the-door cottage. You've worked so hard for it. And the last lot didn't go that far, did it? Rent and bills and things have a huge appetite.'

April sighed. Jix, of course, was right. But it was such a lovely heady feeling to have so much money – and all in one hit. It was a million times better than winning the Lottery.

Elise made a strange little mewing noise in her throat, and indicated the painting. 'The – um – Matlock . . . do you collect him?'

April smiled. Maybe Elise hadn't been ear-wigging that closely – or at least not to the early part of the conversation. 'Sort of. Why?'

'I saw him once,' Elise looked star-struck, 'at an exhibition. He's very – um – hunky. Not like an artist at all.'

'More like a rugby player,' April agreed nostalgically, with a shiver of ancient lust. Noah had always been a bit of a show-off when his paintings were on display. 'So where was this exhibition?'

'Swaffield. Last year. The Corner Gallery. I was working there during the summer holidays before being taken on here full time. He was over from France for a couple of days.'

April and Jix exchanged startled looks. Swaffield was only a couple of miles out of Bixford. They'd missed that one. April wanted to cry. Noah had been so close – and yet he hadn't made contact. She guessed he'd been too busy . . . And now he lived in France, did he? Well, she supposed the loft-living harpy who had taken her place had by now given up her career and was happily parasiting off Noah's new-found fame.

April and Jix had chased so many trails over the years

that had simply dwindled out and gone cold. All their letters had been returned unopened. No wonder. They hadn't even considered that he'd left the country. Noah was obviously settled in some rustic *gîte*, dining al fresco on non-stop Calvados and runny Brie, painting in the sunshine . . .

'He's coming back again.' Elise broke into this Peter Mayle fantasy. 'Noah Matlock. In September. I mean, I thought you might like to know, as you're keen on his work.'

The pristine gallery swirled. Beethoven suddenly became a rap drumming in April's ears. Hoping that she wasn't going to be sick on the waxed lime floor, she swallowed. 'What – er – back to Swaffield, you mean?'

'The Corner Gallery again, yes.' Elise nodded. 'On the twenty-sixth of September – I know because that's my birthday. He's exhibiting his new French stuff. All very Picasso, so I've been told.'

The door opened and Penelope breezed through, an envelope in her hand. She smiled with a refined air of lascivious greed as she handed it over, and April counted the fifty-pound notes and signed the receipt, and none of it registered. The only thing that registered was that Noah would be here, a couple of miles away, and she would see him – and introduce him to Bee – in a little over a month's time.

That evening, the Copacabana was thrumming. It was the running of the Bixford Cup, a prize donated every three months by Oliver, and attracted hugely knowledgeable dog-going crowds. A big race meeting meant that all the celeb owners were out in force. Martina had decided the cocktails tonight were to be champagne only, and April had served Blue Velvets to Jimmy White, Tibetan Monkeys to Ronnie

Wood and, surprisingly she felt, a couple of very pretty La Vie En Roses to Vinnie Jones.

While the other cocktail waitresses were going through their quarterly swoon over the clutch of famous faces, April could see only one. Beautiful and battered, Noah's image was in her head all the time, and had been ever since she and Jix had left the gallery.

'April!' Martina's roar shattered the on-loop daydream just at the part where Noah had again spotted her across the crowded gallery and rushed, in slow-motion – naturally – towards her, his arms outstretched, his love enfolding both her and Bee for ever.

'Uh?' April blinked wildly.

'You've been stirring that Queen Mum for five damn minutes!'

'Oh God – have I?' April looked down at the champagne and Tanqueray Gin. Despite the fact that she'd been whisking it with the jigger for so long, it looked flat and unappetising. She smiled apologetically at the waiting customer. 'I'll chuck it away and do another one.'

'And you'll pay for it,' Martina hissed. 'OK?'

'Of course.' April gave a blissful smile. The majority of the three thousand pounds, the notes rolled in bundles and secured with elastic bands, was stashed in the chocolate tin – and not in a bank since that could only reduce her overdraft. Tonight, the cost of one Queen Mum was neither here nor there.

Five hundred pounds of the money had already been earmarked that afternoon for hiring a car for Bank Holiday Monday and registering Cair Paravel for his first race under his new ownership at Ampney Crucis stadium. Jix had done both the deals by telephone and at the end of the second conversation had hung up and looked bewildered.

'Everything OK?' April had asked.

'Yeah — I suppose so.' Jix had continued to look flummoxed. 'But that lady I've just been talking to -' he'd gazed at the pad in front of him where he'd been jotting down details — 'what was her name? Oh, yes, Peg Dunstable — she's a bit odd. She says she owns the stadium, but she kept singing Whatever Will Be Will Be at me.'

April had giggled. 'Really? She's probably just the cleaner or something. And, you never know, the song title might be an omen. We'll find out soon enough when we get there, won't we?'

The feature race of the evening was just starting. Through the plate-glass windows April could see the crisscross of the spotlights, and hear the excitement rising in a cloud. The customers were drifting away from the bar, clutching their Kir Royales and Viva Glams, towards the viewing balconies. She took the opportunity of leaning back below the optics and flexing her toes inside the absolute bliss of the pink canvas crossover sandals.

'Don't let my mother see those.' Sebastian grinned at her from the plastic palm tree end of the bar. 'She'll have a fit.'

She hadn't seen him arrive. April really wanted to squirm her feet away out of sight. She certainly didn't want to indulge in light-hearted banter with Sebby. He'd been over-friendly for weeks now. She gave a girlish giggle. 'I know! But they're so comfortable.' God! Now she really did sound as if she was in her dotage.

Sebastian nodded in a distant sort of way. She couldn't blame him. There wasn't much he could say to that, really. He looked lovely, April thought, in black jeans and a white T-shirt. She unpeeled herself from the back of the bar.

'Sorry — did you want a drink?'

'No, thanks all the same. I'm waiting for Brittany to meet me here, then I'm taking her out to supper.' Sebastian sighed. 'Which means somewhere in Chelsea where there'll be at least half a dozen other A-listers and a load of paparazzi.'

'And you don't enjoy that?'

'I hate it. But for Brittany it goes with the territory. Sometimes I'm sure that she encourages them – lets them know in advance where she'll be, you know?'

Possibly, April thought, tidying the swizzle sticks in a mindless way. Maybe she'd do the same if she thought her face would be all over the papers the next morning. It must be a heck of a buzz. 'So where is she at the moment? Getting glammed up?'

'Hopefully belting back down the M40. She's been on a recce.'

April looked blank. 'Oh, right.'

'She's sussing out the stadiums that have tendered for the Frobisher Platinum. She's been to Oxford today.' Sebastian hitched himself onto one of the bar stools. 'It's all a bit embarrassing really, because, of course, my parents want it to be here – and think that because Brittany and I are – well – seeing a lot of each other, that it's a foregone conclusion.'

'Oh well, yes, I suppose they would . . .'

April suddenly wished there would be an influx of drunken footballers all wanting Gilda Tops. Anything rather than having to sit here chatting to the dreaded Sebastian, who at any minute was bound to fire off a barrage of questions about Bee and Cair Paravel. Sadly, everyone had decamped to watch the Gillespie Cup.

She shrugged. 'And it isn't, then? A foregone conclusion?'

'Not at all.' Sebastian looked quite shocked. 'Brittany is doing everything above board. All the tracks that have tendered are being inspected and considered in the same way. I've been along with her to most of them, but there are still plenty to see.'

April nodded and mopped up pools of water where the ice-making machine had got a bit overexcited. She knew all this, of course, from Jix. It was all so damned difficult, pretending all the time, having to remember exactly what she was supposed to know. 'Um – so Oliver and Martina would obviously be really upset if this – er – Frobisher thingy went somewhere else.'

'Livid!' Sebastian looked horrified. 'Bloody devastated. But Brittany's her own person. She'll make the final decision. I just wish I could explain that to them. They're really pushing us together all the time in a bid to secure the Platinum Trophy. To be honest, I feel totally manipulated.'

April pulled the bowls of pistachios into neat rows and wondered just how long it would be before Sebastian realised he was chattering with wild indiscretion to one of the Gillespies' more junior employees.

'Yes, it must make it a bit tricky for you, sort of running with the fox and the hounds, I suppose . . . It'll be chronic if Brittany decides to stage the race somewhere else and then you have to explain it to your parents.'

They looked at each other – both letting the awfulness of the situation sink in. It occurred to April that maybe Seb wasn't quite so appalling after all, and she could certainly empathise with his fear of the combined wrath of Martina and Oliver should Bixford not be the selected stadium.

The orgasmic roar from beneath the viewing balcony indicated that the Bixford Cup had been run and won. In less than five minutes, the designer brigade would be back clamouring for Big Apples and Prince Williams. April straightened her mob cap and tugged the frou-frou skirt down over her knickers and moved slightly away from Sebastian.

'Hi!' On cue, Brittany breezed round the plastic palm tree, dressed in see-through black and swinging a Lulu Guinness handbag. She kissed Sebastian on the cheek. 'Sorry to have kept you. The traffic was murder. Are you ready to go? I'm starving!'

Sebastian uncurled himself from the bar stool. 'Me too – although I'd be happier with pie and mash than a minuscule piece of transparent ham and three artistically arranged cubes of beetroot.'

Brittany wrinkled her nose in disbelief. 'Once you've downed the first bottle of Chardonnay you won't know what you're eating.' She glanced at April without recognition, but smiled anyway. 'I'll remove him, shall I? It looks as though you're going to be busy.'

It did. The hordes were pouring back towards the bar. April sighed. It would mean she wouldn't be able to fantasise about the Noah reunion for ages . . .

Sebastian motioned his head in a farewell gesture, and as they left April heard Brittany's well-modulated voice giving the precise lowdown on the pros and cons of Oxford stadium.

'So, where's the next one on the list?' Sebastian asked, as he steered her away from a leering bunch of men in big suits.

'Oh, I thought we'd go to that one that sent us the plans for their restructured stadium. They sounded so sweet. The – what was it called? Oh yes – the Benny Clegg place. Should be fun.'

April heaved a sigh of relief as she reached for the shaker and two bottles of Moët. If Brittany had said Ampney Crucis it would have completely ruined her perfect day.

chapter thirteen

'They certainly look impressive.' In the eyrie office Jasmine leaned over Peg's shoulder, being very careful not to dislodge today's bouncing blonde ponytail. 'Are you sure Damon will be up to it?'

The plans for the new Benny Clegg Stadium were spread across two tables. Jasmine and Peg had approached several local building firms with regard to the refurbishment, and eventually accepted the tender from Ampney Crucis's answer to McAlpine: Damon Puckett.

'Course he will, pet,' Peg said stoutly. 'He knows exactly what cash we've got – and exactly how long he'll have to finish the job. If we close the stadium immediately after the August Monday meeting, we can be up and running again in two weeks.'

'Two weeks!' Jasmine nearly tumbled from her chair. 'Good God, Peg – this is Damon we're talking about. It'll take him two weeks to unpack his sandwiches! Look how long he took to build that extra bit on to the Crow's Nest Caff! They were out of action for months!'

'That was because of his hernia. And the paucity of his workforce. I told him it was bloody stupid timing – building an extension at the same time as the Glastonbury Festival.'

'Not everybody's labourers clutter off after Glastonbury

in the works van to join a convoy of New Agers in the Brecon Beacons, though, do they?' Jasmine frowned. 'Damon always picks such strange people. How do we know that they won't do it this time?'

'Because August is the Reading Festival and they don't go to that because they don't like heavy metal – and because Ewan is acting as foreman.'

Jasmine grinned. 'If he ever manages to tear himself away from Clara's futon, you mean?'

Peg pulled a face. 'To be honest, pet, I'm not sure that that little rekindled liaison is a good idea.'

'They both seem ecstatic about it.'

Ecstatic, Jasmine thought, was putting it mildly. That night they'd all met up at the beach hut, and Jasmine had expected there to be a lot of cold-shouldering and huffing and playing hard to get, had been like the last serious partying and pulling opportunity on a Club 18–30 holiday. No sooner had Ewan and Clara clapped eyes on one another than they were chewing each other's faces and shedding clothes. Feeling very ancient, Jasmine had exchanged affronted glances with Andrew and retired immediately to the privacy of the hut.

When she'd emerged in the morning – after a horrendous night of alternately fighting off Andrew's amorous advances and listening to him spouting vitriol about Ewan and berating her for her lack of takings that evening – she'd discovered Ewan and Clara curled together on the veranda, all sort of welded together and looking like a piece of modern sculpture, and very bug-eyed. They seemed to have remained in that blissful state ever since.

Peg tutted. 'Ecstatic they may be, and Ewan is an angel, but he's still a married man. Not that I ever liked Katrina that much, but there were vows taken that should not be broken.'

Jasmine shrugged. She really didn't want to get involved in moral issues — at least not Ewan and Clara's. She still had her parents to worry about. She hadn't been home again, but had seen her mother twice sitting at the bar in the Crumpled Horn, wearing clothes a decade too young for her, and sipping something cloudy with impaled cherries from a retro glass. Philip had proved immensely difficult to pin down, and Jasmine was still no nearer finding out whether or not the Merry Orchard Shopping Plaza was going to be a reality.

'I'll really need to speak to Dad.' Jasmine pushed her hair back behind her ears. 'Especially if we're seriously going ahead with the plans so soon.'

The plans weren't as drastic as she'd first imagined. The corrugated tin roof was going to be replaced with something more weatherproof, the rickety stands were going to be strengthened and have proper steps and seating and a glass-fronted viewing gallery, there would be a lavatory block at either end, and proper lighting. Trackside, the wood-wormed railings were being rejuvenated with plastic, and Gilbert's hot-dog stand was getting a permanent site and extending its menu. There was even going to be brand-new kennel accommodation for the visiting greyhounds, and a podium built in the centre of the circuit for presentations.

It probably still wouldn't drag the place into the twenty-first century, Jasmine thought, but it would definitely move it on a touch from the nineteenth. And Benny would have loved it.

Folding the plans. Peg leaned from the window. White puffballs of cloud danced along the sea line and the wet sand was the colour of honey. Peg sniffed rapturously. 'Going to be nice for a while, thank heavens. I couldn't abide much more of that rain. Let's hope it holds off until after the bank holiday.'

Jasmine silently agreed. However, the business hadn't been too bad, despite the weather. There were still plenty of holidaymakers desperate for something to do, and they'd dripped from their boarding houses in surprising numbers. She knew, though, that Peg's agenda was completely different: it wasn't the lack of people through the stadium's turnstiles that depressed her when it rained, it was the lack of appropriate Doris Day apparel. Doris, it appeared, had never really gone in for wet-weather gear, and Peg's mood was infinitely sunnier when she could scramble into her floral shirtwaister and a pair of ankle socks.

Peg hauled herself in from the window, pulling the ponytail into place. 'Fancy a spot of lunch, pet? Ewan says they've gone continental at the Crumpled Horn and are offering pizza.'

'Really? That's daring of them. Still, I don't think pizza will last long on the menu when the boat blokes come in looking for fry-ups and shepherd's pie, do you? And I'll have to say no to the invite – I mean, I'd love to try it out, but I'm going to see if I can catch Dad as he leaves work for lunch.'

'Best of luck, then,' Peg said. 'Will you be telling him what we're up to?'

'Of course. Although I'm sure he already knows.'

'From smarmy Andrew, you mean?'

Jasmine shook her head. 'Definitely not from Andrew. I haven't breathed a word of it to him.'

Peg looked shocked. 'Honestly? Good Lord, pet, don't you think you should? After all, you're supposed to be marrying the man. There shouldn't be secrets.'

No, Jasmine thought, as she left the stadium. There shouldn't be. But there seemed to be an awful lot. And not just between her and Andrew either.

*

The council offices, built on the Ampney Crucis-Bournemouth road, and looking like every other municipal building in the country, were disgorging their desk-bound employees like so many ants into the midday sunshine.

Jasmine hung back in the car park, watching as pale-faced people hauled themselves into hatchbacks and headed for an hour's freedom. Philip's car was parked beneath the huge reflective windows, in the space allotted for senior officers. Not sure whether she should wait for him to emerge, or march in and demand to see him, she opted for the latter. At least that way, she reasoned with herself, he couldn't escape so easily, could he?

'Philip Clayton?' The shaven-headed prepubescent on reception, whose name badge said he was Aaron Perks, looked down his list. Even his fingers had acne. 'Planning?'

Jasmine nodded. This child was probably about twelve, obviously new, and fortunately didn't have a clue who she was. 'Is he still here? I don't have an appointment, but if you ring through and tell him it's Jasmine . . .'

The boy looked at her rather unflatteringly. Women giving merely first names and wanting to see high-ups without appointments obviously registered as mistresses in his book. Jasmine, in her baggy combat trousers and big T-shirt, clearly didn't fit the remainder of his mental picture. However, being new, he diligently punched out the number.

The wait seemed interminable. Aaron picked at a scab on his neck. Fortunately, an answer from planning prevented him moving on in his excavations. 'Hello. You took ages! It's Aaron. Is Mr Clayton still there, please? Oh, right – well could you tell him there's a – a lady to see him. Says her name's Jasmine . . . What? I dunno, do I?' He stopped and surveyed Jasmine up and down before continuing his conversation. 'Yeah, I suppose so. Is she? Christ. OK, I'll tell her.'

He replaced the receiver. 'Mr Clayton's secretary says he's still in a meeting and would you wait down here?'

'That's fine. Yes, I'll wait.' Jasmine stared him out, knowing full well that Verity, Philip's long-time, bolster-bosomed and loquacious secretary, would have told the spotty Aaron that Mr Clayton's daughter was plump and plain. It was rather unflattering to realise that he'd so readily accepted her identity from the description.

She drifted away from the reception desk towards the seating area – all beige leatherette and plastic trailing plants. Aaron, who had broken off from a period of frenzied scratching, had three lines ringing at the same time. Taking the opportunity of skipping across the marble tiles while he was preoccupied, Jasmine headed for the lifts.

Planning was on the top floor. Jasmine had always thought this was rather risky, given the suicidal tendencies of the back-hander brigade. However, up here where the air was rare, there were fewer people to stop her and ask what she was doing. It must, she'd always thought, be like trying to get into the Oval Office in the White House. Porch extensions and loft conversions were obviously Ampney Crucis's answer to being in charge of the global nuclear holocaust.

She pushed open the door to Planning – Executives Only. CAD machines whirred with geometric screen savers on vacated desks, several blueprints were being regurgitated from a copier, and somewhere in the empty office a phone was ringing. Jasmine was pretty sure that it was Aaron trying to track her down, or at least warn Verity that the holy portals were about to be invaded by someone large and shaggy.

'Heavens!' Verity powered her way from the inner sanctum at that moment, wearing something hand-knitted in fondant pink. Jasmine blinked. Verity was a big knitter.

She always knitted Yvonne tea cosies for Christmas. Jasmine had worn them for years as winter hats. 'Jasmine! Dear! I personally suggested that you should wait in reception. I thought Aaron said that you'd been informed of the instruction?'

'He must have got it wrong then.' Jasmine returned the faux smile, noticing that Verity was in the middle of squirting Eau Savage into her well-displayed cleavage. 'Is Dad still in his meeting?'

'No, no, fortuitously that finished just a second or two ago. He's just preparing to be leaving for lunch – ah! Here he is!'

They both turned and stared at Philip as he strolled through from his office. Verity had practically emptied the scent bottle by now and the fumes had reached killer toxicity levels. Jasmine wondered why her father had his shirt buttoned up wrong.

'Jasmine!' Philip didn't smile. 'This is a surprise.'

'Er – yes, isn't it? Look, sorry to catch you on the hop, but I never seem to be able to find you at home. Um – I wondered if we could talk?'

'Well – I was just going to take Verity to lunch. Business, of course. Is it important?'

This was just so strange, Jasmine thought, speaking to her father as if she were some junior employee, like Aaron, who had a problem with the filing system or something. She suddenly felt very lonely. 'Well, yes, really. But mine's business too – so maybe we could all go together?'

Verity looked as though she'd rather be dining with Dr Crippen.

Philip shrugged. 'Up to Verity, of course, but yes, maybe we could have a little time together. As long as it's nothing to do with that bloody greyhound stadium.'

'Nothing whatsoever,' Jasmine beamed. 'Verity? Are you going to come as well?'

'Well, to be honest, seeing as it was my luncheon invitation to start with, I rather feel it is I who should be offering to include you.'

Jasmine rapidly worked out the syntax. She hoped that Verity worded the planning department's letters with more fluidity and thought that she probably didn't.

Suddenly irritable, Jasmine sighed. 'Well, no, it's Dad's lunch and I want to talk to him and you two have all the time in the world to discuss car parks and multistorey shopping centres and things, don't you? So, are we all going?'

Jasmine couldn't be sure, but she had a feeling her father was shaking his head. When she looked at him he appeared to be twitching slightly.

'Have you been bitten?'

Verity coughed. Probably the Eau Savage rapidly clogging her airways, Jasmine thought hopefully.

Philip shook his head more publicly. 'A touch of prickly heat, maybe. Verity? Are you going to join us?'

'No, I personally don't think I will. You two pop along to the Crumpled Horn for a nice little tête-à-tête. I hear they're doing pizza.'

'And you'll be all right?' Philip looked solicitous.

'I'll be perfectly fine, thank you.' Verity wriggled her two-ply candyfloss shoulders and looked martyred. 'I've got some Ryvita in the desk.'

The Crumpled Horn was packed with its usual mixed lunchtime trade of tourists and local workers. All the pizza had gone.

Jasmine had sat beside Philip in the air-conditioned car for the ten-minute journey and they'd talked warily about generalisations. It had given her even more of the

161

sensation of a minion being entertained by a potentate.

Once ensconced in the same window seat as she'd occupied on the day of Benny's funeral, Jasmine agreed to have whatever Philip was having and watched as he made his way to the bar. The feeling of loneliness engulfed her again. It would have been so nice to have a proper father-daughter relationship with him, but it was far too late now. He'd always been distant and censorious, and Yvonne had always been busy and panicking about germs and what the neighbours thought. Benny had stepped in and been mother, father and friend.

It shocked her to realise in that happy, warm, laughing place that she didn't actually love either of her parents.

'I've ordered shepherd's pie,' Philip announced, returning with a pint of Old Ampney for her and a whisky for himself. 'I got salad with yours.'

'Great.' Jasmine would have preferred chips. 'Dad, let's not beat about the bush here. I know what's going on. Can we be grown up about this?'

Philip sucked in a mouthful of whisky and coughed alarmingly. Jasmine thumped him on the back until his breathing returned to normal.

He was still gasping, but didn't look as though he was about to have a seizure. His eyes, however, were still watering. 'About what?'

'The Merry Orchard Shopping Plaza.'

Philip exhaled and strangely, Jasmine thought, smiled. He swallowed, wiping his eyes on a paper napkin. 'Ah – right – yes, of course. I wondered when that would come up. What have you heard?'

'What everyone else has heard, of course, but I need to know the truth.'

'Truth? Truth?' Philip looked agitated. 'Who knows what the truth is?'

'Well, you, presumably, seeing as you'd be the one to pass the plans.'

The shepherd's pie arrived then, and there was a lot of shuffling of plates and glasses and cutlery around the table. As soon as they were organised again, Philip wolfed down half a dozen of his chips, then nodded. 'I thought you said it had nothing to do with the bloody greyhound stadium.'

'I lied. I'm good at that. I think I must have inherited the skill from you. No, let me finish . . .'

Their plates were empty by the time she'd stopped talking. Philip had looked alternately shocked and outraged – especially at the bit about her piling Benny's inheritance into the revamping of the stadium – but she hadn't let him get a word in.

'So, that's it. The Benny Clegg Stadium will start its resurrection immediately after the bank holiday. If you – or whichever speculator you've done a deal with this time – thinks they're going to knock it, and my beach hut, down, then you'll have a fight on your hands.'

Philip swirled the last of the whisky round his glass. 'You're just like him, you know.'

'Who?'

'My damned father! Stubborn, single-minded, bloody tenacious.'

'Really?' Jasmine glowed. 'God – thank you. You couldn't pay me a bigger compliment. So? Have the plans been passed, or was that just another of your nasty schemes to upset my first night as a bookie – and any hopes I might have for a real future?'

Philip's fist crashed on to the table, making the plates rattle. Several people stared. 'Jasmine! Being a bookmaker is not a real job! I do not want a bookie for a daughter! Have you any idea how humiliated, degraded, and embarrassed I was at school and college by being a bloody bookie's son?'

She shook her head. 'Why should you be? Grandpa was strong and honest and kind and funny. What more could you want from a father?'

'One who didn't live in a council house and make his money from setting odds on bloody greyhounds!' Philip looked near to tears. 'All my classmates had fathers with their own businesses, they all owned their own houses, they had holidays abroad, and went to London to see shows at half term. They – '

'Jesus, you're just a snob. Grandpa must have worked so hard to be able to send you to school and college, and all you could do to repay him was sneer and be ashamed of him!' Jasmine was shaking with anger. 'Look, I don't want to hear any of this. You've got to live with the fact that Benny gave you everything and you never, ever said thank you – and now it's too late. I'm so glad I'm not living at home any more!' She stood up, catching her knees painfully on the underside of the table and uptipping the glasses. 'Just tell me whether the Merry Orchard Shopping Plaza is or isn't going ahead and I'll leave you to your sad snobby life. Just tell me whether or not the north-east corner of Ampney Crucis is due for total annihilation and I promise I won't embarrass you ever again.'

Philip exhaled. His face was white. Jasmine still felt no pity for him. He pursed his lips. 'Very well, then. No doubt you'll hear this soon enough now the press embargo has been lifted. No, it isn't.'

'Really?' Jasmine felt the grin unfurling and knew it would be ear-to-ear within seconds. 'It really isn't happening? Really, truly? Is that because the greyhound stadium is part of the heritage of Ampney Crucis? Is it because the planners can see the sense in the stadium bringing tourists and money into the village? Is it – '

'It's nothing to do with the poxy stadium!' Philip roared,

making a holidaymaking family on the next table jump. 'It's because of the sodding beach huts! The namby-pamby conservationists on the council – and didn't I say at the time of the last local elections that it was a mistake to vote in Lib Dems and Greens? – have decided that that damned ramshackle row of decrepitude is our answer to bloody Southwold! They've slapped a bloody preservation order on them!'

Practically doing handstands all the way down the cliff steps, Jasmine couldn't wait to spread the glad tidings. Leaving Philip to settle the bill, she had only remembered long after she'd left the Crumpled Horn that she'd meant to ask him about the separate bedrooms bit. Still, first things first. She'd tell Peg and everyone the brilliant news, then she'd ponder over the disintegration of her parents' marriage. There were only so many things a girl could deal with at one time.

Perching on the veranda steps, she flipped open her mobile phone and punched out Peg's number, staring out at the flat, glittering expanse of the sea. Children skittered in and out of the shallows while their parents lounged in deck chairs, rubbing in Nivea and soaking up the welcome return of the sun.

'Peg? It's me, Jasmine. We're OK! Yes, honestly! The stadium is safe! The shopping plaza isn't going to happen. Oh God! Don't cry – you'll set me off . . . What? Oh, yes – tell Roger and Allan and everyone. I know! Yes, fine – I'll see you this evening and we'll have a proper celebration then . . .'Bye.'

Deciding that she really ought to drag this week's washing to the Launderette – the lack of machines was one of the few drawbacks of living in the beach hut – Jasmine unlocked the door and negotiated the furniture. After changing into a pair of knee-length shorts and a denim shirt of Andrew's which she knotted at the waist, she bundled all the laundry into a black bag, helped herself to the last doughnut in the miniature fridge which Clara had given her, and jumped joyously from the veranda.

Hoicking the bag across her shoulders, she felt that a walk into the village along the water's edge would be much more pleasant than struggling up the cliffs with her bundle and forcing her way through the tourists at the Crow's Nest and Eddie Deebley's. The sand was warm under her bare feet, and she smiled beatifically at the children sticking flags into the tops of sand castles, then looked back fondly at the row of brightly coloured beach huts that was her salvation.

'Oh, sorry!' She stumbled across an elderly couple who were blowing up a Lilo behind the Punch and Judy stall. 'I really must look where I'm going.'

Picking her way more carefully now through the sun-worshippers, she headed for the shoreline, having to skirt a complete square of stripy windbreaks. She smiled to herself. Probably honeymooners not wanting to be disturbed. She felt a pang of envy. How wonderful it must be to be so much in love with one person that you just wanted to exclude the rest of the world.

'Ooh! No! You can't do that! Not here!'

The giggle from the depths of the windbreaks made her stop in her tracks. All the fond and sentimental feelings ebbed away. She felt violently sick.

The giggle was huskier now. Almost a growl. 'Oh, well – maybe – but it's risky . . . What if someone sees us? Oooh, yes – that's lovely . . .'

Clutching the black bag, Jasmine turned and belted blindly back up the beach. High-jumping the pensioners with the Lilo, she ran towards the cliff steps.

What the hell was her mother doing here? On the beach? Hidden in the windbreak love nest? With someone who definitely wasn't her father?

Her phone rang. Irritably, she dragged it out of her pocket. On autopilot she snapped it open. 'Yes?'

'Jasmine, pet. It's Peg. In the light of your wondrous news, I've taken the liberty of immediately ringing that nice little girl — Normandy, is it? — at Frobisher's and suggested they make their inspection sooner rather than later. She's agreed to move everything forward, and they're going come down for the August Bank Holiday meeting! Isn't that wonderful?'

chapter fourteen

The greyhounds, shoulder to shoulder, swerved round the top corner of the Ampney Crucis track. A solid swoosh of colour beneath the dark sky, their progress was followed somewhat shakily by the moth-strewn floodlights.

Roger leaned across the gap between the joints, yelling above the raucous bellows of the crowd. 'This one looks like it's going to be a close call! Looks like Trimmy's got his nose up front. What did you do on him?'

Jasmine glanced at her board. 'Oh, damn. Twenties.'

Allan shook his head on the other side of her. 'Trim Tone always gets up there with the leaders – didn't you check the form?'

Jasmine hadn't. She'd been walking about in a haze of unhappiness ever since that afternoon. Now, on the penultimate race of the evening, still the only thing she could hear was Yvonne's voice cooing sexily from the depths of the windbreaks.

'Mistakes like that'll cost you,' Roger warned her, tipping his Panama to the back of his head. 'What's up? Too much champagne earlier?'

'I wish . . .' Jasmine groaned, watching as the white-jacketed Trim Tone swept across the finish line, a whisker in front of the pack.

Almost immediately, as Gilbert announced the result, the winning tickets were being waved in a fluttering forest beneath her nose.

'Bloody hell,' Clara, who had been doing the writing-up in a state of post-champagne and post-Ewan euphoria, woke up at last and jerked her head towards the satchel. 'I don't think I've got enough in here to pay them out.'

Jasmine groaned again. This evening's meeting should have been a breeze. Everyone else was in serious party mode after the news about the demise of the Merry Orchard Shopping Plaza. Even Clara had seemed pleased, although Jasmine reckoned that had far more to do with Ewan than delight at being done out of a retail outlet. As it was, because of Yvonne, Jasmine had wrongly calculated every race, been surly towards the winning punters, and twice shouted at Peg.

'You'll have to go to the cashpoint,' Clara hissed, up to her armpit in the satchel. 'And withdraw some of your inheritance. We'll never make the last race if you don't.'

Jasmine emerged from a bunch of holidaymakers reeking of suntan oil and fish and chips, all of whom had unloaded the last of their spending money on Trim Tone. 'I haven't got any inheritance money left. I gave it to Peg for the refurbishment.'

'Bloody hell. All of it?'

'Most of it. And the rest is earmarked for an illuminated sign over the entrance gate – from me to Grandpa. That's what I wanted to do.'

'What about your earnings, then? They must have accumulated considerably by now. Or have you pledged all those to Peg, too?' Clara frowned, flapping her hands at a teenage boy who was trying to burrow his way into the satchel. 'Excuse me – can I help you?'

'I had a tenner on Trimmy. That's two hundred to come

back and me stake. You wasn't going to do a runner, was you?'

'What? Of course not.' Clara looked scandalised, and deftly counted out the notes. 'Now, say thank you.'

'Bugger off.' The boy pocketed his winnings greedily. 'I never says thank you to damn grasping bookies.' He winked. 'Not even if they're pretty hot babes.'

Clara jabbed a finger in Jasmine's shoulder. 'Stop grinning. Even if he was referring to you, you're not into cradle-snatching, are you?'

'To be honest, I'm up for anything that isn't Andrew at the moment. And,' she stared after the boy's rear view, 'he's got a great bum.'

'Christ.' Clara shook her head. 'It's going to be lock up your sons for the mothers of Ampney Crucis, is it? Not before time, if you ask me. You never had a splurge when the rest of us did, did you?'

'Don't remember. When was that?'

'Ooh – somewhere between being thirteen and fifteen.'

'No, then, I didn't.' Jasmine poked out her tongue. 'Some of us were far too busy keeping our Clark's sandals clean and collecting Sindy dolls. Still, can we lay off my lack of splurging until later, while I concentrate on making some money?'

Clara looked again at the depleted satchel. 'Sounds good to me.'

Jasmine chalked up the runners for the last race, wondering whether she should cut the odds on all of them so that she wouldn't have to pay out too much on whichever dog won, and if she did so, whether she'd actually have any customers at all. Roger and Allan, offering longer odds and better prices, would surely take all the punters.

'Oh God, Grandpa. What do I do now?'

She closed her eyes. She could see Benny's warm grin. She could hear Benny's voice inside her head. He sounded as though he was laughing. 'First of all, cheer up. Life's a breeze. Be happy – that's what I wanted you to be – always. Then lengthen the odds, my love. Take the mugs' money, as much as you can. That's the only way.'

Of course! She'd watched him do it so many times! Cooking the books, he'd told her. What being a bookmaker was all about – gambling everything, making a book which hopefully would finish with only one winner – the bookie. Opening her eyes, Jasmine feverishly rubbed out all her chalked up figures and started again. She also began to smile. Benny was there with her, she knew he was. She could almost feel his presence.

Roger and Allan stared at her in bewilderment, peered through their bifocals at her board, looked askance, then, not to be outdone, changed their figures too. Jasmine lengthened hers again. So did Roger and Allan. And again. This time Roger and Allan didn't.

'What the hell are you doing?' Clara squeaked.

'Covering my losses. An old trick of Grandpa's. Don't go all Young Exec on me now, please. Trust me . . .'

The long odds seemed to do the trick. At least for the moment. As it was the last race, it was now-or-never time for the punters, and they were eager to recoup any earlier losses. Gilbert was extolling the virtues of the six dogs across the Tannoy, Doris was doing the business on 'Sentimental Journey', but somewhere in the background, Jasmine could annoyingly still hear Yvonne's purring voice. Yvonne, it seemed, was splurging indiscriminately.

She clapped her hands over her ears. That was two voices in her head now. It was beginning to get a bit crowded. She'd probably end up like Joan of Arc, barking mad and leaping onto bonfires outside the Crumpled Horn.

'Jasmine!' Andrew pushed his way through the crowds. 'Is what I've heard the truth?'

'Doubtful,' she shouted back, still snatching five-pound notes with gay abandon and mouthing, 'Thirty pounds to five, four hundred and two,' over her shoulder at Clara. She looked at Andrew, all earnest in his cream chinos and mustard-coloured Fred Perry polo shirt. His question sounded like one of those tracts plastered up outside St Edith's by the new vicar. However, his expression was so serious, she felt it would be cruel to tease him. 'No, sorry. What exactly have you heard?'

'About this – this stadium?' Andrew was about three punters back by now, being elbowed out of the way by a contingent of women with Lancashire accents and fierce perms. 'About you and these silly old duffers,' he recklessly indicated Allan and Roger, 'and loony Peg all putting your money into a refurbishment?'

'Quite true,' Jasmine sang happily, lengthening the odds still further as the punters continued to pile in. She could just see Andrew's apoplectic face disappearing behind a sea of bri-nylon. 'Who told you?'

'Never mind who told me! That money was supposed to be for our future! Next year, when we get married, I thought you'd invest some in the dealership. We were going to buy a house . . . Your money would have moved us up into the next council-tax bracket –'

'Andrew,' Jasmine interrupted, 'this is neither the time nor the place. Meet me later – at the hut. I'll explain it to you then. Now go away and leave me alone . . .'

'Spoken like a woman truly in love,' Clara muttered, merrily stuffing wodges of notes into the satchel.

Allan and Roger glared at Jasmine. 'What did he call us?'

'No idea,' Jasmine chewed her lower lip. 'But whatever it was, can you save garrotting him until later?'

The kennel handlers mercifully appeared at that

172

moment, leading the dogs for the last time that night, and the betting became even more frenzied. After five further minutes of frantic money-taking, Jasmine glanced up, but couldn't see Andrew anywhere. Either he'd taken her advice and sloped off to the beach hut, or he'd been trampled to death by the posse of Vera Duckworths.

As the greyhounds were led behind the traps, Allan and Roger were regarding her with severe doubt. She frowned. 'What?'

'Benny would have a fit over those prices,' Allan said dolefully. 'That's a dumb trick.'

Jasmine pushed her hair behind her ears. 'It's not. He told me to do it, actually. Take a ton, risk paying out a ton, but hopefully make a profit.'

'If Half A Sixpence wins, you won't be making anything except a fool of yourself, my girl.' Roger joined in the censure. 'You've got him at fifties. And anyway, what exactly did that boyfriend of yours call me?'

Bunny, bless his plimsolls, snapped back the hare's lever at that minute, and the traps sprang open. The greyhounds belted away on the first of their two circuits, and Jasmine exhaled with total relief.

As it was a longer race, the crowd had more time to whoop up the atmosphere. Jasmine decided not to watch the first lap at all. Neither, it seemed, did Clara. Ewan, looking dishevelled and gypsyish, had materialised out of the crowd and was playing havoc with the buttons on her sundress. It looked very much like they were about to have a no-holds-barred splurging session.

Tutting, and horribly aware that she sounded like some ancient dowager aunt, Jasmine turned away and dared to squint at the greyhounds' progress. They were going round for the second time. Half A Sixpence in the striped jacket was slightly ahead.

The crowd was frenzied now, jumping up and down, encouraging their particular choice home with colourful epithets. Jasmine squeezed her hands together and prayed, Please, please God – anything other than Half A Sixpence.

The screams grew louder as the dogs blurred past, a jag of bright colours in the soft dusk. Jasmine held her breath.

'Blueberry Muffin by a muzzle!' Allan made an arthritic attempt to punch the air. 'I had him on evens. That's a result for me.' He looked across at Jasmine. 'What about you? What did you have for his SP?'

'Ten to one,' Jasmine was still trying to do the calculations in her head. It was no good asking Clara to help. She and Ewan had disappeared to splurge in private. 'I think I'll be OK . . .'

Paying out was slower than usual as she had to do it single-handedly, but eventually everyone seemed satisfied – and she peeped inside the satchel. She wasn't a hundred per cent sure, but it looked as though there may just be more money in there than she'd started with. She puffed out her cheeks. It had been a close call. A real gamble. And, if she was honest, one heck of a buzz. She grinned: this was what it was all about, the thing that had kept Benny going all those years – the risk, the excitement . . .

'Got away with it, did you?' Roger was grinning. 'Bit of a blast, actually, when it happens.'

Allan joined in. 'Congratulations, my love. Now you really know what being a bookie is all about, don't you?'

Jasmine jumped from her pallets, still hugging the satchel, and kissed them both. Then gathering everything together under both arms, she trundled rather inelegantly away to join the crowds queuing to get out through the turnstiles. Having dumped her paraphernalia in Peg's office, and beamed good night at everyone, she suddenly realised that she hadn't thought anything at all about her mother's affair for at least an hour.

Still as high as a kite, Jasmine slithered down the last few of the cliff steps, took a long appreciative look at the black satin ripples of the sea, then skittered along the sandy track in front of the huts.

Andrew was sitting on the veranda in the pale lemon moonlight.

Jasmine grinned and swung the satchel on to his lap. 'There! Tonight's profit, oh, ye of little faith! Have you got a drink?'

Andrew lifted his beer bottle in a mock salute.

'Oh, good. Nothing like a couple of Old Ampneys for celebrations, is there? Lovely as all the bubbly that Peg provided was, I still prefer beer. Another sign of my misspent youth, I suppose.' Jasmine bent to kiss him, then stopped because she probably didn't feel quite that euphoric, and simply retrieved the satchel from his lap instead. 'Did you get one out for me?'

'Ah – no. I wasn't sure what time you'd be back.'

'Whatever.' Jasmine clattered across the veranda and into the hut. 'I'll get one from the fridge . . . Oh, you've had the last one!'

'Have I? Sorry.' Andrew's voice, floating from outside, sounded anything but. 'I didn't realise. Would you like to share mine?'

'No, thanks.' Jasmine had tucked the takings in the back of the drawer, and removed several twenty-pound notes. 'I'll go up to the Crumpled Horn and get some takeouts. I think Clara and Ewan are up there anyway, and I haven't paid Clara yet for tonight.'

'You pay her?' Andrew jerked upright. 'Christ, Jas, you really have no financial sense at all, have you?'

Jasmine gritted her teeth. The 'I'm a real bookie' high was rapidly deflating. 'I've got all the sense I need – financial or otherwise, thank you. And if you're going to have a go at me about Clara, or the stadium, or anything else for that matter, can it wait until I've got some more alcohol inside me?'

She'd thought that Andrew might spring up at that point, blustering apologies, and, like a proper fiancé, offer to walk along the cliff path to the Crumpled Horn with her, as it was late, and dark, and she might get mugged. But of course, he didn't.

Now, she thought, scrambling back up the steps, her fingers sliding easily on the handrail that had been polished smooth by generations of beachgoers: do it now. Each trudging step said the same thing. Do it now. Tonight. Break off the engagement.

Hauling herself to the top of the steps, to where the shale and scrubby grass pretended to be a car park, she looked back down at the row of huts as she walked, their roofs zigzagged in the darkness like a dinosaur's tail. She still honestly couldn't see herself married to Andrew, but neither could she imagine a time when he wouldn't be there, around, in her life. It was just that she really would like to share that life with someone special: not just the joy of making a damn good fist of being a bookie, but also the fears she had about her parents' relationship, and the plans to put Ampney Crucis on the map that were bubbling away inside her head. All that, she thought as she passed splurging couples on the shadowy cliff top benches, and so much more. Things like jokes, and dreams, and sadness, and the stupid little things of life . . . She stopped and sighed. All the things, in fact, that she'd shared with her grandfather.

She reached the Crumpled Horn without the merest

threat of being mugged; but then, this was Ampney Crucis. A mugging would have brought the village to a standstill – the local paper had run headlines on the story of the mysterious disappearance of KitKats from the 8 'til Late for three consecutive weeks.

'Jas! Over here!' Clara, perched skewwhiff on a bar stool shared with Ewan, waved wildly over the heads of the last-orders crowd. 'What happened?'

Jasmine, shoving her way through a mass of Crimplened shoulders, fetched up just beside Ewan's thighs. Ignoring them, and pushing a couple of twenty-pound notes into Clara's hand, she refused Ewan's offer of a drink.

'No, thanks, really. I'm just going to get some bottles to take back to the hut.' A sense of self-preservation prevented her from saying that Andrew had finished off the supplies. 'And yes, I can afford to pay you. The gamble worked well, and that's your percentage. Oh, yes – four bottles of Old Ampney please, to take out,' she leaned across the bar, 'and four packets of smoky bacon. And a pickled egg.'

Clara laughed. 'I see you're still sticking to the healthy-eating plan, then?'

'Of course,' Jasmine raised her voice above 'Mr Tambourine Man', which was belting out from the juke box. It was one of the newest records on the Crumpled Horn's Wurlitzer, and therefore got a considerable share of airplay time. 'I'm no great shakes on the gas ring – and Eddie Deebley's fish suppers and the Crow's Nest's doughnuts manage to supply everything I need.'

'Not everything, surely?' Ewan raised a piratical eyebrow. 'Doesn't Andrew provide something?'

'Not much, believe me.' Jasmine hauled the carrier bag off the top of the bar. 'And possibly not even that for very much longer . . .'

*

The veranda was empty. So was the hut. Happily, Jasmine clicked off the top of a bottle of Old Ampney, opened two packets of crisps, and as a sop to gentility, quartered the pickled egg on a saucer. Then, slumping in one of the canvas chairs and propping her feet up on the veranda rail, she gave a sigh of contentment.

She was just dabbing up the last of the crisp crumbs with a vinegary forefinger when Andrew's head appeared at the top of the beach steps. The rest of him soon followed and he looked at the midnight feast with some disgust.

'Haven't you saved me any?'

'Nope. Sorry. I thought you'd gone.'

He collapsed into the chair beside her. 'I went for a walk along the beach. I needed to do some serious thinking.'

Jasmine swallowed a mouthful of beer. 'And have you?'

'I have. I may have been a little hasty earlier. While you were out, I – um – took the liberty of counting your takings for this evening . . . No, let me finish. Not a particularly good night, was it? But even so, you've made a profit. And the nights that you make a profit outweigh the ones when you don't.'

'Yes, so?' Jasmine was coldly furious that he'd ferreted around in the bedside drawers. Still, it was her own fault. She should be more careful.

'So, even if you're investing your inheritance money in the stadium, that will make you a shareholder. Which, in turn, will bring in some sort of income. Even if you haven't enough capital left to invest in the dealership, your financial status will be considerably enhanced by your annual profit margin, and –'

'Andrew! For God's sake stop talking like *The Money Programme* and cut to the chase.' The lights from Eddie Deebley's Fish Bar bounced across the black sea; the scent of frying and vinegar wafted on the air. Despite the crisps

178

and pickled egg, Jasmine's stomach rumbled. 'What exactly are you trying to tell me?'

He leaned forward, the moonlight making his cropped fair hair look prematurely grey. 'That I think we should look for a house now. Together. With the preservation order on these huts, you could make a small fortune if you sold – and I've got my savings. We could definitely afford something on the Chewton Estate.'

'Dear God!' Jasmine rocked forward. 'I've only just managed to escape from there! Do you honestly think I want to entomb myself back in the Peyton Place of Ampney Crucis?'

Andrew blinked. 'I don't understand . . .'

'My mother and father don't sleep together! My mother is having an affair – something I thought you might know about, seeing as you spend far more time there than I do!'

Andrew, strangely, Jasmine thought, began to laugh. 'Your mother? Oh, God, Jas! No way!'

'She is! I'm sure she is! And don't forget, you said everyone at the damn dealership thought she was top totty or something disgusting!' Jasmine sucked in her breath. This was appalling. She'd honestly thought she'd break off the engagement tonight and now Andrew was trying to weigh her down by tying her ankles to bricks and mortar. She clutched at the final straw. 'And I can't possibly think about marrying you – or anyone – not while my mother is –'

'Yvonne,' Andrew interrupted, 'isn't the guilty party, Jasmine. Oh, dear me, no. I can't believe that you think – look, I never wanted to say this, but everyone else in Ampney Crucis knows what's going on with your parents' marriage. I can't believe that you don't.'

chapter fifteen

'We're all going on a summer holiday . . . la-la-la!' Daff trilled, her face covered by a head-scarf, as Jix and April bundled her out of the door of number 51 and shoved her into the back of the hired Toyota people carrier.

Cair Paravel and Bee were already installed, along with carrier bags full of food, Thermos flasks of iced water, all the beach toys that the charity shop could provide, several changes of clothing, bathing costumes, large towels, and a map of the Dorset coast.

They'd argued the toss over the driving duties, and eventually decided that Jix should take the wheel there, while April did the return trip. It would be impossible, April reckoned, as she leaned over, checking everyone's seat belts and door locks, to gauge which of them was the most excited.

Just as Jix started the engine, Joel and Rusty appeared hand in hand on the doorstep and waved them away, and, despite it being ridiculously early in the morning, Sofia and Tonio, in some very glam nightwear, leaned from the upstairs window of the Pasta Place and called their good luck greetings. Waving like mad, knowing that she'd hold her breath until they'd left the High Street, and the stadium, and the grey parts of Bixford behind,

April couldn't believe that they were, at last, on their way.

Cair Paravel, obviously experiencing an emotional dilemma, thumped his tail ecstatically while at the same time emitting low rumbling growls at the back of Daff's head. This however, left Jix's mum unfazed: even before they'd cleared Bixford South, she was handing out egg sandwiches, and Beatrice-Eugenie, with Cair Paravel now sprawled on top of her, had her nose pressed excitedly to the window, claiming to be able to see the sea. With a huge sigh of relief, April leaned back in her seat and finally exhaled.

Jix, moving the car through the early morning traffic of East London, looked across at her and grinned. 'Never thought we'd do it, did you?'

'No. I must admit I've had kittens for days, just waiting for something to go wrong.'

'Martina was the worst.' Jix indicated to leave the city. 'I thought she'd sussed something.'

'Me too. God, I still can't believe the paddy she threw when I asked for a couple of days off. You'd think there was no one else in the country who could shake a bloody cocktail.'

That, April reckoned, was actually an understatement. Martina had screamed and threatened and blustered, and finally, when April had calmly pointed out that she was entitled to twenty-two days leave a year and had so far only taken ten of them and she'd take it to the union, caved in. As April had never belonged to a union in her life, this had been a bit of a wild card, but Martina had obviously had unpleasant dealings with unions in her past, and went pleasingly white-lipped at the threat.

Jix said he'd had similar problems with Oliver, but surprisingly Sebastian had intervened on his behalf, and said that Jix should certainly take some time off because he'd worked diligently for the family for so long – and how would they ever replace him if he decided to go?

Sebastian had been particularly annoying about the whole thing and, having discovered from the Gillespie Stadium office wall chart that Jix and April were having the same time off, had jumped to all manner of erroneous conclusions. He'd made some very uncool remarks regarding romantic liaisons, which of course they had both strenuously denied, claiming that the days off were simply a coincidence.

April still found Sebastian's *volte face* a little disconcerting. He'd been continually friendly, sitting at the Copacabana's bar and telling April about his days – and nights – out with Brittany. Jix said he'd been much the same with him. They were convinced that he knew about Bee and Cair Paravel and was simply lulling them into a false sense of security. They knew they couldn't trust him. As April had said, Sebby was a Gillespie, and everyone knew that the Gillespies were all born untrustworthy.

Anyway, despite everything the Gillespies had thrown at them, they were off, on their way to Ampney Crucis, for Cair Paravel's first public performance. For ages, ever since they'd decided to enter him for the race, it had been difficult to explain to Daff what they were doing. Naturally, neither of them had wanted to leave her behind, but they had both felt that the agoraphobia would only be exacerbated by the trip.

Jix had looked very doubtful when April had suggested the possibility of fetching her along too. 'I don't know what'd happen to her with all that vast expanse – you know, sea and sky and beach and stuff. I honestly don't think she'll be able to cope.'

But Daff had said as long as they could park the car somewhere near the sea, and she kept her seat belt on while she gazed through the windscreen, she felt that she'd have a whale of a time. They'd explained that the race meeting was at night, and therefore she might be left alone for hours, but again, Daff had maintained that with something to eat and drink, a fairish supply of word-puzzle books and the car radio for company, she'd think she was in heaven.

The journey was taking far longer than they'd anticipated, mainly because Bee, Daff and Cair Paravel all seemed constantly to want to go to the loo. April grinned to herself as Jix resignedly pulled into the fifth set of motorway services; and while she went through the rigmarole of seeing to Bee and Daff – who had to be guided into the Ladies with the scarf over her head, which meant that they miraculously jumped the queues of bladder-bursting holidaymakers who obviously all thought she had something contagious – Jix led Cair Paravel round and round identical ornamental flowerbeds.

It certainly wasn't, April thought as once more they all fastened themselves back into the people carrier, the way the racing greyhounds arrived at Bixford. They, the élite of the doggy world, travelled in kennelled and cushioned luxury, at exactly the right temperature, with precisely the correct amount of meat and vitamins inside them. Cair Paravel, merrily chomping on egg sandwiches and desperately trying to worry the life out of the back of Daff's head, was panting like a steam train and had become feverishly excited.

With Jix in his faded jeans and tie-dye vest and bangles and scarves, and her in her skimpy denim dress and the pink sandals, April was also well aware that they looked nothing like the bejewelled upper echelons of the game, who arrived at the Gillespie Stadium in matching designer bomber jackets with the name of their dog embroidered in neon threads across the back. She and Jix, Daff and Bee looked for all the world like the Raggle-Taggle Gypsies-O about to go mad at the seaside.

April and Jix had spent the last week teaching Bee the route by rote, and since they'd left London she'd been chanting, 'M25, M3, M27 to Cadnam roundabout, A31 through New Forest, then look for a signpost.' By the time they reached Basingstoke, it had started to get a bit wearing.

'Oh, my!' Daff, mercifully interrupting Bee and, ignoring Cair Paravel's teeth which were bared in a manic grin against the back of her neck, leaned forward as they purred through the New Forest. 'This is wonderful! So many trees! All enclosed! Oh, I could live here!'

Jix and April looked at each other in delight. It *was* wonderful, April thought, simply to see Daff so enjoying herself. The escape, albeit a brief one, from Bixford – even if Cair Paravel made a complete ass of himself on the race track – had done them all the power of good. And supposing, just supposing, that he behaved himself, and ran properly, this could be just the start of days out such as this. They could pile into whatever transport they could find, and travel the country. And after next month, April thought blissfully, when she'd been to the Corner Gallery at Swaffield and told Noah about his daughter, then he could join them too.

Sighing with deep contentment, she wriggled down more comfortably in her seat, sang along to 'Postman Pat', and knew that she hadn't been this happy for years.

Ampney Crucis was probably like none of them had expected. Certainly, when April had visualised it, she'd known it would be small, but had imagined it to be a scaled-down Bournemouth or Southend: very lively, with

tons of attractions for the tourists, and shops and amusement arcades and funfairs and – well – a typical brash
British seaside resort.

The minute that Jix turned the Toyota on to the Ampney
Crucis road, April fell hopelessly in love.

The narrow road wound away downhill towards the
signposted village, shaded beneath overhanging chestnut
trees; and the roadside verges were head-high with curly
acid-green ferns, which escaped the confines of their white
picket fences and brushed against the windows of the people
carrier. One side of the road was woodland, with sandy
pathways just visible, twisting up and down beneath the
trees, and a stream bubbling and crashing alongside them.
Opposite, there were houses, a higgledy-piggledy mixture
of tall red-brick villas and tiny cottages, all with picture-
book gardens. On the horizon, past the few shops, there
were pine trees towering into the very blue sky. Banks of
gorse and bracken flopped indolently across pavements,
and even the air was calm, floating in through the open
windows with a sort of heavy languor.

Jix, driving slowly, looked across at April. 'There's no
traffic. No people. It's like – like a film set . . .'

'No it isn't – it's like heaven.' April felt the lump
growing in her throat. This was it. The place she'd come
with Noah and Bee, once they were a real family, once
September was over, and find the roses-round-the-door
dream home.

Daff was staring out at the quiet streets, the tiny shops,
the square grey church as they passed. Tears slid down her
plump cheeks and April touched her gently. 'Daff? What's
up?'

'Nothing, sweet. I'm just being silly . . . It's so lovely
– like you see on the telly – like villages I thought I
remembered from the past, but thought I'd probably got

confused about. Oh, you know, rose-tinted glasses and all that. My mum and dad brought me to places like this when I was young Bee's age, and I've never forgotten them, but this – this is even better than that.' She sniffed. 'It's the most perfect place in the world.'

Cair Paravel, who had been sleeping since the New Forest, snoring, his whiskers twitching, woke up and rumbled a warning growl at Daff.

She dabbed at her damp eyes with a tissue. 'See! Even he agrees with me.'

April had the map on her knees and as the people carrier approached a crossroads in the centre of the village, she tapped Jix's arm. 'Left, I reckon, if we're going to see the sea. The greyhound stadium is further on, but we've got plenty of time to discover that later.'

As they turned left, the light changed instantly. The sky was luminescent, and where the end of the road dropped away, there was a sense of nothingness. April tried to swallow the lump in her throat again. The wind-stunted pine trees on either side of the street swayed slightly, dipping away on the near horizon, forming a tiny valley at the edge of the cliffs. There was a pub called the Crumpled Horn on one side of the road, and a traditional beach café on the other, and then nothing but this image of pale, quivering infinity.

'Mummeee!' Bee's shriek shattered the silence. 'Is that it? Is that the sea?'

Jix turned round. 'Yep, Bee, that's the sea. You can just see it through the trees, can't you? It looks like the sky's turned to liquid, doesn't it?'

April chewed her lips. Jix's voice was husky. It would never do for them all to be in tears at the same time.

The cliff-top car park was almost deserted. Still, April reckoned, as it wasn't quite nine o'clock this was probably to be expected. No doubt as the day progressed, hundreds of cars would line up along the shingle and tufty grass – and hopefully some of them would stay on for the greyhound meeting. Nearly nine o'clock. Still more then twelve hours to go before Cair Paravel hit the race track; twelve hours, April thought blissfully, unfastening her seat belt and unbuckling Beatrice-Eugenie, to explore this little piece of paradise.

With Cair Paravel clipped securely to his lead, and Daff ensconced behind the steering wheel, staring out with no fear at the vastness in front of her, Jix, April and Bee wandered to the edge of the cliffs.

The vast, quiet beauty took April's breath away. The sun was climbing steadily in a cloudless sky, already tingling her shoulders, and below her, a set of sand-encrusted wooden steps twisted their way down the cliffs towards a row of brightly coloured wooden beach huts.

'Blimey!' She nudged Jix. 'Look at them. Aren't they the business? God, imagine how brilliant that must be – having one of those for your holiday, sitting in splendour. Oh, and look! There's some more steps leading down from them to the beach, and – my God – look at the colour of that sand!'

She wanted to jump up and down and shout with delight. Never, ever had she felt this sense of freedom. The coastline curved away in both directions, disappearing round gorsy headlands, forming a perfect curve of pale golden sand. The sea, like shot silk beneath the sun, was splodgy with moving colour – green and grey and turquoise and pale blue – flecked with spindrift foam where the gentle waves formed and fell over an ocean bed gully. With a pang of recognition, April thought it was exactly like Noah's painting – the very painting that had made it possible for them to be here in the first place.

She'd have to tell him. In September she'd tell him about this place, and how exactly right he'd got the ocean's colours – and then she'd bring him here to see it for himself – and she knew that he'd fall in love with it, and Bee – and hopefully with her all over again – and the dream would become a reality.

Putting this future bliss on hold, April hauled herself back to the present. Cair Paravel had his snout lifted to the air, inhaling the new scents greedily, his whippy blue tail doing its rotor blade impression. Bee was wide-eyed and speechless. Jix looked much the same.

'Shall we get all the gubbins, then?' April asked. 'And make our way down to the beach? We might as well pick a good spot while it's quiet.'

Jix, his hair blowing in the breeze like a television shampoo advert, eventually dragged his eyes away from the view and looked embarrassed. 'Yeah – it'll be brilliant . . . Um – did your parents take you to the seaside when you were a kid?'

'Not often. A couple of times, I think. They never seemed happy, though, even then, and a day out always seemed to end in them having rows and me crying. Then later, they always seemed to be too busy – and we never had proper holidays or anything. Just weekends with friends of theirs who lived in the country. Why? Did yours?'

'When Dad was alive, yes.' Jix, with Bee on his shoulders, headed back towards the people carrier. 'But he died when I was five, and that's when Mum started to lose her grip on things. Her agoraphobia got so bad soon after that that we never went anywhere much.'

April smiled, understanding. 'So this, today, is as much an adventure for us as it is for Cair Paravel, isn't it?'

'Yeah. Probably more so. It just seems so sad, doesn't it? People of our age have probably been jetting off on package holidays all their lives, but we've hardly ever seen the sea, even in England.'

'I'll let you into a secret, then. I've never been abroad. Never even been on a plane.'

'Nor me,' Jix sighed.

April pulled open the door of the Toyota. Daff was happily engrossed in a word-search puzzle, and listening to Radio 2. She smiled. 'Going to get into your bathers, then? Take Bee in for a paddle?'

'Definitely.' April nodded. 'And we'll take Cairey with us; there doesn't seem to be any restriction about dogs on the beach. Oh, Daff, it's such a pity you can't come as well.'

'I might later.' Daff nodded towards the windscreen's view. 'It looks lovely down there. Maybe if I closed my eyes I could make it. Once I'd done the steps, I'd probably be fine just sitting on the beach.'

Jix gave his mother a hug. 'Done deal! We'll go and test the water – and then come back for you.'

It took them two bundling journeys to get everything they needed from the people carrier on to the beach, with both Beatrice-Eugenie and Cair Paravel working themselves up into a frenzy of excitement, and Jix and April pausing every few steps to gather up dropped buckets and towels and flip-flops, and to admire the view.

April, clutching Bee's hand tightly, felt overwhelmed with happiness, watching her daughter's chubby legs reach down, so steadily, one step at a time, her eyes fastened as if hypnotised on the constant rush and fall of the sea. She, of course, had the easy part. Jix, who was carrying the bulkiest items, also had to contend with Cair Paravel's sudden joyous discovery of low-flying seagulls.

The sand was pale and smooth, and April, plumping Bee down, kneeled in the coolness and sifted the multicoloured

189

grains through her fingers. Bee laughed out loud, kicking her bare feet into the sand, beating her palms on the beach, entranced by so many new sensations. April, overwhelmed with love, let the tears trickle down her nose, then quickly forced herself to arrange the towels, open Cair Paravel's water bottle, unpack the swimsuits, and generally pull herself together.

'Cossie time, then!' Jix buried Bee's feet. 'And I'll race you into the sea!'

Constantly telling Bee to stand still, and that she mustn't go near the water on her own, and yes they'd all build sand castles in a minute, April wondered fleetingly if she'd be brave enough to bare her body. Oh, to be Bee's age, she thought, as she tugged her squirming daughter out of her shorts and T-shirt, and pulled on the rather pretty and slightly too small second-hand swimsuit. At Bee's age, changing on the beach, however crowded, wasn't a problem: for April, the prospect of wriggling out of the denim dress and her bra and knickers and trying to squeeze into the shiny violet bikini which Naz in the charity shop had assured her would fit like a glove, was a very different matter.

Maybe, she thought, looking back at the cliff top, she should go and change in the public loos. Maybe she'd have to dump the dual responsibilities of daughter and dog on to Jix yet again while she retained a modicum of decency.

Jix had managed to tether the quivering greyhound to an impaled spade, and despite the fact that several other families had clambered down the steps and were setting up camp quite close to them, had shed scarves, bangles, and the tie-dye vest with reckless abandon, and was unzipping his jeans.

'God!' April squinted up at him. 'You're not skinny-dipping, are you?'

'You wish,' Jix grinned. 'Nah. I've come fully equipped.' He held up a pair of frayed denim cut-offs in one hand and a huge bath towel in the other. Wrapping the towel round his waist, he wriggled and contorted his body until his jeans were round his ankles. Removing the towel he grinned again. '*Voilà!* It's all down to dexterity and practice, you see.'

April blinked. If she'd imagined Jix's body at all – which she hadn't, of course – she'd have put money on it being pale, emaciated and weedy. She'd have lost her own bet. The slender, well-muscled torso and the long lean legs that had been hidden beneath the hippie façade came as a complete surprise.

She stopped staring and smiled at him, feeling almost shy. 'Do you know, I was just thinking, I must be the only woman in Bixford who *doesn't* know what you look like without your clothes on.'

'Your loss.' He poked out his tongue. 'Now it's your turn. If you don't get undressed soon your daughter is going to burst with impatience. Do you want me to hold your towel? I promise I won't look.'

'And pigs might . . .' April retorted, grabbing the largest towel. 'Just shut your eyes – Oh, sod it! You made it look so easy.' She wrestled with the towel and various zips and buttons for a few more minutes, then sighed crossly. 'We ought to have one of those beach huts up there; then I could change in privacy.'

And we will, she thought, gripping the towel with her teeth and shimmying her body in the hope that her dress would slide to the floor. When Noah comes back, and I bring him down here, we'll have one of those – maybe the peach one, or that bright red one, or the duck-egg blue . . .

'April, you're making a right dog's breakfast of that,' Jix interrupted the thoughts. 'Here. I'll hold the towel.'

'Oh, God – OK . . .'

Wriggling, highly self-conscious, April tussled with the age-old dilemma of removing one set of bra and pants and getting into another without turning into Gypsy Rose Lee, and all with Jix only inches away. Feeling suddenly very vulnerable, she turned her head to look back up the cliff. The beach huts were opening up their doors now as holidaymakers arrived. People in shorts, encouraged by the heat of the morning, were unpacking cool boxes and shaking out towels and bathing costumes on the wooden slatted verandas.

Concentrating hard on fastening the bikini top under the towel, April noticed the girl dressed sombrely in baggy black, sitting slumped alone outside the prettiest hut – all apricot and red and cream – her dark hair dangling down hiding her face, her shoulders hunched up. April sighed. Poor thing. Probably had a row with her boyfriend or something. What a pity. Being miserable on her holiday – and in such a beautiful place.

'OK?' Jix jiggled the towel. 'Decent?'

'What? Oh yes, I think so.' April moved away from the towel with extreme caution. The violet bikini was very snug, but she hoped it covered all the bits it should.

Jix whistled appreciatively. 'When we go back to Bixford you are going to have to wear that on the debt-collecting round! I know certain people who'd pay well over the odds for a glimpse of you in that!'

Grinning, she punched him. 'Get off! Is Cairey safe there?'

Jix wiggled the spade. 'As houses. He's got water and a biscuit. He'll be fine.'

Cair Paravel, sprawled on all the towels with his biscuit trapped between his front paws, gave a docile thump of his tail.

'Good boy.' April kissed the top of his head. 'You stay on guard. We won't be long.'

The sea, after the scorching summer, was warm as it swirled round their ankles. Bee, shrieking with delight, leaped over the rippling waves, as April and Jix, each holding a hand, swung her up and over the foaming shoreline.

'We ought to get a Lilo from that café place up there,' Jix said. 'I always wanted one when I was a kid but we could never afford it. And you,' he eyed her, 'really should christen that bikini.'

As Beatrice-Eugenie sat down and screamed with excitement as the sea eddied round her legs, Jix tumbled April into the shallow warmth of the water.

'Bastard . . .' she spluttered happily, splashing him back.

'Oy! You! You got a bloody greyhound?'

They both looked at the wizened man in the Aston Villa replica shirt who was standing on the water's edge, gesticulating fiercely.

'Yes, but he's tied up.'

The claret and blue arm jabbed angrily up the beach. 'Not any more, he ain't. The bugger's just eaten my Cornetto!'

With a sigh, April scrambled to her feet. Holding on to her bikini and following the ice-creamless man, she side-stepped dozens of family groups before locating Cair Paravel. He was digging happily in the sand, his tail whizzing like a propeller.

She grabbed his collar and he looked up and smiled at her, the remains of wafer and chocolate decorating his muzzle.

'How much do I owe you?'

The football shirt shrugged. 'A couple of quid should do it.'

'I'll just go and get my purse.' April tugged Cairey away from his excavations. 'And if you come to the greyhound stadium tonight you could put something on him and possibly win a lot more than the cost of an ice cream.'

'On him?' The football shirt looked horrified. 'He ain't even trained proper! Don't you go getting your hopes up on him, gel. He's not a proper racer – he's out of control. He won't be winning nothing, you mark my words.'

chapter sixteen

For Sebastian, August Bank Holiday Monday had so far been a very surreal experience.

It hadn't just been arriving at the Ampney Crucis greyhound stadium and thinking that he must have inadvertently stepped back into a time warp: it had started long before that. Possibly halfway through the morning, when he and Brittany, emerging after a heavy night, intent on dodging the paparazzi outside her West London flat, had discovered that someone had wheel-clamped the Daimler.

'We'll take yours,' Brittany had said, flashing smiles at the photographers and writing a cheque for a Frobisher minion to bail out the car later. 'I can sleep all the way down there, then.'

And she'd done just that, Sebastian mused, now sitting in the bar of the strangest pub he'd ever encountered, listening to the umpteenth rendition of 'Mr Tambourine Man', and watching through the window as the tourists soaked up the scorching afternoon sun.

They'd whizzed down to Ampney Crucis in the Mercedes, with no traffic problems at all on the motorway, and Brittany in her brief sundress, which must have cost about a thousand pounds a square inch, had curled like a Siamese cat beside him, and slept soundly.

Once they'd arrived, Brittany's razor-sharp business

brain had kicked in immediately, and she'd suggested that, as their meeting with the Ampney Crucis Greyhound Stadium board members wasn't until six o'clock, just prior to the evening's racing, they should do a bit of private reconnoitring. This was when the second feeling of disbelief had started to emerge. Ampney Crucis Greyhound Stadium was like something out of an old Peter Sellers film: totally deserted, with no sound but the constant shush of the sea in the background, with birds and butterflies swooping overhead, and the sun spiralling from the crumbling white railings and tumbledown stands.

Sebastian had expected Brittany to hoot with laughter and suggest they made a quick getaway. There was no way on earth, even though the stadium was apparently due for a face-lift, that the Frobisher empire would want to stage their flagship race meeting in a place like this.

'It's rather sweet,' Brittany had said, scuffing at tufts of fern growing through the shingle at the edge of the track. 'Don't you think?'

Sebastian had shaken his head. Sweet it may be, but it would never be able to cater for the *crème de la crème* of the dog world, and the punters, plus the spivs and touts and celeb hangers on, all of whom would follow the Frobisher Platinum Trophy like Eric Cantona's seagulls. As far as he could see, there was no bar, no restaurant apart from the closed-up hot-dog van, and no Tote facilities. The only bookmakers' pitches on offer were three piles of pallets beneath three striped umbrellas, all with well-worn name boards in curlicued writing.

Benny Clegg, Roger Foster, and Allan Lovelock. They sounded – and no doubt looked – like the Three Stooges. He'd laughed softly to himself, wishing his parents could be here to see this. He could imagine Oliver comparing this place with the Gillespie Stadium with all the air of an outraged Derby horse contemplating an Epsom challenge from a Thelwell pony. And Martina – well, Martina would simply never believe it.

'Shall we just go home?' he'd suggested. 'Now. Before it gets any more embarrassing.'

'No, of course not. I've seen much worse than this.' Brittany had looked around. 'Well, not much worse, actually, and probably not as decrepit, but it's got – well – you've got to admit, the place has got something.'

'Woodworm, dry rot, and impending bankruptcy?'

She'd smiled at him. 'I know, Seb, darling, how desperate you and your parents are for the Frobisher Platinum to be staged in Bixford – and believe me, you're up there with the best of them – but don't forget the GRA are very keen to make the dog racing image a friendly, family-outing affair. Places like this have a certain kudos, you know.'

'But you can't seriously be considering –'

'What I'm considering is meeting the people here, as arranged, and discussing their refurbishment plans and their tender. They have as much right as anyone else to my time. That's all. Now, I've got some stuff to do on the laptop and a million calls to make. You don't mind if we park the Merc somewhere quiet and I turn it into a mobile office, do you?'

Sebastian had shaken his head. 'No, of course not. I'm sure I'll find something to amuse myself.'

'I'm sure you will. Have a drink, something to eat, paddle in the sea, watch Punch and Judy . . .' She'd curled herself round him and gently nibbled his lower lip. 'Just don't be late back, Sebby. It's important that we get to the stadium on time.'

And so, Sebastian thought, draining his glass of beer, that was it. They'd parked the car on the cliff top, and he'd left Brittany plugged into her mobile phone and her computer. Arranging to meet her back at the stadium at six o'clock, he wandered off to take in the sights of Ampney Crucis.

They hadn't taken very long. The village itself was incredibly beautiful, very quiet, and totally unspoiled. But it didn't offer much by way of entertainment for someone alone who knew no one. Once he'd stared at the beach, investigated the Crow's Nest Caff and the fish-and-chip shop, and had two pints of some really rather good local beer in the quaint Crumpled Horn, he felt he'd exhausted the possibilities. He looked at his watch. God – it wasn't even two o'clock. What the hell was he supposed to do with the rest of the afternoon?

Deciding that he couldn't cope with another pint – it was curiously strong – or yet another plaintive rendition of 'Mr Tambourine Man' – he already knew that he'd be humming the chorus for the rest of the day – he stepped outside into the sunshine.

It was gloriously warm and the beach below him was packed, brightly coloured bodies plunging in and out of the sea. Sebastian leaned on the railings that were obviously intended to prevent inebriates staggering from the Crumpled Horn and immediately rolling down the cliffs, and sighed. Since childhood he'd holidayed with Oliver and Martina on private islands borrowed from friends in the Caribbean and the Indian Ocean. In adulthood, he'd jetted off to the world's trendiest vacation destinations. Never once had he had an English seaside holiday.

But these people, with their deck chairs, and their children, all looked far happier with the meagre amenities on offer than his rich and bored companions had done with every delight in the world at their disposal. The beach huts were pretty cool too. Like the old-fashioned picture postcards that his grandparents had shown him. It was another world here, away from Bixford and Tacky Towers.

Sebastian fondly watched a young couple with a small child in the distance, running in and out of the water to jump on and off a lurid-coloured Lilo. The girl was slim, with fair hair and a brilliant purple bikini, while the man had long hair and a lean body, and the child ran between them, obviously blissfully happy. There was a dog too, chasing the waves, shaking itself all over them.

They looked like some idyllic family from an Australian soap opera, Sebastian thought, watching them as they scampered back up the beach, carrying the Lilo to where an elderly woman sat huddled in a deckchair with a towel hooded over her head like ET. Was she ill? He hoped not. Illness and death didn't have a part to play on a beautiful day like this. Sebastian smiled to himself as the woman leaned down with admirable dexterity, and helped herself to something from one of the carrier bags. No infirmity there then, thank goodness. She obviously just had an aversion to the sun.

His eyes moved along the shoreline, taking in other similar families, all happily enjoying the very unEnglish bank holiday temperatures. He envied them their ability to be so carefree. Again, he thought, he ached to be part of a happy, uncomplicated family – like the one he'd watched earlier – with a child and a dog and a mother or grandmother sitting cosily in charge of the picnic bags. They were probably all staying at some B&B that Martina wouldn't even deign to enter, and eating fish and chips and huge fry-ups and having the best time it was possible to have.

Feeling highly dissatisfied with his smug, comfortable, parentally organised life, Sebastian unpeeled himself from the railings. There were still more than three hours to go until he could join up with Brittany. It really was scorchingly hot. Irritably he wondered why he hadn't thought about packing swimming trunks and a towel. Possibly because he'd never expected to find clear blue waters and pale clean sand in Ampney Crucis. Of course he could just pop into the Crow's Nest Caff and buy some beach stuff, but it hardly seemed worth it now.

Yawning and stretching, he thought the best thing to do was to look for somewhere cool and shady . . . somewhere he could relax and catch up on the sleep that Brittany's acrobatics had denied him last night.

He drifted away from the sea front, puffing in the heat on the slight incline towards the village. All the seats on display were in very public view, and in the full glare of the sun, and certainly wouldn't serve his purpose. He walked on, his feet heavy, his whole body suffused with a sleepy, opulent, mid-afternoon lethargy. Each step was like walking in a warm bath, and the air was hot on the back of his throat.

A clump of dark trees just along the cliff top seemed to offer the most shade, so Sebastian headed for them, hoping against hope that a dozen other day-trippers hadn't beaten him to them.

They hadn't. Probably, he thought, because when he reached them he quickly discovered that the trees belonged to St Edith's churchyard, and a graveyard would surely not be top of anyone's holiday must-visit list.

The cemetery, set apart from the greystone church, was bordered by trees on three sides. One of these looked out to the sea, and Sebastian felt a childlike frisson of pleasure, watching the shimmering water dancing through the shifting branches. The elders of the parish had kindly provided wooden benches dotted around the tombstoned serenity, and he sank down on the one with the best sea view, grateful for the dark cool green shadows.

God, he was tired. The combination of Brittany's nocturnal antics, the sizzling heat, and the two pints of Old Ampney ale proved just too much. Stretching out, listening to the distant soporific sounds of the sea, and the gulls, and the happy shouts of the children playing on the beach, Sebastian felt his eyelids droop.

He woke with a jump. He could smell pine needles and hot spicy privet flowers. Where the hell was he? He blinked, and slowly remembered. Christ — suppose it was late and he'd missed Brittany and the meeting? He glanced down at his watch in the deep dark silence. Quarter-past four — thank God for that. He stretched, feeling refreshed, and just a bit uncomfortable, then realised he wasn't alone.

A woman, with her back to him, was tending one of the graves against the sea wall. He watched her for a moment as she arranged a tumble of pastel freesias in the vase, and realised that she was talking. Knowing that he was intruding on something very private, Sebastian wasn't sure whether to stay still and hope she'd finish and walk away without even knowing he was there, or to stand up and try to sidle off without her noticing. He certainly didn't want to startle her.

He sat for a moment longer, hardly daring to breathe, hearing the cadence of her voice but not the torrent of words. It sounded like a proper conversation and his heart went out to her. Squinting at the headstone he could see that Mary Clegg had departed this life some twenty-five years previously, but that Benny, devoted husband of Mary, father of Philip and adored and much-loved grandpa to Jasmine, had only joined her in May this year. Four months ago.

He stared at the woman's hunched back again. Poor thing. The grief must still be very raw.

Was this the Cleggs' daughter-in-law, then? Sebastian thought probably not. Although he couldn't see the face, the glossy dark brown hair was girlishly long as it fell forward, and the black T-shirt and jeans indicated a more youthful way of dressing. The granddaughter perhaps? Jasmine? Beautiful name . . .

With another start, Sebastian realised from the quiver of the shoulders as the girl finished arranging the flowers and remained squatting, still talking, that she was crying.

God, this was awful. He really shouldn't be here.

Standing up as silently as possible, hoping that if he stepped off the gravel path and on to the neatly clipped grass he'd be able to exit the cemetery without making a noise, he started to move away. But although he hadn't made a sound, the girl must have sensed the movement, and jerked her head round, staring at him in fright.

'I'm so sorry –' Sebastian whispered, not sure why he was whispering, only knowing that it would have seemed sacrilegious to use his normal volume. From the continuing shocked look in the girl's huge brown eyes, the whisper only further marked him down as a weirdo. He swallowed and tried slightly louder. It sounded horribly like a shout in that quiet place. 'Er – I didn't want to disturb you.'

She pushed the dark hair away from her tear-streaked face. 'Why are you watching me?'

She was just like a puppy, Sebastian thought. Gentle, pretty, and very sad. He tried not to look threatening in any way. 'I'm not, that is, I wasn't. I – er – I was asleep on the bench there. I guess you didn't see me. I – um – woke up and you were there – and – er – I'm just going.'

The girl fished in the sleeve of her T-shirt and yanked out a tissue. Wiping her eyes, she gave him a tremulous smile. 'It's OK. Really. No, I didn't see you there, but I don't think you're the mad graveyard stalker or anything.'

She stopped and considered him. 'You're not, are you?'

He shook his head, feeling desperately sorry for her. 'I was just hot and tired and looking for somewhere cool to catch up on my sleep. Look, sorry to have disturbed you. I'll go now.'

The girl sat on the grave's kerbstone and looked up at him with those huge eyes. 'You don't have to. I've finished now – well, the flowers and stuff – and I've said everything I wanted to say to Grandpa . . .' She stopped, and chewed her lips. 'You must have thought I was crazy.'

Grandpa. So she was Jasmine, then. The name suited her. Sebastian shook his head again. 'No, of course not. I still go and talk to my gramp's grave when things are really bad.'

'Do you? Really? And does it help?'

'Always. He was a star.'

'Mine too.' Jasmine sniffed. 'I miss him so much. I still can't believe he's not around. That I'll never see him again.'

'It takes ages for that part to sink in,' Sebastian agreed, sitting down on the bench again. 'Mind you, I know my gramp is still there for me. He always lets me know . . . I just get this feeling . . .' He stopped. God. What the hell was he doing? Telling all this to a total stranger? Things that he'd never dared voice to anyone ever in his life before. And he'd said gramp rather than grandfather. 'Well, you know . . .'

She nodded. 'Yes, I know. It all comes as such a shock, doesn't it? I mean, my gran died when I was really little so I didn't remember, and then I went on for years, literally years, where no one I knew died. No one. It was like life was this constant thing that would go on for ever, with the same people doing the same things and –'

'That death only occurred on the news or in other people's families?' Sebastian remembered only too well the

203

sense of horror, when he'd realised that people he'd grown up with were not immortal. 'And yet, you still cling on to this vague hope that the people you love will somehow be shielded from death, don't you? Will go on for ever.'

Jasmine nodded more fervently. 'Oh, yes. And do you dream about your – um – gramp? You see, I dream about Grandpa all the time, and I'm not sure which ones are worse – the dreams where he's alive and I wake up and find that he isn't –'

'Or the ones where you dream he's dead, and then wake up and find out it isn't just a nightmare.' Sebastian exhaled. 'Yeah, I have both of those. They're both killers.'

Jasmine nodded and scrubbed at her eyes. 'You *do* understand. Oh, it's such a relief. Sometimes I think I'm going mad and I'll spend the rest of my life waking up in tears.'

'It's grieving and it's natural, and it does get better, believe me.'

Jasmine looked sceptical. 'Does it? I do hope so . . . Um – are you here on holiday?'

'Just a day visit. It's a lovely place. I've never been before.'

'I've lived here all my life. I think it's pretty special too. I've certainly never wanted to move away or live anywhere else.'

She looked at him again, as if assessing his face, then smiled. The smile lifted the top layer of the sadness, and changed everything about her. She was so genuine, Sebastian thought. Totally natural. And she wasn't even attempting to flirt with him, which came as something of a shock. He was used to women becoming a mixture of arch and coy, or blatantly coming on to him. He didn't think he was being big-headed about it. It just happened.

Jasmine fished in the carrier bag beside her. 'Would you like a doughnut?'

'What?'

'A doughnut?' Jasmine looked at him as though he might need to have the concept of fried dough, jam and sugar explained in detail. 'Me and Grandpa always had a doughnut when we came here to tidy up Gran's grave. I've – um – sort of carried on the tradition. Doughnuts, you see,' she continued seriously, 'are pure carbohydrate. People who eat them for comfort have got it absolutely right. Carbohydrates cure depression and shock and sadness.'

Sebastian grinned. 'Do you work for the doughnut marketing board, by any chance? Yes, yes, thanks – I'd love one.'

They munched in silence for a few moments, and Sebastian felt that far from it being odd, sitting in a graveyard with a complete stranger and eating jam doughnuts was the most natural thing in the world.

When they'd emptied the doughnut bag, Jasmine fixed him again with the soulful brown eyes. 'Feel better now?'

'Much, thanks. I think you must be right about doughnut properties. I certainly feel more cheerful. All we need now is something to wash it down with.' He wiped his mouth with the back of his hand. Martina and Brittany would have both shrieked in horror.

'Sorted,' Jasmine delved into the carrier bag and brought out two half-bottles of Old Ampney ale. 'Mind you, it's a bit strong if you're not used to it.'

'I know. I tried some earlier, but I think the effects have worn off now. I'll risk another one.' Sebastian accepted the opaque brown bottle. 'Thanks, again. It's very kind of you.'

Jasmine passed him the bottle opener and he noticed the diamond ring on her engagement finger for the first time. Lucky man, whoever he was, Sebastian thought, having a Jasmine to come home to. Someone who was gentle and would listen and be a friend, and not carp or criticise or expect miracles.

'When are you getting married?'

'Uh? Oh –' she looked down at the ring. 'Next year sometime.'

'Here? In this church?'

She nodded. Sebastian drained his bottle of Old Ampney. He really should be making a move now. Not only would Brittany create merry hell if he was late, but Martina and Oliver expected full and detailed reports on each of the rival tendering stadiums that he'd visited.

He stood up, handing her back the bottle. 'Thanks again. It's been a lovely picnic, but I'll really have to go now. I'm meeting someone and I'll be in deep shit if I'm late.'

'I wouldn't want to be the cause of that.' She smiled and stood up too. 'Anyway, I've got to be making tracks as well. It's been nice talking to you, and I hope you enjoy the rest of your visit.'

'I'm sure I will.' Sebastian motioned towards the headstone. 'And I'm really sorry . . .'

'Yeah, me too. And thanks for talking to me about – well, things, and for understanding. No one else has. I'm very grateful.'

He watched her as she walked away through the churchyard, and hoped that she'd be really happy one day – and that the fiancé would try to take the sadness from her eyes. Then, with the Old Ampney ale still slightly swirling his brain, he headed back towards the cliff top car park.

'Where the hell have you been?' Brittany was glitteringly angry. 'I've been waiting for ages.'

Sebastian glanced at his watch. 'It's only half-five. And you said –'

'Have you been drinking?'

'I've had a drink, yes. I'm not drunk. Anyway, you can

drive to the stadium. And in my role of observer at these sessions I'm not supposed to utter, am I? Therefore, even if I do have a tendency to slur my words a bit, no one's going to notice, are they?' He eased himself into the car, irritably nudging aside the laptop, the mobile, and the folders of paperwork.

Brittany snatched the ignition key and snapped the Mercedes into life. 'Have you been in that pub all afternoon?' The car was skimming recklessly fast over the shale and clumps of grass.

'No, I've had a picnic in the cemetery with a woman I've never seen before and will never see again.'

Brittany glanced across at him as they pulled out on to the sea road and headed towards the stadium. She grinned and snaked one slender hand along his thigh. 'Seb, you're so funny! I suppose that's why I can never stay pissed off with you for long.'

chapter seventeen

Peg's office was bursting at the seams. Ewan sat back in a corner, away from the table, and watched the proceedings with amused interest. As he wasn't a board member as such, he knew that this time Peg had only invited him to sit in because she wanted him to meet the luscious Brittany Frobisher, who was due to arrive, with a companion, at any minute.

Ewan wasn't too sure about the companion. Would it be a Frobisher work colleague, or someone more personal? He hoped it would be the former. He wouldn't have a snowball's chance in hell of seducing Brittany if she was firmly anchored to the side of some equally well-heeled hulk of a man. Not that he doubted his ability in that area, of course, but it was one thing flirting and enchanting someone who was free as the air – and quite another trying to charm someone who was happily attached. Still, he thought, as he watched the hands of the retro fifties clock clamber up towards six, he'd soon find out which it was to be.

Peg, Roger, Allan and Jasmine were poring over the plans and their various copies of the tender for the Platinum Trophy. Ewan looked at them all fondly, and hoped that they weren't all going to be bitterly disappointed. He also wished that Peg had been having one of her more sober

Doris days. One of the sharp black suits and the Peter Pan collars would have probably been far more acceptable to the Frobisher contingent than the Calamity Jane outfit she was wearing.

Ewan looked at the clock again. He hoped that the meeting would kick off on time, because, with tonight's bank holiday racing starting at eight, and him not only having to greet the greyhounds, their owners and trainers, but also supervise the ground staff and the punters, the evening threatened to be pretty hectic.

It had not been a restful bank holiday by any means. Most of the day had been frantically exhausting too. He and Clara had tumbled off the futon at somewhere around lunch time, and had immediately gone to the Crumpled Horn for sustenance. Then they'd returned to Clara's flat and continued their marathon, making love on the balcony, unseen by the day-trippers sitting underneath with their cucumber sandwiches and flasks.

And as well as being greyhound greeter-in-chief tonight, he had also volunteered to help Jasmine with the Benny Clegg writing up, allowing Clara to catch up on preparing a Makings Paper presentation for the morning. It was an exhausting prospect – especially with another night of Clara to come.

However, with at least two weeks of enforced greyhound inactivity ahead due to Damon Puckett and his boys wreaking havoc on the stadium, Ewan had already decided that September was going to be a slate-wiper. Not only would he finally make the break from Katrina, and come out to Peg about his greyhound rescue activities, but he'd also prove to Clara that he wasn't just a freeloading idealist who happened to be able to pass off a reasonable performance under the duvet.

The blissful and no-questions-asked reunion with Clara

– in fact, his whole return to Ampney Crucis – had been a catharsis. But there were still these pressing issues to be settled, and once this evening's meeting at the stadium was over, and Damon and his boys moved in, Ewan knew he'd have plenty of time to play with. There was still one sticking point in all this: Peg's insistence that, should push come to shove, he'd have to seduce Brittany.

Under normal circumstances, of course, it would have been a pleasure, but now he and Clara were reunited, he certainly didn't want to rock the boat. He only hoped that Clara would understand.

'Right-oh, then.' Peg bossily tidied everyone's papers into neat piles in front of them. 'We all know how to play up our strengths and play down our weaknesses, don't we?'

They all nodded. They'd been well briefed. The hands on the clock stuttered upwards to a few seconds before the hour.

Bunny poked his head in from the kitchen. 'Do you want some drinks, Mizz Dunstable? It's durnably hot in here.'

'I'll do it,' Jasmine said, standing up quickly. 'You might trip again, Bun.'

'Good idea.' Peg nodded her plaits as Jasmine disappeared into the kitchen. 'And don't say durnably or anything like it when Miss Frobisher's here, Bunny, please. You know I can't abide bad language.'

Ewan tried not to smile at this total untruth. Nothing quite so refined as durnably had definitely ever entered into Peg's four-letter vocabulary.

The clock's hands flickered into a perfect vertical. There was a sharp rap on the door.

Roger and Allan, showing amazing agility considering their combined ages, stampeded towards it. Peg, the suedette fringes swishing furiously, beat them to it by a nano-second.

'Miss Frobisher! Exactly on time. A woman after my own heart – I can't abide unpunctuality . . . come along in – Oh, and – '

'This is Sebastian.' Brittany Frobisher felled everyone with a dazzling smile, allowing only a flash of consternation at Peg's Wild West appearance to flicker across her face. 'He's going to be taking notes.'

Ewan chuckled quietly to himself. They were obviously very role-reversal then, in the brewing kingdom, with Brittany having a male secretary. Definitely, he reckoned, a case of boardroom and bedroom there. And because he wasn't a man's man, Ewan could appreciate that Sebastian was very attractive to women. Feeling a masculine territorial hostility bristling within him, he opted for concentrating on Brittany rather than the tall and tanned Sebastian, who had arranged himself easily in his proffered chair, and who, if he was romantically linked to Brittany, could be more difficult to shift than a barnacle.

Ewan tried not to stare too obviously at Brittany in the short biscuit-coloured dress, but it was very difficult: she was almost more gorgeous in the flesh than she was in her many photographs. Elegant and assured, she was being introduced now, shaking hands, saying a few words to everyone, and looking as though she was riveted by the answers. Exactly like the royal family, Ewan concluded. Good breeding, beauty and brains in one exquisite package. She was going to be no pushover, that was for sure.

Ewan relished the challenge. All the important women in his life – like all the things that had really mattered to him – had been difficult, powerful, risky. Brittany Frobisher, he thought, would fit into that category nicely. But then there was Clara. He was pretty sure that Clara would have nothing more to do with him if he should stray – again.

Peg had everyone seated and was well into her opening spiel. She was good, Ewan had to admit. Even at her age her voice was strong and persuasive, and Brittany and Sebastian were being treated to the full works about how Ampney Crucis intended to cater for the greyhounds, the media and the punters who would attend the Frobisher Platinum, and being shown the plans for the refurbishment.

None of them seemed to have realised that Jasmine wasn't in the room. Ewan, transfixed on Brittany, certainly hadn't. It wasn't until she clattered in from the kitchen bearing a tray of iced drinks, that he remembered.

'Jasmine, pet!' Peg paused in the middle of describing how the corrugated iron roofing was to be replaced. 'We've started without you. Sorry, but there's a lot to do. Now, this is Brittany Frobisher and her friend Sebastian. Miss Frobisher, this is Jasmine Clegg, another shareholder and – Oh bugger me!'

Jasmine had done a Bunny and dropped the drinks tray.

Ewan, immediately getting to his feet to rescue Jasmine, was beaten to it by Sebastian who practically sprinted from his chair. He and Jasmine gathered the glasses and jugs together with a lot of whispering. There was even some giggling, Ewan detected, over the eel-like qualities of the ice cubes.

Brittany flapped her hand. 'Shall we get on? Sebby is ace at clearing things up – and I'm sure Jasmine knows exactly what's going on and will be able to say her piece later. OK, so I can take away copies of the actual restructuring plans, which is very kind of you, but considering the extra amenities on offer, what safety procedures do you have in place – now and in the future? And press coverage? And car parking facilities?'

The rest of the board members resumed their discussions. Ewan was far more fascinated by the fact that Jasmine and Sebastian, having scraped up all the broken glass, were now chattering quietly together almost like old friends. As they disappeared into the kitchen, his curiosity was very much aroused.

Still, he thought, rather bored by the haggling that was currently going on over sponsorship and advertising bill-boards, it would be nice if Jasmine and Sebastian hit it off, it would suit his plans admirably if Brittany's walker was occupied elsewhere. And Andrew, the smarmy sod, would certainly get his comeuppance.

Ewan shook his head. It just wasn't going to happen, was it? What man in his right mind would jack in the inestimable Brittany for plump and puppyish Jasmine? Oh, Jas was great, of course, but no one would call her beauti-ful, or sexy, or even pretty, would they? She was just Jas – one of the crowd, a good mate. Whatever Sebastian saw in her, it certainly couldn't be measured in seduction terms.

The phone on Peg's desk rang in the middle of Brittany explaining exactly what Frobishers were looking for by way of refreshment facilities for their visiting hordes. Ewan picked it up. It was Gorf, one of the turnstile men.

'We got someone here who'd like a word with the management.'

'Will I do? Everyone else is in a meeting.'

'S'pose you'll have to, then,' Gorf said. 'You'n a Dun-stable anyway. It's some woman – a new 'un – who's got a dog running in the nine thirty. She wants to ask a favour.'

'OK,' Ewan said, 'I'll come down. Tell her to wait round by the kennels. What? Oh, Christ. Are there? A whole family? Right – oh, and check their paperwork, passes, certificates – you know, just in case.' .

He put the phone down. Brittany paused in the middle of explaining the Frobisher presentation podium requirements and raised a perfectly plucked eyebrow. 'Are you leaving us?'

Ewan smiled apologetically. 'Afraid so. I'm – er – sorry to have to dash off but there's a problem downstairs.'

Peg frowned. 'A big problem?'

'One Gorf can't handle.'

'Gorf? How cute!' Brittany beamed. 'Do you give all your ground staff Tolkeinesque names?'

'Tolkie-Who?' Peg frowned. 'Good Lord, we didn't call him that. It's not a nickname, pet. He was christened Gorf. He's got a sister called Waffon. God knows why. Mind, their father was a bit asthmatic . . .' She looked beadily at Ewan. 'Hopefully it's something you can deal with. Shout if you can't.'

Ewan smiled again at Brittany. 'No doubt we'll see more of you and – er – Sebastian later in the evening, when the meeting starts?'

'Unfortunately not.' Brittany met his eyes, holding his stare. 'We're not able to stay. We have another venue to visit on the journey back to London. I hope I'll be able to come and watch another race meeting when your refurbishment is completed. However,' she held out a slender hand, 'I'm sure we'll be seeing each other again some time soon.'

Ewan practically cartwheeled down the stairs from Peg's office. He was in! First base! Yesss! He was still mentally punching the air by the time he reached the turnstiles. Brittany was interested – he knew she was – and Jasmine and Sebastian still hadn't come out of the kitchen!

Gorf, squat and pugnacious, jerked his head towards a Toyota people carrier blocking the main exit. 'Over there. Yon scruffy family. Got a problem with their dog.'

'He's a runner, is he? For tonight?'

Gorf nodded. 'Like I said, in the nine thirty. I've checked

the papers and everything. He's genuine – it's just that the owner needs to ask something before the race.'

'Leave it with me, then.' Ewan felt buoyant. He'd really had very little to do since coming back to Ampney Crucis. Peg had found him made-up jobs to keep him busy, and Clara had taken up the rest of his time, but he'd let his other crusades slip a bit. Now, with Brittany Frobisher obviously interested maybe – just maybe – the stadium would get the Platinum Trophy and he'd be promoted to some sort of manager. Anyway, he could certainly do a bit of troubleshooting in the meantime.

He approached the people carrier feeling very authoritative. A gorgeous blue brindled greyhound scampered up and down on the back seat, scrabbling long thin paws over a middle-aged woman and a small girl and a vast array of towels, carrier bags, and a pink Lilo, still inflated.

'Nice dog,' Ewan said to the driver, who looked as though he belonged to one of the prettier heavy metal rock bands. 'Did someone say there was a problem?'

'Yes, me.' A girl with damp fair hair screwed up on top of her head leaned across the driver. 'We have a favour to ask you about Cairey.'

Cairey? The driver? The woman? The child? Ewan frowned. 'Cairey?'

'Cair Paravel.' The girl indicated the greyhound, who was now trying to thrust his head through the driver's window to lick Ewan's face. 'It's to do with his running. We were training him on the beach this afternoon and we've discovered something, but this is his first race and we're not sure about the rules.'

Ewan groaned. Maybe troubleshooting wasn't going to be his forte after all. A small queue of vehicles was gathering impatiently behind the Toyota.

Gorf clicked his tongue against his teeth. 'Best get 'em

shifted, Ewan. We've got a gridlock situation here.'

Gridlock, Ewan thought, was overegging it a bit. However, he took the point. He leaned back into the Toyota. 'If you drive round the outside of the track to the kennels over there –' he pointed to where a lopsided sign read 'KNLS' – 'and park up, then I'll meet you in a moment and hopefully sort out your problem.'

The people carrier moved away and Ewan exhaled. He knew very little of the rules of greyhound racing; he hoped that the problem wouldn't involve him having to look something up and losing face. Still, he thought, jogging round the track in the Toyota's wake, the girl was rather attractive. It looked like it was going to be a good night all round.

Having completed the circuit, Ewan walked into the owners and trainers' area, loving the smell of the dogs mingling with the salt-tang of the sea, and the circus scent of fresh sawdust. The kennels were already lively and noisy, with the greyhounds being pampered and fussed by their owners. As most of them visited the track at least once every week, it was a very jolly reunion atmosphere, and there was no sign of pre-race nerves, tension, or even the slightest animosity. Ampney Crucis didn't go in for histrionics, and anyone getting ideas above his dog-racing station would certainly get short shrift.

Having seen so many appalling sights during his greyhound rescue campaign, Ewan looked fondly at the thirty or so animals that had already arrived. Every last one of them was loved and pampered and part of the family. Most of them were simply graders who would spend their sprinting years at Ampney Crucis, and the rest of their lives slumbering in front of village firesides. There were no megastars here, but to their owners they were Ballyregan Bob and Mick the Miller all rolled into one elegant, slender bundle. Ewan stroked and patted and fussed them, and tried to push out of his mind the thoughts of the tortured, emaciated, malnourished, exhausted creatures that he'd seen in the last year. They constantly crept in. It didn't matter that he'd helped so many to escape their ill treatment and suffering – he knew he could never rescue all of them, and it hurt.

If he'd told these people here tonight about the things he'd seen abroad, they simply wouldn't believe him. Greyhound racing in this country was so well ordered and controlled and decent that these men and women who loved their animals and the sport would simply dismiss his horror stories as figments of an overactive and grisly imagination. If only . . .

He checked each kennel. He hoped Peg would bring Brittany down here to see the luxury they provided. The dogs were happily ensconced in their temporary enclosures, sniffing each other joyously through the mesh, and the warm evening air was splintered only by the occasional staccato bark from the greyhounds, or a hoot of ribald laughter from the owners. It was all very relaxed.

By the time Ewan had completed his kennel check, and walked into the owners and trainers' car park, Cair Paravel's owner had slid from the Toyota and was heading in his direction. In her short denim dress, lightly suntanned, she was considerably more attractive than he'd first thought. Slapping on his best smile, Ewan waited for her to join him.

'Ewan Dunstable, Stadium Manager.'

'Pleased to meet you.' She shook his hand in a business-like manner. 'I'm – oh, yes, I'm Beatrice-Eugenie Padgett, registered owner of Cair Paravel. He's down to run in the nine thirty, and we – that is, Jix and me – oh, that's Jix in the driving seat. Well, yes, we wondered if there was anything in the rules about the hare.'

Ewan blinked. Christ, now he'd probably have to get the handbook and look nothing like the Stadium Manager he purported to be. And why did these Londoners have to have such peculiar names. Beatrice-Eugenie, for crying out loud! And Jix! They sounded like the sort of very new, very PC names they gave to the presenters on *Blue Peter*. He tried to look efficient. 'Er, what about the hare exactly?'

'Well, Cairey – that's Cair Paravel – he doesn't run well . . . No, I mean, he runs, but he doesn't want to chase the hare, you see. He loves it. He doesn't like the idea of catching it. He just wants to baby it. It causes a problem.'

Ewan raised his eyebrows and sucked in his breath. Jesus! 'Yes, I can see that it would – him being a racing greyhound and this being a greyhound stadium. I mean, we don't actually encourage the dogs to be affectionate towards the hare, otherwise we'd abandon the running part altogether and be having greyhound snuggling events instead, wouldn't we?'

'There's no need to be sarcastic.' The girl glared at him. 'We know it's a problem – but we have discovered a solution. You see, Cairey hates Jix's mum, Daff – that's Daff in the back, waving . . .'

Ewan glanced over to the people carrier. The middle-aged woman was fluttering her fingers at him. She had the inflated Lilo on her head.

He closed his eyes. He thought Cair Paravel may well have a point.

'We discovered,' the girl continued, 'this afternoon on the beach when we were giving him some exercise, that if he can chase something of Daff's he runs in a straight line, like the wind, in the right direction, and with real killer instinct.'

God Almighty, Ewan thought. She's going to suggest that we strap that daft old bat to the electric rail.

'So,' she stopped glaring and gave him a beguiling smile, 'what we wondered is, if for the nine thirty, you could tie this round your hare?'

Ewan looked down at the pink and purple polyester headscarf and thought he was probably going to cry.

'Don't talk to me!' Jasmine snapped over her shoulder after the fourth race. 'Just write down what I tell you. I don't want to hear any of it. Clara's my best friend, and she loves you   and if you screw her up again, I swear I'll kill you.'

Ewan, balancing the ledger on one knee and trying to keep pace with the crowd of bank-holiday punters having a last-minute wager, felt irritable. Jasmine had gone all holier-than-thou over the Brittany thing. And he hadn't had a spare moment to ask her about Sebastian. He'd therefore decided, under the circumstances, to keep very quiet about the hare and the headscarf.

It was a shame, he thought, that Brittany Frobisher had left before the race meeting started: surely the atmosphere tonight would have persuaded her that the Frobisher Platinum could be run just as well here as at any glittery city stadium? The crowds were jam-packed onto the tiered stands, and even the trackside viewing areas were three deep. The night was dark now, and sultry, with the floodlights casting white pools over the sandy track. Roger, Allan and Jasmine had been snowed-under with people having a flutter, the strains of 'Everybody Loves a Lover' were whoopee-doing from the Tannoy and, all in all, it was a true Ampney Crucis party night.

The dogs were being led out for the nine thirty race. Ewan exhaled. He had to do it. He'd promised he would.

'Jas, be a love and cope on your own for five minutes, will you? There's something I've got to do.'

'Phone Brittany on your mobile?' Jasmine's brown eyes flashed fire. 'Forget it, Ewan. No bloody way.'

'It's got nothing to do with Brittany. It's to do with this race — one of the dogs — Cair Paravel. I promised his owner I'd sort something out at the start of his race. They've brought him down from London. See.' He jabbed his finger at the board. 'You've got him at tens, which is a bit risky with him being a stranger.'

'Since when did you know about setting prices? I've got him at tens because Bess Higgins is running Smokey Jo-Jo. He always wins. And if you're longer than five minutes I'm going to tell Clara . . .'

He grinned at her. 'You sound just like you did in the playground. All self-righteous and indignant. You used to beat me up then when I teased Clara, remember? And I promise you I won't hurt her. Now grab this book and I'll be back before you know it.'

Forcing his way through the record crowd, he headed for the traps. The greyhounds were just going behind and he could see the girl — Beatrice-Eugenie — and the rock-star boy, Jinx or whatever his name was, down at the start, looking anxiously at the crowd, searching for him. Cair Paravel, he noticed, had been drawn in trap two, wearing the blue jacket, and seemed far more at ease than his owners.

Ewan nodded his head slightly in Beatrice-Eugenie's direction and, spotting him, she grinned at him in delight. She really was remarkably pretty . . . Feeling like a complete prat, he dragged the headscarf from the pocket of his jeans and, praying that no one was watching him, stepped across the freshly raked sand towards Bunny.

Bunny was just setting the hare on its course, making

220

sure it was firmly attached and that no wires were loose.

'Hi, Bun.' Ewan tried the matey approach. 'Look, I know this is going to sound a bit mad, but could you put this on the hare before you let it go?'

'Uh?' Bunny blinked at the headscarf. 'Is it a joke?'

'No joke,' Ewan said through gritted teeth as the starter on his stepladder showed signs of agitation. 'Just do it. Please.'

'OK,' Bunny took the scarf, and, straddling the rails, with the moth-eaten hare between his knees, placed the pink and purple square over its head. 'Nice colour this, Ewan. My mum's got one of these. Mind you, it ought to have a matching handbag to set it off right . . . You ain't got a handbag, by any chance?'

'No, I haven't got a frigging handbag!' Ewan was trying not to look at the starter. 'Nor a pair of hare-sized sling-backs, nor a cardie for if the weather turns chilly! Just do it, Bunny – and, no, don't bother with tying a bow under its chin. It's an inanimate fur ball. I'm sure it's not too worried about its sartorial appearance.'

'There!' Bunny stood up and admired his handiwork. 'Don't he look pretty?'

The hare looked, Ewan thought, exactly like an East End Ewok. The handbag could have only improved things. However, there was no time to worry about it as the starter had already raised his flag. Beatrice-Eugenie and Jinx, he noticed, were exchanging high-fives behind the podium.

Bunny pressed his button, and the hare, the headscarf fluttering jauntily, bucketed off around the track. Within seconds the traps flew open, and the six dogs tore out into the night, sand flying up in puffs of gold behind them.

By the first bend, Cair Paravel's blue jacket was already four lengths ahead of the rest of the field.

chapter eighteen

April really couldn't believe that September was actually coming to an end. Despite the joy of Cair Paravel's success at Ampney Crucis, the days since had simply crawled by. She'd been marking them off on the calendar at number 51, trying to cram as much into each waking hour as possible, knocking herself out physically so that her six hours of sleeping would be assured. So far it hadn't worked; every night she'd fallen into bed, exhausted by waitressing at the Pasta Place, debt-collecting with Jix, and serving cocktails in the Copacabana, only to be infuriatingly mentally wide awake the moment her head touched the pillow.

All she could think about was Noah. She'd practised seeing him for the first time – her reaction, her approach, her opening lines. Should she take Bee with her, or leave her at home, for the first all-important father-and-child meeting to take place in privacy? Should she get glammed up to compete with the ex-loft-now-*gîte*-living woman, or should she dress as she had when Noah had loved her, in jeans and baggy sweaters, no make-up, and with her hair flowing?

These, and a million other things, had kept April awake for four weeks. But not for much longer. Tomorrow, Noah would be attending his exhibition at the Corner Gallery in Swaffield.

It being her late split shift in the Copacabana, it was nearly nine o'clock before she left the flat for the second time that evening. Cair Paravel, as befitted a champion, was sprawled on the sofa, snarling happily at Daff. Beatrice-Eugenie was sleeping soundly in the truckle bed, still honey-coloured from that glorious day at the seaside, and the only benefit of the split shift, as far as April could see, was that it meant she got back to the flat in time to bath Bee, put her to bed, read her a story, and watch her as she slept.

As Jix was chauffeuring Sebastian and Brittany to a film premier up West, it meant April having to negotiate the High Street and the dingy Bixford back streets on her way to and from the stadium alone in the dark, but tonight, she knew, that wouldn't be a problem. Tonight she felt immortal and untouchable. She was sure if some leery dope-head loomed from the shadows, the elation she felt would enable her to punch him on the nose and send him squawking on his way.

Closing the front door behind her, she breathed in the smoky air, the scent of decaying leaves fighting the smell of diesel fumes. Although the September days were still warm, the nights already had the iced, spiced chill of autumn. With the heels of Sofia's Manolo Blahniks clicking along the pavement – Martina had spotted the pink canvas crossover sandals and banned them two weeks previously – April set out for her final stint behind the bar.

The orange glow of the streetlights was harsh, and clashed discordantly with the yellow brightness spilling from the Pasta Place. Just like one of Noah's paintings, April thought dreamily, as she turned up the collar of Jix's leather jacket and hurried towards the white light in the sky that indicated it was greyhound racing as usual at the Gillespie Stadium.

How different, April thought, as she had all month, to the wonderful track at Ampney Crucis. How different Ampney Crucis had been in every way to grey and dreary Bixford. And what a difference that night had made. Cair Paravel winning the race had been extraordinary – and although the prize money had barely covered the petrol costs for the Toyota, the thrill had been stupendous.

Since then they'd risked the Gillespies discovering Cair Paravel's identity and ownership, and entered him in a couple of minor midweek races at Catford, without the aid of the headscarf, of course, and he'd been left standing at the start. Considering that they were chancing eviction and dismissal by doing so, they'd agreed not to repeat the operation. Disappointed, April and Jix had decided that if he was ever going to make it as a champion sprinter, it would have to be at tiny out-of-city tracks with understanding managers – like that lush Ewan Dunstable – who didn't object to draping Daff's headscarf round the hare. However, they now knew that Cairey had the ability – if not the constant motivation – and could earn his keep.

Jix was going to get in touch with the Ampney Crucis people again and see if they had finished the rebuilding that had been planned, and enquire if maybe they could enter Cairey for a race on a monthly basis, just to keep his hand, or perhaps paw, in. Still, April thought, carefully crossing the busy ring road outside the stadium, when she and Noah got back together and moved to live in Ampney Crucis, all the subterfuge would be over, and all the problems would be solved.

With still half an hour to go before she was due back behind the bar, April followed the late-coming crowds down the stadium's crimson entrance tunnel, with its millions of pinprick wall lights, and out into the brash glare of the amphitheatre. It was like a space station, April thought, all lights and flashing electronic boards under the black September sky, with stainless-steel walkways round the tiers of stands, and the chromium and glass viewing platforms, five restaurants, six bars, and every inch sardine-packed with thousands of noisy people.

Never having been to another stadium before, she realised now just how antiquated Ampney Crucis was. Poor things. They had no chance of Brittany Frobisher choosing them for the Platinum Trophy – which was, of course, a good thing as far as she and Jix and Cair Paravel were concerned. Maybe, in time, they'd get to know of other rural racetracks that few London dog people frequented, and Cairey could become the star of the back-of-beyond circuits.

She watched the race in progress with a professional eye now: the dogs sprinting, bumping and barging round the bends in pursuit of the Day-Glo hare, the feral, deafening roar of the punters, the torrent of commentary from the public address system, the frantic last minute ticktack of the white-gloved bookies, the row upon row of red jackets in the Tote windows. It was like another world. The Gillespie Stadium was a teeming night-time city built round greyhounds, where the staff were numbers on the payroll, not individuals. She and Jix had gawped in amazement at Ampney Crucis at the three solitary bookies' pitches, and no Tote, no bar, no restaurant – and the fact that everyone knew everyone else's names.

Hauling herself up the stairs towards the bar, already tired, her feet already hurting, she prayed that this last couple of hours would be easy – and give her plenty of Noah-dreaming time. Having traded her day off with one of the other waitresses for tomorrow, April wasn't sure that she'd sleep at all tonight. She still had to decide on her outfit, and have a bath and wash her hair and –

'April!' Martina, wrapped in skin-tight sequins, was in corncrake mode. 'You're late!'

'I'm not.' She shrugged out of the leather jacket, and pulled the skirt down as far as it would go. 'I'm actually five minutes early, and'. She looked around the bar. Barry Manilow and 'A Weekend in New England' had it practically to himself. 'It's not busy, is it?'

'But it will be as soon as this race is over. With presentations and everything, it means there's twenty minutes before the next one – and we've run out of sparklers.'

'I'll just have to set fire to the umbrellas, then,' April muttered, easing her pinching toes behind the bar.

It was much as Martina had predicted: the next hour was a rugby-scrum rush. No one however, seemed to miss the sparklers.

Jix's arrival at ten thirty relieved the tedium. In his smart black chauffeur's uniform, the bangles tucked up beneath his cuffs, and with his long hair tied back in a neat ponytail under his peaked cap, he caused quite a stir amongst the micro-skirted Lycra women.

Shoving his way through the crowd, he leaned his elbows on the bar. 'April! Have you got a minute?'

'You'll have to hang on – this is rocket science.' She paused in the middle of pouring a whole flight of B-52s into lowball glasses. It wasn't one of her favourites: the mixture of Kahlua, Baileys and Grand Marnier always seemed to want to separate at the wrong moment.

Eventually managing to get all six drinks looking reasonably the same, and covering any mishaps with two umbrellas and a mini-kebab of impaled fruit, she placed them on a tray and eased her way out into the bar. For once the recipients were housetrained, said thank you and gave her a huge tip. Still smiling her thanks, she tottered back behind the counter and pushed the ten-pound note into her pocket.

The shoes had now cut off the circulation to her toes.

'I thought you were supposed to be in Leicester Square?' She clung on to the bar in front of Jix, easing her feet out of the shoes, and immediately shrinking by six inches.

'I am. I was. I've got to be back there in an hour to collect them when they come out. I just had to tell you something.'

'Couldn't it keep? Oh –' she bit her lip – 'it's not about Noah, is it? They haven't cancelled his exhibition?'

'No – well, not as far as I know. It's nothing to do with Noah.'

April sighed happily. 'OK then, so what is it?'

'Seb and Brittany were at Ampney Crucis the same night as we were.'

'No! God – they couldn't have been! You must be mistaken.'

'No mistake. They chatter away in the back of that car like I'm a proper chauffeur – you know, signed the Gillespie official secrets act and all that. They were talking about the Frobisher Platinum, and about the places they'd been to, and they were discussing who was in and who was out, and all like I'd got my ears stuffed with cotton wool.'

April considered the implications. It had been a month since August Bank Holiday, and they'd both seen Sebastian a lot and Brittany a bit in that time, and nothing had been said. Therefore, even if Seb had been there, he couldn't have seen her or Jix – and certainly couldn't have connected Beatrice-Eugenie Padgett and Cair Paravel with two of his employees, could he? Someone – more than likely Martina – would have definitely sacked them, not to mention evicted them from number 51, if he had.

'Well, supposing you're right, and they were there – we must have got away with it, mustn't we? He can't have seen us. He can't have had a clue.'

Jix shook his head. 'No, by some miracle, I think you're right. I'll tell you, it took all my powers of concentration not to steer off the road when they were talking about it, though. I had to sit there, all impassive, and I thought my heart was going to stop beating. But this is the best bit: Brittany was saying that Ampney Crucis are still in with a chance.'

'You're kidding!'

'No. Seriously. She's seen everywhere now that's tendered, and there are four stadiums left in contention. Us at Bixford, Pullet's near Dagenham, that snazzy one at Chingford that I can never remember the name of –'

'Bentley's?'

'Yeah, that's it. And Ampney Crucis. So, three city ones, and one as far removed as you can get! My money, considering Seb's involvement, was on us. But –'

'There's more?' April grinned, after breaking off to serve a failed professional golfer and two born-again rock stars. 'You ought to do this chauffeuring thing more often. Go on.'

'Well, then Brittany said that she'd heard from that geezer that helped us out at Ampney Crucis – Ewan, was it? – and he's coming up to town to see her apparently. And Sebby didn't seem too concerned to be honest – and then she gets all bitchy and flings this Jasmine thing at him.'

'What, like a bunch of flowers? Or a twig? Or, no, jasmine is a bit shrubby, so I suppose it would be a branch, then. What – in the car? That's pretty dangerous.'

'April – shut up. Jasmine, as far as I could gather, is part of the Ampney Crucis setup and Brittany sounded dead sarky, which means it could be someone Sebby fancied. Anyway, if he's interested in someone from Ampney Crucis, and Brittany gets the nark about it, then it doesn't look good for the Platinum being held either here or there, does it?'

228

April mulled it over. 'No, I suppose not. But then, if Brittany is going to be seeing Ewan, that makes things even more complicated, doesn't it? Does she go with Ampney Crucis because of Ewan? Or against it because Sebby is dallying with the fragrant Jasmine? Christ, it'd finish Martina off completely if we lost out at Bixford because she thrust Sebby and Brittany together and they've each found someone else. A true case of biter bit or what?'

'I know – but I suppose the best part of it is, as long as they're preoccupied worrying about Ewan and Jasmine, and whether or not Bixford will get the Platinum, it'll certainly take the heat off Sebastian finding out about you having Bee and Cair Paravel in the flat, won't it?'

April smiled. 'Too true. God bless Ewan and Jasmine then, that's what I say. Oh, sod it. Here comes Martina – you'd better make yourself scarce.'

Jix unpeeled himself from the bar. 'I've got to be getting back to the cinema anyway. Look, if I don't see you before, good luck for tomorrow.'

'Thanks,' April nodded, watching him as he forged a path through the cocktail drinkers. The Lycra ladies all drooled in unison. It was kind of Jix to be so magnanimous, she thought. He'd never liked Noah.

Martina, dizzyingly resplendent in the skin-tight sequins, looked like an enraged twizzle stick as she wobbled her way towards the bar. Serve her damn well right, April thought, if Bixford lost out on the Frobisher's Brewery sponsorship and the subsequent massive influx of money that the Platinum Trophy would bring in, simply because of her meddling.

'April!' Martina's eldritch screech rocked the plastic palm tree to its man-made roots. 'You get them bloody shoes back on this minute!'

*

September the twenty-sixth, the day that had been ringed in fluorescent marker pen for weeks, dawned blue and golden and misty-warm. April, who having overnight made at least one decision, had opted against the father-daughter introduction taking place at the gallery, and dispatched Bee upstairs to Daff. She'd also taken Cair Paravel out for his run at dawn because she couldn't sleep, and was now shaking from head to foot.

'Stand still,' Sofia said. 'I can't get these damn pins in. God, girl, anyone would think it was your wedding day.'

April, with her teeth chattering, felt that in a way, that's exactly what it was.

Sofia and Tonio, who like Jix had lambasted Noah after his defection with the loft-liver, had turned up trumps. Antonio's brother had a nearly-new clothes stall on Bixford market, and Tonio and Sofia had arrived just as April and Cairey were returning from their morning exercise, with carrier bags full of potential outfits.

Sofia had again donated the Manolo Blahniks – it had been decided that today the glamour must outweigh the discomfort – and was now shortening a navy-blue cashmere sweater dress with ruthless determination.

'It'll look wonderful,' Sofia mumbled through a mouthful of pins. 'Elegant, classy – and like you're now worth a million dollars. Turn!'

April turned. 'I won't need a jacket or anything, will I?'

Sofia shook her head. 'Going to be warm. Just this and the shoes – oh, and a shoulder bag for your hankie for when you bawl. Not a handbag, mind. You'll need to keep your hands free. Turn!'

Antonio came through from the kitchen with more coffee supplies. April, who knew she couldn't eat anything, felt that she'd be jizzing with caffeine fizz for days. Never before had she been so nervous – not even when she went into labour with Beatrice-Eugenie, or when Cairey was about to run his first race.

'Hair up or down?' Sofia demanded when the hem was the right length and the dress had been whisked off to be pressed under a damp cloth.

April, in borrowed Agent Provocateur underwear from one of the other waitresses at the Copacabana, huddled on the sofa with her teeth rattling against her coffee cup. 'Down. Noah liked my hair long.'

'Make-up?'

'Just mascara and a touch of lippy. Noah hated made-up women.'

Sofia heaved a sigh and carried on ironing.

The taxi arrived at ten. April had decided to fork out for a cab from the chocolate tin money, because she knew she'd be far too anxious to cope with buses and the tube. Anyway, she'd thought, if by any chance Noah saw her arrive, it would do more for her image to be stepping from a black cab than to emerge blinking from Swaffield underground station with the rest of the tourists.

With everyone from number 51 waving her off – except Jix, of course, who had to be working at the Gillespies' house that morning – and Sofia and Antonio beaming at their handiwork like proud parents seeing a child off for its first day at school, April gave directions to the cab driver, and shrank back into her seat, feeling sick.

The journey took a little over half an hour, and tottering onto the pavement outside the Corner Gallery, April paid the driver, tipping generously because she knew better than most how important tips could be, then dared to look at her reflection in the gallery's plate-glass window. She had to admit that given the raw material, Sofia had done a stunning job. She looked elegant, assured, and had just the right amount of daytime glamour.

If she could just prevent her knees from knocking, she'd be fine.

The Corner Gallery's windows, white and spot-lit, all proclaimed that world-famous artist Noah Matlock would be attending to discuss his latest work and meet people during the day. It didn't say exactly when, but April was sure she couldn't have missed him. Noah wasn't an early riser. There were two of his paintings on display in the window, neither of which she'd seen before, but she guessed they belonged to his new French period. They were all greens and greys and blocks of granite-coloured shadows.

Trying to stop her tongue sticking to the roof of her mouth, she pushed open the door.

Inside, the Corner Gallery was a smaller version of the one where she'd sold the painting. Noah's pictures were all displayed on three-sided open screens, giving the room the air of a rather haphazard and unfinished maze. The gallery owner — at least April presumed the large woman in the autumn-hued caftan with matching lips and eyelids who was huddled in a corner with several people in baggy suits and thinning hair — was the gallery owner, was energetically extolling the virtue of a triptych of dark squares. Several other people were standing in front of the hessian-mounted paintings, referring back to their catalogues and murmuring.

Black and white photographs of Noah were dotted around the reception desk, and April felt the tears stinging her eyes. She'd had very few photos of him, and those she did have had been put away to show Bee when she was old enough to understand.

His image drew her like a hypnotised snake. These must be recent pictures, obviously taken against the rugged

232

French landscape, but Noah hadn't changed. His gorgeous battered rugby player's face still brooded, his shirt was well-worn denim, his jeans were faded.

Swamped with lust and memories, April turned away from the desk. She wanted to go home. Even if Noah turned up he'd probably have forgotten her, or worse, he'd remember her and not want to know. She must have been mad to do this. Then she remembered the dream: the cottage – and her and Bee and Noah living like a proper family – in Ampney Crucis – and knew that she owed it to Beatrice-Eugenie at least to try.

'Can I help you, madam?' The caftan-wearer rounded the nearest set of screens and beamed kindly. 'Is there a particular painting in which you're interested?'

'Um – no, not exactly. Er – I just wondered if – um – that is, what time Noah was going to be here?'

The caftan woman nodded knowingly. She was obviously used to dealing with Noah Matlock groupies. 'Mr Matlock will be giving a little talk at midday, after which I'm sure he'll be delighted to answer any questions.'

Not mine, he won't, April thought. She worked some more saliva into her mouth. 'I don't actually want to ask him sort of arty questions.'

The caftan-lady tapped her orange lips with a podgy forefinger. 'Well, I'm afraid Mr Matlock won't have time to sign autographs or anything. This is for serious art lovers only.'

Not for serious ex Noah lovers, then April thought. She shrugged. 'Oh, right . . . well, I'll just sort of wander for a bit.'

The orange caftan lady tsked a bit at the term 'wander'. However, one of the balding suits seemed to want to write a cheque, so with a final disparaging glance at April, she wobbled away.

Midday, April thought. She couldn't wait until midday. She'd burst all over the vinyl floor long before then.

More people were arriving now, and April scurried between the display screens, staring at the rather violent daubs of colour. Probably done when he was cross, she reckoned, wondering if he had the same blazing, blinding fits of temper with the loft-liver as he'd had with her. The rattle of glasses and the cool smell of cucumber made her peer round the screen. Waitresses were laying a centre table with French wines, French bread, and rustic salads. The balding people swooped down on them.

April, pretty sure that she was going to be sick, sidled round the next set of screens.

'. . . gets to be a bit of a chore sometimes, to be honest . . . I just want to paint – this sort of public stuff is a drag – especially with the plebs asking pathetic questions . . .' Pause for laughter. 'Oh, no – don't write that down! What? Oh, no – she prefers to stay at home when I'm on the tours . . .'

April felt the floor whooshing up to meet her. Sweatily, giddily, she clung on to the nearest screen.

Noah, with his back to her, was talking to a rather drab woman in a limp grey cardigan who was taking notes.

Peeping back round the screen again, she swallowed. The brown hair was still unruly, almost curly, down to the collar of the denim shirt; the buttocks and thighs, like a fly-half's, were squeezed into stretch denim; the shoulders were broad . . .

The journalist closed her notebook with a sycophantic smile, just as several of the balding suits trundled round the screen.

Noah's shoulders stiffened. 'Question time later, gentlemen . . . Right now I'm going to fortify myself with some of that delicious-looking wine. What? Oh, yeah, thanks –

I'm very proud of them, too. They're good, aren't they?'

Now completely giddy with desire, April propelled herself forward, bouncing off one of the suits.

'Hey!' Noah swung round. 'Careful! Mind where you're — Fucking hell!'

'Hello, Noah . . .'

All April's carefully rehearsed lines flew out of the gallery window. She'd forgotten how huge he was. Feeling dwarfed by his physical presence, and knowing that the suits were all staring, she tried a smile. It didn't work. Noah, looking completely poleaxed, seemed as tongue-tied as she was.

Clearing her throat, she attempted to speak normally. It came out squeaky. 'Er — it's nice to see you again . . .'

'Is it?' Noah blinked. 'Oh, yeah, right . . . You look — well, great. Yeah.'

There was a deafening and profound silence between them. The gallery browsers who had discovered the food and drink were clattering glasses and rattling plates. April suddenly felt an overwhelming urge to throw her arms round Noah and kiss him to death.

'You've — um — done very well . . .' She indicated the hessian screens. 'You must be proud — that is — pleased . . .'

'Yeah. It's gone well. Er . . .' He looked round as though wanting to escape, but failing to find a bolt hole, simply shrugged. 'And you? What are you doing with yourself?'

'This and that . . .' April knew that to talk to him properly, to be able to tell him that he was a father, it would have to be away from here. 'Are you and . . . ?' She couldn't mention the loft-liver; anyway she'd never known her name. 'That is — are you in England for long?'

'A week or so.' Noah looked her up and down. 'And no, Anoushka has stayed in France. You know, you do look exceptionally pretty . . . Tell you what, if you'd like

235

to hang about until this little do is over, maybe we could have a drink together? Just for old times' sake?'

'Oh, yes!' April forgot all about being cool. She forgot the agony of his leaving, the nights she'd cried, the struggle to survive, the awfulness of having a baby alone. She was here, and Noah was here, and he was seducing her with his eyes — and the dream was going to come true. 'Yes, that would be wonderful.'

chapter nineteen

'Oooh – this is the life.' Clara stretched out in her deck chair on the beach hut's veranda, a depleted glass of Chardonnay dangling from one lethargic hand. 'I can't believe that it's officially autumn. It must be even hotter today than it was in July.' Lazily, she raised the glass in salute. 'God bless global warming and all the little holes in the ozone layer.'

'The end of September's always the best time for a heatwave,' Jasmine agreed. 'Most of the tourists have gone, and the beach is practically deserted – not to mention the Crumpled Horn.'

Clara drained her glass, dropped her Raybans down over her eyes, and surrendered herself to the sun. Jasmine, having dared to bare her legs in a pair of cut-off jeans and most of her upper body in a vest, swigged the last drops from a bottle of Old Ampney ale, propped her feet up on the balustrade, and settled down into her canvas chair.

September, as well as being warm enough to warrant 'It's A Scorcha!' headlines in the tabloids, had also, for Jasmine, been wondrously idle. True to form, Damon and his boys were running well behind on the refurbishment of the stadium, so she'd had little to do. Well, she thought, that wasn't strictly true. She'd had nothing at all to do as a bookmaker, but absolutely tons to do otherwise.

There'd been the showdown with Andrew — not to mention her parents — and then her meetings with Peg about putting Ampney Crucis well and truly on the map once the Benny Clegg Stadium reopened. And, of course, there'd been Sebastian.

'So . . .' Clara's voice was drowsy, only just audible above the sleepy rush of the waves and the crying of the gulls. 'You've heard from him again, have you?'

Jasmine smiled to herself. 'I had another letter this morning.'

'How quaintly old-fashioned,' Clara yawned. 'I don't know anyone who writes letters any more. Everyone uses e-mail or mobile phones.'

'As I haven't got e-mail and he doesn't have my mobile number,' Jasmine said, 'he would have found that a bit difficult. Anyway, he likes writing letters. So do I. And he sends me doughnuts on same-day delivery.'

'Christ! Coals to Newcastle or what? Why on earth should anyone send doughnuts to you — when you have a standing order for supplies from the Crow's Nest Caff?'

'These are different ones — any that he finds that have unusual fillings or toppings. He sent me coffee and walnut ones last week.'

Clara sighed. 'God, the last of the true romantics. What-ever happened to bunches of roses and buckets of champagne?'

'I prefer doughnuts,' Jasmine grinned. 'They're far more personal.'

Meeting Sebastian in St Edith's graveyard on August Bank Holiday Monday had been a revelation; meeting him again later at the stadium had been like a dream. A dream, Jasmine had to admit, which had turned a bit sour when she'd realised that he was the delectable Brittany's other half. But then, as he wasn't thinking of her, plain old

238

Jasmine, as a serious contender in the romance stakes, Brittany Frobisher hadn't been overly important in the equation.

And anyway, Sebastian had just been so easy to talk to, and he'd understood her sadness, and – and it was a huge plus, of course – he was, without doubt, the most gorgeous man she'd ever seen in her life.

Clara had been hopping mad at missing out on this tall, lean, tanned vision, with his floppy brown hair and ice-blue eyes, and his lovely crooked grin, and the freckles on his nose . . . Clara, it must be said, was now getting a little bit tired of hearing about them.

'It's the sort of thing you should have done years ago,' she'd groaned when Jasmine was telling her about how sensationally wonderful Sebastian was for the five hundredth time. 'When we were at school. Getting crushes on the most glamorous boys in the sixth form, writing their names on your pencil case, doing that love word-puzzle thing where you cross off corresponding letters of your name and his – that sort of thing. Even if you knew they wouldn't look at you twice.'

'Cheers,' Jasmine had said sharply. 'I do know where I stand, without you having to remind me.'

'Oh, God, Jas – sorry. I didn't mean –'

'Yes, you did. Brittany Frobisher is constantly in the Top Ten Most Beautiful Women in Britain. Sebastian is stinking rich – not to mention drop-dead desirable. I'm well aware that I'm none of those. We're just friends.'

And they were, Jasmine thought now, feeling the sun tingle on her bare arms. They'd been strangers who had become friends in the cemetery when he'd been so kind about Grandpa, and were still friends again later when she'd dropped the drinks in Peg's office. That had been so embarrassing, but she couldn't help it. She'd been out in the kitchen, mixing the lemon barley, thinking about Sebastian, mourning the fact that they'd never meet again – then she'd walked into the office and – well!

And in the month since, he'd written her lovely chatty funny letters, with little cartoon drawings around the edges illustrating some of the things he'd been doing – and he seemed to do an awful lot. She'd been rather disturbed to discover that his parents were *the* Gillespies who owned the monstrous art deco greyhound stadium in Bixford. It seemed that this very fact – plus, of course, his involvement with Brittany – would rule the Benny Clegg Stadium out of any sort of contention for the Frobisher Platinum Trophy. However, because she hadn't wanted Sebastian to be cast as the villain of the piece she hadn't mentioned this to Peg or Allan or Roger. Neither had she mentioned Ewan's brief to seduce Brittany, should it be necessary, to Clara.

'And so,' Clara wriggled down her skimpy bikini top even further, 'what does Andrew make of all this postal snogging?'

'It's not like that – unfortunately. And after what Andrew said about my parents he knows he'll be treading on very thin ice if he even *thinks* anything controversial in future.'

'Jas – sweetie – I know I've said this a million times, but you had the perfect opportunity to dump Andrew that night. Why the hell are you still with him?'

'I don't know really,' Jasmine sighed. 'It's just that when he'd suggested we buy a house together it seemed well, cruel, to tell him that I didn't think I even wanted to stay with him. I mean, it's not his fault, is it?'

Clara slithered down in her chair. 'Give me strength! You'd forgive Attila the Hun for indiscretions! Of course it's Andrew's fault – he's a complete prat. And you're not stupid; you surely must realise that he's only hanging on to you because you're suddenly a lady of substance.'

Jasmine cheerfully patted her ample thighs. 'I've always been that.'

Clara sighed heavily. 'You know exactly what I mean, Jas. He's a money-grabbing toad. Now, unless you're going to talk about the glorious Sebastian, please shut up and let a dynamic career woman catch up on her sleep. Oh, and –' she lifted one frame of the Raybans and squinted across the veranda – 'I do hope you've realised that Mrs Seb Gillespie sounds a damn sight better than Mrs Andrew Pease?'

'Oh pul-eease!' Jasmine pulled a face. 'Now who's being infantile? Not to mention antifeminist. I'm always going to be Jasmine Clegg.'

And that, she thought, was probably the whole sad truth.

The showdown with Andrew, weeks ago now – on the day that she'd heard her mother cooing from behind the windbreak – had certainly changed the relationship. She'd lost her temper completely, and absolutely refused to share the feather mattress or the poppy and daisy duvet ever since. However, Andrew was still clinging on tenaciously to their engagement, and Jasmine was still dithering over the pros and cons.

Andrew had dared to suggest, that night, that Jasmine must have been totally mistaken about Yvonne and – even more outrageously – that it was her father who was having an extramarital fling. Philip, according to Andrew, who said he'd been treated to chapter and verse by a heartbroken Yvonne, had been having an affair for years, and that was the real reason behind the separate bedrooms. Andrew had found out about it, he'd said, when he'd called at the Chewton Estate house and found Yvonne in tears over another potential public humiliation at a council dinner, and had been sworn to secrecy. Yvonne, he'd maintained, hadn't wanted Jasmine to know.

241

Jasmine, however, had scoffed at the whole idea. She'd *known* it was her mother's voice on the beach, and she'd heard her mother whispering into the telephone, hadn't she? And who in their right mind would ever fancy her father? And Andrew had to admit that Yvonne hadn't actually been able to name names, but that the Ampney Crucis gossips had had Moira Cook, councillor for Parks and Cemeteries, down as the main contender for some time.

Moira Cook, as Jasmine had sharply pointed out, was practically in her dotage and had been spotted buying incontinence knickers in the Bournemouth branch of Boots. Anyway, Jasmine had said frostily, both Yvonne and Philip were far too old to be even thinking about sex, let alone doing it. The whole concept was disgusting.

'Then why not ask them yourself?' Andrew had snorted, red in the face. 'Get it straight from the horse's mouth!'

'Not a nice way to describe my mother,' Jasmine had smiled in the darkness. 'Even if it is quite apt – and especially not after you said she was top totty.'

'I did not! I said a lot of my workmates said they wouldn't mind giving her – that is – um – thought that she was very attractive – for her age, of course . . .'

And then after they'd argued about that, she and Andrew had argued even more about spending her bookmaking profits on buying a prenuptial house. She'd maintained fiercely that she was more than happy in the beach hut – and Andrew had retorted that he would never be able to hold up his head at the dealership again if he had to live in a shed.

And that, Jasmine thought cheerfully, watching the waves roll gently onto the pale sand, was how they'd left it. The tiny diamond remained on her engagement finger, mainly because, thanks to Sebastian's exotic doughnut supplies, she'd recently gained a few more pounds and nothing short of bolt croppers would remove it. In fact, she reckoned, it would probably take bolt croppers to remove Andrew from her life too.

She had, a few days after Andrew's revelations, asked both her parents, separately of course, if there was any truth in the rumours. Their reactions, if she hadn't been quite so personally involved, had been quite interesting.

Philip, in the Crumpled Horn, demanding to know where Jasmine had heard such salacious rumours had then choked on his shepherd's pie and turned purple and had had to be revived with three fingers of whisky. Once breathing again, he'd said that he and Yvonne had been happily married for over thirty years, and that he would never, ever, cheat on his wedding vows. Jasmine, knowing that he cheated on his expenses and his tax returns, hadn't been totally convinced. However, the thought of Philip, pompous and pot bellied, rolling naked with the crepey Moira Cook did seem to be way beyond the bounds of even the most fevered imagination.

Yvonne, in her turn, had said that yes, she may have said that Philip was an unfaithful bastard to Andrew on that occasion, but she'd been in a temper with Philip at the time because he was away on another golfing weekend, and she was quite, quite sure that Moira Cook, or any other council crone come to mention it, wasn't in the frame. When Jasmine had rather unwisely suggested that Yvonne, too, may be having a bit of a fling, her mother had giggled and said that unless Mel Gibson moved to Ampney Crucis she was afraid she'd be staying monogamous.

It had all been rather unsatisfactory, really. And now, Jasmine thought, watching the gulls sweep lazily over the shoreline, picking off tiny crabs caught in the shallows of the receding tide, even she was wondering if she may just have been mistaken about the voice from the windbreak. She hadn't imagined the telephone call, though. It was all rather perplexing, but as her parents didn't seem to be on the verge of divorce, she'd decided to let matters lie. She had far more important realities occupying her mind to waste time on speculations.

The decision she'd made to put Ampney Crucis on the greyhound fraternity's map had been down to the meeting with Sebastian as well. Obliquely, of course, but still because of him. Once she'd discovered his Bixford connections, she'd realised that whatever miracle rabbits Damon Puckett and his boys pulled out of the refurbishment hat, the Benny Clegg Stadium would never hold a candle to the Gillespies' super-duper multimillion pound glitterati racetrack.

Therefore, because they obviously wouldn't be getting to stage the Frobisher Platinum Trophy at Ampney Crucis, she felt the least they could do would be to bring in more people – punters, visitors, owners and trainers – from outside the area. People like that family from London whose dog had won after Ewan had tied the headscarf on the hare, for example. There had been a bit of a stewards' inquiry after the race, but the result had been allowed to stand – mainly because there was absolutely nothing in the Greyhound Racing Association handbook about whether or not the hare should be dressed or undressed – and the London couple had gone off proudly with their little trophy and promised to come back.

So, without consulting Peg or Roger or Allan – Jasmine had felt that at their age any build-up of expectation followed swiftly by disappointment may prove fatal – she'd contacted the GRA about the possibility of the Benny Clegg Stadium staging a Six-Pack Night every Saturday. The GRA had responded swiftly with a huge yes, and had sent her a bulky package containing everything she needed to know. It had arrived this morning, at the same time as Sebastian's letter, and Jasmine had propped it on the overcrowded chiffonier and kissed the postman.

All she had to do now was sell this idea to the rest of the board members and start the advertising campaign, and then the problem of dark, wet, winter nights at the stadium with few punters and, for her, little income, would be solved at a stroke. She felt it was a huge step forward – and one which a year ago the Jasmine Clegg who'd worked for Watertite Windows and had been extremely grateful to Andrew for a fumbling and unsatisfactory night of one-sided passion, would never have had the guts to take.

'Clara?' She leaned precariously from her deck chair. 'Are you asleep?'

'Trying hard. Shut up. Unless you want to talk about sex.'

Jasmine didn't. She didn't have any to talk about. 'I just wondered if you knew where Ewan was today.'

'Why? Oh – do you want to talk about our sex life?'

'Not really, thanks. I just needed to get everyone together at the stadium later on. Peg, Roger and Allan are no problem – they'll be there anyway, stalking Damon and his boys and getting in the way. And Bunny and Gilbert'll be fishing off the slipway behind Eddie Deebley's. Finding Ewan is the problem . . .'

'Not for me, it isn't,' Clara said smugly. 'I know exactly where to lay my hands on him.'

Jasmine groaned. Clara and Ewan were hopelessly uninhibited. 'Don't be smutty. It's too hot – and I'm celibate so it's not fair. So, where is he?'

'London, for a few days,' Clara said without opening her eyes. 'He's on a mission.'

Jasmine's heart sank. The mission was, without doubt, called Brittany Frobisher.

Two hours later, glowing from the sun despite larding herself with Factor 10, Jasmine negotiated the jumble of furniture in the beach hut and managed to shower, fall over things, and get changed into a pair of baggy combat trousers and a nicely accommodating T-shirt without waking Clara. Then, leaving a note suggesting that they should meet up in the Crumpled Horn later, Jasmine trudged up the cliff steps and headed for the stadium.

Here, chaos reigned supreme. Damon Puckett and his boys seemed to have conspired to create a bomb site. Jasmine winced at the continuing devastation. She'd last been here a couple of days ago and had hoped it would have started to show an improvement. It hadn't. She was beginning to think that it would never, ever be all right again.

'Hello, pet!' Peg, in shirtwaister and wellington boots, and with a construction worker's hard hat rammed on top of the Doris Day bubble curls, tramped happily towards her. 'Coming on a treat, isn't it?'

Allan and Roger, picking their way more gingerly through the debris in Peg's wake – also wearing hard hats and looking like the geriatric chapter of The Village People – were beaming too. It must be something to do with senility and copious amounts of Wincarnis, Jasmine thought, that gave them all such a rosy perspective on life.

'Er – yes . . . I suppose so. There still seems to be an awful lot left to do. When are they expecting to be finished?'

'Another couple of weeks at least, Damon says.'

'Two weeks!' Jasmine shook her head. 'That'll mean they'll have taken six weeks to do a fortnight's work!'

'You can't hurry craftsmen.' Peg looked shocked. 'They're creating a masterpiece here. Anyway, we want it to be absolutely perfect for the Frobisher's thingy, don't we?'

Jasmine groaned. There was still no way on earth that she could tell Peg that because Brittany Frobisher and Sebastian were an item, the Bixford stadium was going to get the Platinum Trophy – and that all the other applicants were merely window-dressing.

'Oh – er – yes, I suppose so. Anyway, I've got some more good news.'

'Really?' Peg looked very animated. 'Has Andrew tumbled over the cliff and been swept away on the neap tide never to be seen again?'

As Jasmine felt rather treacherous about Andrew at the moment she decided to make no comment. It was worrying to discover that the image of Andrew, buoyed by his own pomposity and an inflated polo shirt, bobbing out into the Solent, painted quite a pleasant picture. She concentrated instead on the demolition site.

The picture here was far from pleasant. Jasmine gazed at the scene with mounting horror. Damon's boys, who, thanks to the Glastonbury trip, now looked like a tribe of Carlos Santanas, were just bringing down the stadium's corrugated tin roof with all the enthusiasm of children pushing over sand castles. The whole thing made Jasmine feel rather sad. So many of her Benny-memories were being swept away with the rubble.

'Isn't there anywhere a bit – er – quieter? Your office?'

'Went this morning,' Peg shouted cheerfully above the sound of tearing tin and concrete. 'We could hole up in the kennels area if you like. Damon's finished over there. But you must wear a hard hat, pet, if you're staying on site.'

Jasmine winced. The hard hat made her look like a boiled egg. However, as Peg was now wheedling one out of Damon and calling him poppet, she felt it would be churlish to refuse.

Once she was suitably hatted, and with Roger, Allan and Peg stumbling over the detritus in a rather unsteady Indian file, they made their way to the kennels, which was currently the only serene corner of the stadium.

Jasmine had to admit that if Damon tarted up the stadium to the same standard he'd employed on the kennels, then maybe things wouldn't be too bad at all. The kennels had always been well-maintained, of course. Peg's love of animals was even better documented in Ampney Crucis than her love of Doris Day. Now, the kennels and runs were larger, and there were more of them. There was also a little sort of office place for the owners and trainers to sit on navy-blue chairs, and a whole spaghetti bowl of wires poking through the rough-plastered walls.

'Just the last cosmetic bits to do,' Peg said. 'A nice coat of candy pink – everyone loves pink, don't they? And the electrics all connected up for the screen in here so that everyone can see what's going on, and wireless trans- mission. Very high-tech, don't you think? Oh, and, I meant to say to you – although Roger and Allan have agreed already so you've been outvoted if you don't approve – on the night of the Frobisher Platinum, we'll have some other bookies, big boys: Ladbrokes . . . Willie Hill . . .'

Jasmine nodded without saying anything. She knew that the new plans included the provision of half a dozen Tote windows. There was absolutely no point in protesting about multinational bookmakers being engaged for an event that certainly wasn't going to happen.

'So,' Peg perched on one of the polythene-wrapped chairs, 'what's your news?'

Jasmine took a deep breath and rattled off the concept of the Saturday Six-Pack Nights. For ten pounds a head the punters would get admission to the stadium and free parking, a racecard, a meal – probably something and chips, which she'd thought Gilbert and Eddie Deebley could combine on – two pints of Old Ampney, a Tote voucher – and a free-admission ticket for a return visit.

'And,' she concluded, 'because the GRA are keen to up the image of dog racing, this will make it available to so many people – families and so on – who might otherwise have thought a night at the dogs was beyond them, or not something they'd enjoy. I've already drafted adverts for the local press, and Clara is going to get Makings Paper to produce flyers and –'

'Absolutely brilliant!' Peg hugged her. 'Oh, pet – what a trooper! What with this and the Frobisher Trophy, we'll really put the Benny Clegg Stadium on the map!'

'Benny would have rightly been proud of you, my love,' Roger said gruffly.

Allan twanged his braces. 'A right little chip off the old block.'

Jasmine swallowed the lump in her throat. She still missed Benny so much. It was awful, to be surrounded by people who cared about her, all her friends, and still feel so lonely.

'Excuse me.' A voice echoed through from the kennels. 'Ms Dunstable? Are you in here? The workman said I'd find you here.'

'Bugger.' Peg straightened her wig. 'Another bloody rep. They swarm in like flies round a cowpat. Always trying to sell me something I don't want.' She turned towards the kennels. 'Yes – I'm here. Come on through, but I'm not buying anything.'

'That's good,' Sebastian smiled, appearing in the door-

way and ducking beneath a particularly lethal bunch of
loose wires, 'because I'm not selling anything.'

Jasmine frantically tugged at the unflattering hard hat,
but it appeared to have welded itself to her perspiring
forehead.

Sebastian's smile turned into a beam as he spotted her.
'Oh, great. I'd hoped you'd be here. I've brought you
some strawberry and cream doughnuts.'

'Oh . . . really? Thank you . . . um . . .' Jasmine gave
up clutching at the hat and beamed back.

She only hoped the beam was steady, because suddenly
the rest of her certainly wasn't.

chapter twenty

Jasmine's next coherent thought was one of relief mingled with frustration. If Sebastian was here then so was Brittany: which was bad for her, but good for Clara, because it meant that whatever Ewan was doing in London, it obviously didn't involve the fragrant Ms Frobisher.

'I've left them in the car,' Sebastian continued to smile at her. 'The doughnuts, that is. In a cool box. I thought they'd go well with some of that beer.'

'Oh, yes – they will . . . I mean – thank you.' Jasmine had another surreptitious go at easing off the hard hat without him noticing. It was difficult when he was looking at her and she was attempting to appear unfazed, and anyway it still refused to budge.

This was appalling – being face to face with the one man on earth who could make her legs wobble, with her head rammed into an upside-down po.

No, she thought as she did isometrics with her forehead, it was even worse than appalling. Because as well as the towering feeling of relief at knowing that Clara wasn't being cheated on, Jasmine was also swamped by the awful realisation that she'd fallen in love.

She exhaled. She'd done some foolish things in her time, but falling in love with Sebastian Gillespie had to take the biscuit. She might as well have a badge pinned to the left-hand side of her T-shirt proclaiming. 'Here's my heart – now break it.'

'It's lovely to see you!' Peg, who obviously had no problems about wearing her hat in Sebastian's presence, was now batting the false eyelashes alarmingly. 'We were just talking about you, weren't we, Jasmine, pet?'

Jasmine, pretending not to be wrestling with the hat or her conscience, sketched a smile. 'Um – yes, sort of . . . about the stadium and things . . . you know . . .'

Sebastian grinned again. Jasmine wished he wouldn't keep doing it. She also wished she'd had far more practice at being overwhelmed by lust, love, or whatever this feeling thundering around inside her was. If she'd splurged sporadically in her teens, as Clara had suggested, then surely she'd have been much more adept at handling this situation. It was far, far too late now to start writing 'I ♥ Sebastian Gillespie' on her pencil case.

Love, for her, had been a timid visitor. As she'd only ever been in love with Andrew, and that simply out of habit, falling in love seemed to be something that Clara did every other month or so, and Ewan did all the time, and the heroines in her favourite Mills and Boon books did with unsuitable men who loved them madly, truly, deeply in return by the end of the novel. Falling in love surely took absolutely ages, after candlelit dinners, and romantic walks in the moonlight, and parties and – well, *knowing* someone. Falling in love didn't happen like a thunderbolt out of the blue. And certainly not to her.

Peg, Roger and Allan were now clustered round Sebastian, their voices all trying to outdo one another as they told him about the Phoenix-like resurrection of the Stadium and Jasmine's plans for the Six-Pack Saturday nights. Jasmine desperately wanted to throttle all of them, to silence them quickly, before they made complete fools of themselves. Seb, with his Bixford stadium connections, would surely be laughing himself silly. Well, no, maybe he wouldn't. He was kind and compassionate, she knew that. But surely, surely, he'd stop them before they went too far?

Anyway, who was she kidding? Peg and Roger and Allan may well be making fools of themselves with Sebastian, but what about her? Wasn't that exactly what she was about to do too? It was some comfort to know that in her letters at least, she'd given him no hint of how she felt about him. Her replies had been jokey and full of Ampney Crucis anecdotes; they hadn't said anything personal at all. Then, of course, she didn't know that she loved him when she was writing the letters, did she? She'd thought he was lovely, yes, and beautiful, and kind, and funny and – Oh, for God's sake!

She tried to take herself in hand with a severe mental talking-to. People like her just didn't fall in love with people like Sebastian Gillespie. Oh yes, but they did, she thought sadly. All the time. It just wasn't reciprocated. The emotion remained a one-sided adulation. And that was exactly how it must stay. She mustn't give Seb any idea at all about how she felt.

Finally managing to wriggle off the hard hat while he was otherwise engaged and lose it behind one of the shrink-wrapped chairs, Jasmine allowed herself the hedonistic and totally destructive pleasure of studying Sebastian at close quarters. Once Brittany – who was no doubt outside having a good giggle over Damon and his boys trying to drag the stadium into a pale Bixford comparison – arrived, the moment would be lost for ever. Wearing faded jeans and a T-shirt, smiling interestedly as he listened to Peg, Seb was unbelievably gorgeous. Jasmine had to clamp her teeth together to prevent the groan of despair escaping. Her imagination and memory simply hadn't done him justice. He was truly wonderful. She'd just bet that Brittany spent lazy Sunday mornings curled beneath Egyptian cotton sheets lovingly counting his freckles . . .

Fighting the sudden desire to see Brittany bobbing across to the Isle of Wight on the same inflated ego trip as Andrew, Jasmine tried instead to concentrate on what Sebastian was saying. It seemed to involve a lot of references to Frobishers, but then she supposed it would. He was probably inviting Peg to the It Girl wedding of the year at Westminster Abbey or wherever it was that It Girls could pack in the most celebrity crowds.

'Oooh!' Peg suddenly broke into the conversation. 'Well! There's a turn up!'

Roger and Allan were puffing out their chests and showing their gums.

'Have I missed something?' Jasmine had already arranged her face into its resigned acceptance mode. 'Are congratulations in order?'

'They are, pet!' Peg hugged her. 'What a splendiferous day!'

'I was just explaining,' Sebastian said, 'that the short list for the Frobisher Platinum Trophy has been drawn up. There are four stadiums in contention – three near London, and yours.'

Jasmine blinked. 'Mine? Ours? Here, do you mean?'

'That's exactly what he means.' Peg was bouncing up and down independently of her wellingtons. 'We're going to be famous!'

'We're only shortlisted,' Jasmine said gently, knowing they'd get no further. She'd bet the beach hut that Bixford was also amongst the finalists. 'But it's wonderful news, and it was very kind of Sebastian and Brittany to come down here to tell us.'

Sebastian shook his head. 'Brittany isn't with me. She's telling the other stadiums the good news. As they were all quite close together it made sense to split up and do it this way. Anyway, I had a doughnut delivery to make.'

Jasmine's shriek of laughter sounded horrendously phoney even to her. She snapped her mouth shut so that the awful noise shouldn't be repeated. And Brittany was in London – and so was Ewan. Oh, sod it.

Peg came to the rescue. 'And the final decision will be taken when exactly, pet?'

'New Year's Eve,' Sebastian said. 'The Frobishers are having a black-tie dinner with dancing afterwards, to which they're inviting all the shortlisted participants, plus the press, of course. It's all good publicity for Frobisher's Brewery, not to mention the winning stadium. Brittany's excellent at stage-managing these things. She's arranging it like a sort of awards ceremony.'

'What – like the Eurovision Song Contest?' Peg squealed with excitement. Everyone in Ampney Crucis knew it was one of her favourite events. She always backed Norway. 'Oh, my!'

Seb smiled gently. 'Well, sort of like that, but maybe not quite so exciting. More like the Booker Prize.'

Peg's face fell momentarily, then she brightened. 'And we're invited? All of us? Up to London?'

'That's how Brittany has planned it, yes.'

Taking his face in both hands, Peg kissed Seb full on the lips. 'If you were only a bit older, pet, I'd give you such a good time!' She let him go and twinkled at Roger and Allan. 'Let's go and tell the news to the rest of the chaps, shall we?'

Jasmine, who wondered if she could get away with kissing Sebastian too and deciding she couldn't had a sudden rather scary vision of Peg, Gilbert and Bunny at a black-tie dinner. Not to mention Roger and Allan, who would probably wear their de-mob suits and – Oh my God! Her, as well. As a board member she'd be expected to attend – and wear a frock and probably a tiara and have to dance gavottes.

Whimpering, she watched as Peg, Roger and Allan returned to their Wilson, Keppel and Betty formation, wheeled smartly on the new lino and shuffled excitedly out of the kennels' would-be reception area – obviously hell-bent on sharing the good news as soon as possible with Gilbert and Bunny.

'So – er – are you going back to Bixford now?' Jasmine asked, blinking at Sebastian as they picked their way out into the afternoon sunshine.

'Not yet. I wondered if you'd like to join me for a drink? To wash down the doughnuts.'

Having to damp down the overwhelming urge to hurl herself into his arms and declare undying devotion, Jasmine managed to shrug noncommittally. 'Why not?'

Oh God, she thought, following his long denim thighs through the bomb site – there were a million excellent reasons why not. All of them linked to her heart being beaten to a mulch.

'They're getting on really well here with the rebuilding, aren't they?' Seb said conversationally over his shoulder. 'This is going to look really swish. Ms Dunstable was just telling me about the Six-Pack setup as well. It'll all draw the punters in.'

'With luck,' Jasmine muttered, trying hard not to fall over. The hat had been embarrassing enough; tumbling to the ground amongst the debris would definitely be the final straw. 'Is the Six-Pack something you do at Bixford?'

'Have done for ages, yes. It's a great way to introduce greyhound racing to families, and people who probably think going to the dogs involves beating a path through thugs and spivs. But this –' Sebastian stopped walking and looked back at the building site – 'this is just brilliant. You can imagine it when it's finished, can't you? Almost feel the atmosphere of the crowds, the dogs running under the lights, the sheer adrenaline rush . . .'

Jasmine walked on, waiting for him to catch up. 'You really love it, don't you?'

'I've never known anything else.'

She clamped her arms to her sides just in case they took on a life of their own and snaked their way round his neck. 'And is Bixford one of the shortlisted stadiums?'

They'd reached the new temporary car park. It was a shingle extension of the beach with flocks of gulls swooping and screaming overhead. The old car park had disappeared three weeks earlier beneath skips and corrugated iron and misshapen lumps of concrete. Several small children were risking life and limb by scrambling cheerfully amongst it.

Sebastian nodded. 'Yes, but that doesn't mean –'

Jasmine sucked in her breath. 'No, of course it doesn't.'

But she knew it did. Brittany Frobisher would make damn sure that the Gillespies got the Platinum Trophy. It made perfect sense. The black-tie awards ceremony was simply a lavish publicity stunt.

'Is your car here?' Seb asked as they scrunched over the shingle. 'Or shall we take mine?'

'No and no.' Jasmine was quite pleased with the jauntiness of her reply. It made her sound almost normal rather than the simpering love-sick fool she felt she was. 'I haven't got a car, and you won't need yours. It's only a short distance to walk.'

Sebastian looked a bit shocked at her car-less revelation. 'You don't drive?'

'Yes, I can drive – no, I don't most of the time. It's

not like London – everything here is really close together. My home, my work, the Crumpled Horn – everything. It's so easy.'

'But what about when you need to go further afield?'

'Oh, I can always use one of my parents' cars, or get one from Andrew.'

'Andrew?'

'My fiancé. He works in a car dealership. Or I could beg a lift with Clara or Ewan . . .' She stopped. She hadn't told him about any of them in her letters. He might remember Ewan from his previous visit to the stadium, but she didn't want to bombard him with unnecessary faceless names. He'd never meet them. 'Anyway, you just won't need the car at the moment. It's a really nice walk.'

Sebastian gave a derisive snort. 'Christ! I haven't walked anywhere for years! I'll probably need mouth-to-mouth resuscitation. OK, hang on then while I just grab the doughnuts.' He headed towards a navy-blue Mercedes convertible, then paused. 'Are we going to eat them on the beach?'

Jasmine took a deep breath. 'Actually, I've got an even better idea . . .'

The walk along the cliff path was one of Jasmine's lifelong pleasures. This afternoon, seeing it through Sebastian's eyes, she was anxious that he should find it wonderful, too.

So far, she thought, he seemed to be enjoying it. The sea glittered with sequins; puffs of butterflies, blue and red and yellow, darted up from the scrubby gorse and ferns beneath their feet; and the maze of narrow, overgrown sandy paths snaked away in all directions.

'It's an amazing place.' Sebastian shifted the cool box to the other hand. 'You're so lucky to live here. But then you already know that, don't you?'

Jasmine did. She was also irritated by the fact that she felt unable to chat to him with the ease that she had on their first meeting, or even the way she did in her letters. She felt that if she dropped her guard, he'd be able to read the conflicting emotions tumbling around inside her. And the thought of watching him and Brittany hosting this sham celebratory black-tie dinner, confident with the social situation and about each other, gnawed uncomfortably at her heart.

'I thought we weren't going to picnic on the beach?' Sebastian said as Jasmine turned onto the cliff steps.

'We're not.' She continued to lead the way down. It was quite pleasant to have the upper hand. 'I thought I'd show you where I live.'

They'd exchanged addresses. Sebastian's home – Marliver House, The Green, Bixford – she'd imagined as being like her parents' house on the Chewton Estate. The beach hut would probably therefore come as something of a shock.

'Oh, right, that'd be nice. You've never said what your place is like – although I suppose the address being 12 Beach Walk should have given me some sort of clue that it was near the sea.'

'Very near.' Jasmine grinned to herself. 'Turn left at the bottom of the steps, along this path – no, not on to the next set of steps – they just lead down to the beach . . . here we are . . .'

She stopped walking. Sebastian almost collided with her. Although she hadn't turned round, she could sense that he was perplexed. Having only a momentary pang of doubt over the wisdom of inviting him to the beach hut – it would be awful if Clara was still there, stretched out as she'd been when Jasmine had left her, lithe and oiled and wearing only a thong – she grinned over her shoulder.

'We just need to squeeze between these – the blue one and this one.'

She stepped into the cool shadow of the gully between the huts and stepped out again at the front of the row. The sun-scorched veranda was mercifully empty of everything – including Clara.

Sebastian was looking at the ice-cream row in total astonishment.

'Here? You live here? In a beach hut?'

'Yep.' She unlocked the door. 'Oh, and if you're coming in, I'd better warn you that it's a bit crowded.'

Sebastian climbed on to the veranda, stepped into the hut and gazed around him, wide-eyed. Jasmine, rescuing the cool box, finding plates in the over-the-sink cupboard and bottles of Old Ampney in the fridge, had to squeeze past him with every manoeuvre. It was lovely.

He still hadn't said anything, but she was aware of him looking at the chiffonier and the walnut clock and the Staffordshire highwaymen, and her grandparents' photo, then through the doorway to the bedroom and the tangle of poppies and daisies where she'd forgotten to make the bed, and back to the fat armchair and the sofa and the tiny television and all her worldly possessions.

He sucked in his breath. 'It's fucking fantastic.'

'I'll take that as a compliment then, shall I?'

'Too right –' Sebastian exhaled. 'Jasmine, this is amazing. You can see the sea from the bedroom and from, well, everywhere – and –' He stopped and shrugged. 'It's just the most bloody perfect home I've ever seen.'

'Thank you. I think so as well.' She beamed at him, all awkwardness evaporating. It didn't matter that she loved him and he would never know. They were friends, and they'd always be friends. Love would only mess that up. 'It belonged to my grandparents. Grandpa left it to me. I'll never leave it.'

'God – nor me. I mean, that is, if I were you . . .'

Sebastian was studying the pictures on the walls, the photographs, the images of Benny. 'Is this you and him? He looks great. You take after him, don't you? Oh, and this has to be you when you were at school! You haven't changed a bit! Are these all your friends?'

Jasmine nodded. 'Me, Clara, Ewan and Andrew – yes. We've know each other all our lives.'

'Really? What, Andrew the fiancé – you mean you've known him for ever?'

She nodded again, wanting to change the subject. 'So, what's your house like? Old? Modern? No – don't tell me – you live in a mansion, don't you?'

'Georgian.'

'Georgian what?'

'I live in a Georgian mansion.'

'Yeah, right.' Jasmine eased her way round him, searching for the bottle opener under piles of envelopes and old newspapers and magazines. 'With hot and cold running flunkies.'

'Seriously,' Sebastian said. 'I live in an apartment in my parents' house – due to laziness rather than any deep sense of filial duty. It is a Georgian mansion. Sadly my mother's sense of history is slightly out of sync – so inside it's all very Louis Quinze meets Epping. You know – everything that can have a coating of gold leaf and a curly ormolu gets glitzed.'

'Are you kidding me?'

'Unfortunately, no. I call it Tacky Towers.'

Jasmine stared at him for a moment, then laughed. 'Not in your mother's hearing though, I bet.'

'She'd kill me,' Sebastian agreed. 'She thinks her taste is impeccable. And if you don't mind I'd really rather not think about it. This is a million times better. Is there anything I can do to help?'

'Get an appetite – I'll never eat more than two of

these . . .' Jasmine opened the cool box and almost moaned with greed at the sight of a dozen doughnuts liberally crammed with plump strawberries and whipped cream. 'Do you think I'm that much of a glutton?'

'I think you're a lady with a healthy appetite, which is a rare treat.' Sebastian picked up the plates. 'And it's a dream come true to find someone who shares my doughnut addiction.'

Jasmine happily returned his grin. Why did she instantly feel more relaxed here with Seb – a man she'd met twice in her life – than she ever did with Andrew? She pushed the plates and glasses towards him. 'Could you take these out on to the veranda as well, please? There's a table and some deck chairs . . . I just want to go to the loo . . .'

Squashing herself into the tiny bathroom, she dived into her make-up bag. Now was not the time for the full slap, of course, but a coat of mascara and a touch of lipstick could only improve things. She kneeled on the lavatory seat, peered into the tiny mirror, and screamed.

Red-faced from the sun, and with the top circle of her hair flattened by the limpet grip of the hard hat, she looked exactly like Friar Tuck.

Ten minutes later, with as many improvements made in as short a time as possible, she sauntered back out of the hut. Sebastian was sprawled on one of the deck chairs, looking languid and utterly at home, and Jasmine allowed herself a moment of pure lustful staring. It was all she was going to get, she thought ruefully, especially as she'd spent the best part of the afternoon with him looking like someone about to go trick-or-treating.

He glanced up and smiled. 'I've put yours in the shade. Over there, behind that stuff from the stadium. Hang on, I'll go and get it. You sit down . . .'

Jasmine sat. She wasn't going to come over all strident and feminist – no chance. Andrew had never, ever waited on her. 'Thanks. What stuff from the stadium? Oh, right! The boards and stool and pallets.'

Sebastian removed the doughnuts and Old Ampney from beneath the trappings of Benny Clegg – the Punters' Friend, and placed them on the table in front of her. 'And is there anything else madam requires?'

Oh, yes, she thought dazedly. Oh, bloody yes. 'No, thanks. This is great . . .'

Sebastian sat down again and raised his beer glass. 'Here's to you – and to the new stadium. Are you going to keep the Benny Clegg stuff here as a sort of memorial to your grandfather?'

Pausing to lick cream from her fingers, Jasmine shook her head. 'No, as soon as the rebuilding's finished I'll take then back, I'm not going to be modernised.'

Sebastian, his mouth uninhibitedly full of strawberries, looked puzzled. Jasmine wanted to laugh. Of course, he'd assumed that she was simply a stadium board member when they'd met, and he'd worked out the connection between Grandpa's headstone and the Benny Clegg bookmaking pitch, but she hadn't told him – not then, and not since in the letters.

'I'm Benny Clegg now.' She reached for her bottle of beer. 'That's why I'm so involved with the stadium. I'm a bookie.'

If she'd said she was a hot contender for the next Pope, Sebastian couldn't have looked more amazed. The stunned expression gradually dissolved into one of astounded delight. He stood up, towering over her for a minute, blocking out the sun, then bent down and kissed her lightly, softly, briefly on the mouth.

He tasted of doughnuts, of strawberries and cream, and

263

beer and sunshine. Jasmine, suddenly wanting to bellow
the chorus of 'My Favourite Things', dazedly kissed him
back.

chapter twenty-one

It certainly hadn't turned out as April had expected. The drink with Noah – for old times' sake – hadn't been the emotional reunion full of explanations and apologies, ending in declarations of undying love, that she'd fondly imagined. The art groupies and the caftan lady had turned up only minutes after she and Noah had sloped off to the wine bar, and all chance of intimacy was lost.

Not only had she not been able to tell him how much she still loved him, but Beatrice-Eugenie's existence hadn't got a look in either. Noah had been bundled away to do press interviews and had mouthed that he'd ring her – soon – and disappeared in a swell of adulation.

Now, four weeks later, he hadn't phoned, and April was sure she'd never see him again. Jix, Daff, Sofia and Antonio had all been sympathetic, but the 'I told you so's' were dangling unsaid. It had all been such a huge mistake, seeing him. It had merely ripped the scab off the healing scar and left her hurt, alone and vulnerable all over again.

And October had been grey and wet and dreary, and Martina had been even more of a cow than ever, and the Copacabana seemed like hell.

Pouring a Cinderella from the shaker over a mountain of ice, April felt as if her one chance of happiness had been snatched away. Noah would now be back in France with the improbably named Anoushka, and she'd robbed Bee of the only opportunity of ever meeting her father. She should have handled it differently, been more assertive, clung on to him when the caftan woman had tried to claim him – anything – damn well anything to make sure they had enough time together.

'Oh, sod! Sorry.' She looked at the mess spreading across the top of the bar. 'I didn't realise I'd overfilled it.'

The customer sighed in a resigned way – as if he'd expected nothing less from a bimbo in a silly costume – and April rubbed angrily at the sticky mess with a J-cloth, praying that Martina wouldn't notice.

'April!' The shriek reverberated around the bar. 'I want a word!'

Oh God – April hurled the syrup-laden cloth beneath the counter and smiled. 'Sorry, Martina, I just overfilled the glass.'

'What?' Martina's heavily embossed eyelids flickered. 'What glass? What are you talking about? You haven't been doling out double measures instead of singles, have you?'

'No – er – it was just a bit of spillage.' The customer had borne away the sticky glass and April quickly shoved a beaker full of brightly coloured umbrellas and twizzle sticks on top of the congealing mess. 'Nothing major. So which word did you want to have?'

'Waitress.'

April sighed. She really hoped this wasn't going to be one of Martina's gimlet-eyed nights where she stood about six inches behind the Copacabana's staff and grizzled about everything, comparing their sloppiness with the *Debrett's Book of How to Serve a Cocktail* while your feet killed you and your knickers showed.

'I'm a barmaid first and a waitress second. I haven't actually dropped a tray or smothered anyone in ice cubes for ages.'

Martina frowned. The little body-pierced bits glittered as her face creased. 'No, that's why I wondered if you'd be interested in doing a bit extra.'

Extra? Where the hell in a twenty-four-hour day was April expected to find time for anything else? If she stayed awake all night the money might come in handy. 'Well, I do work at the Pasta Place as well. I mean, I don't really think I could squeeze in extra hours here at the moment and –'

'No, no.' Martina removed some purple lipstick from her front teeth with the tip of her tongue. 'I wasn't offering extra hours. This is a one-off opportunity. My very, very dear friend Emily Frobisher has asked me if I knew anyone who'd be willing to work waiting on tables at a banquet.' Martina leaned forward cosily and dropped her voice to merely glass-breaking. 'She's apparently had outside caterers in the past who've supplied waiting staff and they have been beyond the pale. Serving from the right! That sort of thing . . .'

God, April thought, how really, really dreadful for poor Emily Frobisher. Fancy getting your roulade and jus dished up from the wrong side! It could ruin your life! She did a few mental calculations. 'And this Emily Frobisher – is she Brittany's mum?'

Martina simpered. 'Actually, yes. They're having a black-tie dinner and ball on New Year's Eve to announce the venue of the Platinum Trophy.' She almost wriggled in excitement. 'Which of course, between you and me, because of Sebby and darling Brittany's little affair, will be here – but we have to go through the motions so that there are no cries of foul – and she's frantic to find proper people to wait table. After all,' she played her trump card with a flourish, 'it's not as if you'll have anything else to do on New Year's Eve, is it?'

Cow, April thought. But it was sadly true. The end of the year would mean staying in with Bee and Daff and watching some dire comedian on the telly hosting something from Edinburgh that had been filmed in a July heatwave. And she could do with the money. And most alluring of all was knowing what Jix had overheard when he was chauffeuring. If he'd heard right, then Oliver and Martina may be in for one hell of a New Year shock.

'It would depend on the money, and transport there and back because I haven't got a car.'

'Ten pounds an hour and transport.'

'Done.'

'Good girl.' Martina waved her bony bejewelled fingers under April's nose. 'I knew you realised which side your bread was buttered. Oh – and I've got some more really exciting news.'

April sucked her teeth. How many fun-filled hours of sweating over a hot banqueting table could she take? 'I really can't fit any more hours in.'

'This isn't to do with work. You'll probably read all about it on the society pages. Well, I mean, that is if you read the proper papers.' Martina smoothed down tonight's clinging twinkly dress. 'We're talking broadsheet superstar status here, not tacky tabloid.'

April sighed. Martina was in full show-off overdrive. As they were used to celebrities frequenting the stadium, April could only assume they were about to be visited by someone of mega-importance. Martina always managed to have her photograph taken with them and appeared frequently on the gossip pages, leering spikily up at famous people like an evil emaciated pixie.

268

'Really? And which superstar would this be? Tom Cruise? Little Leonardo? Cher? Madonna?'

'Not celluloid celeb,' Martina looked shocked. 'This is really highbrow stuff. Noah Matlock.'

The Copacabana became a swirl of noise and colour. April, who had never fainted in her life, clung on to the polished counter and took gulping deep breaths.

Martina's voice sounded quavery and distant. 'Of course the name'll mean nothing unless you're a patron of the arts.'

April took more breaths.

'He's an artist. Famous. Does abstracts,' Martina said by way of explanation. 'Very acceptable with the dinner party crowd now. Hugely famous, in fact.'

April nodded. It made her giddy. 'Yes . . . I know . . . Er – um – what about him?'

'I'd read about him in the Sunday supps,' Martina was tidying the cherries and orange and lemon slices. 'I've asked Oliver for one of his paintings for my birthday.'

Christ, April thought dizzily, pop along to my flat and take your pick. Was that all? For one awful moment she'd thought Noah was going to stride into the Copacabana, or present the prizes for the last race or something. 'Oh, lovely . . . Ah, yes – excuse me a sec . . .'

April staggered unsteadily along the bar to serve a clutch of customers. She mixed and poured piña coladas on auto-pilot. Why the hell couldn't Martina have wanted a David Shepherd elephant painting? Why couldn't she have just said she was getting a little bauble from Cartier for her birthday? Why the hell had she decided to go arty-trendy and mention the forbidden Noah word?

April dawdled as long as she could over the drinks, but sadly, Martina was still waiting when she'd finished.

'And,' Martina continued, 'it turns out that he actually

lived here – in one of the flats we owned, can you believe – some years back. Of course that was Oliver's side of the business and then Sebby took it over and we've never bothered about the tenants' names unless they cause trouble or don't pay their rent – but, my God, I wish I'd known then that we had a celeb amongst the riffraff.'

'Well – um – Noah wasn't famous then – er – that is, I mean, I suppose he wasn't that famous then . . .' April coughed. Even if she told Martina that she knew Noah Matlock intimately, every beautiful perfectly formed inch of him, Martina wouldn't believe her. And honestly, what was the point? She tried to change the subject. 'Do we need more Cointreau?'

'Nah –' Martina cast a cursory glance at the liqueurs. 'There's enough there for tonight. Anyway, it gets better. I'm going to get it autographed. My birthday present.'

Why the hell couldn't she shut up? Why on earth did she want to turn into Mrs Nice-and-Chatty tonight? 'Yes, well, don't all artists sign their work?' April sometimes wondered about Martina's intelligence levels. 'I mean, it wouldn't be worth much without the signature, would it?'

Martina clicked her tongue against her teeth. 'I don't mean just the painting. Of course I know that'll be signed – I mean Oliver is going to ask Noah Matlock to sign my birthday card to go with it.'

April was beginning to lose track. She'd had birthday cards from Noah. They'd always been hand delivered at least a day late and had usually been rather cheap flimsy affairs with sparkle dust on them. She'd kept them, along with his photos, to show Bee when she was old enough to understand.

'Goodness, April!' Martina was suddenly stung into agitation. 'You're being very slow tonight! Why don't you ask me how?'

'How what?'

'How I'm going to get my birthday card signed to go with my painting?'

April sighed and asked.

'Because,' Martina said triumphantly, 'Oliver has a – er – business colleague who has a friend who is a mate of Noah's agent and they contacted him in France . . .'

Whoopee-do, April thought. Through his thug network, she was pretty sure that Oliver could manage to put the squeeze on the entire House of Windsor if Martina had set her heart on a small castle for her birthday.

Martina's eyes were like saucers now. 'And – the very best bit of all – it turns out that Noah is in this country at the moment. In London, in fact. And – oh, well, I know this won't be of much interest to you, of course, but I've got to tell someone – Noah Matlock is downstairs with Oliver at this very minute and we've invited him to supper – Oh, bloody hell! Do be more careful, April! You've spilled the chartreuse!'

The evening dragged on. April was pretty sure she'd mixed Screwdrivers instead of Deathwishes, and Salty Dogs instead of Depth Charges. However, as no one complained she supposed it didn't matter. What mattered was that Noah was here – back in Bixford – and as he didn't know that she worked in the Copacabana, unless she invited herself to supper with the Gillespies, he'd go back to France and never know about Beatrice-Eugenie. April groaned. Assuming that Oliver's connections had wangled the invite, there was no way, this being social, that Noah would be alone. Anoushka, he'd said, only stayed in France when he was on one of his exhibition tours. Of course Anoushka must be with him this time. Bloody Anoushka, who had miraculously metamorphosed from city slicker into pay-sanne peasant at the drop of Noah's 501s.

Race after race took place on the other side of the plate glass, and the rowdy, noisy crowd seemed to have no idea that their drinks were being poured by a zombie. April watched the clock's hands climb round to ten thirty. The last race would soon be over, the serious drinkers would storm into the bar and hang around until midnight. By half-past she'd meet Jix in the stadium, and at quarter to one she'd be home . . .

'Fucking hell!' The explosion of words sounded very familiar.

April turned, and dropped two umbrellas into the ice-making machine. They were immediately chomped up into matchsticks. April really didn't have time to worry. Noah was standing at the bar. Less than a foot away.

Her teeth had riveted themselves together. Despite the fact that she was shaking from head to toe, she managed to force them apart. 'We – um – meet again, sort of . . .'

Noah, it was pleasing to note, seemed even more pole-axed than she did. He ran his hands through his hair, blinking at her as though she was some sort of mirage. Eventually he cleared his throat. 'What the hell are you doing here?'

'I work here. The shop I worked in closed just after you left – like most of them in the High Street. I've been here ever since. Didn't Martina tell you?'

'No she bloody didn't. I needed a drink. I've just escaped from her clawing at me and telling me how much she likes my paintings and how she can't wait to tell all her Inner Wheel Lunch Circle that she's having me for dinner.'

April managed to stretch her mouth into a smile. 'She probably didn't mean it literally.'

'Don't you believe it.'

Of course, there was no reason why Martina would have mentioned to him that one of her staff was called April

Padgett, was there? Martina knew nothing about the affair. Now that he'd recovered from his first shock, Noah was staring at her with a rather weird expression in his eyes. Belatedly she remembered the French maid's outfit and tugged ineffectually at the hem of her dress.

'It suits you . . .' His voice was husky. 'There seem to have been a lot of changes . . .'

More than you'd ever guess, April thought, wishing that the sound of his voice wouldn't play such havoc with her hormones. 'Er, oh yes, loads . . . Would you like a drink?'

Oh, please, don't let him spoil it by asking for a Long Slow Comfortable Screw . . .

'That was my original intention. Do you do beer?'

'Christ, no. You have to go downstairs to Ye Olde Bull and Bush Coaching Inn – it's alongside the Tote – for anything like that. I can do you a Pernod and black, though.'

'I don't drink that any more.' Noah looked a bit shifty. 'Not good for the image. Haven't you got any decent burgundy?'

'If it can't be shaken, stirred, covered in fruit and sparklers, we don't serve it. How about champagne?' April knew she was gabbling and tried to stop. It simply made matters worse. 'I mean, I suppose you're used to champagne now – being a superstar and everything. Oh, and with living in France. It must be just like drinking Vimto. So is that a glass of Moët – or maybe two? I presume you're not alone?'

'I'm quite alone – and I'm sorry I didn't ring you after the exhibition.'

'What?' April's hand rattled on the champagne bottle. Noah always managed to wrong-foot her. 'Oh, I never expected you to. I mean, if you hadn't been in Bixford tonight for Martina's birthday thing I'd never have seen you again, would I?'

'I'm not here for the Gillespies – although it tied in nicely. I'm here for you. I came back to Bixford to find you. I was intending to call in at the flat in the morning.' Noah leaned across the bar and stroked her cheek. 'And no, I won't have the champagne now. I'm having supper with Oliver and Martina as arranged, because they've paid handsomely for one of my paintings and they have some – let's say – extremely influential friends. I'll make my excuses and leave as soon as possible. Just don't bolt the door tonight, honey – I'm coming home.'

'You're bloody insane!' Jix scowled at her through the silky fall of his hair. 'Mad!'

'No, I'm not,' April insisted as they hurried through the sodium-lit darkness of Bixford's back streets. It was a cold night and she huddled inside her coat. 'It's all part of the dream, Jix. He's Bee's dad, and he's got rights. So has she.'

Jix muttered something from the depths of his leather jacket. Then he shook his head. 'He didn't bother to contact you after Swaffield, did he? And now he just turns up, out of the blue, and says he's come to find you? Bollocks. He was over here to feather his nest via Oliver and Martina, walked into the bar, saw you, and took the opportunist route. For God's sake, April, he's lied to you before – and he's doing it again now.'

'No he isn't! What would you know? You weren't there!'

'I wish I had been. Sometimes, for someone who's so tough, you're bloody gullible. He could have phoned you at any time, turned up at the flat at any time – it was his place too, remember – he didn't exactly have to search too hard to track you down, did he? He didn't come to the flat tonight, though, did he? Even though he was in

Bixford? He met you by accident, not design. The man's a complete bastard.'

'You never said any of this when I was going to see him at the gallery, did you? You were all in favour then.'

'No I wasn't.' Jix hunched his shoulders. 'I thought then that he might hurt you, but it's always been your dream – the happy-families thing – and I wasn't going to pour cold water on it. But he didn't want you then, so why should he want you now?'

'Shut up!' They'd turned into the High Street now, and a sharp wind rattled the debris in the gutters and stung April's face. 'This is my life. And Bee's. Just butt out.'

'With pleasure.' Jix jabbed his key into the lock of number 51. 'Only this time when he's shredded you to pieces don't come looking for sympathy. I won't be there with shoulders to cry on, OK?'

'Suits me.'

April stormed into her flat. Daff glanced up smiling, then, seeing the angry faces, looked concerned and gathered her word-puzzle books together without speaking. Cair Paravel, stretched out on the rug in front of the television, raised his head and growled cheerfully at Daff's ankles, then thumped his tail towards Jix and April.

Jix bent down and stroked him. 'Rip the bastard's throat out, there's a good boy.'

April continued glaring until Jix and Daff had left, then checked on Beatrice-Eugenie, fed Cair Paravel, and turned into a small whirlwind. Cushions were plumped, newspapers shoved out of sight, dust removed, all but the dimmest lamps extinguished. Satisfied that Noah wouldn't think she'd allowed the flat to fall into a complete schlep tip in his absence, April ripped off her French maid's outfit and headed for the shower.

Wondering whether being naked beneath her dressing

gown would look a little too obvious, and deciding it would, she dressed again in a pair of jeans and a fraying rainbow sweater that had once belonged to Jix. Clean and casual, she thought, just as she'd been when Noah had first fallen in love with her. No make-up then, and her hair all fluffed out and tumbled . . . She looked at herself in the mirror. Her eyes glittered and the glow of her cheeks owed nothing to Max Factor. He'd be here soon – back in the flat where they'd laughed and loved. Back where he belonged. And surely, once he'd found out about Bee, and April had told him about the Ampney Crucis paradise she had planned for them, he'd never leave her again, would he?

Lighting her last cigarette, she poured a large glass of wine, curled on the sofa, and waited.

April couldn't imagine how she'd managed to fall asleep, but somehow she supposed she must have done. The room was cold and silent and for a split second she couldn't work out quite why she was there. Then she remembered. Her mouth tasted foul and her neck was stiff where it had become lodged against a cushion. She stretched and shivered, then squinted at the clock. Half-past three. With a sudden pang she realised that Noah wasn't coming.

Levering herself to her feet, close to tears of anger and disappointment, she knew she'd have to shoot the bolts on the door, slide the chain in place and shut Noah out of her life for ever. Cair Paravel rolled on to his back in his sleep, his belly grey and pink and mottled, and she stepped over him. At that moment she heard the key in the outside door of number 51. Cair Paravel, still prone, pricked his ears. April held her breath. It could be Joel and Rusty returning home after a night out. It probably was. She mustn't, mustn't, build up her hopes . . .

Cair Paravel rolled over and sat expectantly on his haunches as the key now slid into the flat door. Mesmerised, April watched as it swung open, and Noah stood on the threshold just as he always had. As he had for so many months in her frenzied fantasies.

'I knew there was a good reason for hanging on to my keys. Come here, honey, and give me a kiss.'

With a little cry she flew across the room and launched herself into his arms.

'Hey, that's some welcome.' He smoothed her hair away from her face. 'Sorry I'm so late, but Martina's worse at interrogation than old Paxo. Oh, this is wonderful . . . It's still the same . . . And you've kept the paintings!' He gazed round the flat. 'Christ, you'll never know how much I've missed all this. Nothing's changed – oh, except that . . .'

Cair Paravel had shrunk back on to his stomach, his muzzle laid between his paws, his ears folded flat. A low warning growl rumbled from his throat.

Noah frowned. 'I thought we weren't allowed to keep animals in here.'

'We're not. It's a long story. Oh God, you didn't tell Martina about me – about you and me – did you?'

He shook his head. 'Not a word. It's something best kept secret. I mean, if I'm going to be staying here, the fewer people who know the better.'

The words filtered through. April caught her breath again. 'Staying? You're going to be staying?'

'Too right I am.' He let his lips slide down her neck, nuzzling his mouth into the hollow above her shoulder blade.

April melted. Oh, it was so long since she'd felt like this . . . 'Have you left Anoushka, then?'

'She's still in France, honey. There'll be plenty of time to finalise things in the morning. First things first . . .' He continued the nuzzling. 'Mind you, it's a shame you've taken off the French maid thing. What a turn-on. I don't suppose you'd like to slip into it again, would you?'

About as much as she'd like to slip into a vat of maggots, April thought, but if Noah wanted her to . . .

Cair Paravel growled again and Noah raised his head. 'Can't he sleep outside?'

'He'll be fine once he gets used to you. Honestly.' She pulled Noah's mouth back to her neck, not wanting anything to spoil the moment. 'Oh God, I've missed you so much.'

'Me too, honey,' Noah lifted her off her feet and swung her round. 'And we've got an awful lot of catching up to do . . .'

Carrying her, heading for the bedroom, he side-stepped Cair Paravel's half-hearted attempt to nip his knees. 'The dog's a damn liability. Is he business or pleasure?'

'A bit of both,' April said dreamily, loving the feeling of Noah's arms around her and his strength emphasising her fragility. Oh, the bliss of being frail for once, and seduced, and not having to think or worry. 'He's won a race.'

Noah kicked open the bedroom door with all the panache of Rhett Butler. April, relaxed in his arms, thought it was exactly like he'd never been gone. He'd always come over all masterful, especially when they'd had a row.

'Fucking hell!' Noah stood inside the bedroom door, dropping April unceremoniously on to the bed. 'What the hell is that?'

Beatrice-Eugenie, her hair static from the pillow, sat bolt upright in the truckle bed, scrubbing at her sleepy eyes with bunched fists.

April, overwhelmed with love for both of them, beamed up from the duvet. 'She's your daughter, Noah. Bee, darling, say hello to your daddy . . .'

chapter twenty-two

The honeymoon period was just entering its third week. April had to admit that, delirious as she still was to have Noah back, it wasn't all roses and Mantovani.

The flat, which had seemed so intimately right for just the two of them, was now hopelessly overcrowded. Bee's toys seemed to delight in sneaking into dark corners where Noah could stub his toe on some particularly immovable lump of plastic, and Cair Paravel, by sheer dint of his size, seemed to sprawl across all of the available floor space at the most inconvenient times.

Sadly, Cair Paravel hadn't changed his opinion of Noah since the first night and was even more hostile towards him than Daff. Unlike Daff, Noah loathed Cair Paravel in return, and insisted on him being banished to the walled yard for long spells during the day, or locked in the kitchen if it was raining. April kept sneaking him back into the living room, desperately sorry for the bewildered dog and petrified that someone would discover his existence because he howled so much.

She and Noah had had some fairly heated arguments over Cair Paravel, but she'd stood firm, saying that Cairey had as much illegal right to be at number 51 as anyone, and then Noah would stomp off to the bedroom and sulk.

And it wasn't just Cair Paravel either: Beatrice-Eugenie, usually sunny and adaptable, squirmed with shyness or burst into tears or both whenever Noah opened his mouth.

'Don't be so loud,' April implored. 'She's not used to raised voices – nor is Cairey. Just keep the volume down a bit.'

And Noah insisted on having sex all the time. Everywhere. Trying to keep Bee and Cair Paravel from poking curious eyes and damp noses in where they shouldn't be was becoming a huge problem. Consequently, April couldn't relax, and began to dread every snatched rough and tumble. As she'd refused to make love with Noah in the bedroom with Beatrice-Eugenie sleeping so close in the truckle bed, amorous encounters now took place rather awkwardly on the sofa. April was sure that she had uncut moquette permanently embedded in every part of her body.

Then there'd been the hoo-ha over the *Oceanic* painting. Noah had practically had a rolling-on-the-floor heel-drumming tantrum when she'd told him that she'd sold it. She didn't tell him why she'd sold it, or what she'd done with the money, but pointed out angrily that as she had never expected to see him again, it hadn't occurred to her that she'd need to seek his permission over its disposal. Then he'd turned petulant and said that his early works were much sought after and he could have negotiated a higher price, and that she mustn't, under any circumstances, sell the others. And April had shrugged and said they were Beatrice-Eugenie's inheritance, weren't they? And Noah had looked a bit doubtful, but had smiled and nuzzled her neck, and they'd ended up on the sofa . . .

'So, what's his lordship up to today?' Sofia asked as April untied her Pasta Place pinny at the end of the lunchtime shift. 'Taking his daughter out?'

April pulled a face. Sofia knew exactly what Noah thought of fatherhood. It ranked in popularity somewhere around being first in the queue at the vasectomy clinic.

'Doubtful. He's probably just watching telly.'

'Doesn't he ever go out then?' Tonio handed April a mammoth cappuccino. 'Has he caught Daff's aggorryphobie thing?'

April sipped gratefully at the froth. 'He doesn't want anyone to know he's staying here. He says he gets hounded by the press wherever he goes, and that this is his bolt hole. He just needs a break from all the publicity.'

If it hadn't been so sad, April thought, she would have found it funny. Now she had a child, a dog, and a man, all living at number 51 — none of whom were supposed to be there.

'God alive!' Sofia snorted. 'Some man he is, then! Letting you keep him! Watching you do three jobs a day while he sprawls in front of the box!'

Antonio raised his eyebrows. 'She's got a point, April, *cara*. Isn't he doing any of his paintings or anything?'

'All his stuff is still in France. He says the flat's too small for him to work in now. He says he's used to proper studios with the right light . . .' April sighed. Noah, for all his new wealth, hadn't yet contributed anything to the living expenses. She'd have her tongue ripped out by wailing banshees before she'd admit it to anyone.

The dream, harboured for so long, was turning very sour. Even in their cosy moments, late at night when she'd returned from the Copacabana and after Noah had insisted on having hasty sex before she removed the French maid's outfit, there was something vital missing. She'd told him about Ampney Crucis but he hadn't seemed particularly interested. He'd scoffed at the thought of Cair Paravel ever

281

becoming anything other than a four-legged liability, and Bee just seemed to irritate him.

As well as all this, he'd been rude to Daff, and Joel and Rusty, and now April saw none of them apart from a few brief good-morning exchanges in the hallway. Jix hardly spoke on the debt-collecting rounds, and although he still waited to escort her home from the stadium, he walked on ahead, his hands shoved deep in his pockets.

April, desperate for everything to be all right, was still convinced that once she and Noah moved away from the claustrophobic confines of number 51, the fragments of the roses-round-the-door, happy-families dream would all clunk neatly into place.

Noah's introduction to Bee, though, had probably been the most disappointing of all. It had taken him a scaringly long time to accept that she was his daughter, and then he'd been more angry than enthralled. And Bee had burst into tears when he'd tried to pick her up, and since stubbornly refused all April's attempts to get her to call him Daddy.

Noah's early efforts at fatherhood had all seemed to involve loud and hearty hand-clapping games, which lasted less time than his lovemaking, and only increased Bee's fear. Far from the blissful father-daughter idyll that April had imagined, Noah and Bee currently seemed to have reached a stand-off point, each ignoring the other as much as possible.

Outside the Pasta Place, the October afternoon was grey and windswept. April wouldn't have been at all surprised to see tumbleweed rolling aimlessly along the grim pavements. It was all a world away from the perfection of Ampney Crucis – but she knew that even if she took Noah there now, he still wouldn't see it at its best. They'd have to leave that particular treat until the spring.

282

'Oi!' Antonio suddenly leaned from the window. 'Jix! Come in and have a cup of coffee! Warm yourself up!'

April and Sofia exchanged glances. April very much doubted if Jix would want to spend any more time than necessary with her. She spoke quickly. 'He's probably just going to start the money-collecting. I don't expect he'll have time.'

'You not going with him then?'

April exhaled. 'I'm supposed to be – but to be honest, it's all getting a bit turgid now. With us not really being friends, you know.'

However, Jix appeared in the kitchen doorway, muffled in the leather jacket and several colourful long chenille scarves, and grinned at Antonio. 'Thanks for the offer, but I'll have to say no. I've got tons to do, and –' he looked across at April and withdrew the grin – 'I wanted to talk to you.'

'I'll just go and put my boots on before we start pounding the pavements and harassing people. Don't worry, I wasn't going to skive.'

'We're not debt-collecting this afternoon. I want to borrow Cair Paravel.'

April smiled. 'Oh, great. Poor boy could do with a good run. Are we taking him to the park?'

'We're not taking him anywhere. I am. I'm sure you're far too busy waiting hand and foot on bloody Picasso to spend any time with anyone else.'

'Jix, I know you think I've neglected Cairey –'

'I don't think, I know. And not only the dog, but Bee as well. What the hell are you doing, April? You were a brilliant mum, and I thought you adored Cair Paravel –'

'I am! I do!' April looked hopefully round for backup from Sofia and Antonio but they'd beaten a tactical retreat into the restaurant. 'You know I do! It's just that things are taking a bit of time to settle down. Noah –'

'Don't mention his bloody name to me!' Jix roared with uncharacteristic force. 'The man is nothing but a pimp, a lowlife, a complete waste of space. I can't stand by and watch you ruin Bee's life or Cair Paravel's. What you do with your own is up to you.'

'Don't you dare tell me how to bring up my child! Or how to look after my dog! I know you and Noah have never seen eye to eye but –'

'Cyclops wouldn't have been able to see eye to eye with that slimy bastard!' Jix looked away. 'Now, can I have Cair Paravel for the afternoon or not?'

April put her mug down slowly, well aware that she should be defending Noah more, but simply not having the energy. She really didn't want to fall out with Jix. The withdrawal of his friendship was bad enough. 'Yes, of course. But if you want to take him for a run, I could collect Bee and come with you. We could all do with some fresh air.'

Jix shook his head. 'And listen to you witter on about Noah all the time? No thanks. You've made your choice, and none of us seems to figure in your life much any more . . .'

'It's just a settling down period! Noah's –'

'April, please listen to yourself. Noah's scum, you're behaving like an idiot – and I won't allow you to muck up everyone else. Just fetch Cairey – I'll wait outside.'

Glaring at him, April snatched her coat from the rack and, knowing that Sofia and Antonio were watching her with worried eyes, stomped out of the restaurant.

As she'd expected, Noah was sprawled on the sofa, channel-hopping. He didn't look up as she came in. Leaning over, she kissed the top of his head. 'Hi. I'm not stopping. I'm taking Cair Paravel out.'

'Whatever . . .'

He was so gorgeous, she thought, so physically perfect. That's what she'd fallen in love with – the outer shell of the man, and the glamour of him being an artist, and the fact that he'd taken her away from her unhappy home life. For these things she'd been prepared to overlook his occasional tempers, his laziness, and even, eventually, his unfaithfulness.

Hurrying through to the kitchen and collecting Cair Paravel's collar and lead from the hook behind the door, she wished that Jix and Daff and everyone else could understand. She and Noah belonged together. They'd created Bee together. Once they'd moved to somewhere bigger, everything would be all right.

She came back into the living room. 'Is Bee having a nap?'

Noah still didn't look up from the television. 'She's upstairs with Daphne. I took her up just after you left. She kept grizzling for you. It was getting on my nerves.'

Counting to ten, April rattled the lead. 'OK, I'll go up and see her. And Cairey?'

'Out in the yard. He's too big to be cooped up in here and I don't like the way he stares at me. The animal's crazy.' He propped himself up on one elbow. 'So, now we've got the place to ourselves for a while – how about a little cuddle?'

'Can't.' April backed away from the sofa. 'I said, I'm taking Cair Paravel out – oh, and then I'm on early shift at the Copacabana tonight, so do you think you could get something ready for tea? And clear up a bit in here?'

But Noah was staring at the television screen again, his shoulders hunched.

Once April had dashed into the hall, clambered upstairs, and found Bee and Daff happily cutting out chorus rows of dancing ladies with their hands and feet joined together from the *Mirror*, and eating strawberry ice cream at the same time, and been assured that they'd be fine for the rest of the afternoon, she then retraced her steps, collected Cair Paravel from his exile in the yard, and met up with Jix.

'Don't say anything about Noah,' she frowned at him. 'Please. I want to come with you. I want this to be like it was before.'

Jix, who had bent down to kiss Cair Paravel, flicked his hair out of his eyes. 'It can't be, though, can it? Everything's changed. It's what you wanted. How you wanted it to be. Whether I approve or not doesn't matter – it's been your dream for so long . . .' He suddenly stared up at her. 'I suppose as long as you're happy, it shouldn't bother anyone else.'

'But it does,' April sighed. 'It bothers all of you. You just don't know Noah like I do . . . No, sorry. We're not going to talk about him.'

'Suits me.' Jix scuffed the ground with the toe of his DMs. 'Look, sorry I shouted. I don't usually get riled . . . I shouldn't shout at you.'

'Is that an apology? OK – it's accepted. I don't want to fall out either. So what have you got planned?'

'Two clues.' Jix stood up and almost grinned.

April felt a pang of relief. It was going to be OK. If she and Jix could just be friends again, then surely every-thing else would be all right? 'So, Miss Marple, what are they?'

Jix dug deeply into the pockets of the leather jacket and flourished a square of material and a set of keys under her nose. Cair Paravel, who had been entwining himself round April's ankles, snuffling happily, seemed to twig before she did. He whined blissfully and stood on his hind legs, his front paws on Jix's shoulders. Then he growled low in his throat, while licking his way frantically through the hair and scarves and several necklaces.

April laughed. 'God, he's sussed out what you mean. I obviously need more clues than he does! What the hell is going on?'

Emerging from Cair Paravel's attentions, Jix grinned. 'Mum's headscarf – and the keys to my very own van. You're not the only one who's been salting away their tips under the bed. Yours may have been for your Picasso reunion – mine has been far more prosaic. Transport. I thought it was about time I was mobile, and Mum had such a great time when we went to Ampney Crucis that I thought we should get out more often and –'

April hugged him. 'You're a star! I had no idea . . .' She stopped, stepping back, embarrassed. She shouldn't be hugging Jix. It was almost like being unfaithful. And she wouldn't have had any idea about what he'd been doing, would she? For the last three weeks the world could have stopped turning and she wouldn't have noticed. 'And the headscarf?'

'It's for Cairey – or rather for the hare at Bentley's. I've entered him in the four thirty this afternoon. I thought it was about time he at least got his head out of the clouds and rejoined the real world.'

April almost capered with glee on the pavement. She'd missed all this so much. Noah would have a fit if he knew – but what the hell? This was her life – hers and Jix's and Cair Paravel's – and it had nothing to do with Noah . . .

Jix's van, which was parked in the Pasta Place's lock-up, was a revelation. Having apparently previously been owned by a couple of New Agers who were now in prison after a rather excitable anti-hunt protest, it could have been custom-made for Jix. Painted purple, and liberally splashed with bright yellow daisies, it had a walnut interior and fake-fur zebra-print seat covers. There were even fluffy dice. April and Cair Paravel scrambled happily into the cosy warmth.

Bentley's Stadium, on the Essex borders, was only a short drive away. Far smaller than Gillespies, but much more modern than Ampney Crucis, it had put itself on the map by holding very popular Tuesday afternoon meetings throughout the year. The coach park was full, and consequently, the crowd that greeted them as they piled from the van consisted mainly of pensioners, shift-workers, and done-up women looking for a spot of afternoon delight.

'Remember you're Beatrice-Eugenie Padgett,' Jix reminded April in a whisper as they handed over registration documents, veterinary certificates and the fees.

'I've remembered,' April whispered back. 'And what if I hadn't come with you? Were you going to be Miss Bee?'

'Too right,' Jix simpered in a Julian Clarey falsetto. 'They'd have just had to assume that I had hormonal troubles . . . Now, let's get him into the kennels, go through the owner-trainer bit, and see if we need to slip the starter a tenner.'

'Uh? Bribery? I thought he was being run fair and square?'

'For putting the headscarf on the hare,' Jix said. 'They may not be as accommodating here as that Ewan geezer at Ampney Crucis was. If they turn down hard cash to dress up the bunny, you'll just have to do your vamp bit – O K?'

April shuddered. She'd been role-playing with Noah for far too long. It would be reassuring to know that he was actually turned on by her body, in jeans and sweaters, just as much as he was by the French maid's outfit . . . She decided not to think about it. Not now.

Being in time to watch two races before the four thirty, they settled Cair Paravel into the kennels, explained that they didn't have a separate trainer, made sure that his handler seemed friendly, then decamped to the rails to watch the proceedings.

The crowd was huge, and although the skies were pewter and the wind cold, the atmosphere was buzzing. April bought a racecard and looked with pride at Cair Paravel's name listed for the four thirty in trap one.

'He's got the red jacket,' she said to Jix. 'It'll look lovely on him.'

'Yeah, and as long as the hare is wearing a headscarf, we might just get a result. Do you want to hang on here while I go and chat up the officials?'

She nodded. 'Actually, I think I might have a bet on the next race. Just a couple of quid. What do you fancy?'

Jix looked shocked. 'Gambling's a mug's game. We're here to win money – not chuck it away.'

'Oooh! Now who's gone all prim and proper? Go on – I'll pay your stake. I'm going for Mighty Mabel in trap three.'

Jix peered at the racecard over her shoulder. He smelled of warm leather and lemon shampoo. 'Trap six. Never Say Die. But only a two-pound bet, April. OK?'

She watched him force his way through the afternoon throng until he was swallowed up by the crowd. It was lovely to be friends again. The niggling little worries over Noah seemed so unimportant now. April grinned to herself as she headed for the trackside bookmakers. Things would all work out right in the end, she was sure of it.

The stadium lights were on, cutting through the gloom, giving the circuit the air of a Christmas market. Because it was an afternoon meeting, the hardened gamblers didn't seem to be much in evidence, but there were still huge queues at the ranks of bookies, with everyone seemingly eager to join in the fun. Used to the shoving and elbowing at Gillespies, April wriggled her way along the bookmakers' pitches, checking the odds on the three and six dogs at each one. Deciding that Jeff Mansell – estab. 1803 – and looking it, would be the best bet as he was offering starting prices of nine to two and five to one respectively, she put a fiver on each, and was back at the rails before Jix returned.

He pushed his way in beside her just as the greyhounds were being led behind the traps. 'I think they thought I was running some sort of drug cartel. At one point I thought they were going to call in forensic and carry off Mum's best scarf in a plastic bag like they do on television detective films.'

'But did you manage it?' April was hopping from foot to foot. 'Is it OK?'

'Yeah, actually. Apparently – like Ewan said at Ampney Crucis – there's nothing in the GRA rules, and as it's not giving Cair Paravel an unfair advantage – after all, the other five dogs will chase the hare quite naturally – they've agreed. What about you? Is my two quid safe?'

'My two quid, you mean? Yeah, as houses.'

The greyhounds were all in the traps and the starter raised his arm. As they flew out into the darkening afternoon, April was swept up in the shouts and yells and frenetic atmosphere. The three and six dogs were neck-and-neck round the first bend, blurred against the pale sand, with the others all whisker-close behind. Jix had his arm round her shoulders as they leaned forward with the rest of the crowd on the rails, screaming their favourites home.

'It's the six dog!' Jix punched the air in triumph. 'How much have I won?'

April pulled a mocking face. 'And I thought you weren't

a gambler. Thirty pounds, actually, with your stake back. Enough to buy your mum a hundred new headscarves from Naz at the charity shop.'

Jix was staring at the odds displayed on the illuminated screen, muttering under his breath. 'You put a fiver on, didn't you? You can't afford to do that – oh, unless Noah's giving you pocket money, of course.'

'He isn't,' April said shortly. 'And I enjoyed it and we've made a profit. So stop grouching and let's collect our winnings before we watch Cairey do his stuff.'

Still grinning, and with their arms linked, they thrust their way into Jeff Mansell's very lengthy payout queue.

Just over half an hour later, Cair Paravel did indeed look splendid in the red jacket. Jix and April watched him proudly as he paraded, looking happy and tranquil, trotting beside his kennel handler in front of the packed crowds. His tail wagged jauntily, and he gazed around him, grinning through the straps of his muzzle, loving every moment of his brief fame beneath the spotlights.

'. . . and in trap one we have Cair Paravel,' the Tannoy echoed. 'A two-year-old blue-brindled dog . . .'

April, overwhelmed by love for him, wanted to rush out and hug Cair Paravel and tell him he was a diamond. That he was, without doubt, the most beautiful, funny, kind, wonderful dog in the world.

'Are you crying?' Jix looked at her in concern.

She shook her head. 'No – well, a bit. He looks so lovely and brave and happy, doesn't he?'

Jix wiped her tears away with the softly frayed cuff of his leather jacket. 'I know. He's a real star. Look, they're just wrapping the scarf round the hare. And I don't think anyone else has noticed, thank God.'

Cair Paravel had, though, April realised. He could sense

Daff. His nose twitched, and he bounced even more buoyantly on his slender toes, psyching himself up for the chase. Jesus, she thought, if he gets that wound up over something of Daff's, what on earth would he be like with Noah? Putting a hasty lid on the mental picture of a fang-bearing Cair Paravel belting hell for leather round the track after one of Noah's prized Patrick Cox boots, she concentrated on holding her breath and praying.

It was really autumnal-afternoon dark now, and the floodlights sliced through mist and smoke. The chattering voices joined together, seeming to rise in a cloud which lay trapped beneath the sulphur layer as the disembodied Tannoy voice built the tension.

Then they were all in, and the hare – with Daff's headscarf far more discreetly tucked round it than it had been at Ampney Crucis – skittered off on the rail. The crowd was hushed for a split second, then the gates flew up and the greyhounds poured out, and it looked as though they were running on air.

April wasn't sure if her shouts were silent; she couldn't hear her own voice. She could hear Jix, though, screaming in her ear, and everyone else screaming round her. Cair Paravel, legs pumping, ears flat, was a length and a half ahead of the field within seconds and gaining on the headscarf with every loping stride. He was a red and blue flash against the brightly lit sand, then the pack seemed to gain on him, and he momentarily disappeared as all six dogs crashed together, parted, and ran on.

'He's still ahead . . .' Jix panted in her ear. 'He's going to do it . . .'

He did.

April peered at the winner's cheque in the gloom of the van as they jogged home to Bixford. It was made out – as the previous one at Ampney Crucis had been – to Bee. It would add nicely to Beatrice-Eugenie's building society account.

'Not a huge amount, but with your gambling winnings, we've definitely made a profit. And it's been real fun.' She sank her head gratefully back into the mock-zebra, stroking Cair Paravel's slender nose. He opened liquid eyes and gazed up at her so she kissed him again. 'He's such a performer.'

Jix negotiated a roundabout. 'I think we should enter him for the Frobisher Platinum.'

'What? We can't! It'll cost a fortune just for the fees. We've both worked at Gillespies for long enough to know that the most prestigious races attract the wealthiest owners and –'

'We've got money – my savings and yours. Go on, April, at least think about it.'

'I'm thinking. I'm thinking. But what about the heats? There'll have to be hundreds to get it down to just six dogs for the final.'

'So? If they're not announcing the venue until New Year's Eve, and the race is due to be run on Valentine's Day, there'll only be six weeks for the heats. We can enter him in one out of town – and see how he does . . .'

April thought. And thought some more. 'OK. Why not? Brilliant. Yeah – we'll go for it. Oh God – but what about training? Surely he'll have to be trained properly for something huge like the Frobisher, won't he?'

'If it ain't broke, don't fix it.' Jix pulled the van up at a set of red traffic lights. A yuppie in a Jag in the next lane looked across in horrified disdain. With a 'love and peace' gesture, Jix beat the yuppie to the green light by a whisker. 'Cairey's done just fine so far with the headscarf and the bicycle, hasn't he? I don't think we should change a thing.'

And for the remainder of the journey home, April and Jix sang the wrong words to various Top Ten hits and laughed a lot. Cair Paravel, having clambered over their heads, curled round on the back seat, his head on his paws, and slept the deserved sleep of a champion.

The euphoria was still raging by the time they reached Bixford and number 51. Leaving Cair Paravel with Jix, April, knowing she was going to be horrendously late for the Copacabana, dashed into the flat.

'Noah! Sorry I'm so late. Can you pick Bee up from Daff's for me? And feed her? I'll just get changed and then run like hell. I might just make it –'

The flat was silent. The television was switched off. There were two envelopes on the coffee table.

Lighting a cigarette with shaking hands, April picked up the two notes, not knowing which one would cause more pain: the one with April scrawled across the front in Noah's handwriting, or the second, addressed to Miss A. Padgett, hand-delivered and bearing the Gillespie Stadium address.

The cigarette tasted sour and April stubbed it out, opening Noah's letter with a sick feeling in the pit of her stomach. Scanning the lines, the sick feeling lifted almost immediately like a Prairie Oyster meeting the effects of a killer hangover.

Noah simply said that he'd decided to return to France to sort things out with Anoushka, that he'd be back really soon – with his painting stuff – and that he apologised for being churlish, but he'd been bored. Once he'd started working again, fulfilling his creative drive, he wouldn't be such a mean sod to live with. He also added that he loved her, and would only be gone for a few days and couldn't wait to be back again.

April's fingers resumed the shaking as she opened the

Gillespie envelope. She simply couldn't afford to lose her Copacabana job now.

It was typed, and signed by Sebastian, and said that he'd been anonymously but reliably informed that April was not only subletting her flat to a male tenant, but that she also had a child and a dog living on the premises. He was sure that April was aware these were strictly in contravention of the tenancy agreement, and would she please contact him at the earliest opportunity to discuss the implications.

chapter twenty-three

The invitation to attend the opening of the refurbished Benny Clegg Stadium in Ampney Crucis on 5 November had arrived on Sebastian's desk the previous week. It wasn't totally unexpected, as Jasmine's letters had kept him up to date with the progress – or not – of the building work. However, as the invite was deckle-edged and gilt-embossed, had come from Peg Dunstable and included Brittany, he'd guessed that this was nothing to do with Jasmine.

Sebastian had also imagined that Brittany would not want to attend, amused as she'd been over his friendship with Jasmine. However, like most women he knew, she'd surprised him.

'Of course we must go,' she'd smiled teasingly, perched on the edge of her wrought-iron bed wearing nothing but Clarins. 'They're short-listed for the Platinum after all. We really should beetle off down there and see what they've done to update the antediluvian amphitheatre in our absence.'

'It's not a race meeting.' Sebastian had studied the invitation again. 'It's an official opening and celebration party.'

'All the more reason to be there.'

'And would this enthusiasm have anything to do with seeing Ewan again?' Seb had asked the question without really knowing why. He wasn't sure whether Brittany and Ewan were having a fling. He wasn't sure he even cared.

'No more than your attending has anything to do with seeing Jasmine,' Brittany had replied, standing up and curling her naked, expensively moisturised body against him. 'It should be really interesting, don't you think? There could be plenty of fireworks . . .'

So, here they were, hammering down the M27 again, in the November afternoon gloom, heading for Ampney Crucis. Brittany had opted to drive this time and Sebastian, who usually hated being a passenger, was surprised to feel drowsy and relaxed in the Daimler's opulence.

He really was looking forward to seeing Jasmine. It seemed so long since that balmy day in September when he'd kissed her – not with passion, but with pride. He had been completely knocked out by the fact that she was a bookie: by her casual chuckled admission that she had taken on the eponymous Benny Clegg mantle. It had been amazing enough to discover that she lived in a beach hut, but being a bookie to boot . . . He exhaled – making Brittany jab a quick glance across the leather and walnut.

Seb closed his eyes. He'd previously found Jasmine astonishingly friendly, good fun to be with, and fascinating to talk to, the information that she was a bookmaker simply served to move her sky-high into the stratosphere of his admiration. She'd seemed as surprised as he'd been himself, by both his reaction to her profession and the kiss, but not at all embarrassed. She certainly hadn't swooned and screeched that her devoted fiancé would be scandalised if he ever found out. She'd merely gently kissed him back, then smiled. The kiss hadn't been repeated, and they'd resumed their easy-going bantering and shared doughnuts as if the momentary slip away from mere friendship had never happened.

Now, almost dozing in the comfort of the limousine, Sebastian felt curiously elated that he would soon be with her again. Probably because she was so unusual – an artless, honest woman without a hidden agenda. He grinned to himself. Martina and Brittany would both squawk for England if they knew how he thought of them, but Jasmine was so different. She'd openly shared her emotions and her hospitality with him – and expected nothing in return. Not that he thought there was anything he could offer Jasmine, to be honest. As far as he was concerned she had it all. The perfect life.

'Do you want some music on?' Brittany was driving fast as always, in control, concentrating. 'Or are you happy to zizz in silence?'

'I'm easy – as long as it isn't the Clash.' Quickly he opened his eyes and tried to look wide awake. Brittany always drove even faster when listening to the Clash and he wasn't sure his nerves could stand it. 'Have you got anything more – um – melodic? Early Led Zepplin?'

'You must be getting old . . . hang on.' Brittany took her eyes from the road and rattled calmly through the CD holder. 'This should send you off to sleep.'

It was Nirvana's *Nevermind*. Not the lullaby that he'd have chosen, but pleasant enough. The afternoon was rapidly closing in, with dark clouds meeting over a pale grey sky, and a restless wind buffeting the sides of the car across the open motorway. Sebastian hoped it wouldn't rain. Not that he thought rain would dampen the spirits of Peg and Jasmine and the rest of them at the Benny Clegg Stadium, but simply because it was Guy Fawkes Night.

He'd had enough disappointing damp squibs on bonfire nights in his childhood never to want that feeling of anti-climax inflicted on others. Of course, Martina and Oliver had always insisted on him being taken to nice upmarket politically correct public displays, where the fireworks were safely ignited by an unseen hand and the smell of cordite was smothered by wafts of Chanel.

There had been other earlier firework parties at his grandparents' house, though, where he'd been allowed to run round the garden making rainbow arches in the darkness with sparklers, and light the blue touch paper on wobbly rockets jammed into milk bottles. There had been tumbling, leering guys, their grotesque masks melting in the white-hot flames, and his nan dishing out scalding delicious floury potatoes baked in the bonfire ashes, and mugs of hot chocolate liberally laced with whisky.

These were the times he remembered most – and then the intense agony when his grandparents had died and this blissful part of his childhood was gone for ever. Martina and Oliver had always done their best, he knew, but they thought that the best equated with the financial amount involved. Because of his grandparents, Sebastian knew very well that it didn't.

The sound of Nirvana became a soothing mantra in the background, and Sebastian allowed his mind to drift over more recent matters. He really hoped he hadn't upset April. The meeting had been awkward, and he'd hated having to haul her into the office like some grubby fourth-former who'd been caught cheating in exams and being forced to admit all to the headmaster.

Left to his own devices, he would definitely have ignored the anonymous phone call, which had informed him that April was breaking her tenancy agreement. It had been unfortunate that his father and several other Gillespie Stadium directors had been in his office at the time. The voice on the phone had been disguised – Sebastian still couldn't swear whether it was male or female – and had imparted the information in a very matter-of-fact way.

Sadly, Oliver had picked up on the Gillespie end of the conversation and with much pointing of stubby fingers, had insisted that Seb dealt with it pronto. Then Oliver had turned to name-dropping and let the other board members know that the world-famous artist Noah Matlock had once lived in a Gillespie flat – and that he'd bought one of his overpriced daubs for Martina's birthday and had even had the bloke to dinner at Tacky Towers.

Sebastian had felt pretty bad at this point. Again, he'd thought, he collected the rents from the properties – via Jix or the bank – without even knowing who his tenants were. He'd never known that Noah Matlock had lived in the High Street. Whether the tenants were famous or not shouldn't matter, though. They were real people and as their landlord he played a huge part in their lives, but had never even bothered to find out who they were. It really didn't seem right.

Anyway, the letter had been hand-delivered to April's flat, and April, looking pale and apprehensive and, Seb reckoned, far prettier in her jeans and frayed multicoloured sweater than she ever did in that ludicrous cocktail bar get-up, had arrived the next day.

She'd gazed around his luxurious glass office overlooking the track. 'I've never been here before. I was thinking as I came up in the lift, I've worked at the stadium for so long and never been anywhere near the offices.'

'I've been thinking along the same lines recently,' Seb had admitted. 'Not about the offices, of course, but how frenetic our lives become so that we don't have time to get to know people. We just do our own blinkered rat-run and take no notice at all of anything else. There's no standing and staring time any more.'

April had looked at him quizzically. 'Is that your dream, then? Time to stand and stare?'

And he'd had to agree that, yes, it was. A more easy-going, *laissez-faire* way of life all together.

'Mine, too.' April had perched on one of the square wooden chairs. 'That and a proper family and a cottage by the sea.' She'd looked him straight in the eye. 'Anyway, we're not here to trade dreams, are we?'

And he'd said no they weren't, and almost apologised for sending the letter, but explained about the phone call.

April had continued to stare at him without blinking. 'I think it was from someone who had just got confused . . . Jix's daughter – you know, you saw us with her in the summer? – sometimes spends time at the flat – and we, that is Jix and me, walk a greyhound for a friend. I think you saw us with it too, didn't you?' Her head was on one side now, waiting for him to take this in. 'I'm sure that someone has put two and two together and come up with breaking of tenancy agreement, don't you?'

Sebastian had grinned, and said yes, he guessed that's what it was. Oh, but what about the man? The informant had definitely mentioned a man.

April had beamed at him. 'Oh, I wish! Sadly, as you know from the hours I work, I'm manless. It was probably just the guy who came in to check out the satellite dish. It's always going wrong and wobbly. He's there a lot, you know . . .'

And Sebastian had heaved a huge sigh of relief and said yes, of course, that must be the answer, and April had stood up and shaken his hand and almost skipped out of the office. And then Seb had wandered behind his desk and played with the chromium executive stress toy that Brittany had given him, knowing that he hadn't believed a word of it.

The truth was more likely to be that Jix's daughter stayed overnight sometimes, and likewise the friend's dog

– both of which weren't allowed, but honestly, who cared? The man – well, maybe April did have men staying over? It hardly constituted subletting, did it? April, Seb reckoned, had rehearsed her answers very well, but there was someone out there – the voice on the telephone – who must dislike April very much indeed.

'Thinking of Jasmine?' Laughing, Brittany reduced the Nirvana volume.

'No, April Padgett.'

'Who?'

'April Padgett. She's a waitress in the Copacabana. You've spoken to her a few times. She lives in one of our flats. I was just wondering who would be malicious enough to want to get her evicted.'

'Christ,' Brittany looked across the car, 'why can't you have kinky fantasies like normal men?'

Ampney Crucis still managed to look chocolate-box pretty, even in the rapidly falling autumn darkness. The roads were now banked with leaves, red and golden beneath the diffused orange glow of the streetlamps, and the mist swirling in from the sea blurred the bleak seasonal edges, giving the entire village a gentle soft focus. Sebastian felt a surge of pleasure at being back here. Ludicrous, of course, but it felt just like the first day of the holidays. He grinned to himself. Childhood bonfire nights and seaside holidays? He was only thirty – surely that was far too young to be treading the nostalgia trail?

'Are we going straight to the stadium?' Brittany was cruising along the coast road now, 'or do you want something to drink first to fortify the nerves?'

'Stadium, I guess. I suppose as it's a party there'll be food and drinks there, and anyway your driving didn't scare me too much this time.'

Brittany flicked him an astute glance. 'That's because you've been preoccupied with other things for the majority of the journey.'

They'd passed the Crumpled Horn, and the Crow's Nest Caff, and were crawling along the cliff road. Somewhere, Seb thought, down there in the darkness, was Jasmine's beach hut. He wondered if she would be in there, getting ready, or whether she'd already be at the stadium with Peg and the others, welcoming the guests. Probably the latter, he thought, Jasmine not being the type to spend hours agonising over hair and make-up and which outfit would be best to knock people dead.

Not like Brittany. Her black Versace trouser suit, worn with black rhinestone boots, and with the floor-length black leather coat so casually slung on to the rear seats of the Daimler for wearing later when the wind blew in from the sea, would keep a Third World country in food for a year.

The Daimler cruised towards the end of the cliff road and purred into the new car park. The place was already jam-packed with cars, vans, bicycles and several coaches.

'Wow!' Sebastian simply couldn't hide his astonishment. 'What a transformation.'

Brittany switched off the engine and leaned back in her seat. 'The proles have certainly been busy.'

'Don't be a cow.'

'I'm joking.' Brittany uncurled herself from the car and shivered in the rapid temperature change. 'I'm impressed. It's pretty stunning.'

Seb stood on the shingle, with the wind from the unseen, roaring sea ruffling his hair, and relished the standing and staring. Doris Day, in surround sound, was inviting everyone on a Sentimental Journey. It seemed stirringly appropriate.

While the car park was ringed with soft floodlighting,

the stadium blazed with spotlights, white-hot, like a desert city shimmering beneath a midday sun. Above the new black wrought-iron gates, a glorious golden lined-out and curlicued sign proclaimed 'Ampney Crucis Welcomes You to the Benny Clegg Stadium'. An illuminated brightly coloured stylised painting of racing greyhounds, at least ten feet long, curved over the entrance. It was just like stadiums had been in the old days, Seb realised, remembering nights at Hackney with his gramp, when he'd walked under greyhound arches such as this. Peg and Jasmine and the rest may have chosen to tart the place up, but they hadn't ignored the dog-racing roots. It put Gillespies ultramodern chrome and steel and glass coldness to shame.

Having shown their invitations to a whiskery woman on the gate, and followed Brittany towards the new open-fronted bar, Seb's first thought was that he'd never be able to find Jasmine in the crush. The entire population of Dorset must have turned out tonight.

The refurbishment, which had looked so unlikely ever to be completed in September, certainly hadn't detracted from the informal, cosy atmosphere, and despite Jasmine's voiced misgivings, it appeared that Damon Puckett and his boys did in fact know their stuff.

All the rails had been replaced, the track was weed-free, there were proper lavatory blocks, and the hot-dog van had metamorphosed into a neon-bright fast-food cabin. The corrugated roof was still corrugated, not now with flapping sheets of tin, but some lustrous pale substance, the stands were sturdy and painted red, white, and blue, and a glass viewing area adorned the boxes overlooking the winning post. Sebastian thought he could see tables and chairs behind the glass, presumably all in place for Jasmine's Six-Pack Saturdays.

Clutching a plastic glass brimming with Old Ampney,

Sebastian found a quietish corner. Doris was crooning about Moonlight Bay and Brittany's eyes were sparkling.

'It's absolutely superb.' She wrinkled her nose over the top of her beaker. 'I can't quite believe it. It's like stepping back in time, but with all mod cons. They've even got Tote windows in place. The media would love this . . . And look at the size of that bonfire!'

A huge pyramid of wood and pallets and various other large combustible items, was set in the centre of the track where the presentation podium had been. Seb could almost smell the acrid wood smoke and taste his nan's potatoes . . .

'Christ!' Brittany spluttered. 'This stuff is lethal. Pops would adore it. This gets better and better . . . Look, Seb, do you mind if I just go and put myself about a bit? I'd quite like to find Peg Dunstable. We'll catch up with each other later in time for the fireworks.'

She kissed his cheek, and was gone into the throng. Possibly to find Peg, Seb thought, more likely to look for Ewan. Did he mind? He thought he probably didn't. Slowly, Sebastian drained the remains of his Old Ampney and decided he was pleased to be alone.

He watched the crowds, all talking loudly over Doris Day, grinning, clutching drinks and fast-food containers. Martina would rather die than offer her guests anything less than a good Romanian Merlot and smoked salmon bagels. He wished she were here to see this. She would be socially outraged. It was all wonderfully pleasant, lounging here, sheltered from the sea breeze, muffled in his thick sweater, having to do nothing but people-watch in the darkness. Life at the Gillespie empire was becoming more and more exhausting and less and less satisfying. Organising corporate hospitality at the stadium, being landlord of dozens of Bixford properties, and travelling the country checking on the efficiency of the motorway service stations'

Gillespsie Guzzler vending machines, no longer held Sebastian in thrall. This, however, was balm for his frazzled soul.

It was while he was crowd-skimming that he saw Jasmine.

He knew he was smiling even though she couldn't see him, and felt foolish. The smile stayed in place, though. Illuminated by the floodlights, she was chattering to a group of people, laughing, and waving her hands towards the bonfire. Through the shifting gaps in the crowd, he could see that she was wearing jeans and an oversized navy-blue Guernsey, and her dark hair swung around her face as she moved. Seb watched her, fascinated. Jasmine Clegg was as far removed from Brittany and most of his other girlfriends as she could be, but none of the slender, designer-clad, perfectly turned-out women in his life had had half the effect on him that she did.

With a start he realised that he recognised the faces surrounding her. Ewan Dunstable, of course, he'd already met, but the other two were the school friends from the photo in the beach hut. He couldn't remember the girl's name, but the stocky man with the fair cropped hair must be Andrew, the fiancé. Sebastian felt a knot of jealousy tighten in his stomach. Jasmine had her perfect life here, with friends she'd known all her life, and the man she was going to marry. She didn't need him.

Turning away, he crumpled his plastic glass and threw it into a waste bin. Of course he should have realised that Jasmine would be with Andrew tonight. After all, he himself was with Brittany. What the hell had he expected to happen? That Doris would whisper 'Secret Love' and the crowds would part and he and Jasmine would run, in slo-mo, straight into each other's arms?

'Sebastian? Seb? Oh, great! It is you! I said to Clara I

thought it was! How long have you been here? What do you think of the stadium, then? Swish, or what?'

He looked down into Jasmine's large brown eyes. 'I think that your grandpa is doing handstands in Heaven.'

Her face crinkled into a huge grin. 'Me too. I cried so much when they put the Benny Clegg sign up – did you see it? – but I've got used to it now. He'd really love it. I mean, he does love it. He's here, I can feel it. Oh, come and meet Clara. And Andrew. And Ewan, who of course you've already met but –' She stopped and peered into the crowd. 'Oh, Ewan seems to have wandered off, but come and meet the others, anyway . . .'

Swept along on her boisterous enthusiasm, Sebastian found himself tugged through the crowd. He knew that he didn't want to meet Andrew at all, and he was pretty sure that Ewan and Brittany were together somewhere, but it would have been churlish to refuse Jasmine's invitation.

Clara, dark and sultry, had obviously heard a lot about him and kissed him expansively on both cheeks. It wasn't, Sebastian thought, extricating himself, the genteel luvvie air kissing that went on in Brittany's circle. Clara went for the full monty. Andrew, who hopefully hadn't heard anything about him at all, nodded and sketched a smile. Fortunately, there was no time for clipped small talk, as Doris ceased 'Que Sera'-ing, and the Tannoy system crackled into life.

'Ladies and gentlemen.' Peg, in the blonde French pleat wig and a 1950s crimson two-piece, appeared beside the bonfire, artistically back-lit by several people carrying torches. Her voice wavered across the stadium. 'It is my very great pleasure to welcome you all here this evening. Many of you are regulars, but many of you are not, and I hope that you all approve of the changes we have made! I know that several of you were concerned that updating the stadium would detract from its originality, and from the traditions of Ampney Crucis, but I'm sure you'll agree that the finished result is quite spectacular.'

There was a roar, and a massed stamping of feet and clapping of hands.

'It is also my pleasure,' Peg yelled, 'to invite Jasmine Clegg, who has spent all of her life in the village, and has been a stalwart of this track since she was old enough to walk, and who is the granddaughter of the late and terribly much missed Benny, to open this greyhound stadium which bears her grandpa's name.'

Jasmine had turned pale.

'Didn't you know?' Seb asked her.

She shook her head. Andrew, Sebastian noticed, was shoving her forward. Shaking him off, Jasmine hurried towards the track and ducked under the rails.

'Poor thing,' Clara said. 'She hates anything like this. She was the same at school. Never put her hand up in class because she didn't want to draw attention to herself.'

'I'm not surprised she doesn't want to draw attention to herself here,' Andrew muttered. 'After all, it's only a two-bit dog track when all's said and done.'

Sebastian stared at him. 'Aren't you proud of her, then? Of what she's done? Of taking on this refurbishment and setting up regular meetings? And even more, becoming a bookie – and a trackside bookie at that? Not a cosy office-bound number. She's taken on a job that most men would flinch at.'

'Oh, yeah,' Andrew nodded, 'I'll give you that. But it's nothing to be proud of, as such, is it? As a career, I mean. Mind you, she's made a mint of money – and that does impress me.'

Seb, really wanting to leap on Andrew and pummel him into the newly laid turf, was prevented from doing so by

Jasmine's wavering voice echoing through the darkness.

'I just want to say thank you to all of you for coming to the party tonight. And to say thank you for your support in the past – and I hope that you'll all enjoy the bonfire and the fireworks – oh, and the greyhound racing at this stadium in the future. Er – especially the Saturday night Six-Packs.'

'You'd think she'd have worn something a bit smarter,' Andrew grumbled. 'Being up there in front of all these people. She looks like a bag lady.'

Sebastian clenched his fists and his teeth.

Clara showed no such restraint. 'Butt out, Andrew, you prat! Jas looks lovely – and she didn't know Peg was going to throw this at her, did she? And even if she had, she wouldn't have tarted up for it because Jas doesn't do smart. Now shut up – she's going to say something else. Listen!'

Jasmine, looking petrified under the lights, held the microphone closer. 'Oh, and – um – I just want to say that my grandpa Benny Clegg was the most wonderful man in the world ever – and that this new stadium is the best memorial he could ever have. I just wish he was here to share it . . . Um – and thank you . . .'

To a tumult of clapping, Jasmine handed the microphone back to Peg and stepped away from the bright lights. Clara and Sebastian applauded like mad; Andrew less so. The roars, as Jasmine picked her way back from the centre of the track, would have done justice to a homecoming trophy-winning football team.

'Bless!' Clara gathered Jasmine into her arms. 'That was wonderful. Don't cry – you'll ruin your mascara.'

'You were great,' Seb smiled at her, suddenly wanting to cuddle her too. He wondered why Andrew didn't. 'You handled that really well.'

'I should have said more,' Jasmine sighed. 'And I'm desperate for a pint.'

'I'll get it,' Andrew seemed pleased to escape. 'Anyone else?'

Clara and Sebastian shook their heads. Jasmine's teeth were still chattering. A biting wind was swirling up from the sea. Sebastian really hoped it wouldn't rain before the fireworks.

Peg and her torchbearers, probably Allan and Roger, were setting light to the lower tiers of the bonfire now, with much whooping from the crowd. Huge tongues of orange and blue flames rushed into the dark sky.

'She's put petrol on it,' Jasmine sighed. 'I knew she would. She'll probably incinerate the whole damn stadium before we even open.'

'Who's doing the fireworks?' Clara asked. 'Gilbert – or have they asked Eddie Deebley again?'

'Not after he burned down the bus shelter on Millennium Eve with that display rocket, no.' Jasmine shook her head. 'Bunny's doing it.'

'Christ, I hope they've got paramedics on standby.'

Andrew still hadn't returned with Jasmine's drink. Seb wondered whether he should offer to go as backup and decided against it. The bonfire's flames were stretching into infinity now, and even at this distance, he could feel the welcome warmth on his face. Suddenly, with a mighty roar, a cascade of colour screamed into the sky, and Armageddon came to Ampney Crucis. Explosions of light, blinding neon fountains, waxing and waning cushions of fire, all accompanied by a crescendo of staccato thunder bursts, rocked the Benny Clegg Stadium to its newly laid foundations.

'Oh dear,' Jasmine said. 'Bunny's let them all off at once . . .'

*

It was nearly midnight when the party finally started to break up. The brief, but impressive, fireworks display had given way to dancing round the bonfire, and the sort of singalong that Sebastian had fondly imagined had been dead and buried with the demise of *The Black and White Minstrel Show*.

Brittany hadn't made a reappearance; neither had Ewan. Clara, looking singularly unconcerned, had hugged Jasmine, kissed Sebastian a lot, then left to look for him. The fact that Andrew and the promised pint of Old Ampney hadn't materialised either seemed to have been forgotten. Seb had made several journeys to the bar for himself and Jasmine, and was now feeling merrily light-headed.

'You're not driving, are you?' Jasmine attempted to focus on his face.

'No. Brittany is. I guess I'll just have to hang around and wait for her. I – um – think she might be with Ewan.'

'So do I.' Jasmine squinted up at him. 'Bugger, isn't it? Oh, damn – and it's starting to rain.'

The wind was pushing across the open expanse now with vicious little gusts, each new onslaught bringing with it a sheet of icy rain. Jasmine shuddered inside her Guernsey. 'We'll get soaked if we hang around here. Why don't you leave a note for Brittany on her car and come back to the beach hut and wait for her?'

Seb grinned. 'Is that a proposition?'

'Yeah.'

'Great.'

They staggered back along the cliff path in the darkness, Jasmine linking her arm through his and pointing out the potential pitfalls. The sea boiled and crashed invisibly beneath them and the rain, now horizontal on the wind, slashed at their faces. Slithering down the steps, Sebastian had never felt so happy.

The beach hut offered welcome shelter. Stumbling slightly among the overcrowded furniture, Jasmine lit the lamps and switched on a prehistoric electric heater. Her hair was plastered to her head and little rivulets of rain ran down her face.

'You look dreadful.' She wrinkled her nose at Sebastian. 'Designer jeans, designer sweater, all ruined. You might have to take them off . . .'

'That's a bit forward of you.'

'Is it? OK.' She clanked two bottles of Old Ampney from the fridge and expertly flipped off the tops. 'I just thought you could dry them in front of the heater before Brittany comes to claim you. And you don't have to sit there in your boxers and socks, you know. I do have vast supplies of big boyish clothes.'

'Boxers and socks sound fine to me.'

'Men are so naff!' Halting in the process of handing him his bottle of beer, Jasmine managed to glare. 'No socks, OK?'

Sebastian laughed, attempted to unlace his trainers, and immediately fell over on to the sofa. Reaching out to Jasmine, he pulled her down beside him. She curled against him, her wet hair resting on his cheek. He couldn't see her face.

'We can't sleep together, can we? Because of Brittany and Andrew?'

'No,' her voice was muffled. 'I suppose we can't. It's a bit of a sod having principles. But there are no rules about cuddling, are there?'

'None at all.'

Sebastian hugged her, listening to the wind screaming and punching against the beach hut, thrusting in straight from the English Channel. He closed his eyes. The rain thrummed a torrential tattoo on the roof and Jasmine was in his arms. It was what he'd always wanted without realising it. This was his dream. He just wanted to stay like this for ever.

chapter twenty-four

'Haven't you got anything other than the Moody Blues?' Brittany, sitting alongside Ewan as the car headed for Bixford, drifted her long fingers through his CD collection. 'I'm not really into this born-again hippie stuff. God – you haven't. You must be their number-one fan . . . You really should update your musical tastes.'

Ewan sighed. Spending time with Brittany was becoming rather a chore. She reminded him of a much-less-brittle and marginally-more-driven Katrina, and as – thanks to an excellent solicitor and a lot of Peg's money – his wife was soon to be his ex-wife, he really would never want to repeat that particular marital experience. Not, of course, that he and Brittany Frobisher were going to be plighting their troths, but honestly, the woman was an ace nagger. He'd told her so, many times before, and did so again.

'Sorry,' she frowned. 'I'm just used to being in charge.'

'With Sebastian?'

Brittany grinned. 'Definitely not with Sebastian. He's very much his own man. Anyway, I don't think he cares enough about me to allow himself to become hen-pecked.'

'And does that worry you?'

'No.' She leaned back in her seat as the urban sprawl of East London rushed to meet them. 'Well, not in a heartbroken, weeping-copious-tears-into-my-pillow sort of way. It bugs me a bit because I'm used to calling the shots with the brewery business, and having people dancing attendance on me all the time, so I expected to be able to do the same with him – but there, that's me being a spoiled brat. Seb's a bit of a spoiled brat too, so we'd never have made a real go of it. Shame. He's miraculous between the sheets.'

Ewan, who really didn't think he could take yet another blow-by-blow account of Sebastian Gillespie's sexual prowess, turned the car towards the city. He immediately felt the claustrophobia enveloping him as Bixford approached. He was so much part of Ampney Crucis now, that not being able to see the horizon, and to find the sky low and grey rather than iridescent and never-ending, always came as something of a shock. There were Christmas decorations everywhere, and although it was only the end of November, the festoons across Bixford High Street were already faded and tatty, like a bedraggled carnival queen on a wet Bank Holiday Monday.

Ewan looked across the car. 'And have you told Sebastian what you're really doing with me?'

'Nope. I've managed to evade the issue. Have you told Clara?'

'Fat chance. I need to get this right out of my system before I tell her. Then it'll be over. In the past. Nothing she needs to worry about.'

'A final fling, so to speak?' Brittany shrugged. 'A bit risky, if you ask me.'

It was a lot less risky for his continuing masculinity, though, Ewan reckoned, knowing Clara, than his original planned seduction of Brittany Frobisher. Brittany had surprised him with her enthusiasm for becoming involved, although at first the whole thing had been full of misunderstandings. Thanks to Peg's insistence that Ewan should seduce the Platinum Trophy out of Brittany, and Brittany's quicksilver brain realising exactly what he was supposed to be doing, their first meeting had been highly embarrassing. Still, they understood each other very well now, and if Brittany's commitment was born more from boredom than desire, it really didn't matter.

'Just along here . . .' Brittany said suddenly. 'Past these shops. There's some waste ground just by the entrance to the park. No one will see us. Not, of course, that this is my neck of the woods – I wouldn't want you to think that. It's just that, well, since I've been seeing Seb, I've got to know the area well, and when you said Bixford I knew immediately where it was.'

Pulling the car onto the sort of rubble-strewn terrain much loved in gung-ho blood-and-thunder films, Ewan switched off the engine. It was all very depressing. A thin, icy sleet spat spitefully against the windscreen. All they had to do now was wait.

'I've never done undercover work before,' Brittany said happily. 'It's a pleasant change from lunches and parties and first nights and fashion shows.'

This was the first time that Ewan had taken Brittany on this sort of excursion. It was the last time he'd be doing it too. He'd made that very clear. Oh, he'd be more than happy to be on the periphery in the future, but he had no intention of ever sailing this close to the wind again. Still, Brittany had proved to be reliable at giving him the area information he needed, and surprisingly discreet, and they'd become good friends.

At first, when he'd thought he may have to seduce her to get Ampney Crucis into the running for the Frobisher Platinum Trophy, he'd been plagued by doubts. He certainly didn't want to risk losing Clara – and he was sure that Jasmine knew that he saw far more of Brittany than he ever let on. He was just glad that they'd now reached the end of their assignations without anyone getting hurt.

For Peg's sake, Ewan still tried to find out as much from Brittany about the chosen host for the Frobisher Platinum Trophy. Brittany was irritatingly adamant that the selection still hadn't been finalised – and was subject to a complete embargo until the New Year's Eve dinner. She had, however, been very impressed with the Benny Clegg Stadium at the opening party, although a lot less impressed with eventually discovering her Sebby curled up on the beach hut's sofa with Jasmine, both sound asleep and clinging to each other like the babes in the wood.

They'd apparently not even drunk their beer. Ewan thought this sounded serious – especially knowing Jasmine's capacity for Old Ampney – and had suggested that Brittany could have walked in on a marathon lovemaking session. But Brittany had said no, she somehow doubted it, as they were both fully clothed, and rain-splattered, and more than a little hung over when she eventually managed to wake them.

On second thoughts, he'd decided, aware of Jasmine's old-fashioned moral values, and her tendency to hang on to bloody Andrew even though anyone with half an eye could see that they were completely wrong for each other, Brittany was probably right.

'Oh, I'm definitely right,' Brittany had said, smiling in satisfaction. 'As I've always said, Sebastian is an amazing lover. If he and Jasmine had been having sex, believe me she wouldn't have been half so grumpy as she was when we left her. It would have taken days to wipe the smile from her face.'

Ewan decided he probably wouldn't pass this scrap of information on to Jasmine – just in case.

The Moody Blues were just coming to the end of 'I Know You're Out There Somewhere'. Ewan always felt it could have been written for him and Clara. Still, they'd found each other again, hadn't they? Each time he heard the song it made him wonder about all those I'll-love-you-for-ever lovers who had then parted over something silly and lived for the rest of their lives regretting it, remembering, wondering if the other person ever thought of them . . .

'There!' Brittany clutched at his arm. 'There's a greyhound! Is it the right one? They all look the same to me. Thin and pretty – like Kate Moss.'

Ewan peered through the rivulets of sleet sliding down the steamy windscreen. Oh, yes . . . this could be it. The informant hadn't given much of a description, Ewan knew, but then they rarely did. No one ever wanted to become involved. Still, it was enough to have had it reported. The ill-treatment of any animal made his blood boil; the cruelty to racing greyhounds that he'd witnessed during his travels abroad had made him determined to do all he could to help these gorgeous, vulnerable, almost spiritual creatures.

Rubbing a spyhole in the window, Ewan peered out at his quarry. He felt his anger rising. The dog certainly looked dejected, with its head down and its tail between its legs. It was being led towards the park by a girl wearing a flapping plastic mac with the hood up, and too-big wellingtons, and who, if her body language was anything to go by, was also in the slough of despond. The greyhound's coat was black-slicked by the sleet, and if it was the dog he'd been tipped-off about, it was apparently being kept in a one-bedroomed flat, for God's sake, and had been locked outside howling in a tiny yard for weeks on end.

'OK, go for it.' He nodded to Brittany. 'Take some

photos – don't let her see you – and we'll follow her when she comes back and find out where she lives. Bastards! I'd like to string up the lot of them.'

Brittany, clicking away happily with the Polaroid, had pulled her leather coat up to her chin, and her Kangol beret down to her nose. Ewan personally thought that this was taking undercover surveillance a smidgen too far, but he didn't want to dampen her enthusiasm.

They'd first got into conversation about his greyhound rescue activities completely by accident. Needing both Peg's offered accommodation and employment – not to mention the hefty loan to divorce Katrina – Ewan hadn't wanted to refuse to flirt with Brittany Frobisher. It had put him in something of a quandary because of Clara, so he was mightily relieved that the situation hadn't arisen. By then, though, he'd seen Brittany at Ampney Crucis and spoken to her, and been surprised to find that behind the glitzy paparazzi image was a woman with strongly held views on animal rights.

He'd told her of his exploits abroad, rescuing, nursing and rehoming the half-dead greyhounds that he'd snatched from the illegal circuits, and seen her eyes fill with tears. It had moved him considerably, and when she'd asked to become involved, but only if Ewan would ensure her complete anonymity, he'd been more than happy to rope her in. So far, Brittany had successfully used her A-list celeb contacts, and her It Girl chums to raise enormous funds for the greyhound rescue shelters.

The girl and the greyhound hadn't returned from the park, and he wondered for a moment if they'd simply left by another gate. The sleet had turned to icy hail now, slashing wickedly at the windscreen, and he was sure that no one would choose to stay out in it any longer than was absolutely necessary.

'Tell me,' Brittany pushed the camera and the disgorged photographs back into the glove box, 'why don't you tell Clara what you're doing? It's nothing to be ashamed of. On the contrary, I'm sure she'd be very proud.'

'She may well be – I hope she is. Clara loves animals, hates cruelty . . . yes, I'm sure she'd be a hundred per cent behind me. But Katrina – my almost-ex – definitely wasn't. It wasn't just that she had no feelings for animals, but she thought my time would be better spent, a) making money, and b) keeping out of trouble. I couldn't risk Clara feeling the same way.' He looked at Brittany. 'Soppy to the point of complete wetness, I know, but I do love Clara very much. I want it to be perfect. I couldn't bear it if there was a flaw – so I reckoned that if I didn't tell her then I wouldn't know.'

'You're just like Seb.' Brittany spoke without rancour. 'He's searching for the perfect love too. Silly sod. But – and please tell me to mind my own business here – but if this relationship with your Clara is going to be so idyllic and eternal, don't you think it'd be a good idea to know how she feels about the things that are important to you before you commit?'

'Mind your own business.'

'Asking for trouble . . . Hey! Angels at two o'clock or whatever it is they say in those old war films!'

Ewan looked in the direction Brittany was pointing. Bingo! The girl, indistinguishable because of the voluminous plastic mac, and the greyhound, wetter and more miserable-looking than ever, were trudging back towards the High Street. Leaning forward, rubbing a larger spyhole, Ewan watched as they crossed the main road, paused outside one of the bleak three-storey houses while the girl found a key, then disappeared dismally inside.

'So now what?' Brittany pulled off her beret and fluffed

at her short layered hair. 'Do we go belting in like the SAS and fire accusations like bullets?'

'Sorry, no. What we do is note the address and bide our time.'

Brittany looked disappointed. 'God, is that all? No storming the barricades or bringing in RSPCA reinforcements or anything?'

Ewan, who had scribbled '51 High Street, Bixford' on the back of an envelope shook his head. 'Nothing like that at all. There are no set rules, of course, and yes, we'd report definite acts of cruelty to the appropriate authorities, but in cases like this I prefer more direct action. The dog is my prime concern, so once I've watched a couple more times, I'll pick my opportunity and move in.'

'You're going to snatch it?' Brittany's eyes shone. 'What – in a midnight raid?'

'I think you've watched one too many Bruce Willis films,' Ewan grinned. 'But, yes – that's more or less what I intend to do. Hopefully, before long, when the poor thing is tethered in the yard, we'll find a way in and rescue him without anyone knowing. He'll be well looked after. Then we'll see what happens. The owner, if she tries to reclaim it, will be met by the full clout of the law.'

'Super,' Brittany sighed. 'Although I'd hoped for a bit more action. So, what now?'

'I'm going back to Ampney Crucis and Clara. What about you?'

'I should go into the office, I suppose.' Brittany looked at her watch. 'What with this, and Seb, and organising the Platinum Trophy, I haven't done much real work for ages.'

Ewan was impressed. It never failed to surprise him that under the designer layers and the gossip-column inches, there was a very hard-working and astute company director. 'Shall I drop you off at Frobisher House, then?'

Brittany shook her head. 'I'll need to go home first and collect some things. I could do with a shower. We've a shareholders' meeting this evening so it could be a long night. Would you mind popping across town?'

'The least I can do.' Ewan started the car. 'And thanks for helping out today.'

'My pleasure,' said Brittany, snuggling into her leather coat as the Moody Blues began to tell everyone about their Wildest Dreams.

Brittany's flat — her little *pied-à-terre* she called it — was in London's latest fashionable quarter. Ewan was slightly dismayed to see a couple of wet and frozen photographers hanging around outside. However, Brittany greeted them gaily, posed prettily, and then beckoned Ewan in through a maze of porters and security devices.

'Poor things,' she said as they hurtled upwards in a silent and perfumed lift. 'Their editors insist they hang around all the likely spots all the time. They're from the glossy star-goss mags. You know, that'll come out as "Brewery Heiress Brittany returns from Christmas Shopping Trip" or some such crap. They'll have loads of fun trying to work out who you are, though. You'll probably be billed as "Brittany's latest dark and dangerous dalliance". I hope Clara doesn't take that edition — you could be seriously in the shit. Ah — here we are . . . This is me.'

The flat — more like an enormous sweeping palatial superstar penthouse, Ewan thought — overlooked the city from a wall of plate glass. Expecting it to be filled with the latest stark and minimalist designer furniture, Ewan was rather impressed by its cosiness. Everything was large and colourful and cushiony. It was very warm and snugly barricaded against the foul weather lashing from outside.

There seemed to be fresh flowers everywhere, and lots of photographs, and the mantelpiece was stuffed with invitations.

'Make yourself at home,' Brittany called. 'I'm just going to get showered and changed. Oh, and if you could be a poppet and put the kettle on, we'll have a cup of tea before we both depart for pastures new.'

Ewan, who really wanted to get back to Ampney Crucis, and who was still worrying about whether the greyhound would be shoved outside in this appalling storm, felt he had no option other than to obey. Brittany was back in full autocratic mode.

He was just pouring Earl Grey into *Chicken Run* mugs when Brittany appeared in the doorway. The smell of expensive body lotion had preceded her, and she wandered into the kitchen swathed in a towel, her hair slicked back from her face.

'Super. You don't fancy a change of career, do you? You'd make a lovely house-boy.' She took the mug from him and kissed the tip of his nose. 'Clara is a very lucky woman. You've got a pretty face, a gorgeous bod, a brain, and compassion. That's some package.'

Ewan, who knew that in the past a come-on such as this would have had only one conclusion, backed slightly away. 'Clara will be pleased to hear that you've endorsed me so highly.'

Placing the mug of tea on the large oak table, Brittany let the towel slip. Ewan blinked at the beauty of her nakedness. They stared at each other in silence.

'You're going to turn me down, aren't you?' Brittany looked slightly surprised.

Ewan shrugged. 'Yeah, I am — and no one is more amazed than me . . .'

'Your loss.' Brittany bent down and retrieved the towel

323

again. 'And probably mine. Clara's gain. One day you may regret this.'

One day, Ewan thought, he might – but somehow he doubted it. It was his trial of fire and he'd passed with flying colours. 'Look, I don't think I'll hang around for the tea, if you don't mind. Thanks for everything you've done for the dog rescue stuff – and, well, everything, but it's a long drive and the weather is lousy and –'

Brittany, clutching the towel loosely against her, kissed his cheek. 'Bugger off back to Clara, you smug sod. The greyhounds will still get my financial support, don't worry. And no doubt I'll see you at Pop's dinner at the stately pile on New Year's Eve – if you're coming with the rest of the Ampney Crucis brigade, that is. Which I suppose you will be, you being on the payroll. Only I'd prefer it if you didn't bring Clara. I really hate to see people in love.'

He laughed. 'Really? So you and Seb definitely aren't . . . ?'

'Christ, no. He's in love with Jasmine – but I'm not sure that he knows it yet.'

Three hours later, after a long, slow and arduous journey in which the hail turned to sleet and then back again, and the Moody Blues had sung their greatest hits more times than he'd care to remember, Ewan pulled up outside Clara's loft.

Ampney Crucis was deserted in the storm, and the sea, slate grey and restless under the onslaught, crashed listlessly onto the beach. There were lights on in most of the houses and the Crumpled Horn had a fully bedecked Christmas Tree visible through the windows beside the roaring log fire. Ewan was delighted to be home.

Clara looked up from the long, white sofa where she'd obviously been reading. 'Hi. Everything OK?'

324

'Fine. No, better than fine.' Ewan sat beside her. 'Absolutely bloody fantastic.'

'Really? I was worried about you. The weather's so atrocious. Where have you been?'

'London. Sorting out some final bits and pieces of my life.' He slid his arms round her. 'Are we eating in tonight? Or do you fancy skipping across to the Crumpled Horn for a meal?'

'Sounds great.' Clara stretched in his embrace. 'And perfect for you now they've included veggie burgers on the menu. Add a bottle or two of burgundy and you could make me a very happy woman.'

He kissed her. She didn't question him, ever. They'd known each other for so long – and the fact that he'd let her down before only served to make him more aware that he must never hurt her again.

She kissed him back, nuzzling her lips against his throat. Clara, he thought hazily, could arouse him more by the lightest touch than Brittany Frobisher could do with the whole of her exquisite naked body.

'Do you want me to ring Jas?' she whispered in his ear. 'And get her and Andrew to meet us in there as a foursome, or shall we just go solo?'

'Could it be just us tonight? I sort of want you all to myself. For tonight and for always.' He eased himself away from her slightly. This was it. This was what he should have done long ago. He took a deep breath. 'Clara, will you marry me?'

chapter twenty-five

'Nine to four the field for race seven!' Jasmine yelled against the biting northerly wind. 'I'm offering Simply The Best at fives! Place your bets now!'

The Benny Clegg Stadium, on the last Saturday before Christmas, was crammed to its newly embellished rafters. Despite the continuing Arctic weather, the punters were out in force. Tonight, on the final Six-Pack Saturday of the year, everyone seemed determined to throw themselves into the festive spirit and hopefully win back some of their seasonal overspending.

The floodlights sliced silver paths through the December darkness, and despite several thermal layers, Jasmine was frozen both inside and out. Allan and Roger, used to years of working in this weather, were almost invisible on either side of her, snuggled into sheepskin coats and balaclavas, but for Jasmine, her first winter as a bookie-proper had come as an awful shock to the system. She almost wished that just for tonight she could be one of the red-jacketed Tote ladies, cosy and sheltered behind their Perspex windows.

Several people, their faces purple and their hands blue, thrust notes at her, and mumbled their selections through rigidly clenched teeth. Jasmine uncurled her fingers enough to take their money and hiss, 'Eleven pounds to five, twenty three' to Muriel, who was now employed as her permanent writer-upper.

Having worked for forty-odd years on the fruit and veg stall in Ampney Crucis market, Muriel, a crony of Peg's, was well used to inclement weather. Dressed in a velveteen pixie hood, donkey jacket, zip-up ankle booties and fingerless mittens, Muriel still looked just as likely to dole out five pounds of King Edward's as the winnings on the last race.

Clara, who was definitely a warm-weather person, had made all sorts of excuses not to turn out and keep the ledger as soon as the temperatures started to dip. Anyway, Jasmine reckoned, Clara and Ewan – since the engagement – had been like damn Siamese twins. It was almost impossible to spot the join. Still, at least it must mean that Ewan had stopped his Brittany thing – which must also mean that Brittany and Seb were reunited. She sighed and pushed her thoughts away from that path. It was lovely enough that Clara, proudly displaying a very ostentatious opal and jet engagement ring, was talking about a definite Easter wedding and a hoped-for next-Christmas baby.

The greyhounds started to parade for the seventh race. Jasmine looked at them with intense pity. They'd just been dragged, without warning, from the sumptuous luxury of the centrally heated kennels into the freezing night. Poor things. Even though she knew that they were all loved and well cared for, tonight they appeared more shivery and undernourished than ever, with their knees knocking and their tails uniformly down.

The punters, at least, seemed to be having a good time. The Six-Packs had gone down really well, with coaches disgorging people from all over Dorset and beyond every Saturday night. In the illuminated eating area, behind the glass stand, Jasmine watched them all now tucking into

...ir chicken and chips and downing their Old Ampney ale as the heating roared at blast-furnace level. She fervently wished that she could join them.

Gilbert, who, harnessed with Eddie Deebley, had made a more-than-passable job of providing meals for the many visitors, was reeling off the list of runners over the Tannoy. Jasmine knew that he was wearing, as were Bunny, and Gorf – who had been promoted from security to starter – a Santa Claus hat. Peg had tried to persuade Jasmine into one too, but after the fiasco with the hard hat, which would haunt her for ever, she'd resolutely refused.

'You lose most of your body heat through your head,' Peg had warned. 'You could get frost bite in your brain.'

Jasmine had said she'd risk it.

Peg was bouncing around, looking very festive in a red velvet get-up trimmed with swansdown, plus, naturally, the ubiquitous Santa hat. Several fir trees, ablaze with flashing fairy lights, were dotted about the stadium, all seriously overloading the mains circuit, and the music echoing from the Tannoy in between races had been changed to a perpetual loop of *Doris Sings Christmas*. For Jasmine, the night's twenty-third rendition of 'Little Donkey' was just beginning to pall.

The greyhounds were in the traps now, and Gorf had raised his green flag. Bunny, his Santa hat touching his forest of eyebrows, was poised with the hare. Three more races and that would be it until after the New Year. Jasmine sighed. No more racing until she'd got through potentially the two worst days of her life – her first Christmas without Benny and New Year's Eve at Frobisher Palace.

The roar as the dogs sped free was frozen solid, a zillion droplets of breath instantly crystallised in the crisp night air. Jasmine watched as the greyhounds scurried round the first bend, close together as if for mutual warmth, and bounded on into the straight. Everyone was standing up behind the glass panels, their meals abandoned, soundlessly cheering on their favourites. The stalwarts, too hooked or too drunk, or both, to notice the cold, were yelling from the rails. The six-packs had certainly improved the fortunes of the Benny Clegg Stadium. Jasmine just wished that Peg would stop heaping her hopes on their staging the Platinum Trophy too. It simply wasn't going to happen.

The screams, as the greyhounds completed their far-side circuit and rounded the last bend before the finishing post, grew louder and more frenzied. Jasmine did mental calculations and hoped that Love-A-Dove, the six dog, would win. It didn't.

'Simply The Best,' muttered Muriel, blowing on her fingers. 'Five to one. Bollocks.'

'So, what about Christmas, pet?' Peg, with her Santa hat now at a rakish angle, was doling out treble measures of single malt in the fiery warmth of her new office. 'Have you decided yet?'

The greyhound meeting was over, the coach parties had left, and the floodlights were out. Gilbert, Gorf and Bunny were clearing up. Everyone else had gone home.

'I've tried not to think about it.' Jasmine rolled the Glenmorangie round her tongue. 'Clara and Ewan have asked me to go to them, but if I'm honest, I'd rather stay in the hut on my own.'

Peg didn't immediately insist that Jasmine shouldn't be alone on Christmas Day. Peg understood. 'Might be for the best, pet. Nasty time, Christmas, for memories. And with Clara and young Ewan being so happy it could get a bit wearing. What about your mum and dad?'

'Not even in the frame. I mean, even when I lived at home, I always spent Christmas Eve night and all of

Christmas Day with Grandpa . . .' She stared into her glass, willing the tears not to fall. 'We had little routines, silly traditions, you know . . .'

Peg leaned across and patted her hand. 'I know. And Andrew?'

Jasmine sighed. 'We've never had Christmas Day together, so I don't see why we should start now. I mean, Andrew always just used to see me on Christmas night at Grandpa's for an hour or so, because he liked to spend the day with his family. He hasn't suggested that I go to his parents' this year or anything awful. Or even that he comes to me in the hut. He did say some time ago that maybe we should both go to Mum and Dad's – but that was before they looked likely to be the next candidates on the *Jerry Springer Show*.' She took another gulp of whisky. 'I really think I'll stay in the hut with the telly and get very drunk and eat myself silly and just be glad when it's all over.'

'Sounds a good plan to me. And we'll have the lovely swanky do at the Frobishers to look forward to, won't we?'

Jasmine tried to look enthusiastic. 'We will. And what about you? Are you having Christmas Day with Ewan and Clara?'

'I am, pet. Clara's promised to do a full vegetarian roast just for Ewan. I'm pleased that they've got engaged. I'm still angry with him for not marrying her in the first place. It's all so messy – the divorcing Katrina business.'

'And expensive.'

'That too,' Peg agreed. 'Look, maybe you should come along to Clara's on Christmas night or something – just so that you won't have to spend the whole day alone.'

'Maybe.' Jasmine downed the rest of her Glenmorangie in silence. There were only two people she wanted to

330

spend Christmas with and, of course, they were both out of the question. Benny was dead and Sebastian wasn't.

She'd had a Christmas card from Sebastian. It was very pale, a solitary log cabin beside a frozen lake all surrounded by snow drifts. He'd written, 'This is the nearest thing I could find to a beach hut in splendid isolation by the sea. Not a patch on the real thing. I hope your Christmas is all that you want it to be and more. I won't insult you by suggesting you relive your happy memories – it's far too soon. I'll be thinking of you. Love, Seb.'

She'd lingered on the word 'love' and then decided that unless he'd put yours sincerely, there weren't many other card-signing options open to him. He'd also sent her six doughnuts looking like plum puddings, complete with dripping glazed icing and a sugar-crafted holly sprig on top.

Peg yawned noisily. 'Oh, excuse me, pet. I must be getting old. I used to be able to take running the stadium and a few whiskies and the mayhem of Christmas all in my stride. Once we've got the Frobisher Platinum out of the way I think I'll loosen the reins a little – hand over more responsibility to you and Ewan . . . Oh, don't look like that. I'm not retiring. It's just that you've done so much already to make this place successful, and I can see that you younger ones have the clout and guts to keep my dreams – yes, and your grandpa's dreams – alive. We're all knocking on – me, Roger, Allan, Gilbert – and we may still have the enthusiasm but we haven't got the get-up-and-go.'

'You'll be here for ever.' Jasmine felt drowsy now, the Glenmorangie and the warmth of the office wrapping her in a cosy blanket.

'We're none of us here for ever, pet. But the stadium, hopefully, will be. That's why I'm looking to the next

generation. Ewan will have children, you'll marry someone –'

'Andrew.'

Peg exhaled. 'If you say so. Although I thought you
were going to break off the engagement some time back?'

'I was. I kept trying to find the right moment. There
wasn't one.'

Peg stood up and kissed her. The papery skin smelled
of loose powder and rouge. The swansdown was moulting.
'Just don't marry the wrong man, pet. You've taken some
brave decisions since Benny died. You've ignored your
parents and damn Andrew, and flown in the face of conven-
tion by taking on more here than most people would have
ever thought possible. You've carried on the true Benny
Clegg tradition and you're a successful bookie. Don't throw
all that away by marrying Andrew because you think that
not doing so would hurt him.'

'I don't think it would,' Jasmine sighed. 'It's just that
we've always been together. And I know he really hates
me being a bookie. But he likes the money I'm making
and –'

Peg pulled away and held up her hands. 'Jasmine, pet,
listen to yourself.'

'I can't finish with him at Christmas!'

'Why not?' Peg was gathering her bags and coat and
scarves together. 'Most people are at each other's throats
over the festive season. At least you and Andrew will
have a good reason. Now, do you want Bunny to see you
home?'

Jasmine shook her head. 'No thanks. The last time he
did that, I then had to walk home with him because someone had been reading Harry Potter to him and he thought
that there were bad wizards lurking in St Edith's graveyard.'

*

The next morning the gale was still howling and the sky was still slate grey. Jasmine, snuggled beneath the poppies and daisies, could hear the sea tugging restlessly at the shingle and the occasional angry squawk of a gull as a gust of wind blew it off course.

She looked at Sebastian's Christmas card on her bedside table. She loved him. And because she loved him, she couldn't carry on being engaged to Andrew. It wasn't right. Not, of course, that she thought by breaking off her engagement Seb would then immediately be hammering at her door with Tiffany diamonds and a life-promise. That may well be the Mills and Boon dénouement she always read with such satisfaction, but she was well aware that it simply wouldn't happen in real life.

Jasmine punched her pillow. In real life, she'd finish with Andrew, and stay friends with Seb; but at nearly thirty and not prepared to take second best, not to mention being no great shakes in the beauty stakes, she'd spend the rest of her life single and sinking slowly into eccentricity. It was quite a pleasant prospect, really. She'd manage alone, being a bookie, and loving Sebastian Gillespie in the same distant and hopeless way that she'd once loved the Bay City Rollers.

Everyone had been telling her for ages that she and Andrew were wasting their time – she knew it and so did he. It just needed one of them to be brave enough to make the first and final move. And, of course, Peg had been absolutely right about Andrew last night. It made her sad, though, she thought, looking at the school photo of her and Andrew and Ewan and Clara. It should have worked out. For all four of them.

She pushed back the duvet and shivered. The shutters and door all rattled alarmingly in the wind, and the slats in the floorboards now emitted irregular icy blasts round her ankles. It may not be the lap of luxury, she thought, scuttling out into the kitchen to put on the kettle and ignite the heaters, but she truly never wanted to live anywhere else. And if she had to live here alone for the rest of her life then things weren't all bad.

The radio burbled comfortably in the background as she washed and dressed in as many layers as she could squeeze into. Four days until Christmas. She'd bought her presents in a one-off blast in Bournemouth some weeks ago, and they were all piled behind the sofa, wrapped and ready. Most of them she would dole out at Peg's traditional party at the Crumpled Horn on Christmas Eve, but the golfing sweater for her father and the diet cook book for her mother would prove the perfect excuse for calling now and explaining about her plans for a solitary Christmas.

Crunching toast and strawberry jam, and warming to her theme, Jasmine convinced herself that Sunday morning would be the ideal time to catch both her parents at home. She hadn't seen them for ages, although Andrew still called in regularly to the Chewton Estate house and kept her updated on the matrimonial developments. There had been no indication that either of them was about to decamp with an extra-marital lover, so she assumed that it had all been a lot of fuss over nothing. Maybe her father had been dallying with the decrepit Moira Cook, and maybe her mother had taken a lover to score points. Jasmine sighed. She'd never know, and even if they had, it all seemed to be over now.

Dragging Benny's waxed jacket from its hook behind the door, she stuffed Yvonne and Philip's Christmas presents into a carrier bag, then turned down the heaters and switched off the radio. Gloves . . . She'd need gloves for the trek across the village. Fumbling deep into the pockets of Benny's jacket she came up with a fistful of sweet wrappers and several scrumpled up tissues. So where had she left her gloves? She stared down at her hands. There was something wrong. Something missing.

She gawped at her bare fingers in total surprise. Andrew's engagement ring was no longer there . . . Was it a sign, a portent, an indication that her body knew the relationship was over even if the rest of her didn't? She shook her head at such flummery. So what on earth had happened to it?

Wondering momentarily if she'd lost enough weight for the ring simply to have slipped from her finger, she dismissed the notion straight away. Not that she was given to regular weigh-ins, but on the trip to Bournemouth she'd jumped recklessly onto the scales in Boots, only to see the red digital read-out spiral into amazingly high metric figures. She'd then got off, put down her shopping bags, taken off her coat, her shoes and a jumper and tried again. This time the red kilos had translated satisfactorily into somewhere around her normal eleven and a half stones.

The only logical reason for the ring to have moved was because her hands were so damn cold, that her fingers looked like wizened matchsticks. And so where the hell was it? Knowing that she'd had it on last night, it must be here in the beach hut somewhere. Retracing her steps from kitchen to living room, from bedroom back to kitchen and not finding it, she sighed in exasperation.

'Oh God, Grandpa, what do I do now? How can I go and tell Andrew that I want to break off the engagement but that I can't give him the ring back? He'll think I've hocked it or something.'

She shoved her hands deep into the pockets of the waxed jacket and her fingers closed round something small, circular, cold and solid. She smiled and withdrew the ring. 'Cheers, Grandpa. Any more advice?'

None seemed forthcoming, so Jasmine slid the ring safely inside her glove, then picked up her carrier bag and stepped out onto the veranda.

The walk had taken her breath away. Every part of her was numbed. Jasmine wished it would snow. Surely a good snowfall would take the biting edge off the temperatures? Anyway, she loved the snow. A white Christmas, snugged up in the beach hut, dreaming of Sebastian, would be lovely. Not that it ever snowed at the proper times any more. Last year it had been relatively warm all winter and then snowed in April. She and Benny had built a snowman in the middle of the greyhound track and given it Gilbert's fedora and a string of pearls nicked from Peg. They'd thought it looked a touch like Eddie Izzard.

A month later Benny was dead.

Brushing away the tears, and deciding to call into the cemetery on the way back from Andrew's for a lengthy chat with the headstone before visiting her parents, Jasmine trudged on towards the outskirts of Ampney Crucis. Andrew shared a house with several of his dealership colleagues, though she rarely went there because it was always scuzzy and she felt everyone laughed at her. Occasionally she'd spent the night there with Andrew, after a party, and had always been made to feel very unwelcome the following morning. Andrew's workmates were all target-blind in the loo, never cleaned the bath, and farting out the tune of the National Anthem while watching *Baywatch* seemed to constitute their main entertainment.

She rang the doorbell. All the curtains were sort of dragged together, so the chances were that no one was yet up. She rang again. The wind was pushing debris against the doorstep and rattling a discordant melody amongst a heap of empty wine bottles and lager cans inside the gate.

Eventually, the door was pulled partly open. Nick, one of the dealership boys, peered at her round it. His hair was on end and his eyes were almost closed. Jasmine thought he was possibly naked.

'Er – is Andrew here?'

'You're too late for the party, sweetheart. That was last night.'

Party? What party? 'Yeah – I know. Um – can I see Andrew, please?'

'I'll go and ask him. Who shall I say is calling?'

'Just get him.'

The door closed again. Jasmine seethed. Even if she'd known Andrew and his flatmates were having a party, she wouldn't have gone. She'd been working anyway. But surely he might have mentioned it to her?

The door opened again. Andrew, looking even worse than Nick had, stared at her as though she was the last person on earth he wanted to see. 'Jas?'

'Good party, was it? Can I come in?'

'Yeah, well, um – no, not really . . .'

'Tough.' She pushed past him into the hall. With the curtains closed and the lights off, the darkened house smelled rancid – of stale smoke and stale beer and stale vomit. She looked at him. 'Is there somewhere we can talk? Not down here – your room?'

'Not my room.' Andrew, dressed only in Y-fronts and someone else's T-shirt, hurled himself at the bottom of the staircase.

'Have you got someone else in there?'

'No.' Andrew looked very pale. 'But Jon and Richard have.'

'What? Both of them?'

'Yeah. Nick pinched their room, you see, for him and – well, you wouldn't know her – and then they piled into

337

mine with – um – well, you wouldn't know them either, so I've slept on the sofa –'

'With us . . .' A very thin girl in grubby Sloggi vest and pants, and with most of her make-up round her chin and twiglets in her hair, staggered into the hall. 'Me and my sister. Oh, and her friend, and her friend's mate from work.'

'Not that we were – like – together,' Andrew said quickly. 'Were we?'

'Christ, no.' The thin girl gave Andrew a disparaging glance as she disappeared into the downstairs loo. 'It was just there were no more beds free and we were all zonked.'

Jasmine felt very old. And extremely angry. 'Why didn't you invite me?'

'Don't shout, Jas, please. I've got one hell of a headache. You were working. And you wouldn't have liked it. You don't like my friends. Look, give me half an hour to pull myself together and we'll go to the Crumpled Horn and talk. O K?'

'Not OK.' She shook her head. 'I've got millions of things to do. Actually, I just came to give you this.' She wriggled off her glove and pushed the ring into his hand. 'Sorry. I should have done it a long time ago, shouldn't I? Now you'll feel better.'

Andrew stared at the engagement ring. 'You don't want to marry me?'

'No. I don't think I ever did, not really.'

'But you can't do it now!' Andrew almost howled. 'I've bought you a Christmas present! What shall I do with it?'

'Give it to her.' Jasmine, feeling light-headed and joyously liberated, nodded towards the thin girl who'd emerged from the loo holding her nose. 'I'm sure she'll love a set of three hankies and some cheapo bath foam.'

'How did you know? Oh . . .' Andrew looked crestfallen.

Jasmine grinned. 'See you around, no doubt. And no hard feelings. Bye . . .'

She closed the door behind her and burst into tears.

More than an hour later, having sat on the kerbstone of Benny's grave in the freezing wind, and given him chapter and verse of the break-up, Jasmine felt a lot less wobbly. It was really strange, not being part of a couple any more. No more Jas and Andrew. It would take a lot of getting used to. She stood up. Just her parents to sort out, then she'd go back to the beach hut and ring Clara and tell her. And then – and then, what? For a frightening minute the future seemed to stretch ahead full of nothing. Jasmine gulped in the icy air. The feeling would pass, she knew it would. She'd get used to being alone. She'd even enjoy it. Probably.

It took another twenty bitterly cold minutes to reach the Chewton Estate. Maybe, she thought, puffing like mad, the time was right to invest in a small car. She'd made a decent profit since she'd become Benny Clegg, and her building society account was looking reasonably healthy. And now she wouldn't be needing any of it as the deposit for the house she and Andrew were supposed to have. And she wouldn't be able to borrow cars from Andrew for her journeys in future, would she? Yes, she thought, definitely. My early New Year's resolution: I'll buy a car in January. The future was already looking a bit less scary.

There were two cars parked outside her parents' house. Her mother's and Andrew's. Jasmine groaned. It hadn't taken him long to come to spread the glad tidings, had it? And her father's car wasn't there, which probably meant he was out playing golf – even in this weather – and she really didn't want to see her mother alone, or Andrew at all.

Dithering for a moment, hesitating on the edge of the drive, horribly aware that various neighbouring net curtains were twitching, Jasmine decided to march straight in, hand over the presents, ignore Andrew, and beat a hasty retreat. Anyway, her nose was running from the cold and she could do with using the loo.

The swimming pool, left uncovered and undrained, had a thin crust of ice which rippled strangely in the wind. The garden was unkempt, all the summer flowers left to go to seed and now rattling their stalks together, lace-topped and neglected. Feeling guilty, Jasmine realised that she hadn't been here for ages. And things must have got serious if both her parents had let the garden run riot. She should have cared more about their problems. She shouldn't have been so wrapped up in the greyhound stadium and being a bookie – and Sebastian. She'd had weeks while Damon and his boys were doing the rebuild to pop up here and be a real daughter . . .

She paused by the kitchen door. Walk straight in or slope off back round the front and ring the bell? Straight in, she decided: the neighbours had had their floor show for today. The kitchen was empty. There were signs of breakfast scattered around, but no smell of lunch being prepared. Andrew must be pouring out his heart to Yvonne in the sitting room. In a fit of cowardice, Jasmine thought about leaving the Christmas presents on the kitchen table and just creeping away. It was her mother's voice, suddenly raised, that stopped her.

'. . . no, I won't keep my voice down! I'm bloody angry! How dare he do this to me! I'll be a laughing stock! What?'

There was a low rumbly male voice – obviously Andrew's. Jasmine couldn't make out the words. Her father was in the doghouse, though, that much was obvious.

'Moira Cook!' Yvonne shrieked. 'God – I wish! Yes, yes, I know what you told Jasmine. She came here and asked me if it was true, remember? I said it wasn't because – dear God, Moira Cook! The woman's dead from the neck down!'

More Andrew rumblings.

'That's wicked!' Yvonne laughed. 'Oh well, yes, I know Philip has trouble getting it up, but even so –'

Jasmine wanted to stuff her fingers in her ears. She shouldn't be listening to this – and neither should Andrew. What the hell was her mother playing at?

Yvonne's laugh was closer now, as if she was about to walk into the hall. 'OK, OK – I'll give you that. Well, she's welcome to him. I hope they'll be very happy together. And of course she's got her own place so he won't be coming back here . . .'

The voice receded. Andrew laughed too. Jasmine felt she might join in, hysterically, at any moment.

'Anyway, he's finally gone to fat Verity – the woman's thighs are like lard slabs! I've seen her in the gym. Mottled cellulite! Like two salamis. What? Yes, well, there's a blessing . . . no more poxy knitted tea cosies.'

Jasmine's head reeled. Her father had left. Her father had gone to live with Verity, his secretary. Verity of the bolster bosom and the knitting needles. He'd been having an affair all the time! Andrew had been right! Oh, her poor mother –

'And now I'm a free man . . .' Andrew's voice was suddenly very close. He must be standing just inside the sitting-room. 'Aren't you going to console me?'

Yvonne giggled. And cooed, 'Andy, darling, of course I am. I must say my daughter may be a huge disappointment in all other areas, but she does have impeccable timing.

And, of course, after a suitable interval, you'll be able to step neatly into Philip's shoes . . .'

What the hell was that all about? Surely – no . . . Jasmine's hair stood on end. There was a sick, cold feeling snaking into her stomach. That come-on laugh of her mother's, that cooing voice – she'd heard them before. On the phone . . . on the beach . . .

Andy? Her mother called Andrew Andy? Oh dear God – no!

Rooted to the spot for a split second, Jasmine then sucked in her breath and stormed into the sitting room. Her mother, in a tiny silk nightie, was curled into Andrew's arms – obviously not for the first time – making little moaning noises as he kissed her throat.

Gagging, Jasmine stared at them. She didn't feel hurt. Just angry and disgusted. The anger won the battle. She looked down at the carrier bag still clasped in her hand, and with a cry of fury, she whirled it round and round her head like a demented dervish, then let it go. It zoomed across the room and caught both her mother and Andrew neatly on the side of the head.

'Happy Christmas, you bastards!' Jasmine roared. 'Happy bloody Christmas!'

chapter twenty-six

Christmas Eve in the Copacabana was getting out of hand. Martina had hired a whole batch of mini Santa outfits with obscenely short skating skirts and white fur-trimmed hats – and insisted that the waitresses should all wear them with their black fishnets and white thigh-length boots.

'I look like I should be walking the beat round Sussex Gardens,' April grumbled, mixing a potentially lethal shooter of Cuervo Gold, sambuca and Tabasco. 'And I'd make more money.'

'You would that, love,' the recipient of the Flatliner waggled a piece of mistletoe across the bar. 'Gissa kiss.'

'OK, but I've got halitosis and herpes – oh, changed your mind? Shame. Who's next?'

The Christmas Eve dog racing was over. Oliver had scheduled an early meeting, in the hope that everyone would then pour away from the tracks and into the Gillespie Stadium's many bars to continue their celebrations. It had worked very well. At least, for Oliver and Martina's already bulging bank balance. April, who still had masses of Christmas things to do at home, had never felt so exhausted.

All night, a girlie group dressed as reindeers had been chanting their way nasally through some really sugary festive favourites – and currently Santa Claus was Coming to

Town – again. April, already punch-drunk, kept impaling green cherries on the umbrellas and setting fire to the olives. The swizzle sticks had disappeared hours ago, and the last of the sparklers was smouldering at the base of the plastic palm tree.

This would be, without doubt, the worst Christmas of her life.

Noah hadn't come back. She hadn't heard from him, and now never expected to. She assumed he'd returned to Anoushka and the *gîte* and the proper studio, and had forgotten all about his family in Bixford. It was almost a relief. Beatrice-Eugenie and Cair Paravel were certainly far happier without his loud, crashing, moody presence in the flat; Jix and Daff were regular visitors again; and Joel and Rusty had resumed their dropping-in for late-night drinks and chats. And, if she were honest, April was absolutely delighted about not having to perform sexual gymnastics on the sofa every night when all she wanted to do was crawl into bed and die.

But, she still loved him. The love that she'd felt for Noah had been so all-consuming that she knew it would take ages to work its way out of her system. And it also meant that the Ampney Crucis cottage-by-the-sea dream had gone too, which made her doubly miserable. In the April-Noah Utopia plan, she'd fondly imagined that this Christmas, with Noah and Bee together, would be like some happy families television advert. Noah would fill Bee's stocking at midnight, and then they'd stand in the bedroom doorway, arms entwined, gazing with mutual love at their peacefully sleeping progeny.

Then there was going to be Christmas morning, with the flat awash with festive wrapping paper, and gales of laughter. And they'd all go for a walk together, and come home ravenous, and have a proper Christmas dinner with crackers and everything, and slump afterwards in front of the telly, the room dimly lit by the twinkling lights on the Christmas tree in the corner . . .

And, to make matters worse, not only was she going to be facing yet another Christmas alone, but April was pretty sure she'd got a stalker.

She'd seen him, either slouched in his car on the waste ground near the park when she took Cair Paravel for his pipe-openers, or hanging around outside the Pasta Place. April was pretty sure she recognised him – although he was always careful to keep his distance and hide his face – and was trying to place him. She'd decided he must be a customer – either from Antonio and Sofia's restaurant, or the Copacabana – and squinted now at everyone she served, just to watch their reaction. More scary was the thought that it was someone she may have unintentionally upset during the debt-collecting. She hadn't mentioned him to anyone yet because he hadn't actually done anything and he may not be watching her at all, but she was careful never to be alone after dark, just in case.

In fact the only good thing to have happened recently, April thought dizzily, as she flew backwards and forwards behind the bar, passing Toxic Wastes to customers who had ordered Head Rooms, and snatching Vanderbilts back from hardened Widow's Kiss drinkers, was that Cair Paravel's training was coming on a storm.

Since the win at Bentley's, and the decision to enter him – come hell or high water – for the Frobisher Platinum Trophy, Cair Paravel had become the embodiment of canine speed. He still needed something of Daff's to get him into the right frame of mind, and April and Jix had gone through umpteen headscarves and had just started on fluffy slippers. However, thanks to either or both of them trudging out with him in all weathers to put him through his paces, Cair Paravel now ran in a straight line, chased the hare with enthusiastic hatred, and his times were improving with each session.

As soon as the venue for the Platinum Trophy was announced on New Year's Eve, April and Jix had planned to enter Cair Paravel in the furthest distant qualifying heat. That way, they reckoned, if Sebastian should still be sniffing around, no one would discover that an illegally kept and dubiously owned dog was being put forward to run in the most prestigious greyhound race of the century, or at least not until it was far too late.

The worst thing that could happen would be if Brittany Frobisher chose to hold the Platinum here at Bixford, of course. If that calamity occurred, they may have to resort to their emergency contingency plan of reregistering Cair Paravel in Antonio's name.

At least she seemed to have got away with keeping Cairey – not to mention Bee – in the flat. Whoever had informed Sebastian that she was in breach of her tenancy agreement had scored a spectacular own goal. The subletting bit didn't matter now that Noah had gone, but Sebastian had swallowed her story really easily. She had wondered momentarily if it hadn't been a little too easily, and whether Seb was trying to catch her out, but there had been no repercussions, and she was as careful as ever to make sure that Bee and Cairey remained under wraps, so she hoped that was one problem that shouldn't bother her again.

She and Jix had tried to work out who would have been nasty enough to inform on her, but honestly couldn't think of anyone. As far as she knew she had no enemies, and no one stood to gain anything from her eviction. She had wondered whether the stalker could have anything to do with it, but had dismissed that as fanciful nonsense. The two things couldn't possibly be connected, and anyway –

'April!' Martina, wearing flashing antlers, was nodding violently across the bar. The gyrations gave a curious strobe effect to her body-pierced diamonds. 'You're using the wrong glass!'

'Sod it . . .' April stopped pondering, and immediately decanted the Double Jack into the appropriate receptacle, then added a mountain of ice to make up for the shortfall. She smiled at the customer. 'Would you like a cucumber twist? We seem to have run out of everything else.'

Midnight came and went. Everyone had screamed 'Happy Christmas!' at everyone else, kissed total strangers, and carried on drinking. April, thinking frantically of all the things she still had to do at home, wished they'd all fall into a coma.

At half-past twelve, when the licence ran out, Martina indicated that thankfully it was time to put up the shutters. April, whose feet were squashed into a pair of someone else's white boots, could have cried with relief. After a further frenzied fifteen minutes of wiping and washing and thrusting things out of the way, she grabbed her coat and limped painfully down the stairs.

'Please, please, please God,' she prayed, 'let Jix have waited for me. Please, please, please don't let me have to walk home on my own. Please don't let me come face to face with the mad axeman – not tonight. I've still got presents to wrap . . .'

The stadium was deserted, just the security lights blazing as always, and the freezing wind which had roared for weeks, rattled and whined its way though the high wire fences. Jix, in leather and chenille and wearing a garland of mistletoe, unpeeled himself from the darkness at the bottom of the escalator doors.

'Happy Christmas.' He kissed her cheek.

'And you.' She kissed his cheek in return, desperately relieved to see him, and wrinkled her nose as they hurried through the imposing gates. 'God! You smell like the scent counter at Harvey Nicks has exploded on you! And,' she peered at him, 'you've got about twenty different shades of lipstick smeared everywhere.'

'I do love Christmas,' Jix said happily, linking his arm through hers.

'I hate it. Thanks for waiting, by the way. I was dreading walking home alone. You always get so many weirdos hanging around at Christmas.'

'Do you mean me?'

'Nah,' April laughed. 'I meant special seasonal weirdos.'

'You get weirdos all year round here.' Jix steered her across the ring road. 'Have you done Bee's stocking yet?'

She shook her head. 'I haven't done anything. There doesn't seem to have been a spare minute. I'll have to work like mad when I get in to make sure Father Christmas has been before she wakes up, and I'm totally knackered. Still, at least I've got three days off now. What about you? Are you all done?'

'Oh, you know me – I go minimal on Christmas pre-sents. Mum gets slippers and books, Bee gets whatever she wants, and you get – well, you'll have to wait and see . . .'

April smiled in the icy darkness. Jix usually gave her hippie presents of patchouli or dream-catchers or joss sticks. She'd bought him a multicoloured striped scarf about twenty feet long – à la Doctor Who – from Naz at the charity shop.

'I thought I might have been chauffeured home in style tonight.'

'Sorry, shanks's pony is the best I can do. I knew I'd be offered a few drinks; I didn't want to risk losing my licence. It'll do you good to walk – you spend far too much time in idle sloth.'

'When I'm rich and famous,' April grimaced, hobbling in the too-tight boots, 'I'm going to be carried everywhere on one of those chairy-things with servants on either side handing me a fag and a cup of tea.'

'You should have asked Noah to shell out for one before he scarpered.'

They scurried, heads down against the wind, into the High Street. Jix and Daff had been very kind about Noah's non-appearance. April knew that they were both pleased that he'd gone, but also knew how hurt she felt and hadn't openly gloated.

'I bet Bee's still running rings round your mum,' April said, sliding the key into number 51's lock. 'This is the first year she's been old enough to know about Father Christmas and she was determined to stay up and wait for him.'

'So am I,' Jix grinned, following her into her flat. 'Oh, frigging hell!'

'Happy Christmas, hippies.' Noah reared up from the depths of the sofa. 'Oh, and April – so enticingly gift-wrapped. Come here, honey, and let me get to the surprise . . .'

April stayed rooted to the spot. 'Where's Bee – and Daff? And what about Cair Paravel?'

'Daphne was somewhat surplus to requirements when I arrived, so she's gone back upstairs to her own little hutch. Bee is in bed.'

'You put her to bed?'

'She got in on her own. I merely told her to go.'

'Noah – it's Christmas Eve! Well, no, it's Christmas Day now. She's waiting for Santa! And she never goes to bed on her own.'

'So I gathered.' Noah raised his eyebrows at Jix. 'I don't know about you, but we're just off to bed too. We've got weeks of catching up to do.'

Jix, shaking his head, gave April a horrified glance and walked out of the flat.

April counted to ten. 'Where's Cairey?'

'Outside in the yard. He wanted to go out. As soon as I arrived he was scratching and whining at the door. I couldn't believe you'd still got him, to be honest. Oh God — don't let him in. Animals should live outside.'

'No they shouldn't. It's freezing out there.'

April opened the back door, and the cold immediately hurt her throat. Cair Paravel had been huddling on the doorstep and practically tumbled inside. Fussing him, making sure he had his blanket in the corner by the cooker and plenty of water and a biscuit, she firmly closed the kitchen door. Having tiptoed into the bedroom and checked that Bee was well tucked in as well, and asleep, April kicked off the crippling boots and walked gingerly back into the living room.

For the first time she noticed the piles of luggage stowed in the far corner of the room by the Christmas tree, and the strapped and buckled folders containing Noah's canvases, and the familiar battered cases of paints and brushes. This was no flying visit.

'Why didn't you tell me you were coming back?'

'You knew I was. I told you so in my letter. I just couldn't say when exactly. Anoushka proved a little — let's say — difficult. Anyway, we eventually reached an amicable arrangement, and I got a last-minute flight, and here I am. Now, come here and give me a kiss.'

April shook her head. Why wasn't she more ecstatic to see him? She'd lain awake for nights on end, listening for his key in the lock. She'd pounced on the phone each time it rang, and had practically snatched the mail from the postman's hands in the mornings. Every day, she'd dreamed that Noah would come back. And now he had.

He reached out for her. She wriggled away. 'Don't, Noah. Please. I've got so much to do. Presents to wrap, you know.'

'I still want to unwrap mine.' Noah's grip was strong on her arm as he thrust her down onto the sofa. 'Don't struggle too much, honey. I don't want to rip that sexy little dress . . .'

Ten minutes later, April fell off the sofa, clutching her clothes against her and threw herself into the bedroom. There was no time for a shower, which was what she wanted more than anything, to get the smell of Noah — sour wine, sweat and garlic — out of her body. Oh God, this was a nightmare. Who was it that said you got what you deserved? What the hell had she done wrong to deserve this?

'Mummy . . .' Bee's head poked out from under the truckle bed's covers, 'has he gone away now?'

'Who? Father Christmas?' April struggled into her dressing gown and sat on the edge of the bed. She kissed the top of Beatrice-Eugenie's halo of hair. 'Not yet, poppet. He hasn't even been yet. Look, your stocking is still empty.'

'Not Father Christmas,' Bee struggled into a sitting position, gripping her hands tightly round April's neck. 'Noah.'

April exhaled. 'No, Daddy's still here. He won't go away again.'

Bee gave a shuddering sigh and gripped tighter. 'He's not my daddy. He said so. And he said Father Christmas wasn't real.'

Bastard, bastard, bastard, April thought, settling Bee down again, with merry laughter and soothing words about

Noah only teasing her, and she'd find out whether Father Christmas was real or not in the morning when she saw all the presents he'd brought.

Twenty minutes later, with Bee at last sleeping peacefully, she stormed out into the living room. Noah, half dressed, was just emptying the dregs from the bottle of wine that she'd bought to go with Christmas dinner.

'What the hell do you think you're doing?'

'I couldn't find any half decent wine anywhere –'

'Not the bloody wine! With Bee! How dare you tell her there isn't a Santa Claus?' April began dragging the presents she'd bought over the last months for Bee from the cupboard, and wrestling with two huge rolls of wrapping paper. 'It's the most magical night of any child's life! How dare you?'

Noah drained his glass. 'I merely told her the truth. No point in filling her head with lies. At least I was here to do it. I wasn't dressed up like a tart in some tacky cocktail bar on the most magical night in any child's life.'

April bit back her fury. There was no point in rising to his bait. She certainly didn't want Beatrice-Eugenie's early memories of Christmas to be associated with rows and raised voices like her own were.

'You know damn well why I have to go to work. And why did you say you weren't her father?'

'Christ, April. I don't know. She irritated me. She doesn't like me, and I'm crap with kids. Stop making a fuss – I'm here, aren't I?'

Oh, yes, April thought, savagely ripping off pieces of Sellotape with her teeth, you're definitely here . . .

Christmas Day morning was as far removed from April's rose-tinted dream as it was possible to get. Fortunately Noah stayed in bed and slept, as Bee and April and Cair

Paravel sat on the floor beside the Christmas tree and opened the presents. It was a huge relief to see that Bee's faith in the miracle of Santa Claus had been fully restored as she tore off handfuls of wrapping paper and held up each new delight for April to inspect.

Cair Paravel rolled happily amongst the discarded paper, completely ignoring the squeaky rubber bone which April and Jix had given him. However, it seemed to April, that both Beatrice-Eugenie and Cair Paravel seemed to know that their celebrations must be muted. Although April had closed the bedroom and living-room doors, both the little girl and dog kept stopping in their enjoyment, looking towards the hall, and listening.

Still, with carols on the radio, and a sharp frost outside, it was pretty seasonal. April, who had yearned for a family Christmas as long as she could remember, wondered why the reality was never, ever as good as the dream.

Noah emerged at just before midday. The sleep seemed to have restored some of his good temper, and he appeared reasonably happy, squatting on the floor, playing with Bee's toys. Bee, though, April thought as she watched them together, wasn't relaxed, and treated Noah with a distant politeness, flinching each time he roared with laughter. Cair Paravel didn't pretend at all. Carrying his squeaky bone in his mouth he haughtily returned to his blanket in the kitchen, sank on to his stomach and grizzled deep in his throat.

'Sorry about last night –' Noah looked up at April as she handed him a mug of coffee. 'I was a git. I was knackered and a bit disorientated. We'll make it work, honey, I promise you.'

'We'll have to,' April nodded her head in Bee's direction, 'for her sake, won't we?'

Noah stretched out on the floor. 'Guess so. And I'm so

sorry I didn't bring any presents for you or Bee. It was all so last-minute.'

'That's OK. We didn't get anything for you either. Well, we didn't know you'd be here, did we?'

Noah feigned a grin, but looked, April thought, a bit miffed that he didn't have a secret stash of presents from his doting family hidden away.

'No . . . no . . . I suppose not. I'll have to buy you something after Christmas. Perhaps we'll go to the sales. Anyway, I've been thinking, you know we talked before about moving away? Getting somewhere bigger than this, so that I can work in peace and you can – well, you can do whatever it is you want to do?'

April nodded, feeling a small surge of happiness at last. 'Oh, yes. I told you about Ampney Crucis, didn't I? It's the most perfect village – like out of a storybook – by the sea. Bee and Cairey loved it there, and the light would be right for you to paint and –'

'April, April . . .' Noah held up his hands. 'I don't want to live in some decrepit English backwater. I'm talking about going back to France. All of us. It's the only place for me now. I could never settle here permanently.'

April continued to smile, but inside she felt sick. France? Abroad? Leave everyone she knew and be alone with Noah? She really wanted to laugh. It was the dream she'd been working for ever since he'd left her, and now he was handing it to her gift-wrapped, and she wasn't at all sure that she wanted it.

She forced a laugh. 'God, that'll take a lot of getting used to. But can we talk about it later? It's gone one – we'll be late for dinner.'

'Dinner?' Noah leaned back against the sofa. 'I can't smell turkey roasting or stuffing or sprouts or anything. I presumed we were going to eat tonight.'

'No,' April closed her eyes. She should have told him before but she'd been sure he'd object. 'Dinner's at half-past one. I'll just go and feed Cairey, then we're all going to Antonio and Sofia's.'

The Pasta Place was silent. Everyone turned and stared as April came in. She knew that Jix would have warned them about Noah, but she'd hoped they'd try to be friendly just for her sake.

Sofia had gone way over the top with the Christmas decorations, and the tables were pulled together and covered with a holly-sprigged cloth. Glasses and cutlery sparkled under the flicker of dozens of dark red and green candles, and there were crackers beside each plate. The mingled scents of roasting turkey, and bacon and prune stuffing, and roast potatoes and chestnuts, all wafting from the kitchen made April drool. Bee immediately broke away from her and scrambled into the seat between Jix and Daff, proudly showing off the most portable of her presents. Joel and Rusty, at the far side of the table, nodded their heads at her, smiled at Bee and ignored Noah. Sofia, who was changing the Christmas CD on the stereo, did the same.

'April –' Antonio poked his head out from the kitchen, surrounded by clouds of fragrant steam, 'can I have a word, *cara*?'

She closed the door behind her. Nine massive dinner plates were arrayed on the counter. Two turkeys sat golden and fragrant on their carving dishes, and there were half a dozen vegetable tureens piled high.

'This is amazing!'

'But our uninvited guest isn't.' Antonio sharpened the carving knife on a steel with swift, vicious movements. 'Oh, I know you had to bring him – Jix explained. And

355

if he's your choice, then so be it. But a word of warning: if he upsets anyone here today I will slit his throat, OK?'

April nodded silently. She didn't doubt it.

Antonio tested the blade of the knife by running it along his finger. April almost expected to see the flesh fall neatly apart.

'Noah Matlock was a moody bastard long before you came to join him here.' Tonio didn't look at her. 'He was always arrogant and often unpleasant. You were good for him, *cara*, and he was nicer with you around. But you should have let sleeping dogs lie. You should never have tried to get him back. We all know him very well, don't forget. His fame has only made him worse. Now, smile, princess – for the *bambina's* sake – and we'll have a happy Christmas meal all together, won't we?'

'Yeah, of course we will.' April smiled dutifully. 'I just wished you'd said all this earlier, though. Like when I first moved in with Noah years ago. It would have saved a lot of trouble.'

'And would you have listened, *cara*? No bloody way. You're a woman and you loved him. You wouldn't have listened to anyone, would you? Now, remember the smile, and grab that nearest dish of veg. It's Christmas.'

The meal went far better than April could have imagined. By the time she'd returned from the kitchen, everyone was at least talking. Sofia had poured the first of many bottles of wine, they'd pulled crackers, at Bee's insistence, and everyone round the table, including Noah, was wearing a paper hat.

In true Italian tradition, the feast lasted for ever. The food was amazing, the wine plentiful, and the mood grew more merry and relaxed. April noticed with amusement that whenever Noah started bragging about his paintings, someone always cut in and talked him down.

They exchanged presents across the plates, and Bee had twenty times more than anyone else. Noah, of course, didn't have any. April gave him a sideways glance but he didn't seem to mind too much. Jix wound his Doctor Who scarf round his neck, wearing it throughout the meal, flicking it artlessly over his shoulder with a Diana Dors motion every time it looked like trailing in his gravy. It was only at the stage where they were all trying manfully to cram mince pies and cream down on top of everything else, that April realised Jix hadn't given her a present.

She sighed over the silliness of men – did he really think she cared? – and because Antonio and Joel and Noah were by then all having cigars with their coffee, she lit a cigarette.

Jix and Noah glared at her with twin stares of disgust and she laughed out loud for the first time that day.

It was dark when they all staggered back towards number 51. With Joel and Rusty on either side, Jix wrapped his scarf round Daff's face for the short outside journey, and they parted in the hallway, peeling off to their respective flats with almost cheery Christmas greetings.

Noah slumped on the sofa. 'That was much better than I'd anticipated. Wonderful food.' He patted the cushion beside him. 'Come and sit here.'

'In a moment. Bee's nearly asleep – I'll put her to bed. Oh, and I'd better let Cairey out for a wee in the yard first. He must be bursting – Oh!' April stood in the kitchen doorway. 'He's not here – and I closed the door so he can't be in the bedroom.'

Noah looked over his shoulder. 'What? Oh, I put him out in the yard just before we left. I thought it was best.'

April yanked open the back door, cursing Noah under her breath. 'Come on, Cairey, poor boy . . . You must be so cold . . . I've brought you the biggest doggy bag you've ever seen — turkey and sausages and bacon and —'

April stopped. The yard was empty. Cair Paravel had gone.

chapter twenty-seven

J asmine sat beneath the glittering chandeliers and waited to wake up. As everything since before Christmas had passed in a sort of dream, she saw no reason why New Year's Eve should be any different.

The Frobishers' house – no, she shook her head. Wrong word. Stately home? No, wrong shape. Small palace? Not that, either. She played with the bread roll sitting in the centre of her side plate. OK, yes, the Frobishers' castle – that was it – was like something she'd been taken to see on school visits.

It had suits of armour in the hall, and portraits of ancestors, and dead animals on the walls, and sweeping staircases, and about six million oak-panelled rooms with fireplaces big enough to conceal Rutland.

All twelve representatives of the Benny Clegg Stadium had hired a minibus for the journey from Ampney Crucis to Surrey and had booked overnight rooms in a nearby Travel Lodge. Now, sitting between Bunny and Gilbert round a Camelot-sized circular table in the banqueting hall, Jasmine tried not to stare at the splendour. It was very difficult.

There were four main tables – for the four Platinum Trophy short-listed stadiums – with five smaller tables or the greyhound organisations and the press and other interested parties, dotted between them – and the top table on a sort of raised platform. Ampney Crucis had the table immediately to the right of the Frobishers' podium, while Bixford were to the left. Pullet's and Bentley's, the other contenders, were in the far corners. Peg had got quite excited about this, but Jasmine thought it showed no preference in the pecking order – probably just Brittany's clever way of being able to keep an eye on Sebastian and Ewan at the same time.

The Gillespie contingent hadn't yet arrived, although, with the exception of the top table, most of the other tables were already full, and a rather wispy-looking man in a shiny David Essex suit and a red neckerchief was mournfully strumming classics on a six-stringed guitar and looking as though he was about to run out of repertoire.

Aware that everyone round the Ampney Crucis table was surreptitiously watching her for the first sign of irrational behaviour which might just indicate a full-blown mental collapse, Jasmine refused to meet their eyes.

After storming out of the Chewton Estate house, with her mother and Andrew in hot pursuit crying that she'd got it all wrong, and the neighbours' net curtains going up and down like marionette strings, Jasmine had eventually shaken them off and fled back to the graveyard.

Pouring it all out to Benny – with some tasty four-letter epithets – she'd felt marginally better. Then she'd gone to the Crumpled Horn, put 'Mr Tambourine Man' on constant replay, and downed five pints of Old Ampney without stopping. Staggering back to the beach hut, she'd drawn wobbly moustaches on her mother's photos and ripped up Andrew's and fallen into a rather giddy sleep on the sofa.

Clara had arrived noisily at the hut after lunch, intent on taking Jasmine to do some last-minute Sunday shopping and had been treated to hung-over chapter and verse. Being Clara, she'd immediately made a lot of black coffee, added a Lenin beard to Yvonne's photos, set fire to the remains of Andrew's, and dragged Jasmine off to buy a shock frock for the Frobishers' do. Retail therapy, Clara had insisted, was exactly what was needed.

Which was why, Jasmine thought, she was sitting in a castle, merely feet away from the only man she'd ever love – or at least she would be when he arrived – wearing something floor length and skintight in scarlet satin which pushed her breasts out like the figurehead on a sailing ship and was split to the thigh. Oh, and the fact that it had cost at least the winnings on five races hadn't added to her happiness much either.

Everyone else had been wonderful when Clara had told them the dire Yvonne-and-Andrew and Philip-and-Verity news. They'd rallied round, and made sure that Jasmine was left alone when she wanted to be, and not when she didn't. Christmas Day had been and gone in a sort of blur, and Philip and Verity, holding hands, had bravely arrived at the beach hut on Boxing Day to explain the situation. As Jasmine knew more about the situation than they did, it was a rather strange conversation. And her father had got quite agitated about Yvonne and Andrew, but Verity had giggled, and patted his knee in a calming, motherly way.

After their visit, Jasmine had to admit that her father looked happier than she'd seen him look for years, and Verity was nice and comfortable – and at least her father would now never run short of warm hand-knitted woollies.

The banqueting hall was noisy: splinters of far-flung conversations rising and falling, chair legs being scraped back across flagstones, and cutlery being knocked to the floor with a clatter. The wispy guitarist had just started rather recklessly on 'Una Paloma Blanca'. Jasmine could just see the whole place erupting vociferously into the more popular version and considerably lowering the Frobisher tone.

She smiled round the table. They all looked very swish – Clara in black, Peg in a sugar-pink chiffon copy of something Doris Day had worn to a 1957 awards ceremony, and Roger and Allan's wives both in a sort of mustard paisley material much beloved for 'posh frocks' by ladies of a certain age. Gorf had brought his sister, Waffon, and she'd worn her best dungarees and a diamanté bow tie. All the men were in evening dress – all hired from the same place – and all almost fitting, even Bunny's, although because of his feet he'd had to wear plimsolls. Peg had said it didn't matter a jot just so long as they were black and he didn't fall over the laces.

Ewan, of course, looked the most sensational of all in his suit – although by the way he and Clara were scrabbling at each other beneath the white linen tablecloth, Jasmine couldn't see it staying on for too long.

With a huge commotion, the double doors flew open and the Bixford brigade made their entrance. Jasmine held her breath. They looked, she thought, rather like the Krays on a day trip – tough, glamorous, and stinking rich.

Oliver and Martina she recognised immediately from Sebastian's descriptions. Oliver's suit obviously wasn't hired, and no doubt the cost of Martina's frock – neck-to-ankle sprayed-on purple sequins to match her aubergine spiky hair – could have wiped out the national debt. The remainder of the party looked very East End and done up too. They all gave the impression that this late entry had been deliberately planned, strolling in, laughing and talking, relaxed. Jasmine, scanning them and trying not to show it, felt her heart plummet. Sebastian wasn't with them.

No doubt he was frolicking about in the acres of corridors with Brittany, already knowing that Bixford were going to walk off with tonight's spoils, and totally familiar with every nook and cranny of both Brittany and the Frobishers' home. Jasmine pulled her bread roll apart angrily, scattering the crumbs on the table cloth. Both Peg and Clara were watching her, so she swept them into her hand and hid them under the plate.

The waitresses were circulating now; filling up wine and water glasses, pouring everyone a promotional pint of Frobisher's beer — which Jasmine thought wasn't a patch on Old Ampney — replacing bread rolls, flicking out napkins. They looked wonderful, an army of pretty girls in short black skirts and tight waistcoats, all smiling and moving as if on well-oiled castors.

One of their waitresses, with tendrils of fair hair escaping from her bun, kindly replaced Jasmine's roll and swept the crumbs from beneath her plate with an amazing sleight of hand. She didn't smile, and her eyes were red-rimmed under the coat of make-up. Probably a man, Jasmine thought with sisterly solidarity. Bastard.

Ewan, Jasmine noticed, jerked his head up when he saw the waitress and kept on staring. The waitress frowned. Jasmine growled at him for good measure, and nodded her head towards Clara. God, she was glad to be manless.

Oh, no she wasn't, she thought, a split second later as Sebastian came into the banqueting hall. He smiled briefly towards his parents, and then slid elegantly into his chair round the Gillespie table. Brittany would probably not be far behind, but until she appeared, Jasmine drank him in. The evening suit looked superb on him — even better than it did on Ewan. Clara had swivelled her head round and stared as soon as he'd arrived, and now looked wide-eyed across the table at Jasmine.

'Wow. Hot or what?'

Jasmine smiled smugly.

'Jesus . . .' Clara, still gawping at the vision of Seb scrubbed up, had her mouth open.

Ewan, Jasmine was pleased to notice, had immediately stopped eyeing up the waitress and was belatedly attempting to bring Clara to heel.

The doors opened again – it was like a posh pantomime, Jasmine decided – and this time the guitarist struck up the 'Blue Danube' as the Frobisher family glided in. Jasmine wasn't sure of the connection, but possibly they just liked Strauss, or maybe the guitarist had forgotten the chords to 'Jerusalem'. Emily Frobisher had her hand resting delicately on her husband, Rod's, arm – Sebastian had filled Jasmine in on all the names in one of his letters – and they were followed by a phalanx of Frobisher minions. Brittany, glittering and breathtakingly beautiful in pale blue, brought up the rear.

They swerved sinuously between the tables, smiling at everyone, having a few polite words with some, managing to climb on to the podium and take their top table places without the slightest stumble. Jasmine watched, and reckoned they must do this sort of thing all the time. Anyone normal would have teetered on that top step.

Brittany was seated between her parents, and had the microphone in front of her. Jasmine raised an impressed eyebrow; Brittany was certainly in charge of this whole shebang, then. She wasn't just the pretty packaging for Rod Frobisher's multimillion-pound business. Ewan nearly fell off his chair, trying to turn round and smile at her, Jasmine noticed with some disgust. Fortunately, Clara noticed too, and started nibbling his ear.

At some unseen signal, the waitresses swarmed in again once more topping up glasses and sliding Parma ham ar warm leaves with croutons on to each plate. Their red-eyed waitress still looked miserable, but managed to be very efficient. Again, Ewan looked at her intently. This time, the girl looked back at him and almost smiled. Jasmine wanted to slap them both, but especially Ewan. This was neither the time nor the place.

Just as she was advising Bunny on the best way to tackle his croutons and explaining that the lettuce was supposed to be hot, Sebastian crouched down beside her.

'I didn't see you straight away. God knows how I missed you in that dress, though,' he smiled up at her as Bunny merrily skittered croutons across the table like marbles in a pinball machine. 'You look amazing.'

'Thanks. I'll probably pop out of it the minute I move. You look really nice too.' Her mouth had gone dry and her stomach started looping the loop. 'And your mother is staring.'

'There's probably some social law about gossiping with other tables while starters are being served. She'll look it up. Thanks for your Christmas card – and these . . .' He stuck out a leg and pulled up a couple of inches of his black trousers, displaying Jasmine's gift of a pair of Union Jack socks that tinkled out God Save the Queen if you rubbed your ankles together. 'They were my best present.'

'I ate my doughnuts,' Jasmine said. 'Before Christmas.'

'Good. They'd have probably gone off if you'd saved them. So, how was it? Your Christmas, I mean.'

'Not bad. I broke off my engagement and my parents split up.'

'Christ.' Sebastian stared at her. 'Seriously?'

'About as serious as you can get.' Jasmine smiled at the concern in his eyes. She also had a mad urge to lick his freckles. 'Um, my mum and Andrew were – that is, are – having an affair, you see, and my dad moved out because

365

he was having an affair too, and is living with his secretary. She's quite nice, actually, and she knits.'

'You're joking – aren't you?'

Jasmine shook her head and held up her left hand. 'See – no ring. I'd finished with Andrew before I knew about the affair, which makes me feel a lot better. Andrew is history – except, as Clara kindly pointed out, he may one day be my stepfather . . .'

'Fucking hell!'

'You just said fucking.' Bunny frowned crossly at Sebastian. 'That ain't fair. Mizz Dunstable said I wasn't allowed to.'

'Sorry.' Sebastian held up his hands to Bunny. 'I shouldn't have either. My apologies.'

'That's all right. Apology accepted.' Bunny grinned, instantly losing his grip on a cherry tomato. 'Ooh! Fucking thing!'

'You'd better go back to your seat,' Jasmine said to Sebastian. 'Your parents are looking murderous.'

Seb stood up. 'They'll see it as fraternising with the enemy. We'll fraternise on the dance floor later, shall we?'

'For commiserations or congratulations?'

'I was thinking more for pleasure. And you're sure you're all right?'

'I'm fine. Really, truly. But thanks for asking.'

Jasmine watched him return to his table. So, she noticed, did most of the women in the banqueting hall, especially Brittany.

Sorbets came and went, so did roast meats on beds of thyme and sorrel mash with baby vegetables, and more sorbets, and *crème brûlées*, and coffee and petits fours – along with bottle after bottle of wine. Jasmine and Sebastian smiled at each other frequently. So did Ewan and Brittany. And Brittany and Sebastian. Somewhere in between the second sorbet and the pudding and all the smiling, the waitress with the red eyes disappeared.

'What happened to her?' Jasmine asked her equally pretty replacement. 'Was she not feeling well?'

'April? No idea. Just said she had to dash off and would I mind taking over. She's been really upset this week, mind you, because she's lost her dog – but I don't know if she's gone home. God knows how she's going to get back there, if she has. We all come from Bixford and we had a coach.'

'Poor thing,' Jasmine said, immediately full of sympathy for the red-eyed April.

Bixford, though? Why on earth would the waiting staff be bussed-in from Bixford, for goodness' sake? Unless, of course – she shot a glance across to the Gillespie table – it was something to do with them. A bit of a sweetener. Wasted, in Jasmine's opinion, because Bixford were going to walk away with the Platinum anyway. Still, you had to admire Martina and Oliver's style.

'Where's Ewan?' Peg paused in removing gelatine leaves from her petit four. 'I haven't seen him for a while.'

'He went to the loo,' Clara waved an inebriated hand. 'He's probably got lost in the maze of corridors.'

It was getting closer and closer to midnight. Again, Jasmine knew from one of Sebastian's letters that Emily Frobisher had planned this evening along the lines of a similar bash put on by the Queen at Sandringham. Not, of course, that Her Majesty was sponsoring a greyhound race, but the premise was much the same: eating, then speeches, then dancing in the attached ballroom to a big band, followed by a disco for the young and sprightly, all culminating in a full English breakfast for those still standing at daybreak.

Jasmine was pretty sure they'd all have passed out long before that.

The other contenders' tables were getting quite rowdy,

as the time for the twelve o'clock announcement approached and the excited tension increased. There was a lot of giggling and speculation round their own. However, apart from wondering whether Brittany would do the deed before or after the witching hour, Jasmine felt very little curiosity. Ampney Crucis, being out in the sticks – and the coastal sticks at that – meant they'd come in a resounding last. She just hoped Brittany would read out the result in reverse order, then at least they'd have the pleasure of being first in something.

'Ladies and gentlemen!' Brittany stood up and took the microphone. The room scuffled into a ragged silence. 'This isn't going to be a long-drawn-out process. I have no intention of prolonging the agony – or the ecstasy – and once the announcement has been made, I'll speak to the victorious team alone later, so that you can all enjoy the party.'

There was a lot of foot-stamping and clapping.

'My parents –' Brittany indicated Emily and Rod. More foot stamping – 'my parents, are delighted to see you here this evening, and have obviously been extremely supportive while I've worked behind the scenes to make my choice. However, they wish me to stress that it is essentially a traditional New Year's Eve party and that on the last stroke of midnight, the haggis and whisky will be piped in. There will also be champagne for the toasts – and then if you'd like to make your way through to the ballroom we'll continue the festivities there.'

The clapping grew louder. There were whistles from the Pullet's table, and whoops from Bentley's.

Brittany, shuffling her notes, suddenly smiled across at Sebastian, and Jasmine felt a jag of misery.

'Ewan's going to miss the best bit if he's not careful.' Peg seemed to have got a petit four caught in some of her pink netting and Gorf and Waffon were picking it out. 'Shouldn't someone go and look for him?'

The Ampney Crucis contingent – including Clara – all stared at the tablecloth. None of them, it seemed, was prepared to miss the 'best bit' simply to rescue Ewan from the Frobishers' lavatory.

'So, without dragging it out,' Brittany spoke loudly, 'I've had a lovely time going to the dogs this year.' She paused for the roar of laughter. 'And I've made some very good friends in the process.' A quick glance at Sebastian. 'Choosing four stadiums for the short list was difficult enough, and picking one from those four, almost impossible. However, and it was a very close thing, one stadium just had the edge over the other three. One stadium is able to provide everything that Frobishers require to stage this – the biggest new greyhound trophy race to be introduced for over one hundred years.' Another pause. The room was silent. The tension now was bow-string taut. 'We looked for somewhere that would reflect the Frobisher way forward, and at the same time retain the greyhound-racing traditions. We also wanted a stadium which had the facilities to welcome the crowds that this prestigious event will no doubt attract, without turning it into yet another corporate hospitality bonanza. What we were looking for was somewhere with style.'

Jasmine glanced over at the Gillespie table. Oliver was leaning across the wine glasses and ashtrays, conferring with three of the other portly and polished hit-men types, while Martina was grinning and mentally running through her acceptance speech. Sebastian had his head down. Hah – Jasmine thought – can't look me in the eye now, can he!

'So, as I said,' Brittany continued, 'one stadium met all these criteria. One stadium had everything I wanted. One stadium will be hosting the Frobisher Platinum Trophy on Valentine's Day. And that stadium is –' she swept a teasing glance at all four tables – 'the Benny Clegg Stadium at Ampney Crucis!'

There were screams from Peg and Clara and Bunny – and possibly from Martina. Jasmine sat completely pole-axed. She wouldn't get excited because it wasn't right. Brittany had got it wrong – surely she had? Suddenly the room erupted, and everyone was shouting, pushing towards them, slapping their backs, yelling congratulations.

'And I'll meet up with you all later to discuss the finer points.' Brittany was beaming across at them. 'But in the meantime, enjoy the rest of the night – and congratulations to you all for putting on such a splendid show.'

Peg and Roger and Allan were dancing round the table. Because Ewan was still missing, Clara was kissing Bunny and Gorf.

'Jasmine . . .' Sebastian's voice filtered through the may-hem, just as the clock and the crowd started the midnight countdown. He was very close to her. 'Well done. I'm so pleased for you – and you really deserve it. I bet your grandpa is having one heck of a party and – Oh, bugger . . .'

Whatever else he was going to say was drowned out, not only by the gonging of the clock, but also by the loud skirl of the pipes, as a kilted bagpiper wailed in a file of waitresses carrying haggis and whisky and flutes of champagne.

'Happy New Year!'

The banqueting hall erupted for a second time. Sorrows were being drowned with a vengeance. Now everyone was gulping whisky and champagne and eyeing the haggis with suspicion. There seemed to be a lot of kissing and hugging and dancing going on in a very small space. The noise was unbelievable.

Jasmine stood up and moved tentatively away from the table. The dress didn't split. Sebastian was even closer to her. She smiled at him. 'Happy New Year.'

He bent his head towards her, his hands reaching for hers. But the kiss didn't happen.

'Oh, no you don't,' Brittany said, grabbing Seb and kissing him thoroughly. She looked over his shoulder at Jasmine. 'You got the Platinum – I think I deserve the celebratory snog, don't you?'

Jasmine shrugged. 'Seems like a bit of a consolation prize to me . . .'

'Me, too,' Brittany smiled, and wriggled away from Sebastian, who was looking slightly irritated.

Jasmine laughed. She decided that she liked Brittany. 'Thanks – for choosing us, and everything. I still can't quite believe it.'

'You had everything I needed, and what's more you did it all yourself,' Brittany said. 'Turned the stadium around, making it a going concern, but without taking away its unique atmosphere. I had the easy part, just playing my usual role, but you had to take giant steps. That's why I so admire you. And believe me, there's no sentiment in this game. I picked the best stadium for the event. It's going to be wonderful – and because there's only six weeks to go, we'll have to spend a lot of time together on the organisation. Will that be OK – if I keep popping down to Ampney Crucis with my people?'

'Of course it will.' Jasmine nodded. 'You'll be more than welcome.'

'And me?' Sebastian looked from one of them to the other.

'Sebby,' Brittany patted his cheek, 'for once in your life you're the loser here. As far as the Frobisher Platinum es, that is. But if you're offering your services, I'm sure

Jasmine will find plenty of things to keep you busy in Ampney Crucis.'

Moving away to kiss Peg's cheek and shake all the other Ampney Crucis hands, Brittany, Jasmine noticed with amusement, gave Martina the widest possible berth.

'Do you want to discuss the win with Peg and the others?' Sebastian asked. 'Or can we dance?'

Jasmine gave her consortium members a rueful glance. 'I don't think there's any point in discussing anything with any of them at the moment. They were plastered before the announcement — they're totally wrecked now.' She smiled at him. 'And the dancing? I can dance, sort of. I don't know about you. Whether the dress will stand it is anyone's guess.'

'I can't wait to find out . . .' Seb grabbed her hand, and tugged her through the brightly coloured, noisy throng towards the ballroom.

The corridors went by in a sort of blur. Vaguely Jasmine wondered if Ewan was still staggering about in the warren, looking for a way out.

The ballroom was three times the size of the banqueting hall, and seemed to be hung with battle banners and whole boughs of greenery and even more chandeliers. A forty-piece dance band was on the stage, expertly trumpeting out a selection of Glenn Miller favourites.

Jasmine shook her head. 'There's no way the frock will cope with jitterbugging.'

'Good,' Sebastian grinned, twirling her round. 'That's just what I wanted to hear.'

chapter twenty-eight

'You stupid bastard!' April grabbed Ewan's bow tie and pushed him back against the Frobishers' pantry wall. A lot of tins clattered from the shelves and rolled round their feet. 'What the hell did you think you were playing at?'

Ewan, making a sort of strangled gulp, tried to remove her hands from his throat. 'I – um – for Christ's sake, woman! Let go! I – thought the dog was being ill-treated. You're bloody choking me! I'd – we'd – had a tip-off.'

'God!' April, suddenly realising that she was in serious danger of actually throttling Ewan, reluctantly released her grip on his tie. 'I've been out of my head for the last week! I thought he was dead! I love him so much! I haven't been able to eat or sleep or think straight – oh God! And now the dancing's started – and I'm supposed to be working until dawn – and I'll never see him again! Oh, you stupid, stupid sod!'

Ewan took deep breaths. 'Christ, if the dancing's started that means it's New Year's Day now – and I didn't kiss Clara at midnight – and, oh, shit – it means they've announced the winner.'

'That's the least of your worries.' April glared at Ewan in disgust.

She'd recognised him straight away, as soon as she'd tarted serving the Ampney Crucis table at the beginning of the evening, and she'd smiled, feeling sad, because he'd been so good to them when Cair Paravel had run his first race all those months before – with the hare and the headscarf and everything. And Ewan had smiled back at her without much recognition in his eyes.

Which, April admitted, had to be a blessing with the Gillespies sitting so close. Then as her visits to the table increased, so did Ewan's recognition, and her own suspicions. There was something familiar about him, and not just as dishy Ewan Dunstable from Ampney Crucis, especially when she caught him in profile against the candlelight. She'd been serving up the meat course when it had all snapped into place.

Sliding the vegetable tureen on to the table, she'd leaned towards him, pretending to straighten his napkin. 'You've been watching me.'

'What?' Ewan had looked startled. 'No I haven't. I mean, well, I might have been, you're very pretty, and I certainly didn't expect to see you here, but it's a small world and –'

'Not tonight,' April had muttered under her breath. 'At home in Bixford. You've been hanging around where I live . . .' She'd looked across him at Clara. 'I'm sure your girlfriend would be really interested to know what sort of pervert she's mixed up with.'

The rest of the table, laughing and talking and exclaiming over the food, didn't seem to have taken any notice of this exchange.

'You're mistaken.' Ewan had shaken his head. 'I've never hung around where you live – I haven't got a clue where you live – and apart from seeing you at Ampney Crucis for that race – Oh, my God! Did you say Bixford?'

She'd straightened up and stared at him. 'Changed your mind, have you?'

374

Ewan had turned whiter than the tablecloth. 'Christ, look, can we talk? Not here – I mean, later, outside somewhere?'

'Oh, yes. You'd better start talking – but I've got no intention of meeting you anywhere. You're seriously weird.'

'I'm not. Believe me. Let me tell you . . . I've got to explain –'

April had surveyed him. She didn't want to be alone with him – he'd terrified her for weeks. And she'd thought he was so nice, as well. It just went to show that you never could tell. Daff always said it was the nice ones . . . But if he was her stalker – and she was sure he was – there had to be some explanation, surely. And she wanted to hear it.

'Come out to the kitchens. There are about ninety thousand people out there to rescue me if you turn funny. But if the explanation isn't twenty-four carat, then I'll be calling the police first, and grabbing that mike from Brittany and informing the whole room, including –' April had looked at the huge engagement ring on Clara's finger '– your fiancée, second. OK?'

So Ewan had eventually turned up at the kitchen door, and after getting one of the other Copacabana girls to cover for her on the Ampney Crucis table, April had dragged him away from the crashing, steaming, shouting mayhem of the cooking and dishing area towards the relative privacy of the pantry.

'I said I was going to the loo,' Ewan had tried, and failed, to look relaxed. 'So they shouldn't miss me for a while. Anyway, this won't take long.'

'Too right it won't. Why have you been stalking me?'

And then, it had all poured out. April, who'd previously ly thought that Ewan had been one of the dirty raincoat brigade, suddenly realised the full extent of his felony.

Desolate since discovering the loss of Cair Paravel, having tramped the streets of Bixford, putting up posters, and searching everywhere with Jix and Joel and Rusty and Sofia and Antonio – Noah had said he was far too busy doing sketches for a new series of paintings to become involved – she'd given up all hope of ever finding him alive.

Cairey must have somehow scrabbled over the wall because bloody Noah had locked him out in the yard, and probably run straight out on to the ring road, all laughing face, and lolling tongue, and silly splaying legs and – and she'd shut the rest of it out of her mind.

If he'd been run over she supposed the driver hadn't stopped. She and Jix had made terrified searches of all the bushes and waste ground round the road and not found a body. April, distraught, knew this meant that Cairey must have crawled away somewhere else to die, alone and in pain . . .

And now her fury was so incandescent that she could hardly breathe – now this bloody stupid man was telling her that he'd stolen him! No – not even that – rescued. Rescued! As if Cairey, the most spoiled canine baby that had ever lived, needed rescuing!

And there was worse to come. Not only had he been 'rescued' but he'd also been practically rehomed!

'I could kill you!' She hissed at Ewan. 'I really could kill you!'

'I'm so sorry. We had a tip-off – a telephone call – to say that he was being kept in a flat, and not looked after properly, and that he was left howling in a confined yard in all weathers. I followed it up. Everything I saw seemed to confirm it. What was I supposed to do? Ignore it? It's what my life has been for ages – rescuing dogs in that position.'

'He didn't need rescuing!' April screamed for the hundredth time, wondering again who'd made that phone call. 'And didn't you have anything better to do on Christmas Day, for Christ's sake?'

Ewan looked at her. 'If you'd seen some of the sights that I have, you wouldn't ask that.'

'No, OK,' April had conceded. 'But still, Christmas Day –'

'I didn't do the – er – rescue personally. We have a network of people. They know exactly what to do and when to do it.'

'And that makes it better, does it? Stealing a dog that is perfectly well cared for and much loved and –'

'He was shut outside in the dark and in freezing temperatures when my colleagues found him.'

'But I didn't know that! That was my – um -- boyfriend. Not me.'

Ewan frowned. 'What? Jinx, or whatever his name was? I thought he seemed like a nice bloke.'

'Christ! Not Jix! Jix isn't my boyfriend! Jix wouldn't do anything like that – he loves Cairey as much as I do. Noah – I live with him -- he shut Cair Paravel out without me knowing.'

Ewan shook his head. 'Look – um – oh, yes, Beatrice-Eugenie -- I didn't mean –'

'Who?' April frowned, then laughed. 'Oh God, that's not me. My name's April. Beatrice-Eugenie is my daughter. We registered Cairey in her name because – oh, well it's a long story. All I want to know is how do I get him back?'

Ewan looked first confused, and then worried. 'I know where he is, of course, but as I said, he's been earmarked for rehoming.'

'Ah, there! I bet you didn't check that, did you?'

'What?'

'The earmarking! Cairey's got his ear tattooed, like all registered racing greyhounds! I bet you didn't even think —'

Ewan looked completely crestfallen. 'I honestly have no idea. We'd do a check normally, naturally, but I don't know if my colleagues have or not, with it being the holiday period. Anyway, now you know he's OK, it's New Year's Eve — and I really should be getting back in there and —'

April shook her head. 'You're going nowhere until I get Cairey back. How far away is he? Oh God — not down in Dorset?'

'No, it was some of our local people who rescued — er — well, you know — um — took him. We have a network of safe houses all over the country. He's in Barking. No — really . . .'

'Barking?' April's head reeled. 'That's not far from Bixford — but it's bloody miles away from here, isn't it? Where are we, anyway?'

'Somewhere in the leafy glades of poshest Surrey. Er, sort of Epsomish, I think.'

April walked away. The pantry was almost the size of her flat at number 51. She stared at four shelves of bottled plums. It was wonderful to know that Cair Paravel was alive and well, of course it was. He must be so bewildered, though. Being yanked away from the yard and whisked off by strangers: people who wouldn't know that he loved egg sandwiches, or having his tummy tickled, or that he had to have his blanket tucked under in a special way so that he could slide his nose into it while he slept.

She whirled round on Ewan. 'We're going to get him. Now. Where's your car?'

'In Ampney Crucis. We had a minibus up here — and, anyway, I've had far too much to drink to be able to drive anywhere. Look, if I give you directions, you could go and —'

'We came on a coach!' April yelled. 'From Bixford! I don't even know where I am!'

'But at least you haven't been drinking . . . and anyway, it's the early hours of the morning, so my – um – Barking counterpart is probably asleep and –'

'Ring him and wake him up, then.' April flapped her hands. 'You're bound to have a mobile. People like you can't exist without mobiles. Ring him, tell him you've made a mistake – tell him you've scared the shit out of me and pinched my dog. Tell him we'll be there!'

Ewan sighed. 'OK, I'll ring him. Maybe we could go tomorrow –'

'We're going now!' April was almost in tears. 'You ring him and I'll find someone with transport – and if you run away I'll tell your lovely girlfriend and everyone in that room exactly what you've been up to! Just the pervy bits, of course.'

Making sure that Ewan was punching out numbers on his mobile, April braved the kitchen. The chefs were yelling at each other and the waitresses, there were unwashed plates and dishes and cutlery and pots and pans on every surface, and in the corner, the wispy guitarist and the kilted piper were drinking champagne from each other's glasses, their arms entwined.

'I want a car!' she announced loudly to no one in particular.

'Me too, dear,' the guitarist sighed.

The piper shook his head. 'I'd like a nice little bungalow in Esher.'

'I want to borrow someone's car for about – oh – an hour.' April had no idea how long it would actually take to get from the Frobishers' to Barking, home to Bixford, and then for Ewan to drive back here again. Tough hat he'd been drinking. If he got caught it was nothing

379

less than he deserved. 'It's a matter of life or death.'

'You can have mine if you like,' one of the washer-uppers said mournfully. 'I'll be here 'til next Tuesday at this rate.'

'Brilliant.' April kissed him. 'Which one is it? I mean, there are about a thousand cars outside.'

'It's the gold Cavalier under the oak tree at the top of the drive. I parked it out of sight.'

'Has it got petrol?'

'Petrol, yes. Tax and MOT, no.'

April shrugged. What the hell? She pocketed the keys. 'You're a star. And I promise to return it.'

'Don't matter too much,' the washer-upper said. 'The owner don't know I've got it, anyway.'

Deciding not to give any of this information to Ewan, on the grounds of what he didn't know couldn't possibly hurt him, April belted back to the pantry.

As she drove inexpertly, in a possibly stolen and definitely not roadworthy car, round the M25 in the early hours of New Year's Day, April started to fill Ewan in on Cair Paravel's training regime, and the plans she and Jix had for his future.

Ewan looked down at the floor of the car. 'Hang on a minute – have you taken your shoes off?'

'Mmm,' April sighed blissfully. 'They were killing me. They're not mine anyway. I needed black T-bar straps with a kitten heel for tonight to go with the uniform. Joel in the flat upstairs borrowed them from a bloke he works with – no, don't ask – anyway, I was saying . . .'

Because she found both the M25 and the Cavalier quite frightening, and because it was easier to drive and talk than drive and tremble, April continued to tell Ewan all about how well Cairey had done in his few races, and how hi training was coming on, and how they'd decided to enter him for the Frobisher Platinum heats.

'Don't mention the Frobisher Platinum!' Ewan groaned. 'It's like being the only person in the country who doesn't know who won the election.'

April allowed him a sympathetic glance. He'd acted from the best of motives, after all. And he hadn't even complained too much when she'd told him he'd be navigating because she'd never done this stretch of the M25 in her life. He had begged to be allowed to let Clara and Peg and Jasmine know where he was going in case they were worried, but April, sure that once Ewan returned to the Ampney Crucis mob she'd never extricate him again, had refused. He'd also said that his rescue friend in Barking had been most annoyed to be disturbed in the middle of the Kendall MacNulty Hogmanay Special on ITV2, but that he would be waiting for them.

'With Cairey?'

'With Cairey,' Ewan confirmed. 'And yes, he has checked the tattoo. And we've removed him from the rehoming list. And I am terribly, terribly sorry. But even if you aren't mistreating him, your bloody boyfriend certainly was.'

April gripped her hands tighter on the wheel. 'Yeah, I know. Jix kept telling me I was mad . . . I just put up with it because I loved him. OK, OK – don't start. Everyone has had a go on the subject. I'll deal with it. We're going to move away and live in the country. The French country.'

'You don't sound particularly delighted.'

'I'm not. Oh God – I don't know – it's such a long story . . .'

'You might as well tell me,' Ewan yawned, leaning back in his seat. 'We've got plenty of time.'

*

By some miracle, they arrived in Barking still in one piece and without being arrested. Irritatingly, April had found Ewan excellent company, and even more irritatingly he'd come down heavily on the side of Jix and Antonio and everyone in begging her to think seriously about her future with Noah. He'd understood, he'd said, about the long-term love thing and the happy-ever-after dream — but he'd made the same awful mistake with his ex-wife — and had been so lucky to escape and get back together with Clara. He wouldn't wish that sort of heartache and upheaval on anyone.

April really didn't want to think about Noah at the moment anyway. He'd been very calm about her working on New Year's Eve. Far too calm, really. She'd have liked him to have protested just a bit, and said that as it was their first New Year back together, he'd got something special planned. But he hadn't. He'd seemed perfectly happy to stay in with the television and baby-sit Bee while she went to work. Jix had been invited to Joel and Rusty's party upstairs, and as it didn't mean a trip outside, Daff was going too. She had been quite excited about being the only woman.

'This is it,' Ewan said eventually. 'The one with all the lights on.'

April was out of the car, sprinting barefoot up the path, and hammering on the door before Ewan had released his seat belt. And if she'd thought that Ewan was an unlikely animal right's activist, then the elderly man who opened the door was even more so. He looked like — and probably was — a retired schoolmaster, balding, rheumy-eyed, and with the compulsory beige cardigan and baggy cords.

'You've come for Evelyn, I take it.' He peered uncertainly through hefty bifocals. 'We were watching television. I like a proper New Year's Eve show, with dancing and swords, don't you?'

'Oh yes, definitely. Er – is Evelyn your wife?'

'Avis is my wife, Evelyn is your greyhound. You'd better come in.'

April got as far as the hall. Cair Paravel, whom she'd just spotted sitting on a cushion in front of the television with several cuddly toys and what appeared to be the carcass of a wild boar, hit her before she got any further.

'He recognises you then,' the schoolmaster said happily. 'That's nice. I like a satisfactory conclusion.'

April couldn't say anything. Mainly because of the joyous tears, but also because having an ecstatic greyhound in her arms meant she couldn't breathe or see or even stand up.

Ewan squeezed past her and shook the schoolmaster's hand. 'Nice one, Aubrey. Sorry about the mix-up – and to have disturbed you and Avis'

'Not a problem, dear boy.' Aubrey blinked back tears behind the bifocals. 'As long as they're reunited, and we know he's being looked after. He's a lovely dog. What did you say he was called?'

'Cair Paravel,' April managed to mutter through a mouthful of blue hairs.

'Ah, C. S. Lewis! Grand chap!'

Managing to return herself and Cair Paravel to almost normal positions, still stroking him, determined never, ever to let him out of her sight again, April spat out the remaining brindled coat. 'Why on earth did you call him Evelyn?'

'Looks the image of Evelyn Waugh in his early days,' Aubrey said. 'Grand chap, too.'

'Aubrey taught English,' Ewan said rather unnecessarily, 'and now that everything's sorted, I think we should be making tracks . . .'

Waving goodbye to Aubrey, and with Cair Paravel dangerously spread across both their laps in the front seat,

April wiped her tears, blew her nose, and set off for the homeward part of the journey.

'You don't mean,' she said, indicating to rejoin the A13, 'that Aubrey scaled the wall in my yard and hauled Cairey over? He must be seventy if he's a day.'

'Avis does the commando stuff,' Ewan said, removing a slender blue paw from the pocket of his tuxedo. 'She belongs to the WI.'

New Year's Eve had apparently been and gone at Bixford. Everywhere, including number 51, was in darkness. April assumed that Bee and Noah had both gone to bed and that Joel and Rusty's party had ended without the need to call out any of the emergency services.

Cair Paravel, still stretched across April and Ewan's laps on the front seat, had fallen asleep somewhere near Plaistow, and continued to snore contentedly.

'Shall I come in with you?' Ewan asked. 'And explain to whatshisname about all this?'

'Best not.' April was forcing her feet back into her shoes and shaking Cair Paravel awake. 'Hopefully Noah will be asleep and I'll be able to do all the explanations in the morning.' She slid out of the car, dragging the dozy Cair Paravel after her. 'Right, when you get back to the Frobishers', can you leave the car where we found it? And give the keys to the washer-upper with the nose ring and the Arsenal tattoo on his neck?'

'Should be easy to spot,' Ewan said, sliding into the driving seat. 'And I'm truly sorry about all this – and especially that I scared you.'

''S OK,' April grinned through the window. 'Everything's going to be all right now. And anyway, I think what you do – the rescuing stuff – is really great. You're pretty cool.'

'Thanks.' Ewan started the Cavalier. It sounded very noisy in the silent grey street. 'You'd better get indoors. It's freezing – oh, and if by some miracle Ampney Crucis have got the Frobisher Platinum and if by some other miracle young Cairey here makes it through the heats, I'll be seeing you on Valentine's Day, won't I?'

April blew him a kiss. 'You bet. It's a date. Take care driving back, won't you?'

'Too right.' Ewan released the hand brake. 'Mind you, I sobered up hours ago – on that first bit of the M25 when we did two miles on the hard shoulder . . . Good night.'

April watched the Cavalier's taillights turn the corner of the High Street and slide on to the ring road. She actually did hope Ewan got back to the Frobishers' in one piece and without being breathalysed. She didn't want anything else on her conscience.

As quietly as possible she slid her key into the lock of number 51, tiptoed across the communal hall, and, praying that Cair Paravel wouldn't bark and that Noah wouldn't wake up, she unlocked the door to the flat. Everything was completely silent.

Switching on only one of the table lamps, she scuttled across the living room and opened the kitchen door. Cair Paravel, with a lot of scrabbling toenails, bounded joyfully towards his blanket, leaped on it, turned round three times, then sank down on to his haunches with a sigh of pleasure.

April kissed him, and wiped away the tears again. He was home and he was happy. And so was she. Well, almost.

Without switching on any more lights, she peeped into the bedroom. There was no sound. No sound at all. Not Noah's low rumbled snore, not Bee's restless movements . . . April clicked on the bedroom light. Both beds were empty and untouched.

She blinked, not immediately feeling the shock. She was

dead tired, and overemotional. There had to be a reasonable explanation. Noah, however casual about his paternal role, wouldn't have let anything happen to Bee, would he? Oh God! The shock suddenly kicked in and April's imagination went into overdrive.

They'd gone to the hospital! Bee had probably choked on an illicit peanut, or swallowed some of Noah's paint, or electrocuted herself with the Christmas-tree lights or –

She flew out of the flat and up the stairs, hammering on Daff and Jix's door. There was no reply. Knowing that Jix sat up, reading and listening to music long after Daff had gone to bed, April hammered again. Nothing. Of course, they'd been to Joel and Rusty's party. They'd probably had loads to drink and were both comatose . . .

Feeling more sick than she'd ever done in her life, April flew up the next flight of stairs. Joel and Rusty's door got the same treatment. They'd probably passed out, too, she thought, almost choking on the mingled perfume of cloying scented oil and hot Indian spices. She'd got Cairey back and lost Bee! She shouldn't be at work! She should stay at home like a proper person and take care of her family! It was divine retribution or something.

The door opened a couple of inches. Daff, wearing a very jaunty paper hat with yellow feathers, peeped out. 'Oh, hello, sweet. You're back early. I thought you were staying down there until –'

'What's happened to Bee?' April's tongue seemed to be far too big for her mouth. Her legs were shaking. 'Is she in hospital? Daff – what's happened?'

'Happened? Nothing that I know of. Bee's here, April! Steady . . . Oh, come along in, sweet . . . Look, she's here. She's quite safe. She's as happy as a sand boy . . .'

April, still clutching the doorframe, peered into the flat. Bee, dressed in her pyjamas and with a party hat low or her brow, was sitting on the floor between Jix and Rusty, playing Monopoly.

April tried to speak but couldn't. Her knees were knocking and her heart was thundering and she was sure she was going to pass out. She managed to grab hold of the back of the sofa.

Bee looked up at her and smiled. 'Mummee! I've stayed up late and I've won! Did you bring me a present?'

April nodded. 'A big greyhound present.'

'Cairey?' Bee's eyes were round. 'Cairey's home?'

April nodded, knowing she was going to cry again.

'Honest?' Jix was on his feet. 'You're not kidding? I mean, it's not a replacement like Mum used to do with my goldfish when they snuffed it?'

April shook her head. 'The genuine article -- no, please don't ask me about it. I'll tell you later. But he's fine . . . What the hell is going on here, though? Where's Noah?'

Daff perched on the arm of the sofa. 'Well, to be honest, sweet, it's been a bit of a mix-up. Lovely party, though, and the boys did us proud – but they were all couples, April. Mixed couples. I thought it was going to be all Boy George and bitchy.'

Joel appeared from the kitchen carrying a coffee pot. 'We do have straight friends, Daff, as I kept telling you. Oh, happy new year, April.'

'And you . . . Yes, so?'

'Well, we were having a grand time, when your Noah comes upstairs with madam there – oh, about ten o'clock I reckon – and says he's going out, and could we keep an eye on her? So we take her in and she's had a whale of a time. He said he'd leave you a note.'

April gratefully accepted a cup of Joel's strong black coffee. 'He probably has. I didn't look. I wonder where he's gone – he certainly didn't have any plans.' April felt

387

the caffeine surge dizzily through her body. She really didn't care. She was home, Cairey was home, and Bee was safe. If Noah had decided to go out and celebrate on his own she really didn't care.

Twenty minutes later, with Bee clutching half a dozen hotels, she made her way downstairs again. The flat was still in darkness. Feeling guilty at the relief surging through her, she left Bee giving Cair Paravel a welcome cuddle and a million kisses in the kitchen, and turned the living-room lights on.

Everything was as it had always been. Everything except the blank spaces along the far wall. All Noah's paintings had gone.

Taking a deep breath, she looked round for the note. There wasn't one this time. There didn't need to be. His buckled canvas carriers, the paints, the brushes, were all missing too. And the suitcases from behind the Christmas tree. April bit her lip. He'd done it again. Left her without saying anything. Only this time he'd taken the paintings. The paintings that were her and Bee's insurance for the future.

Angrily, she walked into the bedroom, tugging off the waitressing skirt and waistcoat, and switched on the light. Bastard, she thought. Total tosser. Noah's clothes, normally tumbled everywhere, had vanished. The top of his bedside cabinet was empty. She rattled open the wardrobe doors: – everything of Noah's, every trace of him, had disappeared. Slowly, she turned round, too tired to try to make sense of her feelings tonight. She'd have to think about it all in the morning. Worry about the implications. Then she stared at the bed in horror.

The chocolate tin money box from under the bed was upended, completely empty, on her pillow.

chapter twenty-nine

'Come on, Cairey! Come on! Oh God – I can't look!'
April closed her eyes as the traps sprang open.
The shouts and screams of the thousands of spectators skewered into her brain. Only 480 metres – the length of this heat – were all that now stood between Cair Paravel and a place in the Frobisher Platinum Trophy final.

It was just over four weeks since Noah's defection. Four weeks in which April had taken stock, licked her wounds, and tried to hold herself together. Because she was responsible for Bee and Cair Paravel, life had had to go on after a fashion, even though she had been left with little money and even fewer dreams. Which was why, on the coldest January night that anyone could remember, she was standing with Jix in a downpour of icy rain at Hove greyhound stadium, and praying for Cair Paravel to win.

Immediately after the new year break, the heats for the Platinum Trophy final had been held at stadiums across Great Britain: from Swindon to Sunderland, from Sittingbourne to Perry Barr, and at all points in between. Hundreds of greyhounds had been entered in hundreds of elimination races, and now there were just thirty-six left in contention. Thirty-six dogs running in six heats at different venues, all at the same time tonight. The winning dogs from these last six races would be the fêted finalists at Ampney Crucis on Valentine's Day.

April and Jix, fitting in split shifts and extra hours to enable them to take time off, had already accompanied Cair Paravel and Daff's headscarf to more than twenty preliminary Frobisher Platinum races across the country. They'd been delighted when he'd won at first, then astounded as he kept on winning, then hardly daring to hope that he might just make the final heats.

Thanks to Brittany's relentless PR machine, the race had caught the imagination of both the press and public alike. It was something different for the newspapers to hook into: a fun event, a bit of light relief on the coldest, darkest days of the year. The media had been following the build-up to the Frobisher final with huge interest: after all, it was the first time that greyhound racing had been made so available to the general public, and going to the dogs was being heralded as the new gardening/make-over/docusoap television phenomenon.

And now there was just this race to go . . .

'Open your eyes,' Jix's voice, muffled by the Doctor Who scarf, yelled in her ear, just audible above the other surrounding yells. 'April! Look!'

She looked. The greyhounds were approaching the finish line. Cair Paravel, romping through the rain, wearing the black-and-white striped six jacket, was a neck ahead of the Hove pack. It was all over in a flash.

'He's won!' The tears mingled with the rain drops. 'Hasn't he?'

Jix hugged April and she hugged him back and then they were being pulled and pushed through the crowd to the presentation podium. The floodlights filtered through the deluge and the darkness, and Cair Paravel, sopping wet, squirmed against them ecstatically as cameras popped white explosions all round, and someone in a bowler hat shook their hands and gave them a statuette and a cheque.

April, her arms constantly round Cair Paravel's neck, experienced it all with a feeling of disbelief. It was like seeing it happen to someone else. Like watching the events taking place at the end of a long, dark tunnel.

'She don't look too good . . .'

'Is she all right up there?'

'Look out, mate, she's going to keel over . . .'

The inside of the van was dark and warm, and April could hear the rain drumming on the roof. She opened her eyes. Cair Paravel, sitting in the back seat, was peering at her mournfully across the faux zebra covers. Jix, beside her, was wearing much the same expression.

She blinked dizzily. 'Did I faint? Really?'

'You did, really. Scared the shit out of me – and everyone else,' Jix said. 'The St John Ambulance guy was really annoyed to find you had a pulse. He looked very keen on a bit of mouth-to-mouth. Mind you, the press thought it'd make a great story – they all had to ask me how to spell Beatrice-Eugenie.'

'Don't make me laugh . . . My head hurts.' April took deep breaths. Cair Paravel licked her face with a warm, slow tongue. 'I've never fainted in my life – come close a couple of times, but never –'

'It's hardly surprising, is it?' Jix poured her a cup of water. 'No, just sip it or you'll be sick. I bet you're not eating properly, and you never stop working, and with everything else that's happened . . .'

April flapped her hand at him. 'Don't nag me. I need the money. Now more than ever. And I can't change any of it, can I?'

'He can, though.' Jix fondled Cair Paravel's ears. 'Now

he's in the Platinum final, he could win you a fortune.'

April smiled wistfully. It was a lovely dream, but she wasn't going to dwell on it. She hadn't had a lot of luck with dreams lately, had she?

The letter had arrived from France exactly a week after Noah's new year disappearing act; although by then, April really hadn't needed to read the contents. She'd been made a fool of again, and it was all her own fault. She was beginning to get used to the feeling. However, this time, Noah certainly hadn't pulled any punches.

Dear April,

I'm sorry it had to be like this. It was over between us so long ago. I'm afraid I let my lust rule my head when I saw you again at the exhibition. I suppose, if you had been content to have been a bit on the side, then we could have left it like that – me dropping in at the flat for a few days when I was in England – just for sex – no strings. But that was never your style, was it? You wanted the full hearts and flowers, trumpets and rainbows – and I just didn't feel the same. And, of course, Bee just complicated matters. I'm too selfish to be a parent. I'm too selfish to want to share my life. Anoushka gives me the freedom I crave, the independence I need to create. I took the paintings because they were mine. I came back solely to get them. This probably sounds very cruel, but Anoushka and I had it planned. My early work – as you obviously know – is much sought after, and I wasn't prepared to let it go. I brought all my stuff so that you'd think I was staying. Sorry, again – a rat's trick. I hope you find what you're looking for – but it certainly won't be with me.

Noah.

PS. Don't think about selling your story to the tabloids –
I've already negotiated the contract.

PPS. I took the chocolate-tin money because I was short of
readies. Bee showed me where it was. And most of it came
from the sale of *Oceanic*, didn't it? So, legally it was mine.

PPPS. If you want to get that bad-tempered gangly mutt
back now I'm gone I think he's at some greyhound rescue
place, unless they've already put him down. I tipped them
off that he was being mistreated. Sorry. I just couldn't stand
him being in the house a minute longer.

April had sat in silence after reading the letter, staring out
of the window at the grey High Street, as the rain lashed
down. It was the end of her dream. She'd thought that
was what hurt most – that Noah had destroyed her future,
leaving her nothing to aim for. It didn't matter how many
times Daff had said she should count her blessings, all her
energy had been piled into reuniting her family, finding a
proper home, living in cosy comfort. She'd worked so
hard, and being exhausted all the time hadn't mattered,
because there was a purpose. Now, with nothing, all she
felt was a weary sadness.

The anger, she'd known, would come later. She'd loved
Noah very much, and she knew that she'd made far too
many excuses for him. But everyone else had been right –
and this time there would be no second chances. She hadn't
cried, or ranted or raved. She'd merely mourned the death
of the dream.

Jix had read the letter later that day. 'Do you want to
keep it?'

She'd shaken her head.

'What about the others? That crap he wrote about the
ocean painting? Anything else – or do you want to keep
them to show Bee when she's older?'

April had smiled ruefully. 'Possibly best not to. I'll tell her one day, of course. But I'll never colour her judgement. I'll let her form her own opinions about him – but no, go on – destroy the lot. It'll make me feel better. They're in a box on the top shelf of the wardrobe. Leave the photos – not for me, but for Bee. She'll need to be able to have something to identify with.'

Jix had disappeared, and April heard him tearing the letters into tiny pieces and then flushing them down the loo. She'd wished that she could flush away her humiliation half as easily.

Returning, Jix had stood in the doorway. 'Please try to forget him, April. Not yet – I know it'll take time – but try. He never deserved you.'

And she'd turned her head to the window and watched the rain.

Jix took the cup of water away from her. 'Feeling better?'

'Yes, thanks. I just got a bit overexcited, I expect, and it's so cold tonight.'

'God knows why this couldn't have been organised in the height of summer.'

April smiled as much as her wobbly lips would allow. 'Because, apparently, according to the Copacabana gossip, Frobishers are launching a new beer to go with the trophy – called something mad like Cupid's Cuddle Cup – well, no, not that – but along those lines, it being held on Valentine's Day. I suppose the whole Platinum thing is a brewery marketing ploy anyway. I mean, it must be easy to get people to drink gallons of beer on a red-hot summer day – but a damn sight more difficult in the depths of winter.'

As Jix started the van, Cair Paravel flicked his ears and curled round happily on the back seat, sleepily thumping his tail. April felt as though she wanted to join him and sleep for a week.

'I wish we could just stay here until I felt less tired. I wish I didn't have to go to work tomorrow – or ever again.'

'You'd get bored.'

'Eventually, maybe. But it'd be fun finding out what it's like to be a proper mum.'

They drove away from Hove, and April was vaguely aware of the motorway signs flashing past. She hadn't told anyone about the illegal drive with Ewan on New Year's Eve. She wondered how he'd explained his absence. No doubt he'd tell her when they saw each other again at Ampney Crucis. She watched the lights sparkle on the statuette in her lap, and grinned. It would go with all the others beside Bee's truckle bed. And the cheque would be put into Bee's building society account in the morning.

Courtesy of Cair Paravel, April thought, Beatrice-Eugenie Padgett was now the main breadwinner in the family.

Jix glanced across the van. 'Still awake? Look, I know you don't want me to nag, but you're wearing yourself out. You're knackered, you're miserable, you're screwed up – you need a holiday.'

'Yeah, right. Thanks to Noah, I've just lost all my savings, all those tips, all those months and months of slogging and scrimping and saving. I can't even afford to live at the moment – let alone go cavorting about in the Caribbean.'

'No one mentioned the Caribbean, did they? I was just thinking that as we're going to be at Ampney Crucis for the Platinum Trophy, maybe we could go down the day before and stay on afterwards, and have a bit of a break.'

'Ooh, yes.' Mollified, April nodded. 'Actually I can't think of anything nicer at the moment.'

'It won't be the same as before, of course, as it's the middle of winter.'

'Don't care.' April slid luxuriously down in her seat. 'It'd be wonderful. Can we all go – even Daff?'

Jix grinned. 'I can't see her allowing us not to take her, can you? I'll ring round and find a B&B or something. Of course, we'll have to ask for the whole week off work'

'Martina will love that.'

Actually, April thought dreamily, the last few weeks at the Copacabana had been quite amusing. Apart from the fact that she'd hoped to be able to retire, and now thanks to Noah, she'd have to work until she was about three hundred and eighty, it had been fun to watch Martina making a million different excuses why the Gillespie Stadium had missed out on the Frobisher.

And Sebastian was rarely seen: rumours were abounding that he'd resigned from the stadium board, and kicked the Gillespie Guzzler side of things into touch too. April really hoped that Seb was spending all his time with Brittany Frobisher – and not that Jasmine Clegg from Ampney Crucis. Now that Cairey was through to the Platinum final, it would be just terrible to have to face Sebastian at the racetrack and know that, as a result, she'd lose her home.

Mind you, she thought drowsily, snuggling into the seat and being hypnotised by the swish-swoosh motion of the windscreen wipers, it was going to be almost impossible to keep Cair Paravel a secret for much longer. The Frobisher finalists would be announced in the national press in the morning, which would mean that if his ownership was revealed, Martina would fire her by lunch time, and Seb would evict her before tea.

*

The following evening, Martina drummed her talons on the top of the bar and looked furtive. 'A whole week off? Middle of Feb? It's very short notice. Why?'

April, who was still rather shaky, shrugged. 'I haven't been feeling very well lately. I could just do with the break.'

'You're not pregnant, are you? I can't have bar staff who are pregnant.'

April laughed. That was one thing she was sure of. 'I'm definitely not pregnant. But you do still owe me some time off in lieu for New Year's Eve.' She held her breath here. So far, Martina had said nothing about the fact that she hadn't finished her night's work at the Frobishers'. April was pretty sure it had gone unnoticed. One waitress looked pretty much like another to Martina. 'And I know you don't like any of us taking time off in the middle of the busy season, with the build-up to the Greyhound Derby and all that.'

Martina tisked her tongue against her teeth. 'Well, yes, all right. I'll juggle the rosters. If I allow for two of the days being your rest days anyway, I'll give you three days paid leave and two unpaid. Take it or leave it.'

'Taken.'

Martina obviously felt she'd won that round. 'Good. Now go and do some work.'

And April, her spirits soaring, wobbled off on another pair of shoes borrowed from Sofia, and started happily stocking the sparklers, twizzle sticks and umbrellas in their containers. Sofia and Antonio had already agreed to give her as much paid leave as she needed, and the thought of a few days beside the sea at Ampney Crucis, was just what she could do with. The Frobisher Platinum Trophy, and Cairey's involvement, was something she'd think about later. The holiday was a definite — Cair Paravel's victory wasn't. And April had decided that she wasn't going to bet on uncertainties ever again.

The finalists for the Platinum Trophy had been trumpeted in the *Racing Post* and all the sports pages of the dailies that morning. April and Jix had beamed at each other with parental pride at the inclusion of Cair Paravel's name. As well as Bee being registered as his owner, they'd also used an anagram of their own first names as a trainer. So the identity of Cair Paravel, owned by Beatrice-Eugenie Padgett and trained by L. X. Piriaj, would hopefully stay a secret for a while longer.

'April! A word!'

Martina, looking frazzled, was motioning from behind the plastic palm tree. April, pausing in slicing limes, slid her feet back into her shoes and tottered towards her. Please God don't let her have changed her mind about the holiday. 'Is it about my week off?'

'Indirectly . . .' Martina's eyelashes were aquamarine tonight to match her body studs, and they flapped in agitation like the fronds of something more usually found in an Amazonian rain forest. 'I've just pencilled you in on the leave chart, and Oliver informs me that he has given Jix the same week off.'

So? April thought. So?

'Are you going away together?'

'Yes, sort of. Well, not together as in a couple, but yes, we're going to the same place . . . with Daff. You know, Jix's mum? She doesn't get out much and we thought – '

'It is company policy that the staff do not have relationships. Well, I mean, not with each other, so to speak.'

'Oh, we're not. We're just friends.' April floundered a bit, then went for the throat. 'Did you say that Oliver was doing the leave chart? Isn't that Sebastian's job usually?'

'Not any more.' Martina's lips pursed themselves together in an angry pucker. 'You might as well know that since New Year's Eve, and the failure of Gillespies to secure the Platinum Trophy – not that we really wanted it, you understand – Sebastian has relinquished his seat on the board.'

So the rumours were true, then. 'Oh dear – does that make things difficult?'

'Not really. To be honest, his heart hasn't been in it for some time. He's having a rather late attack of adolescent itchy feet as far as I can gather. He just decided to up sticks, move out of his apartment, leave his job here and –'

'Backpack around India? Work in Tesco? Tread grapes in Tuscany? Be a beach bum in Thailand?'

'Christ!' Martina's eyelashes snapped fiercely up and down. 'Nothing as irresponsible as that! He's merely decided to go out on his own for a while, and gain some independence.'

'So does that mean I'll have a new landlord, then? With Sebby off the scene?'

Martina winced, as always, at the use of the diminutive. 'Sebastian's duties will be shared out among the other directors, yes. We'll not be electing anyone new to the board – just in case he decides to come back. In this instance, the property side of things will revert back to Oliver.'

Oh bugger, thought April.

'He's going to be checking up on all tenancy agreements, inspecting properties, you know . . .'

Double bugger. 'So what's Sebastian going to be doing, then?'

Martina preened. 'Brittany, who will no doubt one day be our daughter-in-law, so it's keeping it more or less in the family, has offered him a little job with Frobishers.'

Thank God, April thought. 'Oh well, it's always good to have a change, isn't it? Will he be making beer or something?'

Martina frowned, looking as though she'd probably already been a bit too chummy with a subordinate. 'No, it's no secret that he won't actually be working for the brewery. He's down in bloody Ampney Crucis, masterminding the staging of the Platinum Trophy.'

Oh, double double bugger, thought April.

'This is it, then. You can open your eyes now.' Jix, who had insisted that April shut her eyes the minute they drove into Ampney Crucis, had switched off the van's engine. 'What do you think?'

April, expecting to be parked outside one of the villas along the main road, blinked.

The sea, rushing and crashing below them, looked like molten silver beneath the heavy sky. The wind whistled through the frost-bleached grass on the cliff top, and the strangely shaped trees, all leaning away from the sea, spread skeletal arms across the crisscrossed sandy paths. The Crumpled Horn and the Crow's Nest Caff were just visible round a bend in the twisting shingle road, and several other cottages nestled in a rather higgledy-piggledy row on either side.

'It's a cottage . . .' April stared at the little stone-built house, with its sloping tiled roof, and a holly bush hedge, and a tangle of gorse and heather and ferns in the garden. It was straight out of her dreams. 'A cottage by the sea. Oh, it's beautiful . . . Will there be enough room for us all to stay here?'

'Three bedrooms, according to the brochure,' Jix said, watching her face. 'Two receptions, a kitchen and a bathroom. Loads of room.'

Bee and Daff and Cair Paravel were staring at it too. Cair Paravel had decided that as long as Daff wasn't wearing floral polyester he didn't want to savage her. Daff now spent most of her time in tweed.

April unbuckled her seat belt. 'And the landlady knows about Cairey, does she? There's not a problem with dogs? Or children?'

'Not a problem at all. And there's no landlady. We're self-catering.'

April wanted to laugh and cry with delight. 'You mean we can pretend to really live here for a whole week? All of us? In a cottage by the sea? Oh, wow!'

They all tried to scramble out of the van at the same time, and eventually, with Bee clutching April's hand, and Jix leading Daff, and Cair Paravel leaping between them, they negotiated the overgrown path and pushed open the cottage door.

'It's furnished like a proper home!' April stood in the hall, gazing in complete rapture at the cosiness. 'It's got a fireplace! And big armchairs – oh, and look at the kitchen! Oh, Bee, look – you can see the sea from the windows!'

She dashed away the tears. It was all far too much. This was the place she'd always dreamed of. Tomorrow, Cair Paravel may or may not win the Frobisher Platinum Trophy, but for the next seven days and nights she would be living in paradise.

Daff was busily unpacking things, bustling round the cottage as if she'd lived there for ever. 'April, sweet – you look very pale. Leave Bee here to help me feed Cairey and get things shipshape, and you go and get a few lungfuls of that sea air.'

'I ought to help you –'

'You'll be more help to me when you're feeling stronger. Now run along.'

April ran.

Once outside, she felt that she could run for ever. There were a few hardy souls striding along the shoreline, accompanied by dogs and children, all muffled against the wind. The Crumpled Horn was filled to the seams if the car park was anything to go by, and there were a couple of people visible down by the beach huts. Apart from that, Ampney Crucis seemed deserted. There was no noise except the rushing of the wind and the sea. It was invigorating and savagely beautiful.

April leaned against the railings, staring down at the slope of the cliffs and the wide white spread of the beach below.

'Happy?' Jix, wearing the leather jacket and the Doctor Who scarf with his velvet flares, leaned beside her. He was still carrying his rucksack. 'Is this what you wanted?'

She nodded, unable to speak. All the anxiety and the humiliation and the worries seemed to be swept away in the vastness.

'I know you'd planned to do this with Noah,' Jix said quietly, 'but it's the best I could do . . . No, listen. April – what have you always wanted? Truly?'

She stared out at the ocean. 'You know very well. A family, a proper family, a proper home, to live in a place like this and feel that I belong to something, someone . . .'

'You've got all that.'

'What?' She turned to look at him.

'All of that. You've had most of it for ages. Me and Bee and Mum and Cairey – we've been your family. And now you've got the cottage by the sea.'

She smiled. 'Yeah. It's brilliant, but it's not for ever, is it?'

'It could be. If it's what you want.' Jix scuffed at the stubbly grass. 'The cottage is a holiday home, available on a yearly lease. I've – um – made enquiries. If you're happy with the rest of it, we could stay here and find work. We can both turn our hand to anything – and in a holiday place there's bound to be loads of opportunities. And you left something out just now.'

'Did I? I don't think so.' April was just allowing the rest of it to sink in. She'd wake up in a minute, she knew she would, and find none of this was real. 'Jix – you mean, really mean, we could live here – all of us? No more Bixford or Copacabana or debt-collecting or Gillespies or – '

'None of it. I told you, I've been saving for my dream too. I've got the van, and this is the rest of it.'

Biting her lip, she looked at him. The wind had whipped his hair across his face so she couldn't see his eyes. 'You said I'd forgotten something – what was it?'

He didn't answer immediately. When he did, he wasn't looking at her. 'Love. You always said you wanted to spend the rest of your life loving someone who loved you in return. And no, don't say anything – there's this first . . .' He swung the rucksack off his shoulder, undid the buckle, then handed her a parcel wrapped in holly-and-mistletoe paper. 'It's my Christmas present to you. Because things were so shitty on Christmas Day, and because you and Noah were together, I didn't – couldn't – give it to you then.'

Tearing at the paper with icy fingers, April gazed at the purple box inside. She lifted the lid and was stunned into silence.

Nestling in billows of the softest tissue paper was a pair of shoes. The most beautiful shoes she'd ever seen. Designer shoes, hand-crafted, pale blue and pink entwined strips of leather, with high, slender glass heels with pale blue and pink rosebuds caught inside like jewels in aspic.

She kicked off her boots and slid her feet into the sensational softness. The shoes looked slightly out of place with jeans, but she sighed with happiness. Her feet felt as though they were cushioned in thistledown.

'Probably the first pair of shoes you've ever had that fit you . . .' Jix's voice was husky. 'Um – I thought that as a declaration of love, they'd – um –'

'Oh, thank you so much!' April threw her arms round his neck, crying properly now. 'Thank you . . . Oh God, Jix! They're absolutely incredible! They are just wonderful! Oh, I can't believe it . . .' She stopped. 'What did you say?'

'I love you.' He pulled her back against him. 'I've loved you from the minute you moved in with Noah all those years ago. I know you don't love me –'

She smiled through her tears. 'I never got the chance, did I? Every other woman in Bixford was there before me.'

'Had to do something to pass the time . . .' Jix lifted her face up. 'Anyway, if you're happy with the idea of the cottage on a long-term basis, I thought you might just get used to having me around too.'

He kissed her gently, properly, for the first time. April felt her whole body melt. Shivering, she kissed him back, softly at first, and then not so softly, and then not softly at all.

'Jesus . . .' she whispered into his hair. Her legs were shaking. 'Can we go home now, please?'

'You want to go home to Bixford?' Jix kissed her again.

April held his face between her hands, smiling. 'Never. I want to go home with you. To our family. Our cottage. And I need time to get my head round this love thing, don't I? After all, falling in love with your best friend is a pretty major step.' She looked down at her feet. 'But at least now I've got the right shoes to take it in . . .'

chapter thirty

The Benny Clegg Stadium was ablaze with lights. The normal floods and spots had been joined by thousands and thousands of tiny pink bulbs, rosy pinpricks suspended in ropes like dowagers' pearls in the darkness. Huge red helium Valentine hearts floated in their hundreds against the night sky, and the lasers, in a constantly moving rainbow, spelling out 'Frobisher Platinum Trophy here tonight!' were visible for miles.

At ground level, the coach and car parks were already full, and queues were snaking round the turnstiles and out towards the cliff top. Frobisher's Brewery staff, warmly wrapped up against the continuing icy weather, were moving amongst the waiting crowds, doling out tiny free glasses of their new winter beer – which Jasmine had sampled earlier and quite enjoyed – and peanuts. Doris Day, who had been trilling out all her best romantic ballads in surround sound since twilight, was currently getting the collective feet tapping with 'By the Light of the Silvery Moon'.

All across the stadium, the themes of Valentine's Day and the Platinum Trophy were cleverly intertwined: red roses and pink-cushioned hearts were on every post, pole and railing, while cut-out silver trophies, looking like the overspill from an FA Cup production line, adorned walls, doors, and practically anything else that didn't move. The word 'Frobisher' was everywhere you looked, and still the crowds were arriving in droves.

The Ampney Crucis board members were in paroxysms of delight.

Clara and Ewan, looking quite Torville and Dean in matching red and black outfits, had been appointed greeters-in-chief, and were cheerfully showing all the local dignitaries to the posh seats in the stands, and all the various newspaper competition winners and Clara's massive extended family to the even posher – and warmer – seats behind the glass viewing screens, where Gilbert and Eddie Deebley were serving up chicken and chips and pints of Old Ampney like it was going out of fashion.

The six greyhound finalists for the Platinum Trophy had arrived earlier, and were ensconced in a special part of the new kennel block with their connections. Ewan, Jasmine noticed, had spent quite some time down there, and had come back beaming almost soppily. After the really strange goings-on at New Year, when he had been missing from the Frobishers' party for hours, and had then come back with some cock-and-bull tale of having had too much to drink and fallen asleep in one of the centrally heated lavatory cubicles – which Clara had believed and Jasmine hadn't – Ewan had actually behaved himself amazingly well. Jasmine hoped this silly smile when returning from the kennels was merely because of his love of greyhounds – and had nothing to do with a pretty handler.

Peg was wearing a 1950s style fur coat, much to Jasmine's disgust, with stilt-high black courts and the French pleat wig. Jasmine, who had shunned dressing up on the grounds that as she'd be in the front betting line she just needed to keep warm, was wearing clean jeans, her thickest sweater and Benny's waxed jacket.

As well as the Platinum Trophy, there were eight other races on the card tonight — all also lavishly sponsored, thanks to the hype stirred up by Brittany — and Jasmine, Roger and Allan had watched with a sense of foreboding as the out-of-town bookies set up their very flashy joints, boards and umbrellas along the rails.

'Plenty of business here for everyone,' Peg said, swishing her coat along the ground. 'And it's only for tonight. You'll get your exclusivity zones back for the next meeting. Don't frown so, pets.'

'All right for her,' Roger grumbled. 'This could have been my swan song.'

Allan and Jasmine had looked at him in surprise. 'You're not going to retire, surely?'

'Not now,' Roger blew on his hands. 'Not when yon Ladbroke's laddie is going to undercut me on every bloody dog.'

The fever-pitch feeling was building rapidly. Brittany had just arrived, looking very elegant and not at all cold in a silver trouser suit and huge velvet hat, and accompanied by her parents and what appeared to be the entire remainder of the Frobisher workforce. The paparazzi pack had swooped on Brittany immediately, and she had smiled happily and confidently cracked jokes with them all. A whole area had been set aside earlier in the day for the media, and suddenly the enclosure emptied as microphones and cameras of all types were homed in on the It Girl of the moment.

Jasmine watched and tried not to be envious. Brittany, true to her word on New Year's Eve, had made regular visits to Ampney Crucis, accompanied by a host of Frobisher 'suits and boots', and had proved to be truly amazing at promoting and marketing the event. Having grown to like and admire Brittany more each time they met, Jasmine really tried not to think about what would happen tomorrow when it was all over.

The trouble was, she had got so used to having Sebastian around. When he'd told her, during the dancing on New Year's Eve, that he intended to leave Bixford, and jack in his job at the Gillespie Stadium, Jasmine hadn't really been surprised. Everything she'd learned about him during their friendship had indicated that this was something he really wanted to do. She'd wished him luck in breaking the shattering news to his parents, and he'd said that if she could survive what had happened to her with her parents and Andrew, then what he was contemplating should be a piece of cake in comparison.

They'd danced and talked all night, and over the day-break breakfast, Sebastian had sleepily promised her that he'd be seeing her very soon. Jasmine had returned to the Travel Lodge with the victorious Ampney Crucis crew, more hopelessly in love than ever.

Within two days Sebastian had turned up at the beach hut, with a selection of doughnuts and a holdall, explaining that after the expected parental explosions, he was now working for Frobisher's as a sort of back-room Platinum Trophy promotions boy, and he was at her disposal. She'd swallowed the all-too-obvious retort, hugged him – trying to keep the hug friendly so as not to scare him off – and said that if he didn't mind getting his hands dirty she was sure that Peg and the other Ampney Crucians would also welcome him with open arms.

Jasmine had also been brave enough to suggest immediately that he bagged a room at the Crumpled Horn while he was working at the stadium – just in case he'd intended to stash the holdall behind the chiffonier and leap under the poppies and daisies. As she actually wanted nothing more than Seb in her bed, this, she felt, was quite a grown-up thing to do. Sebastian Gillespie as a permanent sleeping – and waking – partner would be sheer unadulterated bliss. Sebastian Gillespie as a sort of prolonged one-night stand who was going to leave her as soon as the Platinum Trophy was over, was asking for lifelong heartbreak.

So Seb was staying in the Crumpled Horn, and for the last few weeks, while they'd been working round the clock to prepare the Benny Clegg Stadium for tonight, he had slogged as hard as any of them. He had fitted in so easily that it sometimes seemed impossible to remember a time when he hadn't been around. But Jasmine was constantly aware that once the Platinum was over, when all the hoo-ha had died down, Sebastian would be off to spread the Frobisher word elsewhere.

And even worse, she was convinced that Sebastian was not only going to be Brittany's business partner, but would no doubt also resume his role as her part-time lover.

He'd laughed when Jasmine, over a huge fry-up in the Crow's Nest Caff some days before, had voiced this opinion.

'When the hell have I had time to be anyone's part-time lover? I haven't done anything since new year, except work – thanks to you. I collapse into bed – alone – every night, and I'm asleep before my feet have left the floor.'

'You know what I mean . . .' Jasmine had mopped up all the delicious juices with a doorstep of white bread and butter. 'You and Brittany were together in a snuggly-up way before all this happened – and you'll be together again after it's all over . . . I mean, I'm really glad that you've left Bixford, if that's what you wanted to do, and by working on promotions for Brittany you'll have a lovely itinerant life, but –'

409

'But what?' Seb had balanced a mountain of beans on his last piece of fried bread.

'I'll miss you.'

He'd grinned at her. 'I'll write to you – and send you doughnuts. It'll be just like old times.'

And then Bunny and Muriel had turned up, as someone always did when she and Sebastian were together, and said there was some new crisis at the stadium and could she come and sort it?

The stadium had been open for business as usual all through the preparations, and Jasmine, as Benny Clegg – the Punters' Friend, had set odds, negotiated prices, won and lost money on at least ten races, three nights a week, ever since Sebastian had arrived. Still fascinated by the fact that she was a bookie, he hadn't tired of watching her work, and even volunteered to replace Muriel on writing up when she had her tea breaks.

Jasmine had teased him mercilessly. 'God, you ran a multimillion-pound business for your dad – had your fingers in all sorts of iffy pies – you go out with the financial whizz-kid babe of the century – and you still can't pay out quicker than that? And what's that supposed to be? Even Clara was better than you – and she was hopeless.'

And he'd poked his tongue out at her and they'd giggled at each other, and Roger and Allan had shaken their heads over Benny Clegg behaving like a schoolgirl.

'First race in ten minutes, Jas.' Gorf, in his starter's kit of shiny suit and bowler hat and carrying his green flag, tapped her on the shoulder. 'Better start laying some off.'

So, with her chalk flying across the board, Jasmine wrote up the names of the six dogs in the first race, undercut the William Hill odds on each one, and took a deep breath as the punters started piling on their money. Muriel was

410

working like lightning behind her, but even she was having trouble keeping up.

'God, if it's like this now, what on earth is it going to be like by the time we get to the Platinum?'

'Murder,' Muriel said with relish from beneath her pixie hood. 'Sheer bloody murder. But we'll both be going home a darn sight richer than most of these mugs.'

An hour and a half later, with six races behind them, and the crowd seething like maggots in a jar, Jasmine trudged off with the full money satchel to decant her takings in Peg's office safe. There had never been a night like it, and would probably never be another – but it didn't matter. The Benny Clegg Stadium was well and truly on the greyhound map and would always stay there. Jasmine smiled to herself. It was all she had ever wanted for Grandpa, wasn't it? And for her? Well, almost.

On her way back to her post, shoving through the crowds, she was practically knocked senseless by a killer whiff of Eau Sauvage. Verity and her father, both buttoned and belted in woollen overcoats, were shoving in the opposite direction.

'Dad!' Jasmine, completely forgetting herself, threw her arms round his neck. 'God – this is amazing! I never thought . . .'

'Couldn't let this pass, could we?' Philip's voice was gruff as he patted her. 'Damn good show, Jasmine. Not that I approve, but –'

'Oh, get away, Phil!' Verity pummelled his arm. 'You're as proud as punch of the girl. You said so. I for one will be coming here a lot more. Haven't had so much fun in ages. And all the telly people and everything! I've just seen Des Lynam, I think . . .'

'And we've got a bit of news,' Philip smiled indulgently. 'The house – our house, or ex-house, I suppose – is on the market. Your mother and that young bastard have decamped to Bournemouth – couldn't stand the heat. Heard from the solicitors this morning . . . So, you won't have to worry about bumping into them again.'

'Nor will you,' Jasmine said. 'Thanks for telling me, though. Um – maybe we could get together for lunch or something . . .'

'Just what I've been saying,' Verity beamed. 'We'll have you round for a Sunday – next weekend, maybe? I do a lovely roast with all the trimmings and your dad is really partial to my creamed rice pudding.'

Jasmine, knowing that her father had existed for years on Yvonne's ready-cooked low-calorie meals, reckoned he'd fallen on his feet, big time.

'I'd love to,' she said, surprised to find that she meant it. 'Thanks. That'd be great.'

Kissing them both, she hurried back to the rails, wiping away a tear.

Sebastian was standing on her crates chalking up the next race. She stood and looked at him for a long moment. It was the picture she'd keep inside her head for ever: Seb in jeans and a huge navy-blue sweater, his hair falling forward, concentrating. With all the noise around them, and the lights, and the thousands of people, and the yapping of the greyhounds from the kennels, it was like a virtual reality Lowry painting. There'd be something new to see each time she conjured it up.

'What are you doing?' She peered up at the board. 'Oh, right – OK . . .'

'Expected me to have got it wrong, did you?' Seb grinned down at her. 'I wouldn't dare. I've learned a lot in the last weeks, Jas, just standing and watching. I might still be a bit ham-fisted with the paying out, but I'm getting a good idea of how to make a book. See – I've even studied the form here . . . and this one is easily the best, so I've put it in at twos.'

'It's great. Couldn't have done better myself. Are you planning to put me out of business?' She climbed up on to the orange box beside him. 'Or does this mean you're part of Benny Clegg for the rest of the evening?'

He nodded. 'Muriel said you were doing a roaring trade, and could do with a bit of help. It's all amazing, isn't it?'

'Thanks to Brittany.'

'And you.' Sebastian ruffled her hair. 'You've done a brilliant job. I'd never dreamed it could be like this. At Bixford the meetings just happened, organised and run by an unseen committee. There was no hands-on and, for me, no excitement. It was like an every-night-of-the-week soap opera – you could miss dozens and still pick up the threads.'

'We're off again.' Muriel leaned forward. 'Brace yourselves . . .'

The crowds, seeing the prices on the boards, and hearing Gilbert announce the names of the runners, surged forward. Jasmine took a deep breath and once more turned into Benny Clegg.

The atmosphere now was electric. The last race of the evening – the Frobisher Platinum Trophy – had at last been announced. Gilbert had done his build-up and handed the microphone to Peg, who'd given a brief history of the Benny Clegg Stadium and how the whole thing had come about for those who didn't already know. Then Brittany had spoken on behalf of the sponsors and got the loudest applause because she was so famous.

There was then a brief interlude of stirringly suitable dog music – Peg had managed to fish out an obscure copy of Doris singing 'How Much is That Doggy in the

Window?' to fit in with this, and the crowd were raucously joining in on the chorus.

The greyhounds then appeared, one at a time, each led out, not by a regular handler in a kennel coat, but by a very pretty Frobisher promotions girl in shorts and boots and a skin-tight T-shirt. As the weather was so bitter, they got an extra cheer for sheer guts, and almost as much camera coverage as Brittany.

Jasmine had already chalked up the names, and pressed up against Seb on the pallets to watch as each one appeared: Foxy Flo, Clyde the Spider, Luton Lennox, Cair Paravel, Emily's Gem, and Ruby Slippers.

'Beautiful, aren't they?' Jasmine craned her neck. 'And I'm sure we've had at least one of them running here before. Cair Paravel sounds familiar.'

'I'm surprised you can remember with all the dogs that you write up each week.'

'You always remember the strangers. We get the same dogs so often. I'm sure there was something about Cair Paravel . . . something Ewan told me. Oh, well – it'll come back. God, I wouldn't want to be their owners. They must be dying with nerves.'

Gilbert had started naming the owners and trainers. Jasmine, who tried to listen to the information on Cair Paravel's connections, was interrupted by Bunny.

'Jasmine! Guess what? We got the dog what wears clothes in this one!'

Jasmine watched him as he scampered back to the responsibilities of the hare, and wondered if someone had inadvertently upped his medication. Still, there was no time to dwell on it as the crowds, waving tens and twenties above their heads, had surged forward again, and were pressing against the joint, twelve deep. Jasmine, working faster than she ever had before, was still finding it difficult to keep up, and even with Seb and Muriel employed in tandem, she was sure she was losing bets to the Ladbroke's six-strong team.

The prices were changing all the time, but Ruby Slippers, the winner of the Walthamstow heat, was definitely favourite. The other five dogs were much of a muchness, and Jasmine, one eye constantly on the other boards, rubbed and chalked like fury.

They were going behind the traps now and the cold night air seemed to crackle and fizz with tension. Peg, the wig slightly askew, was in the centre of the course on the new illuminated presentation podium with Brittany and several television reporters, and Jasmine smiled. This was her dream: hers and Benny's. They were so lucky. So few people had dreams that really came true. Tomorrow she'd go to the graveyard and tell Benny every bit about it. Tonight, though, she was pretty sure he knew.

'All in!' Gilbert yelled. 'All bets done! Ladies and gentlemen – it's the Frobisher Platinum Greyhound Trophy!'

The screams seemed to rise and linger. Jasmine felt the hairs prickle on the back of her neck. Bunny released the hare, which to Jasmine's eye, looked a little more bulky than usual as it zoomed past in a blur, then the traps sprang back and the greyhounds streaked out.

Sebastian found her hand in the folds of the waxed jacket and clung on to her fingers. 'This is un-bloody-believable.'

She squeezed his fingers back, unable to speak.

The action was fast and furious as, with nothing to choose between them, the greyhounds sliced through the solid wall of sound. Neck and neck, they hurtled up the straight, with possibly the striped jacket of Ruby Slippers fractionally in the lead. The crowds were screaming with no words. Every name had merged into every other name, and as the sand flew under the chasing feet, it looked as if the dogs were simply skimming the ground.

The colours collided, the blue jacket was a whisker ahead, then the black, then the orange and the red. No, the stripes were taking it on the far side. Ruby Slippers had the advantage. One stride. Two. Then the black jacket was up alongside again, stride for stride, leaning against each other coming round the final bend. There was still nothing in it. The crowds were manic in their encouragement.

'Ruby Slippers,' Jasmine muttered through clenched teeth, still holding Seb's hand. 'It's going to be the six dog!'

'No it isn't – look at the black jacket!'

Almost in slow motion, the stripy jacket and the black jacket clashed and collided, as the long powerful legs punched at the ground. The four dog was a nostril ahead now. And gaining . . .

The stadium exploded as the dogs streaked over the winning line.

'Ladies and gentlemen,' Gilbert's voice, cracking slightly, broke through the mayhem. 'The winner of the Frobisher Platinum Trophy is dog number four! Cair Paravel!'

Fireworks, like huge bottles of shaken champagne, were gushing in silver brilliance across the sky, the Tannoy was playing 'Congratulations' at a deadly level, and the noise from the crowd was indescribable.

'Christ,' Seb said, as the hordes started to descend towards the bookies' pitches. 'Can we afford to pay them out?'

'Oh, yes.' Jasmine was buzzing. 'I took most money on Ruby Slippers and Luton Lennox. This is quite a result for us. Let's hope we get 'em paid out in time to watch the presentation.'

They did, just. The media were pushing themselves forward, as Brittany, minus her hat, said her piece. Everyone stopped dancing for long enough to applaud and cheer. Jasmine, with most of the other stadium stalwarts on the edge of the throng, and still holding Sebastian's hand, wondered just why Ewan was on the podium. He was whispering something to Brittany, making her laugh delightedly, and then they both grinned down at the exceptionally pretty girl in the short blue woollen dress who was climbing on to the podium to receive the massive Platinum Trophy and the even more massive cheque.

'Look at those shoes!' Clara, who had joined them, groaned greedily. 'Manolo Blahniks! They must have cost the earth.'

'She'll be able to afford a lot more now,' Seb said. 'After all – Jesus! It's April!'

'April who?' Jasmine squinted towards the podium. 'Christ! She's the waitress from the New Year's Eve party!'

'It gives me the greatest pleasure in the world,' Brittany was saying, draping a sash over a bouncing Cair Paravel, 'to present this, the first Frobisher Platinum Trophy, to Cair Paravel – and his owners and trainers – April Padgett and Jix Bellamy.'

'Not what it says on the race card,' Gorf muttered. 'Says he's owned by Beatrice-Eugenie someone or other and trained by some Hungarian bloke.'

'Beatrice-Eugenie?' Seb was frowning. 'Beatrice-Eugenie? God Almighty! What a scam! Clever buggers – oh, and no one deserves this more. They fooled me, and what's more they've fooled everyone else. God, my parents will crucify them when they get back to Bixford.'

'What the hell is going on?' Jasmine asked. 'Is this illegal or something?'

As Jix joined April on the podium and they all shook

hands and kissed everyone, Sebastian sketched the outline of the story for Jasmine's benefit. She beamed with delight. What a fairy tale! The press would have a field day bonanza with this one.

'. . . And,' Brittany was saying, 'we at Frobisher's are so delighted with the resounding success tonight that we're pleased to announce that the Frobisher Platinum Trophy will be held here, as an annual event, on Valentine's Day, for at least the next five years!'

More whoops and screams and cheers from the crowd. Jasmine clapped her hands with total joy. The Benny Clegg Stadium was well and truly established.

The party in Peg's office was still pumping. Sebastian had introduced Jasmine to April and Jix, who were far more than just joint owners if the way they couldn't keep their hands off one another was anything to go by. Cair Paravel was sitting proudly in a corner, still wearing his sash, gnawing on a T-bone steak and grinning.

Ewan and Brittany gave everyone some very garbled accounts of Cair Paravel having been snatched and rescued just in time – none of which made sense to Jasmine – and Peg had removed her wig for the first time in living memory and was dancing with Rod Frobisher to 'I'll See You in My Dreams'.

Jasmine, remembering now that Cair Paravel had been the dog who chased the headscarf, had hugged April and Jix and said that no one would ever believe their story.

'Mum and Dad certainly won't,' Seb said. 'They'll have purple fits when you go back to Bixford.'

'We're not going back,' Jix said happily. 'We've rented a cottage up on the cliff top and we're staying here in Ampney Crucis and being a family. With Mum and Bee and Cairey, of course.'

'And with the winnings money,' April's eyes were huge, 'I'm going to be able to stay at home and be a proper mum to Bee and everything.'

Seb grinned hugely at Jix. 'Amazing. I'm so happy for you. And, of course, if you're looking for a job, then Jasmine will be able to find you something here, I'm sure. I'll give you the best references in the world.'

It was all very emotional. Clara had taken April to one side and they were enthusing about shoes, Brittany was shaking everyone's hands, and the piles of empty champagne bottles were growing by the minute. Jasmine, who had been trying to piece things together, and getting more and more confused, was simply delighted that everyone was happy.

'So,' Seb was saying to Jix, 'it was April's ex who had Cair Paravel nicked, was it? So it must have been him who informed me about her subletting and having a dog and baby in the flat . . . Bastard.'

Jix shook his head. 'No, that was me, I'm afraid. I've explained it to April now. It was a mad thing to do, and I'm desperately sorry to have caused April such grief: I felt terrible once I'd done it. I shouldn't have interfered. I never have before – but I was off my head over how Noah was destroying her and how she wouldn't do anything about it. So I thought if you were informed, you would turn nasty and throw her out, and I could come to her rescue . . .'

'And it all backfired because I believed her story!' Seb grinned. 'Actually, I didn't, but there was no way I'd ever have chucked her out on the streets. Sorry, mate. Still, things always have a way of working out, and you must love her very much.'

'More than anything in the world,' Jix said. 'April has forgiven me and now we're all away from Bixford, we can

419

see each other the whole time, can't we? Life is going to be just so cool.'

Jasmine, still beaming, drifted away to talk to Roger and Allan, who had obviously made massive profits too, and were talking of taking on extra writers-up. By the time she'd returned to the main bunch of partygoers, Sebastian had gone. So had Brittany.

Instantly deflated, Jasmine was swamped with tiredness. She'd known he'd go, of course, but she'd expected him to say goodbye. Maybe he'd thought it was less painful like this – just to slip away. Less painful for him, maybe – totally devastating for her. Bloody men, they were all the same. Selfish . . .

As the party looked like frolicking on into the small hours, Jasmine made her goodbyes, and stepped out into the icy night. Celebrations were still roaring in the stadium and, skirting the revelry, Jasmine headed for the cliff path.

The beach hut was her salvation. Everything that had rocked her life – Benny's death, her parents' separation, Andrew's treachery – all of it had seemed less painful here. She had a feeling that loving and losing Sebastian might just take a bit more than a jumble of furniture and a fridge full of beer. She climbed wearily on to the veranda.

'What kept you?' Sebastian emerged from the canvas chair in the darkness. 'I'm freezing.'

Jasmine, delighted to see him, but knowing that this was goodbye, unlocked the door. 'I thought you and Brittany had already gone.'

'Brittany has. I haven't.'

'Yet.' She switched on the lights and lit the heater. The night was raspingly cold.

Sebastian leaned against the chiffonier. 'I need a job.'

Peeling off her waxed jacket, Jasmine sighed. 'You've got a job, Seb. With Frobisher's.'

'I've just resigned. It seems to be getting a habit.' He smiled at her. 'So, I'm now homeless and jobless. Any chance of a beer?'

Jasmine reached into the fridge and dragged out two bottles of Old Ampney. Her hands shook as she flipped off the tops. 'You mean you're not going? You're staying? Here?'

'Yes. Yes. Yes. Thanks.' Seb took the beer and raised the bottle. 'Oh, and happy Valentine's Day.' He handed her a white box. 'Actually, they might be a bit squashed.'

Jasmine opened the lid. The box contained three heart-shaped doughnuts. Each one had a word scrawled in scarlet icing. Together they read 'Seb Loves Jas'.

'There wasn't room for the full names, but I do, you see.' He looked anxiously at her. 'Love you. So much. I just wasn't sure . . . Oh, wow!'

With a gurgle of delight, Jasmine threw herself into his arms. He kissed her with a passionate urgency that equalled her own. The Old Ampney spilled across them both.

'Don't worry,' Seb muttered, 'we can lick it off later . . .'

Later, much later, curled naked in his arms beneath the poppies and daises, Jasmine growled with sheer contentment. 'It's going to be a bit cramped living in here.'

'It's going to be bliss.' Seb kissed her gently. 'And, anyway, I can't move out yet; you've only counted a tenth of my freckles . . . Now where are you going?'

Jasmine had scrambled out of bed and padded to the window. 'I knew it! It sounds different! Look, Seb – it's snowing.'

He stood behind her, circling her with his arms, and

they watched the snow, black flakes against the dark sky, turning white as they fell, dissolving into the sea.

'Perfect timing,' Sebastian whispered. 'Now I know I've come home.'

Jasmine twisted away from him and dived back into bed. 'Quick – it's freezing! Leave the curtains open so we can watch the snow. What are you laughing at?'

'Nothing.' Sebastian snuggled up beside her again. 'I was just wondering if I should telephone my mother and tell her that I've just spent the last three hours, and will be spending the rest of my life, making love to Benny Clegg – the Punters' Friend . . .'